I0674879

LET IT GO

by

Aurealia Nelson

ISBN 979-8-89778-878-1

9 798897 788781

20 **S** 23

Staten House

DEDICATION

This book is dedicated to the resilient spirits of Black women everywhere, those who have navigated treacherous landscapes of trauma and emerged stronger, wiser, and more fiercely independent. Your strength inspires me, your stories resonate deeply within my soul, and your unwavering determination to thrive in the face of adversity fuels my writing. To the women who have loved fiercely and bravely, despite the odds, this one's for you. May these pages offer a moment of escape, a glimpse into a world where passion and power collide, and a celebration of the complex, multifaceted beauty that defines you.

This is also dedicated to the unsung heroes of the East Asian diaspora, those who carry the weight of tradition while forging their own paths in the modern world. Your intricate blend of ancient customs and contemporary ambition fascinates me. The delicate balance of honor, family, and personal freedom you navigate daily challenges conventional narratives and enriches the human experience. Your silent strength, your unwavering commitment to family, and the unspoken sacrifices you make to maintain balance, are a testament to an enduring spirit that deserves recognition. May this story, in its own small way, contribute to a more nuanced understanding of your rich culture and the complex lives you lead.

Beyond the specific cultures represented within this narrative, this dedication extends to every individual who has dared to love outside the confines of societal expectations. To those who have dared to embrace passion in the face of prejudice, judgment, and fear; those who have

found love in the most unexpected places; those who have embraced their differences and built bridges instead of walls, I offer my profound respect and admiration. Your courage to love freely, fearlessly, and authentically is a beacon of hope and a reminder that love can conquer any obstacle. May this story serve as a testament to the power of human connection, the beauty of diversity, and the enduring strength of the human spirit. Your vulnerability, your honesty, and your unwavering belief in the power of love, inspire me to tell stories that matter.

CHAPTER 1: WHISPERS OF HARLEM

The scent of shea butter and sandalwood hung heavy in the air, a familiar comfort in Aisha's small but meticulously organized Harlem apartment. Sunlight, filtered through the lace curtains, painted dappled patterns on the worn wooden floorboards. It was a sanctuary, a haven she'd painstakingly built, brick by brick, curl by curl, amidst the relentless pulse of city life. Outside, the rhythmic beat of hip-hop throbbed from a nearby bodega, a stark contrast to the quietude she cultivated within her walls. But the peace was deceptive, a fragile veneer masking the deep-seated anxieties that gnawed at her soul.

Aisha traced the delicate curves of a hand-carved wooden comb, its smooth surface, a stark contrast to the jagged edges of her memories. The comb was a gift from her grandmother, a legacy passed down through generations of strong, resilient Black women. It was a reminder of her heritage, a source of strength, yet it couldn't entirely erase the scars left by Damon, the man who had once held her captive, both physically and emotionally.

Damon had been her first love, a whirlwind romance that had quickly spiraled into a terrifying descent into addiction and abuse. He'd been charismatic, charming, a smooth talker who'd swept her off her feet with promises of a life beyond the struggles of Harlem. He had painted a picture of escape, of riches and glamour, a life far removed from the realities of her modest upbringing. The illusion shattered piece by piece, leaving behind a wreckage of broken trust, physical scars, and a profound sense of betrayal.

The memory of his possessive grip, the chilling glint in his eyes as he controlled every aspect of her life, still sent icy tendrils down her spine. The constant fear, the ever-present threat of his violence, had become ingrained in her being, a constant companion that shadowed her every move. It lived in the quickening of her pulse when a car backfired, in the nervous twitch of her fingers when a stranger brushed past her on the street.

The near-fatal incident, a botched drug deal gone wrong, had been a turning point. She'd witnessed firsthand the brutal reality of Damon's world, a world she'd naively believed she could escape. The memory of the cold steel of a gun pressed against her temple, the chilling indifference in the eyes of the men surrounding her, remained etched into her memory. She'd survived, narrowly escaping with her life, but the trauma had left an indelible mark.

Her escape had been a desperate flight, a scramble for survival. She'd run, leaving everything behind – her belongings, her dreams, the illusion of the life she'd once envisioned with Damon. She'd found refuge in the familiar comfort of Harlem, seeking solace in the embrace of her community, finding strength in the bonds of family and friendship.

Her apartment wasn't just a place to live; it was a fortress, meticulously designed to provide a sense of security and control. The heavy oak door, the reinforced locks, the strategically placed security cameras – these were not just precautions; they were manifestations of her deepest fears. Every night, before she slept, she checked each lock, ensuring that the barriers she'd constructed were impenetrable. The ritual was a way to reclaim a sense of power, a small victory in a world that had once felt entirely out of her control.

Even within her apartment, the reminders of her past were everywhere. The faint scent of his cologne, a ghost of his presence, sometimes clung to her clothes, sending shivers down her spine. She'd tried to purge every trace of him from her life, but certain memories, certain smells, certain sounds, could trigger flashbacks, plunging her back into the darkness of her past.

Her dreams were often haunted by his image – his predatory grin, his menacing eyes. She woke up gasping for air, her heart pounding like a drum, drenched in cold sweat. The nightmares were relentless, relentless attacks that stole her sleep and left her emotionally drained. Therapy had helped, but the scars ran deep, weaving themselves into the very fabric of her being.

Despite the trauma, she'd managed to rebuild her life, piece by painstaking piece. She'd channeled her pain into her work, finding solace in the transformative power of hairstyling. Her salon, a small space tucked away on a side street, was a testament to her resilience, a symbol of her triumph over adversity. Her clients, a diverse mix of women from all levels of society, confided in her, seeking comfort and solace in her warm, nurturing embrace. She listened to their stories, empathizing with their struggles, finding a sense of purpose in their shared experiences. Her skill with scissors and combs was more than just a profession; it was a form of therapy, both for her and her clients.

Her apartment, though a sanctuary, also served as a workspace. A small corner was dedicated to her craft, filled with an array of hair products, combs, and styling tools. The scent of hairspray and various conditioners mingled with the sandalwood, creating a unique aroma that was both professional and personal. It was a space where she felt in control, a space where she could create beauty and transform lives, one perfect curl at a time.

But even amidst her success, the shadows of the past lingered, casting long, menacing shadows that she couldn't completely banish. The fear was a constant, a silent hum beneath the surface of her daily life. It was a part of her, a reminder of her strength, her resilience, and the long journey she had undertaken to rebuild her life, brick by painstaking brick, curl by carefully placed curl. The journey was far from over, but she was determined to keep moving forward, one step at a time, always vigilant, always aware, but never letting the darkness completely consume her. The city lights outside flickered, and for now, at least, the quiet hum of the evening in Harlem was a fragile, hard-won peace.

The air in Minton's Playhouse hung thick with the scent of sweat, cheap bourbon, and anticipation. Aisha, usually content in the quiet solitude of her apartment, had been coaxed out by her best friend, Simone, for a night of live jazz. Simone, ever the optimist, believed a night of soulful music and good company was just the tonic Aisha needed to shake off the lingering shadows of her past. Aisha wasn't entirely convinced, but the promise of respite, even a temporary one, had been enough to lure her out.

The club throbbed with vibrant energy, a kaleidoscope of faces reflecting the diverse tapestry of Harlem. The low, guttural murmur of conversation mingled with the sultry notes of the saxophone, creating a hypnotic symphony that washed over Aisha. She found a small table tucked away in a dimly lit corner, sipping a glass of Merlot, the rich, dark liquid, a welcome comfort. The music swelled, washing over her, momentarily drowning out the persistent whispers of her anxieties.

Simone, a whirlwind of infectious energy, was already chatting animatedly with a group of friends, her laughter echoing through the smoky haze. Aisha watched her, a faint smile playing on her lips. Simone's unwavering faith in her ability to heal was a source of strength, a lifeline in the turbulent sea of emotions.

Then, she saw him.

He stood near the bar, a silhouette against the flickering neon lights, his back to her. Even from a distance, his presence commanded attention. He was tall, powerfully built, with an aura of quiet intensity that set him apart from the other patrons. When he turned, Aisha's breath caught in her throat.

His features were striking, a sharp contrast to anything she'd encountered before. High cheekbones, dark, intense eyes that seemed to pierce through her, and a strong jawline framed by thick, dark hair that fell just past his ears. His skin had the smooth, porcelain quality of jade, a stark difference from her own rich, ebony complexion. He was undeniably handsome, a vision of exotic allure that captivated her senses.

He was dressed impeccably in a tailored suit that hugged his muscular frame, the fabric the color of a midnight sky. A simple silver chain, glinting faintly under the dim lights, was the only visible piece of jewelry. There was an almost regal quality about him, a sense of quiet power and authority that both intrigued and intimidated her.

As he moved, a faint, subtle scent reached her – the clean, crisp fragrance of sandalwood and something else... something faintly spicy, almost intoxicating. It was a scent that lingered in the air, drawing her closer, even against her better judgment.

Their eyes met across the crowded room. There was a palpable tension, a silent acknowledgment of their mutual attraction. It was a moment suspended in time, a charged connection that transcended the barriers of language, culture, and background. Aisha felt a strange pull towards him, a magnetism that was both terrifying and exhilarating. It was a feeling she hadn't experienced since... since Damon. But this was different. This was something else entirely.

He approached her table, his movements fluid and graceful, like a panther stalking its prey. His gaze never left hers, his eyes burning with an intensity that both excited and unnerved her. As he drew closer, Aisha could discern the slight accent in his voice, a subtle lilt that hinted at a foreign origin.

"May I?" he asked, his voice a low, resonant murmur that sent shivers down her spine. He gestured towards the empty chair opposite her. His English was flawless, but the undercurrent of his speech held a subtle mystery.

Aisha hesitated for a moment, her instincts screaming caution. But the pull was too strong, the magnetism too potent to ignore. She nodded silently, her heart pounding in her chest.

He sat down, his presence filling the small space between them. He introduced himself as Kenji Tanaka. He didn't offer a handshake; instead, he simply looked at her, his gaze intense and unwavering, as if he was trying to decipher her soul.

The conversation that followed was a delicate dance, a careful exploration of their differences and similarities. He spoke of his family's business, a chain of beauty supply stores that spanned across the country, an empire built on generations of hard work and shrewd business acumen. He spoke of his passion for art, his appreciation for classic literature, his love of traditional Japanese tea ceremonies.

Aisha, hesitant at first, gradually opened up, sharing snippets of her life, careful not to reveal too much about her past. She spoke of her passion for hairstyling, her love for her community, her dedication to helping others. She described the vibrant energy of Harlem, the rhythm of its streets, the warmth of its people.

Their conversation flowed effortlessly, a seamless blend of laughter and shared stories. Despite their contrasting backgrounds, there was an undeniable connection, a mutual understanding that transcended cultural differences. Kenji listened intently, his dark eyes reflecting her every word, his expression a mixture of fascination and admiration.

As the night deepened, the music intensified, becoming more soulful, more sensual. The air grew heavier, charged with unspoken desires and a palpable sense of anticipation. Aisha found herself drawn to Kenji's intensity, his unwavering gaze, his quiet confidence. He was a world away from the chaos of Damon's life, yet there was a dangerous allure in his world, a mystery she couldn't resist unraveling. The line between fascination and fear blurred as the rhythm of the music and the intensity of their connection began to intertwine, shaping a destiny that neither of them could have foreseen. The night in Minton's was just the beginning. The whispers of Harlem, usually soft and comforting, were now overshadowed by the potent, dangerous, and exciting possibility that was Kenji Tanaka. Aisha's life, once carefully constructed and guarded, was about to be irrevocably changed. She could only hope she was ready for what lay ahead. The jazz music swelled to a crescendo, mirroring the chaotic yet exhilarating symphony of emotions blooming within her heart.

The cab pulled up to a building that seemed to scrape the sky, its glass facade reflecting the city lights like a million captured stars. It was a stark contrast to the brownstones and brick buildings of Harlem, a world away from the soulful rhythm of Minton's Playhouse. Kenji, sensing Aisha's unspoken question, simply smiled, a subtle, knowing smile that held a hint of amusement.

"Welcome to my world," he murmured, his voice a low caress against the night air. He opened the car door for her, a gesture both courtly and inherently possessive.

The lobby was cavernous, opulent, and eerily quiet. The air was perfumed, a subtle blend of expensive wood and something subtly floral. A uniformed attendant, his face impassive, silently took their coats, his eyes subtly assessing Aisha as if she were a prized painting awaiting appraisal. The elevator ascended smoothly, silently carrying them upward, leaving the city lights far below.

Kenji's penthouse apartment was breathtaking. Floor-to-ceiling windows offered a panoramic view of Manhattan, a glittering cityscape unfolding beneath them like a jeweled tapestry. The apartment itself was a symphony of modern elegance and traditional Japanese aesthetics. Sleek, minimalist furniture was juxtaposed against ornate screens and meticulously crafted artwork. A low, soothing melody, the soft plucking of a shamisen, drifted through the air, creating a mood both serene and slightly mysterious.

The contrast between the brutal efficiency of the city below and the peaceful serenity of his apartment was jarring, a testament to the carefully orchestrated balance that Kenji seemed to maintain in his life. It spoke of a duality, a man who moved seamlessly between two worlds, yet remained firmly rooted in both.

Aisha found herself captivated by the sheer beauty of the space, a testament to wealth and exquisite taste. She moved cautiously through the apartment, her eyes scanning the details – a carefully arranged bonsai tree, a collection of ancient scrolls, a single, perfect orchid blooming in a minimalist vase. Every object was placed with intention, a reflection of Kenji's meticulous nature.

"Make yourself comfortable," Kenji said, his voice soft, but his presence undeniably commanding. He poured her a glass of sake, the pale liquid glowing softly in the dim light. The rice wine had a delicate sweetness, a subtle fragrance that resonated with the overall serenity of the apartment.

As they talked, Aisha learned more about Kenji's family, a lineage deeply rooted in both tradition and business acumen. He spoke of the Yakuza, not with pride, but with a quiet respect tinged with a hint of weariness. It wasn't a boastful display of power, but a matter-of-fact acknowledgment of his heritage, a lineage woven into the very fabric of his being. He explained the delicate balance between respecting tradition and navigating the complexities of the modern world, the careful dance between ancient rituals and modern business practices.

His family's beauty supply empire wasn't simply a business venture; it was a legacy, a tapestry woven from generations of hard work, shrewd business strategies, and the silent power of the Yakuza. It was a world of discreet deals, unspoken alliances, and powerful connections, a world far removed from her own. The elegance of the empire masked a dangerous undercurrent, the whispers of a world operating outside the bounds of conventional law and morality.

He showed her a family heirloom, a katana, its blade gleaming under the soft light, a testament to a past rife with both violence and honor. It was a symbol of his heritage, a silent reminder of the traditions that bound him, yet it was displayed not as a weapon, but as a piece of history, a symbol of an ancestry both glorious and complex.

He shared stories of his upbringing, tales of rigid discipline and ancient traditions, the strict expectations placed upon him as the heir apparent of his family's empire. He spoke of the quiet strength of his mother, a woman of immense power and grace, who navigated the complexities of both worlds with an unwavering resolve. His father, a man of quiet authority, he described as a figure of respect but one who communicated more through actions than words. The family structure was strict, hierarchical, demanding unwavering loyalty and obedience.

He spoke of his training, the rigorous physical and mental discipline that had shaped him into the man he was today. The years of rigorous practice were not merely about physical prowess; they were about honing a self-control, a mental fortitude capable of withstanding intense pressure and navigating complex moral dilemmas. The discipline he'd undergone was not just physical; it was a mental and spiritual conditioning, a forging of his character in the crucible of ancient traditions and modern realities.

Aisha listened, captivated, as the layers of Kenji's life slowly peeled back, revealing a complex tapestry woven from tradition, power, and the subtle allure of forbidden desire. She saw the weight of expectation upon his shoulders, the burden of heritage and tradition, the silent pressure to uphold his family's legacy. He was both the embodiment of this legacy and a man wrestling with his own desires and aspirations.

He took her to a hidden alcove, a traditional Japanese tea room nestled within the modern apartment. The air was thick with the scent of incense, the low hum of a water fountain a soothing counterpoint to the city's relentless energy. The ceremony, performed with meticulous grace, was a stark contrast to the boisterous energy of Harlem.

The delicate porcelain cups, the precise movements, the silent respect – it was a ritual, a meditation on balance and harmony. As he served her tea, his touch was light, almost reverent, his eyes never leaving hers. In that moment, the vast gulf of their cultural backgrounds seemed to momentarily disappear, replaced by a shared understanding, a fragile bridge built upon mutual respect and an undeniable attraction.

But the quiet elegance masked an underlying tension, a sense of unspoken danger that lingered beneath the surface. The whispers of Harlem, faint but persistent, seemed to clash with the hushed serenity of Kenji's world, hinting at the complexities and potential conflicts that lay ahead. The intricate dance between their lives had just begun, a dance on a razor's edge where passion and peril intertwined, a thrilling and potentially dangerous journey into the unknown.

He spoke of the responsibilities that came with his position, the weight of expectations borne on his shoulders, the silent burden of family loyalty. The Yakuza were not simply a criminal organization; they were a brotherhood, bound by ancient oaths and codes of conduct. His life was a delicate balancing act, a tightrope walk between the demands of his family and his own desires.

The conversation turned to his personal life, or rather, the lack thereof. He spoke of his commitment to his family, the sacrifices he'd made, the loneliness that often accompanied his position. He had an air of quiet solitude, hinting at a life lived on the edge, where trust was a rare commodity and intimacy a perilous luxury.

He revealed a subtle vulnerability, a hint of a longing for something more, a yearning for a connection that transcended the confines of his carefully constructed world. It was in this vulnerability, in the cracks in the carefully crafted facade of his controlled existence, that Aisha found herself drawn even deeper into the mystery of Kenji Tanaka.

The night deepened, the city lights painting the cityscape in hues of gold and silver. The air crackled with an unspoken energy, a tension that hung heavy between them, a silent acknowledgment of the forbidden allure of their burgeoning connection. The line between desire and danger, fascination and fear, became increasingly blurred. Aisha found herself increasingly drawn to him, mesmerized by his power, yet haunted by the potential consequences of her growing involvement in his complex world. The whispers of Harlem were now overshadowed by the silent hum of his opulent penthouse, a silent symphony of power, mystery, and a promise of danger that held an irresistible allure. The city slumbered below, oblivious to the passionate and precarious dance of desire about to unfold.

The sake warmed Aisha from the inside, a comforting contrast to the cool elegance of Kenji's penthouse. The conversation had flowed easily, a surprising ease given the stark differences in their backgrounds. Yet, beneath the surface currents of polite conversation, a palpable tension simmered, a silent acknowledgment of the unspoken attraction that crackled between them. He moved closer, the scent of his cologne – a sophisticated blend of sandalwood and something subtly spicy – filling the air around her.

He reached out, his fingers brushing lightly against her arm, sending a shiver down her spine. The touch was fleeting, yet it held a weight, a silent promise of intimacy that both thrilled and intimidated her. Her heart pounded a rapid rhythm against her ribs, a drumbeat of anticipation and trepidation. The whispers of Harlem, the familiar rhythm of her life, seemed a million miles away. She was lost in the captivating allure of this man, this enigma wrapped in silk and shadowed by the whispers of the Yakuza.

Kenji's eyes, dark and intense, held hers captive. They were windows into a soul both complex and guarded, a man who wore his power like a second skin yet revealed a vulnerability in the depths of his gaze. He leaned in, his breath warm against her ear, his voice a low murmur that sent shivers down her spine. "There's a beauty in the unknown, Aisha," he whispered, his words a seductive caress. "A risk...a thrill."

His hand found hers, his fingers interlacing with hers, a silent invitation. The touch was electric, a spark that ignited a fire within her, a flame that danced on the edge of control. She felt the weight of his hand, the strength in his grip, a reassuring presence that belied the danger that lurked just beneath the surface of his refined world. This was a man of power, a man who operated in shadows, yet in this moment, there was only the raw, undeniable connection between them.

He led her to a plush, oversized couch, the deep velvet cushions sinking under their weight. The low lighting cast long shadows across the room, creating an intimate, almost secretive atmosphere. The silence between them hummed with unspoken words, with desires both hinted at and barely concealed. His gaze held a depth that went beyond simple attraction; it was a recognition, a silent understanding of something deeper, a shared understanding of a need for connection that transcended the boundaries of their worlds.

The air thickened with anticipation, the unspoken desires hanging heavy between them. He reached out again, his fingers tracing the delicate curve of her jawline, his touch gentle yet undeniably possessive. The intimacy was slow, deliberate, a measured dance between their cultures. His gaze dropped to her lips, lingering there before he leaned in, his breath warm against hers. The kiss was tentative at first, a soft exploration of desire.

It was a melding of cultures, a whispered conversation in the language of touch. His kiss was a blend of Western passion and Eastern restraint, a careful exploration that acknowledged both their differences and their shared desires. It was a kiss that both respected and challenged societal norms. His lips were soft yet firm, his touch both gentle and assertive, a reflection of the careful balance he maintained in his life. He was a man who navigated a world of power and shadow, yet his touch held a surprising tenderness.

The kiss deepened, becoming more intense, more passionate. His hands moved to her waist, pulling her closer, his body molding against hers. It was a dance ancient, yet imbued with a unique vibrancy, a unique intensity born from the clash and harmony of their cultures. His lips moved to her neck, leaving a trail of fire in their wake. His touch sent shivers down her spine, a testament to the raw power of their connection.

The encounter was a slow burn, a gradual unveiling of desires both unspoken and fiercely held. They explored each other, their hands moving in a silent conversation of touch, a dance of discovery that defied language and cultural boundaries. It was a journey of exploration and mutual understanding, a testament to their inherent connection. They moved beyond the tentative, venturing into a deeper intimacy, the air alive with their passion.

Their physical exploration mirrored the cultural interplay of their lives – the delicate grace of Japanese tradition woven with the unrestrained passion of American desire. His mastery of touch was mesmerizing, his expertise a quiet assertion of his power while also demonstrating an unparalleled sensitivity to her needs and desires. He read her body, her whispers, her hesitations, and responded with an understanding that transcended words.

The night deepened, the city outside fading into a muted backdrop to the passionate dance unfolding within his penthouse. It was a journey that revealed layers of vulnerability, a moment of shared intimacy that surpassed any initial concerns of cultural differences. This was not merely a physical encounter; it was a mutual exploration, a quiet conversation in the language of the body, a merging of souls that transcended the boundaries of their vastly different worlds.

As the intensity of their passion reached its peak, Aisha felt a surge of emotion, a complex mixture of exhilaration and trepidation. The fear of the unknown, the whispers of danger that constantly surrounded Kenji, flickered in her mind. Yet, the raw intensity of their connection, the undeniable power of their shared desires, pushed those fears to the periphery. She surrendered to the moment, lost in the intoxicating blend of passion and vulnerability.

Following the intensity, a gentle tenderness emerged. They lay entwined, their bodies still warm from the passion they had shared. In the quiet aftermath, a sense of intimacy settled between them, a shared understanding born from their physical connection. It wasn't just the physical act itself; it was the vulnerability they had revealed, the mutual trust that had blossomed in the space between their bodies, that created an enduring bond.

The morning light filtered through the floor-to-ceiling windows, painting the apartment in hues of soft gold. They lay embraced, their bodies intertwined in a testament to the night's passion. The silence between them was not empty but rather filled with the unspoken language of intimacy, a quiet understanding that transcended words. The contrast between the luxurious surroundings and the raw intimacy of the moment created a profound and unforgettable experience for Aisha.

The quiet moments that followed their passionate encounter were filled with a newfound sense of intimacy. It was a connection forged in the crucible of desire, a bond that transcended cultural differences and spoke to the universality of human connection. Their shared experience, the vulnerability they had revealed to each other, had created a sense of trust, a fragile bridge connecting their vastly different worlds.

Kenji's touch, even in the quiet moments after their passion had subsided, held a tenderness that spoke volumes. He had displayed a gentleness and sensitivity that contradicted the hardened image of a Yakuza member. This intimacy, built upon a foundation of mutual respect and understanding, was a beacon in the shadowy world he inhabited, a glimmer of hope that transcended the darkness that surrounded his life.

Aisha felt a profound shift within herself. Her past, the trauma she had endured, still lingered, but this new connection provided a glimmer of healing, a sense of empowerment that she had been missing. This was a connection unlike any she had ever known, a passionate embrace that helped her overcome a part of her past, a relationship that was simultaneously exhilarating and profoundly grounding. She had stepped into a world she had never imagined, a world of wealth, power, and danger, and discovered a connection that challenged her assumptions and offered a glimpse of a future she had never thought possible. The whispers of Harlem seemed far away, replaced by the hushed echoes of a new beginning, a future that was both exciting and unsettling, a dance on the edge of danger and desire, a thrilling journey into the unknown.

The opulent silence of Kenji's penthouse held a deceptive calm. The lingering scent of their lovemaking still clung to the air, a stark contrast to the chilling dread that began to creep into Aisha's heart. The initial euphoria had faded, replaced by a gnawing unease, a familiar shadow from her past stretching its tendrils into her present. Sleep, when it finally came, was fractured by nightmares, vivid and terrifying replays of the drug dealer's cruel reign over her life. His face, a mask of malice, loomed in the darkness, his voice, a venomous whisper, echoing the threats that had once held her captive.

She would jolt awake, heart hammering against her ribs, sweat slicking her skin, the phantom touch of his violence still clinging to her. The plush silk sheets, the soft glow of the city lights filtering through the floor-to-ceiling windows, were no solace against the icy grip of fear that tightened around her. Kenji, sleeping peacefully beside her, was a comforting presence, his warmth a tangible counterpoint to the icy dread that haunted her. But even his nearness couldn't completely banish the memories, the chilling echoes of a past she desperately tried to outrun.

The following day, a subtle distance settled between them. Aisha's normally vibrant spirit seemed dimmed, her laughter muted, replaced by a quiet reserve. Kenji, perceptive as he was, noticed the change. He observed her subtle flinches, the way her eyes would dart nervously to the shadows, the way her hand would instinctively reach for his in moments of quiet, as if seeking reassurance against an unseen enemy. He understood, instinctively, that her past was not merely a story to be told, but a living, breathing entity, a ghost that haunted her waking moments and tormented her sleep.

He approached her with a gentle patience, a sensitivity that belied his powerful exterior. He didn't push, didn't demand explanations. Instead, he offered a quiet presence, a reassuring silence that allowed Aisha the space to process her own turmoil. He brought her tea, the delicate aroma of jasmine a calming balm to her frayed nerves. He held her hand, his touch a steady anchor in the storm raging within her. He simply *was*, a solid presence, a steadfast rock against the tide of her fear.

One evening, as they sat on the balcony, overlooking the sprawling cityscape, Aisha finally broke her silence. Her voice, at first hesitant, gradually gained strength as she began to recount fragments of her ordeal, choosing her words carefully, revealing only what she felt comfortable sharing. She spoke of the manipulation, the control, the insidious erosion of her self-worth that had taken place at the hands of the man who had once held her captive.

She spoke of the nightmarish cycle of violence and manipulation, of the constant fear of his unpredictable rage. She described the feeling of being utterly powerless, of her very life teetering on the edge of a knife. Her voice trembled at times, her eyes welling with unshed tears, but she persevered, sharing the burden that had weighed heavily on her soul for so long. Kenji listened intently, his dark eyes mirroring the pain she described, his gaze filled with empathy and understanding. He didn't interrupt, didn't offer platitudes. He simply listened, his presence a silent testament to his unwavering support.

As Aisha spoke, Kenji's understanding of her fear grew, and with it, a profound respect for the strength she had shown in surviving her ordeal. He saw beyond the confident exterior she often projected, recognizing the hidden scars that spoke of her resilience and the unwavering strength of her spirit. He realized that her fear was not merely a personal battle, but a testament to the pervasive violence that women often face, and the deep scars it leaves behind. He understood that her hesitations and anxieties weren't weaknesses, but manifestations of her past trauma, a silent testimony to the strength it had taken for her to survive.

He learned about the systemic issues that allowed such predation to occur, and the societal mechanisms that enabled such men to operate in the shadows, preying on vulnerability and fear. The narratives of abuse, of manipulation, of control, formed a stark contrast with the world he inhabited – a world of power, wealth, and privilege. But these stories, these testimonies of pain and survival, resonated deeply within him. They challenged him to confront the reality that even in his world, far from the streets of Harlem, the shadow of violence could stretch its tendrils, reaching into the most unexpected corners of life.

Aisha's vulnerability opened a door into a deeper level of intimacy, a connection forged not just in passion but in shared understanding and mutual empathy. Kenji's response wasn't just that of a lover but also of a compassionate confidante. He offered not only physical comfort but also emotional support, demonstrating a sensitivity and understanding that went far beyond the casual exchanges of a romantic relationship. Their connection deepened, anchored by a shared experience that transcended the cultural differences that initially separated them.

The weight of her past continued to cast its shadow, but now it was a shadow they faced together. Kenji's presence was a source of strength, a comforting presence against the lingering fear. He helped her navigate her anxieties, reminding her of her own strength, gently coaxing her back from the brink of despair. He showed her, in subtle yet powerful ways, that she wasn't alone, that she was loved, and that her past experiences didn't define her future.

Their relationship, born amidst passion and danger, evolved into something deeper, something more profound. It was a journey of healing, a testament to the transformative power of love and understanding. It was a slow and painstaking process, one marked by setbacks and triumphs, fears, and reassurances, but it was a journey they were willing to embark upon, together. The whispers of Harlem still lingered, but now they were intertwined with the quieter, more intimate sounds of hope and healing, a new chapter in a life still unfolding, a life that was beginning to find its own light. The shadows of the past remained, but they no longer held the power to consume her. Kenji was there, a beacon of light in the darkness, guiding her through the maze of her memories, towards a future that promised healing, hope, and the promise of a love that could conquer all.

CHAPTER 2: THE DRAGON'S EMBRACE

The quiet intimacy of Kenji's penthouse, once a sanctuary, now felt like a stage. Aisha, despite the lingering warmth of their shared nights, felt a growing chasm between them, a chasm carved not by distance, but by culture. Her Harlem upbringing, a vibrant tapestry woven with gospel music, street smarts, and a fiercely independent spirit, clashed starkly with Kenji's reserved demeanor, steeped in the ancient traditions and rigid hierarchy of the Yakuza.

It wasn't just the language barrier, though that certainly played a part. Aisha's expressive nature, her tendency to laugh freely, to speak her mind without hesitation, felt jarringly out of sync with Kenji's quiet intensity, his carefully measured words, his almost stoic composure. He moved with a grace that hinted at years of disciplined training, a controlled elegance that was both captivating and intimidating. She, on the other hand, was a whirlwind of motion, her emotions always close to the surface, her laughter a spontaneous eruption of joy.

Their lovemaking, though intensely passionate, also highlighted this cultural divide. Aisha's uninhibited sexuality, a reflection of her upbringing where physical expression was often a form of communication and connection, clashed with Kenji's more reserved approach, steeped in traditional Japanese aesthetics and a profound sense of respect for the body as a temple. He was mesmerized by her spontaneity, her uninhibited passion, but also slightly unnerved by its intensity. It was a foreign landscape to him, unfamiliar and yet undeniably alluring.

One evening, while preparing dinner – a delicious fusion of soul food and Japanese cuisine, a testament to their unusual union – Aisha found herself frustrated. Kenji was meticulously preparing sushi, his movements precise and deliberate, a stark contrast to her own more haphazard approach to cooking. She'd started with a joyful exuberance, humming along to the gospel music playing softly on the stereo, only to find herself irritated by the silence and precision of Kenji's actions.

"Kenji," she said, her voice laced with a playful exasperation, "why so serious? Cooking should be fun!"

He looked up, his dark eyes questioning. "Fun?" he repeated, his voice a low rumble. "Cooking is an art, Aisha. It requires precision, respect for the ingredients, a deep understanding of the process."

"And a little soul," she retorted, adding a generous pinch of cayenne pepper to her collard greens. "Where's the soul in all this meticulous slicing and dicing?"

The silence that followed was heavy, charged with unspoken tensions. Aisha realized then the depth of the cultural chasm that separated them. Kenji's upbringing emphasized discipline, restraint, and a profound respect for tradition. Her own had instilled in her a love of spontaneity, a celebration of life's vibrant chaos.

It wasn't just a difference in personalities; it was a collision of worlds, of deeply ingrained cultural values. She saw it in the way he interacted with his family, the deference he showed to elders, the unwavering loyalty he displayed towards his clan. It was a world governed by unspoken rules, by centuries-old traditions, a stark contrast to the more individualistic, less hierarchical structure of her own community.

Later that night, as they lay entwined in bed, Aisha attempted to bridge the gap. She spoke about her childhood in Harlem, the vibrant community she grew up in, the strong women who had shaped her life. She described the Friday night fish fries, the soulful sounds of gospel music echoing through the streets, the close-knit bonds of family and friends. She painted a picture of a world teeming with life, where emotions were openly expressed, where laughter and tears flowed freely.

Kenji listened intently, his dark eyes absorbing her words. He learned about the struggles, the triumphs, the unwavering resilience of the African American community, a world so different from his own, yet equally rich and complex. He began to understand the source of her exuberance, her spontaneity, her uninhibited passion. It wasn't merely her personality; it was a reflection of her community, a testament to the spirit of survival and resilience that had shaped her life.

He, in turn, spoke about his upbringing, the strict discipline of the Yakuza, the unwavering loyalty demanded by his family, the ancient traditions that governed every aspect of his life. He spoke of the honor, the responsibility, the weight of expectation that came with his heritage. He described the quiet elegance, the controlled intensity, the deep-seated respect for order and hierarchy that characterized his world. He explained that his reserved demeanor wasn't a sign of coldness, but a reflection of his cultural background, a deep-seated respect for tradition and the importance of maintaining composure.

As they spoke, the cultural differences remained, but the distance between them began to shrink. They began to understand each other's perspectives, to appreciate the beauty and complexity of their respective cultures. They saw beyond the surface, beyond the initial misunderstandings, to the shared humanity that bound them together. Their love, initially forged in passion, began to deepen, rooted in mutual understanding and respect.

Their conversations continued, each exchange revealing another layer of their lives, their cultural experiences, their personal histories. Aisha learned about the complexities of the Yakuza, the intricate web of loyalty and betrayal, the delicate balance of power and tradition. Kenji, in turn, was introduced to the rich tapestry of African American culture, its resilience, its vibrancy, its unwavering spirit.

The cultural clash wasn't erased, it was transformed. It became a source of fascination, of mutual learning, of a deeper understanding of each other's hearts and souls. Their differences enriched their relationship, adding depth, complexity, and a unique spice to their passion. Their love became a bridge, spanning the vast cultural chasm that initially separated them, a testament to the power of love to transcend boundaries, to unite two seemingly disparate worlds.

The differences remained, but they were now seen as facets of their individual identities, not insurmountable obstacles. Aisha's vibrant spirit, her unbridled laughter, her uninhibited expression of emotion, were no longer viewed as jarring contrasts but as integral parts of her being, aspects that Kenji came to cherish and admire. Kenji's quiet intensity, his disciplined nature, his deep-seated respect for tradition, became aspects of his personality that Aisha understood and appreciated. Their love was a testament to their ability to embrace their differences, to find harmony amidst the apparent discord. It was a beautiful testament to the transformative power of love and understanding, a journey of mutual respect and growth, a bond forged not just in the fires of passion, but in the crucible of cultural exchange. Their journey was far from over, but they were navigating it together, learning, adapting, and growing together, united by a love that transcended the boundaries of culture and tradition. The cultural clash had not destroyed their love; it had deepened it, enriched it, making it stronger and more resilient than they could have ever imagined. Their love story was becoming a unique masterpiece, painted with the vibrant hues of two vastly diverse cultures, a testament to the beauty of diversity and the power of love to overcome all obstacles. The tapestry of their relationship continued to weave itself, becoming richer and more intricate with each passing day, a testament to the enduring power of love and understanding.

The sleek black car pulled up to a sprawling estate that seemed to defy categorization. It was a breathtaking juxtaposition of modern opulence and ancient Japanese architecture, a testament to the Yakuza family's wealth and their deeply rooted traditions. Gleaming black granite met weathered cedar wood, minimalist lines contrasted with intricate carvings, creating a visual representation of the clash between Kenji's two worlds – the high-powered, modern business empire and the ancient, secretive life of the Yakuza.

As the car door opened, a wave of apprehension washed over Aisha. This was Kenji's world, untainted by the casual ease of his penthouse apartment. This was the heart of his family, the source of his power, and potentially, his greatest vulnerability. Stepping out, she felt the weight of their unspoken scrutiny, a pressure that was both palpable and unnerving.

Kenji's hand, warm and reassuring, tightened around hers. He squeezed gently, offering a silent promise of support as they walked toward the house. The imposing structure loomed, a silent guardian of secrets and traditions that Aisha was only beginning to understand. The air itself felt thick with expectation, a potent blend of incense and unspoken rules.

They were greeted by Kenji's mother, a woman whose beauty was as sharp and elegant as a katana. Her eyes, dark and piercing, held a hint of apprehension and something Aisha couldn't quite decipher – a guarded curiosity, perhaps? There was a regal bearing about her, a quiet strength that commanded respect. Her silk kimono, a vibrant tapestry of crimson and gold, spoke volumes about her position within the family. The subtle nod she offered Aisha was more of a concession than a genuine greeting.

"Aisha," Kenji said, his voice a low rumble meant to be both reassuring and a warning. He translated his mother's words to Aisha, a careful explanation of the appropriate level of deference and respect required within their traditional family dynamic. This was not the casually affectionate Kenji she'd grown to know. This was the Kenji bound by duty, heritage, and the unyielding expectations of his clan.

The interior of the house was as striking as its exterior. Modern art clashed with ancient scrolls, sleek polished floors reflected the light from exquisitely crafted lanterns. The air hummed with an unspoken energy, a delicate dance between the old and the new. The family members they encountered were a fascinating mix of age and ambition. Elderly men, their faces etched with the wisdom – or perhaps weariness – of a long life, sat quietly observing. Younger men, sharp dressed and strikingly handsome, exuded an air of quiet intensity, their eyes constantly scanning, assessing.

Aisha felt like a specimen under a microscope, each of her movements, each of her words dissected and analyzed. She found herself instinctively mimicking Kenji's more reserved demeanor, a subtle shift in her posture and a conscious attempt to temper her usually exuberant expressiveness. The cultural clash intensified here, palpable in the silent judgments and the measured responses.

Dinner was a tense affair. The traditional Japanese meal was meticulously prepared, a testament to the family's attention to detail and their deep respect for their culinary heritage. But the silence during the meal felt heavy, burdened by unspoken words and the weight of centuries-old traditions. Aisha's attempts at light conversation were met with polite but distant responses, leaving her feeling increasingly out of place, a stark outsider in their tightly knit world.

One of Kenji's younger brothers, Hiroki, caught her eye. His stare was sharp, assessing; a silent challenge masked by a façade of polite neutrality. She could sense a resentment simmering beneath the surface, a mixture of disapproval and barely concealed hostility. Later, Kenji explained that Hiroki, ambitious and fiercely loyal to the family, viewed Aisha as an intrusion, a threat to his brother's allegiance and his own standing within the clan.

The evening unfolded with a carefully choreographed dance of politeness and subtle power plays. Aisha watched, fascinated and increasingly apprehensive, as family members interacted, their conversations filled with veiled references and unspoken allegiances. She caught glimpses of the intricate web of loyalty and betrayal that underpinned the Yakuza family, a world of carefully cultivated relationships and unwavering fealty. The respect shown towards the elders was absolute, their pronouncements treated as undeniable fact.

As the evening wore on, Aisha's initial discomfort morphed into a growing unease. The weight of the family's expectations, the unspoken judgment in their eyes, created a pressure that was almost suffocating. She felt like a fragile porcelain doll in a room full of seasoned samurai, her every move observed, scrutinized, and potentially judged. The quiet intensity of their world was unlike anything she had ever experienced. It was a world of silent obedience, unwavering loyalty, and a rigid adherence to tradition that seemed to clash violently with her own fiercely independent spirit.

Yet, amidst the tension and the unspoken disapproval, there were also moments of unexpected warmth. Kenji's grandmother, a frail but remarkably perceptive woman, offered Aisha a rare smile, a gesture that felt like a silent acceptance, a subtle sign of approval in this sea of watchful eyes. She spoke to Aisha in soft, broken English, her eyes conveying a deep understanding that transcended words. Her words, translated by Kenji, were simple but heartfelt: "He chose you, and that is enough." This simple statement offered Aisha a sliver of comfort amidst the overwhelming pressure.

Leaving the family estate, Aisha felt drained. The encounter had revealed the depth of the complexities within Kenji's world, a world that was both alluring and terrifying. The veiled threats, the subtle displays of power, and the constant assessment of her worth had left her feeling exposed and vulnerable. Kenji held her close, his silence as comforting as his words, his presence a reassuring shield against the storm she'd just weathered.

Back in the quiet sanctuary of their penthouse, the contrast was stark. The modern minimalist design, the soft lighting, the comfortable silence felt like a refuge from the opulent yet suffocating atmosphere of Kenji's family home. They shared a quiet meal, their conversation subdued but comforting. Aisha felt the need to confide in Kenji, to express the feelings of unease that had been building throughout the evening. She described the veiled hostilities, the unspoken judgments, the palpable sense of being constantly evaluated. She explained her concern that her independent spirit, her vibrant personality, might be seen as a threat to the rigid order of Kenji's family.

Kenji listened intently, his dark eyes reflecting the complexities of his own feelings. He acknowledged her fears, explaining the intricacies of his family's dynamics, the fierce loyalty that binds them together, and the unspoken rules that govern their lives. He spoke of the challenges of reconciling his modern life with his family's ancient traditions, the constant pressure to maintain the delicate balance between his own desires and the expectations of his clan.

Their conversation stretched into the night, a bridge built across the chasm of cultural differences and unspoken tensions. Their love, initially ignited by passion, was now being tested by the crucible of cultural clash and family expectations. The path ahead remained uncertain, fraught with challenges and potential conflicts, but their mutual understanding, their shared love, served as a beacon in the darkness. Their connection, strengthened by vulnerability and mutual support, became a testament to their resilience and their unwavering belief in the strength of their bond. The weight of his family's expectations, though heavy, couldn't extinguish the flame of their shared passion, a flame they vowed to protect as they navigated the treacherous waters ahead.

The penthouse, a haven of sleek modernity, became their sanctuary. The muted lighting, the soft jazz drifting from hidden speakers, and the absence of the suffocating weight of Kenji's family home created a space where they could shed the masks they wore in public. Here, their passion ignited into a fiery blaze, a breathtaking exploration of intimacy that transcended cultural boundaries.

Their lovemaking was a dance, a sensual choreography blending the familiar with the unexpected. Aisha's initial apprehension melted away as Kenji guided her, his touch both gentle and insistent, his lips whispering promises in both English and Japanese. He taught her the subtle art of Japanese massage, the ancient techniques designed to soothe and awaken the senses, a prelude to their more passionate encounters. His hands, strong and sure, moved with a practiced grace, coaxing pleasure from her body with a fluidity that was both mesmerizing and breathtaking.

Their nights were filled with whispered secrets and shared laughter, their bodies entwined in a tapestry of sensations. He introduced her to the nuances of Shibari, the ancient Japanese art of rope bondage, a practice that was both exhilarating and deeply intimate. The silken ropes, expertly woven around her limbs, weren't instruments of restraint, but rather tools of exploration, highlighting her curves, emphasizing her vulnerability, and intensifying the sensations. The act of surrender, the trust inherent in the practice, deepened their connection, creating a bond of shared vulnerability that transcended the physical.

Aisha, in turn, introduced Kenji to the uninhibited passion of Western eroticism. She taught him the language of her body, the nuances of her desires, a language he eagerly learned, his responses both intense and surprisingly tender. Their exploration was a journey, a shared discovery, a celebration of their differences and their growing intimacy. She found him capable of such intense passion, so uninhibited in his expression of desire, that it shattered any preconceived notions she'd held about East Asian men. He was both powerful and tender, a dichotomy that captivated her completely.

Their intimacy wasn't solely physical; it was a fusion of souls, a deep connection forged in the crucible of shared experiences and mutual respect. They spoke for hours, sharing stories of their pasts, their hopes, and their fears. Aisha, slowly opening up about her traumatic past and her lingering insecurities, found solace in Kenji's unwavering support. He listened patiently, his dark eyes reflecting a depth of empathy that was both comforting and profoundly moving. He, in turn, shared details of his life within the Yakuza, the complexities of loyalty and betrayal, the burden of family expectations, and the constant threat of violence that loomed over his world.

The vulnerability they shared in those intimate moments became a powerful bond, a testament to the strength of their burgeoning love. They found a safe space in each other's arms, a refuge from the pressures of their respective worlds. The contrasts in their backgrounds, initially a source of apprehension, now served as a foundation for their growing understanding and appreciation of each other's unique perspectives.

One evening, as the city lights twinkled outside their penthouse window, Aisha found herself tracing the intricate tattoos that adorned Kenji's back, each a symbol of his heritage and his place within the Yakuza. She ran her fingers along the delicate lines, feeling the raised texture beneath her fingertips. The intricate designs spoke of a history steeped in tradition, loyalty, and a code of conduct that was both fascinating and terrifying. He turned, his eyes filled with a tenderness that softened the harsh lines of his face.

"They are a part of me," he murmured, his voice low and husky. "But they don't define me. You... you see beyond them, don't you?"

Aisha nodded, her gaze locking with his. "I see you, Kenji. The real you. The man behind the tattoos, the man behind the expectations of your family. The man who makes me laugh until my sides ache, who makes me feel safe, who makes me feel... loved."

Their passion continued to evolve, mirroring the growth of their relationship. Their intimacy became a sacred space, a refuge from the complexities of their lives. The blending of their cultures, initially a source of apprehension, now fueled their desires, adding depth and richness to their experiences. They explored techniques from both their heritages, each encounter a unique and intimate exploration of their shared desires.

Aisha discovered a sensual confidence she had never known, her body responding with a vibrancy she hadn't believed possible. Kenji, in turn, found a freedom in his expression of desire, a release from the rigid expectations of his family and the constraints of his world. Their lovemaking became a testament to their individual growth and their deepening connection, a fusion of cultures and desires that was as powerful as it was beautiful.

Their conversations deepened, too. They delved into the complexities of their cultural backgrounds, Aisha sharing her understanding of African American culture, its strengths, its struggles, and the unique blend of resilience and joy that defined her community. Kenji, in turn, provided insight into the intricacies of Japanese culture, its emphasis on tradition, honor, and the sometimes suffocating expectations of conformity. They discovered common threads, shared experiences of prejudice and discrimination, and a mutual understanding of the struggles inherent in reconciling tradition with modernity.

Aisha learned about the strict code of honor within the Yakuza, the unwavering loyalty demanded of its members, and the constant threat of violence that hung over their lives. Kenji, in turn, discovered the strength and resilience of Aisha's spirit, her fierce independence, and her unwavering commitment to her own values. He admired her ability to challenge societal expectations, her willingness to embrace her individuality, a quality that was both captivating and inspiring.

Their love was a testament to their resilience, a beacon of hope in the face of adversity. It was a relationship forged in passion, tested by cultural differences and family expectations, yet strengthened by their shared vulnerability, mutual respect, and unwavering commitment to each other. Their intimacy, both physical and emotional, became a sanctuary, a space where they could be truly themselves, free from the judgments and expectations of the outside world. It was a love story as unique and captivating as the two individuals at its heart, a testament to the power of love to transcend cultural boundaries and forge a bond that defied definition. The journey ahead remained fraught with challenges, but their love, rooted in mutual respect and understanding, offered the promise of a future where their differences were celebrated, and their passion burned ever brighter.

The humid night air hung heavy, thick with the scent of exhaust fumes and something else, something acrid and faintly sweet that prickled Aisha's nostrils. She'd followed Kenji's instructions meticulously, parking her beat-up Honda Civic several blocks away from the designated meeting point – a deserted alley tucked behind a row of dilapidated warehouses. The silence was unnerving, punctuated only by the distant wail of a siren and the skittering of rats in the shadows. Her heart hammered against her ribs, a frantic drumbeat against the quiet menace of the surroundings. She gripped her phone tighter, its cold metal a small comfort in the clammy darkness.

This wasn't how she envisioned spending a Tuesday evening. Earlier, nestled in Kenji's arms, the world had seemed a distant, less threatening place. The memory of his warmth, the lingering scent of his cologne – a blend of sandalwood and something subtly masculine – calmed her slightly, but the unease remained. Kenji had been unusually tight-lipped, his usual playful demeanor replaced by a grim seriousness that had sent a shiver down her spine. He'd merely said it was "business," a word that, in his world, often translated to something far more complicated and dangerous.

She'd agreed, partly out of trust, partly out of a desire to understand the life that lay hidden beneath the surface of his charming exterior. She'd seen glimpses of it before - the sudden tense phone calls, the hushed conversations in a language she didn't understand, the almost imperceptible shift in his posture when certain names were mentioned. But tonight felt different; this felt like a plunge into the heart of the storm.

The alley was eerily quiet. The only light came from a flickering streetlamp at the far end, casting long, distorted shadows that danced and writhed like restless spirits. Aisha pulled her jacket tighter, the thin fabric offering little protection against the chill night air. She checked her phone again, a small digital clock displaying the time – 11:47 pm. Kenji was late.

Then, she heard it – the low rumble of a car engine, growing steadily louder as it approached. Her breath hitched in her throat. Two figures emerged from the vehicle – hulking men, their faces obscured by shadows. They moved with a practiced efficiency, a silent menace that sent a wave of cold dread washing over her. One of them carried a large duffel bag, its contents unknown but undoubtedly significant.

Without thinking, Aisha raised her phone, her fingers fumbling with the recording app. It was a reflex, a habit she'd developed years ago, a tool of self-preservation. She'd learned early on that sometimes, the only way to protect herself was to document everything. The small red dot on her screen, the silent witness to the unfolding scene, became her only ally in the encroaching darkness.

The exchange was quick, brutal, efficient. The two men engaged in a low, guttural conversation, the words muffled and incomprehensible. Aisha could only see their silhouettes, but their body language spoke volumes – tension, suspicion, a palpable sense of danger. She felt a cold knot tighten in her stomach, her body trembling slightly. The muffled words, the furtive glances, the sudden change in the air - everything screamed danger.

Suddenly, a high-pitched whine cut through the night air. It was the sound of a car speeding towards them. Aisha froze, her fingers gripping her phone so tightly that her knuckles turned white. She instinctively squeezed her eyes shut, bracing herself for the inevitable impact. But it never came.

Instead, she heard the unmistakable sounds of a struggle, punctuated by grunts, curses, and the sharp thud of bodies hitting the concrete. Aisha opened her eyes cautiously. The two men were grappling with another figure – a shadowy form that moved with blinding speed and terrifying efficiency. They were completely outmatched.

The fight was over in a matter of seconds. The two men lay sprawled on the ground, groaning in pain. The shadowy figure moved silently towards Aisha, stopping just inches away. Only then did Aisha realize it was Kenji. His face was grim, his eyes reflecting the harsh glare of the streetlamp. He was breathing heavily, his body taut with exertion, but his eyes held no fear.

He looked down at her phone, the small red dot still glowing, and a flicker of something – amusement, perhaps? – crossed his lips. "You're quite the documentarian," he murmured, a hint of a smile playing on his lips. The tension momentarily dissipated; his words, even laced with a dark humor, brought a surge of relief.

The following hours were a blur of frantic calls, whispered explanations, and the hushed movements of people moving in the shadows. Kenji orchestrated the scene with a level of coolheaded competence that both amazed and terrified her. His world was a labyrinth of danger and intrigue, one she was only beginning to glimpse. His efficiency in handling the aftermath of this near-deadly encounter, however, was something else entirely.

He'd had the men taken care of quickly, efficiently, quietly. He didn't offer specifics, but Aisha gathered that the men were not just criminals, but were connected to elements far more dangerous, far more powerful. The implication hung heavy in the air, the gravity of her accidental recording sinking in with every passing moment.

The adrenaline began to subside, leaving Aisha feeling drained and exhausted. The weight of the evening's events pressed down on her, the chilling reality of her near-death experience slowly settling in. Kenji's silence on the matter was unsettling, his focus solely on ensuring their safety. The feeling of vulnerability gnawed at her.

He led her to a waiting car, a sleek black sedan that seemed to materialize out of the darkness. The driver, a man whose face remained obscured by the shadows, nodded curtly to Kenji before whisking them away from the scene.

The ride was silent, broken only by the hum of the engine and the occasional squeal of tires as the car navigated the city streets. Aisha stared out the window, the flashing city lights blurring into streaks of color. Her mind raced, replaying the events of the evening, the near-miss, the sudden violence, and the silent efficiency of Kenji's actions. The recording, an innocent act of self-preservation, had inadvertently plunged her into the heart of a world far more dangerous than she could have ever imagined.

The sense of impending doom lingered; it was no longer

just the thrill of discovering Kenji's world; it was now about surviving it. Aisha looked over at Kenji, his face illuminated by the faint glow of the city lights. He seemed to be lost in thought, the usual playful glint in his eyes replaced by a serious expression. His hand reached for hers, his fingers interlacing with hers, his touch conveying a silent reassurance, a promise of protection.

"We need to talk," he said, his voice low and steady, a stark contrast to the turmoil raging within her. The weight of his words, the unspoken implication, hung heavy in the air. Aisha knew, with a certainty that chilled her to the bone, that the accidental recording was just the beginning. The game had changed, and she was now a player in a game she didn't understand, a game where the stakes were life and death. The comfort of his hand in hers, however, offered a fragile anchor in the storm. His touch was a lifeline in the darkness, a promise of protection and a reassuring sign of their unwavering connection. The future was uncertain, fraught with peril, but at least she wasn't facing it alone.

The car pulled up to a secluded apartment building, the kind that boasted more shadows than light. Kenji squeezed her hand, a silent reassurance in the suffocating silence. He didn't speak, but the tension radiating from him was palpable, a tangible force pressing down on her. He hadn't explained the situation in the alley, only that it was "taken care of." The vagueness was unnerving, leaving her in a state of uneasy anticipation.

As they stepped out of the car, the city's cacophony washed over Aisha, momentarily drowning out the whispers of fear inside her. The building's entrance was a darkened maw, promising little comfort. The air itself felt thick with a silent menace, a prelude to the storm that was brewing. Kenji led her through the dimly lit hallway, past closed doors that seemed to pulse with unseen energy. The atmosphere was a heavy mixture of apprehension and something else, a dark anticipation that prickled her skin.

Inside the apartment, the contrast was stark. Modern, minimalist design, cool, neutral tones, a world away from the grimy alley where she'd nearly met her end. But even in this sanctuary, Aisha couldn't shake the feeling of being watched, of being under siege. The quiet hum of the city outside seemed to pulse with a dangerous rhythm.

Kenji poured her a glass of something amber and fragrant, a Japanese whiskey that warmed her from the inside out. The liquor eased the tension in her muscles, but not in her mind. He sat opposite her, his eyes intense, scrutinizing, searching. The playful spark that usually lit his features was gone, replaced by a grim determination that was both intimidating and oddly comforting.

"They know," he finally said, his voice a low rumble that resonated in the hushed apartment. The simplicity of his statement sent a shiver down her spine, the words echoing the cold fear she'd been trying to suppress. They knew about the recording. They knew she held the key to their downfall, to the unraveling of a world carefully constructed on secrets and lies.

"How?" she whispered, her voice trembling slightly. The question hung between them, heavy with unspoken dread. How had they discovered the recording? How could they possibly have known? The question was more than just curiosity; it was a desperate attempt to understand the depth of danger she was facing.

Kenji's lips tightened into a grim line. "They have their ways," he said, his voice hardening. "It's not important how. What's important is what we do next."

The next few hours were a blur of tense conversations, strategic planning, and desperate measures. Kenji revealed more about his world, about the intricacies of the Yakuza and the dangerous networks they controlled. He spoke of rival factions, of betrayals and alliances, of a world where loyalty was a fragile commodity and death was always a possibility. He spoke in carefully chosen words, never revealing too much, always maintaining a careful balance between trust and concealment.

He explained that the men in the alley weren't just ordinary criminals; they were connected to a powerful rival gang, their business stretching far beyond petty street dealings. The drug trade was just a small part of their empire, a fraction of their immense reach and influence. The recording, Aisha now understood, was a significant threat, an exposure that could topple empires and ignite a full-scale war.

He showed her a photograph—a grainy image of a man with piercing eyes and a cruel smile. "This is who you're up against," he said, his voice low. "He's relentless. He won't stop until he has that recording."

The implication hung heavy in the air—the man in the photo

was more than just a rival gangster; he was a predator, hunting Aisha with a single-minded determination that was both terrifying and awe-inspiring. The casualness with which Kenji spoke of this danger only served to highlight the gravity of the situation, highlighting the normalcy of such events within his world.

The realization struck Aisha with full force. This wasn't just some romantic entanglement; she'd stumbled into a dangerous game, a life-or-death struggle with high stakes and even higher risks. The weight of her accidental recording was far greater than she ever imagined; it wasn't just evidence, but a weapon.

Kenji outlined a plan – a desperate, high-stakes gamble. They would go on the offensive, trying to anticipate and neutralize the threat before it became insurmountable. He was accustomed to handling such situations, he explained. But he was also underlining the significant risks involved. This was not a game; this was survival.

The plan involved using Kenji's connections, navigating the shadowy underbelly of the city, and relying on an intricate network of informants and allies. It required trust, unwavering loyalty, and a willingness to delve into a world that was both seductive and terrifying. Aisha hesitated for a moment, her fear battling with her determination. The situation was grim; she was facing death, but not alone.

Kenji's hand found hers again, his touch firm, reassuring. "I won't let anything happen to you," he said, his voice a promise as much as a statement. His words, combined with the warmth of his hand, were a lifeline in a world threatened by sudden violence and death.

The following days were a whirlwind. Aisha found herself thrust into a world she never knew existed, a world of clandestine meetings, coded messages, and whispers in dimly lit rooms. She was both terrified and strangely exhilarated; the adrenaline fueled her, pushing her beyond her comfort zone and forcing her to rely on her instincts and her growing trust in Kenji.

The pursuit intensified. She felt their eyes on her, their presence a constant, looming threat. She saw them lurking in the shadows, following her from a distance, their menace a silent, chilling reminder of the danger that surrounded her. Once, she caught a glimpse of the man from the photograph, his eyes cold and calculating, his presence sending a wave of panic through her.

Kenji's strategy was to use Aisha's recording as leverage. They would find a way to turn the tables, to use the evidence to their advantage, to exploit the rival gang's vulnerabilities. It was a calculated risk, a daring maneuver that could lead to their salvation or their destruction. Their movements were carefully orchestrated, every step planned, every move calculated. The fear was ever-present, but their bond deepened with each challenge they faced.

The threat was ever-present, a dark cloud hanging over their heads, but their determination grew stronger with every passing day. Aisha discovered a new strength within herself, a resilience she never knew she possessed. She learned to trust her instincts, to rely on her own abilities, and to navigate the dangerous currents of Kenji's world.

Their bond strengthened with every close call. The erotic tension between them, always simmering beneath the surface, intensified. Their intimacy became a refuge, a sanctuary from the constant danger. Amidst the shadows and the threat of violence, their passion became a source of strength, a testament to their resilience. The danger served to heighten their feelings, their connection forging an unbreakable bond under pressure.

The game was far from over. The threat was real, immediate, and pervasive. But Aisha was no longer just a pawn; she was a player, fighting for her survival in a world of shadows and secrets, her fate intertwined with the captivating and dangerous Kenji. The future was uncertain, fraught with peril, but she had Kenji, and that, in itself, was a formidable weapon in this fight for their lives. She would not yield; she would not be broken. She would survive.

CHAPTER 3: SILK AND SHADOWS

The following days were a blur of clandestine meetings and whispered conversations. Kenji, ever the strategist, moved with a quiet intensity that both captivated and unnerved Aisha. He introduced her to a network of individuals that existed on the fringes of society—informants, fixers, and those who danced dangerously close to the line between legality and the criminal underworld. These encounters, shrouded in secrecy and held in dimly lit backrooms of smoky bars and opulent private clubs, exposed Aisha to a world vastly different from her own. It was a world of power plays, shifting allegiances, and veiled threats, a world where the spoken word held as much weight as the unspoken.

She witnessed the brutal efficiency of Kenji's world, the way he could manipulate events, anticipate threats, and weave his way through the labyrinthine corridors of the Yakuza's intricate operations. He was both ruthless and charming, a duality that kept Aisha perpetually off-balance, captivated by his power yet wary of his methods. His touch, both tender and commanding, served as a stark contrast to the harsh realities of his world. The intimacy they shared was a sanctuary, a momentary escape from the constant pressure and ever-present danger, a potent reminder that amidst the chaos, they had something real and precious. But even in their shared moments of passion, a shadow of uncertainty lurked, a constant reminder of the precariousness of their situation.

One evening, as they sat across from each other in a dimly lit izakaya, the traditional Japanese pub, Kenji revealed a detail that sent a chill down Aisha's spine. The man in the photograph, the ruthless rival gang leader, wasn't simply after the recording; he had a personal vendetta against Kenji's family, a decades-old feud fueled by betrayal and ambition. Aisha's involvement, her accidental possession of the incriminating evidence, had become an unforeseen pawn in this larger game.

The implications were staggering. She was no longer just a witness; she was inextricably linked to a centuries-old conflict, a battle between powerful families that extended beyond the confines of their immediate circle, reaching deep into the heart of Japanese organized crime. This knowledge intensified her fear but also ignited a spark of something else—a sense of purpose, a feeling that she wasn't simply a victim but a critical player in this dangerous drama. The weight of responsibility settled heavily upon her shoulders, the burden of this realization pushing her to the limits of her endurance.

Kenji's strategy involved a daring and risky gambit: to turn the tables and use the recording as leverage against the rival gang, using their greed and ambition against themselves. It required a delicate balancing act—navigating the complex relationships within the Yakuza, anticipating their moves, and exploiting their internal conflicts. Aisha, despite her initial reluctance, found herself drawn into the intricate plan. She discovered a reservoir of strength she never knew she possessed, her fear tempered by a fierce determination to survive. She was learning to trust her instincts, to read between the lines, and to decipher the subtle cues that signaled impending danger.

As the plan unfolded, Aisha faced a moral dilemma. The rival gang's operations extended far beyond drug trafficking; they were implicated in activities that impacted her own community— exploitation, human trafficking, and acts that violated the trust and safety of her people. Aisha, fiercely loyal to her community and deeply rooted in her cultural identity, faced a heartbreaking choice: betray Kenji and turn over the recording to the authorities, potentially jeopardizing his life and possibly failing to dismantle the larger criminal network; or, collaborate with Kenji, taking a significant risk herself, and potentially sacrificing her own safety and risking the lives of others. This choice weighed heavily on her conscience, as it forced her to navigate the complexities of her loyalty to Kenji and her sense of responsibility towards her community, a delicate balance between love, duty, and survival.

The tension escalated. The threat of discovery loomed large, the constant presence of danger making their every interaction charged with a desperate intimacy. Their shared moments of passion, ignited by fear and fuelled by adrenaline, became both a solace and a source of strength. Kenji's touch, his tender words, and his unwavering determination were her anchors in a tumultuous sea of uncertainty. Their love deepened, forged in the crucible of danger, their connection a lifeline amidst the storm. Yet, the weight of her decision loomed over their intimacy, a dark cloud hanging over their otherwise passionate moments.

One night, as they lay entwined, Aisha confessed her internal struggle. The conflict between her loyalty to Kenji and her responsibility to her community tore at her soul. She spoke of the injustices she had witnessed, the suffering inflicted upon her people, the violation of their trust and safety by the rival gang. Tears streamed down her face as she recounted the stories she had heard, the silent pleas she had witnessed; tales of exploitation and human trafficking that shook her to her core.

Kenji listened patiently, his gaze unwavering. He understood her predicament, recognizing the conflict she faced between her personal feelings and her social responsibility. He didn't judge her internal struggle, nor did he attempt to minimize the weight of her decision. Instead, he acknowledged the depth of her loyalty, her commitment to her community, and the weight of her responsibility to her people. He spoke of the sacrifices he had made, the lines he had crossed, and the lives he had touched within his own community. He shared his own experiences, offering a shared understanding of the complex moral dilemmas that emerge when navigating the shadowy world of organized crime.

He revealed a hidden layer to his own motivations. His family's business extended beyond the beauty stores—a network of charitable foundations and community support systems, all operating quietly under the radar, providing assistance and support to underserved communities. His actions weren't merely about personal gain; he was driven by a desire for justice, a need to rectify the imbalances of power within his community. He affirmed that her concern was valid and shared her commitment to protecting her community.

His revelation brought new perspective to Aisha. She realized that their shared struggle transcended personal gain, extending beyond their personal relationship to encompass a broader social justice. They were both fighting against forces that exploited and oppressed the vulnerable. The common ground they discovered solidified their commitment to one another, strengthening their bond in the face of adversity. Their differences in background and culture became strengths, their unique perspectives complementing each other, fostering a powerful alliance.

In the end, Aisha made a choice, a decision borne of both love and principle. Her decision, however, was not a simple resolution. It was a complex calculation—a tactical maneuver made in a high-stakes game of survival. Her choice involved a delicate balance of personal sacrifice and strategic advantage, a risk-reward proposition that could lead to both victory and annihilation. The next move would be crucial, the stakes were impossibly high, and the consequences would be far-reaching. The path ahead remained uncertain, fraught with danger, but Aisha, armed with a renewed sense of purpose and strengthened by her love for Kenji, was ready to face whatever challenges lay ahead. The game was far from over, but Aisha and Kenji, their destinies intertwined, would face it together.

The next morning, the city unfolded before them in a stark contrast to the clandestine world Aisha had been exposed to. The vibrant hues of Tokyo's neon lights felt almost surreal after the dimly lit backrooms and smoky bars of the previous nights. Kenji, however, remained ever vigilant. He moved with an almost imperceptible grace, his eyes constantly scanning the surroundings, a silent guardian ever present.

He took her to a traditional tea house, a serene oasis of calm amidst the bustling metropolis. The aroma of freshly brewed green tea filled the air, the delicate porcelain cups a comforting contrast to the steel-edged world Kenji inhabited. Here, amidst the quiet tranquility, he spoke of his vow to protect her. It wasn't a grand declaration, but a quiet promise, delivered with a depth of conviction that resonated deeply within Aisha.

"Your safety is paramount," he stated, his voice low and resonant. "They will not touch you." The assurance he offered wasn't just a statement of intent; it was a promise backed by the formidable power of the Yakuza. He spoke of the network at his disposal, the men who owed him allegiance, the resources he could command.

But his methods, Aisha soon realized, were far from conventional. While his tenderness towards her was undeniable, his ruthlessness in protecting her was equally terrifying. He orchestrated encounters with individuals whose faces seemed to be etched with stories of violence and betrayal. These were not the smooth-talking businesspeople or the subtly threatening enforcers she'd glimpsed before; these were the hard men, the ones who dealt in shadows and silent promises.

One evening, they found themselves in a secluded warehouse on the outskirts of the city. The air hung heavy with the scent of decay and damp concrete. Kenji, his usual elegance replaced by a cold intensity, conducted a meeting with three imposing figures. The conversation was a low murmur of Japanese, punctuated by tense silences and the occasional sharp exchange. Aisha, understanding little of what was being said, still felt the chilling implications of the discussion. It was clear that Kenji was not merely threatening; he was making deals, bargains struck in the shadows, involving debts paid in blood and loyalty bought with fear.

Later, Kenji explained. He had initiated a series of carefully calculated maneuvers to eliminate the threat, to neutralize the rival gang's capacity to reach Aisha. He had leveraged his family's influence and his own reputation, making deals with rival factions, promising favors, and delivering swift, decisive punishments to those who dared to oppose him. He spoke calmly, almost clinically, about the intricate web of alliances and betrayals he'd woven, a macabre tapestry of power and vengeance.

Aisha felt a strange mixture of fear and fascination. The man who could be so gentle, so tender in their shared moments of intimacy, was capable of such ruthless efficiency. The contrast was jarring, but it was also strangely alluring. It underscored the depth of his commitment to her safety, the lengths he would go to protect her. It was a testament to the intensity of their connection, a bond forged not just in passion, but in shared danger and mutual dependence.

Yet, the dark underbelly of Kenji's world was a constant, unsettling presence. She witnessed the casual brutality, the casual disregard for human life that permeated his world. She saw the fear in the eyes of those who interacted with him, the respect tinged with apprehension that underscored his power. It was a world where loyalty was a currency, where promises were sealed with blood, and where betrayal meant certain death.

Kenji, however, remained a paradox. He could order a man's death with icy calm one moment, then turn around and hold her gently, his touch soft as silk against her skin. He would speak of the cultural traditions and expectations that governed his world, explaining the complex dynamics of the Yakuza, the intricate codes of honor and the unwavering loyalty that bound its members together.

He introduced her to aspects of his life that had nothing to do with violence or crime. He took her to family gatherings, where the atmosphere was markedly different from the tense, clandestine meetings she had witnessed. He shared traditional Japanese meals with his relatives, his warmth and humor radiating through the family gathering. He spoke lovingly of his younger siblings, his parents, and even his extended family. He revealed his softer, more sensitive side to her, showing her a different facet of his life, separate from the dangerous and ruthless life of his profession. The stark contrast between these two worlds fascinated Aisha.

She began to understand that Kenji's dedication to protecting her wasn't simply a matter of romantic love, but also a matter of honor. In his world, to fail to protect someone under his care was a sign of weakness, a transgression that could lead to profound consequences. This realization added another layer of complexity to her feelings for him. She wasn't just his lover; she was also, in a way, under his protection, a responsibility he took seriously. The weight of this responsibility added an unforeseen dimension to their relationship, intensifying the bond between them.

One evening, Kenji took her to a secluded onsen, a natural hot spring nestled high in the mountains. The steaming water, the surrounding serenity, provided a momentary respite from the tension and uncertainty that had become a constant in their lives. As they sat in the soothing waters, Kenji confessed his fears. He spoke of the risks he was taking, the enemies he had made, and the potential consequences of his actions. He admitted that even his formidable power had limits, that he couldn't guarantee her complete safety.

"There are forces beyond my control," he admitted, his voice laced with a vulnerability Aisha had rarely seen. "But I will fight for you, until my last breath." His words resonated with a depth of emotion that went beyond mere words. They were a declaration of his unwavering commitment, a promise etched not just in his words, but in his actions.

Aisha, too, felt the weight of their precarious situation. She had witnessed the dark side of Kenji's world, the casual violence, the calculated ruthlessness. But she had also seen his unwavering loyalty, his fierce protectiveness, his tender love. She was drawn to him despite the danger, perhaps because of it. Their relationship was a tempestuous mix of passion, fear, and an unwavering commitment to one another. It was a love story unfolding amidst the shadows, a love born of danger and fueled by a desperate desire to survive.

His protection, while often ruthless and unorthodox, was absolute. It wrapped around her, a shield against the storm brewing around them, a promise whispered in the silences between their passionate encounters, a constant reassurance amidst the ever-present threat. It was a protection that transcended mere physical safety; it was a protection of her spirit, her dignity, her very being. Kenji's world was dangerous, yes, but within its darkness, he had created a sanctuary for Aisha, a place where their love could flourish, even as the shadows closed in. The next move, however, would be their most perilous yet. The storm was gathering, and the battle for their survival was about to begin.

The air crackled with anticipation, a tangible tension that

vibrated through the crowded streets of Harlem. Aisha, her senses heightened by the adrenaline coursing through her veins, spotted him first. He wasn't Kenji. This was one of Kenji's men, a figure she recognized from a previous clandestine meeting, his face etched with a silent, chilling intensity. He blended seamlessly into the crowd, a ghost in the vibrant tapestry of the city, his eyes constantly scanning, searching. The chase began with the urgency of a heartbeat.

The pursuit was a dizzying ballet of movement, a frantic dance between the pursuer and the pursued. Aisha, guided by Kenji's whispered instructions relayed through an encrypted channel, weaved through the throngs of people, the rhythm of her footsteps echoing the pounding of her heart. The city, once a familiar comfort, had transformed into a labyrinth of danger, every alleyway a potential trap, every shadow a hiding place for unseen threats. The vibrant energy of Harlem, usually a source of comfort and pride, now felt menacing, a cacophony of sounds that muffled the urgent whispers in her ear.

She darted through bustling avenues, the scent of fried chicken and jerk spice momentarily distracting her from the icy grip of fear. She dodged taxis, leaped over overflowing trash cans, and squeezed through narrow spaces between buildings, her heart pounding a frantic rhythm against her ribs. She could feel the eyes on her, the weight of the pursuit pressing down, heavy and suffocating. Each glance behind her revealed the ever-closing proximity of her pursuer, a shadow that clung to her like a second skin.

Their pursuit led them to a forgotten corner of Harlem, a place where the city's vibrant energy faded into a desolate landscape of crumbling buildings and deserted streets. The air here was thick with the scent of decay and forgotten dreams. It was a place where shadows held secrets and silence whispered warnings. She had been to places similar to this in her past life, places that had reminded her of the danger that surrounded her when her former lover was still present. Yet, this felt different. The danger was more calculated, more sophisticated, the threat more precisely targeted.

Suddenly, a car screeched to a halt, blocking her path. Two men emerged, their faces masked, their movements swift and brutal. Aisha's breath hitched in her throat; this wasn't a random street thug, this was organized, professional. This was the kind of precision Kenji had warned her about. It was the cold efficiency of a well-oiled machine, designed to eliminate any threat to Kenji or to her.

But Aisha wasn't unarmed. Kenji had given her a small, intricately crafted knife, its blade as sharp as a razor. It was a tool, a symbol of his protection, a promise etched in steel. It was a deadly reminder of the reality of the world they occupied. It was the sharp edge of love within a deadly profession. The cold steel seemed to pulsate with the rhythm of her fear, the metallic weight strangely reassuring in her trembling hand.

The fight was brutal, a desperate struggle for survival. The air filled with the sounds of shattering glass, grunts of exertion, and the metallic clang of steel against steel. Aisha fought with the ferocity of a cornered animal, her movements fueled by adrenaline and a primal instinct to survive. It wasn't a graceful fight, it was primal, raw, violent. Yet, it was also a fight for her life, a fight for her love, a fight for her future. She danced between and around them, weaving herself between attacks with precision. This felt more like a fight than the fight with her former partner. This time she had a reason to fight. Kenji.

She used the environment to her advantage, utilizing the narrow alleyways and broken fences as cover, creating a chaotic dance that mirrored the intricate beauty and deadly potential of her situation. She ducked, she weaved, she struck with the precision of a warrior, the fury of a woman fighting for her life. Her training as a dancer had always taught her grace and agility, and it aided her now in this harsh reality. The knife, now slick with sweat and blood, became an extension of her will, a testament to her determination. Each blow was calculated, each movement precise, each thrust deadly.

In the midst of the chaos, a gunshot rang out, sharp and brutal. One of the attackers crumpled to the ground, a silent testament to the swift and brutal efficiency of Kenji's intervention. From the shadows emerged Kenji himself, his presence as chilling as the night air. His movements were swift and economical, his eyes blazing with a cold fury. He dealt with the remaining attacker with cold, calculated precision, leaving the remaining man crippled and bleeding. Kenji's entrance was not one of mere assistance; it was a statement of power, a declaration of his unwavering commitment to Aisha's safety.

The aftermath of the conflict was quiet, the stillness punctuated only by Aisha's ragged breathing and the pained moans of the defeated attacker. Kenji, his face impassive, retrieved the knife from her hand, his touch lingering for a fraction of a second. The touch of the knife, still slick with the blood of the attackers, created a strange contrast to the soft touch of his fingertips, a stark reminder of the dangerous dance of love and death they shared.

He led her away from the scene, silently, his arm wrapped firmly around her. The silence between them was a shared understanding, a silent acknowledgement of the precariousness of their situation, the ever-present threat that hung over them like a shroud. The streets of Harlem, once filled with vibrant energy, now seemed eerily silent. The city itself seemed to hold its breath, a silent witness to the dangerous game they were playing.

As they walked, Aisha felt Kenji's presence, a solid anchor amidst the storm. He was more than just a lover, more than just a protector; he was a symbol of her defiance against the darkness, a beacon in the storm. Their journey, however, was far from over. The shadows lengthened, and the next battle loomed on the horizon. The stakes had been raised, and the dangerous game was far from over. The whispers of the Yakuza, the secrets held within the heart of Harlem, the tensions between their two worlds—it was a precarious dance on the edge of a knife, a delicate balance between life and death, love, and loss. Their bond, forged in the crucible of danger, would be tested again and again. But Aisha, for the first time in her life, didn't just feel the danger; she felt the strength she held and her determination to fight. This determination was both a strength and a weakness. This was her life now and she would fight for it till the very end. The dangerous game had only just begun.

The following days were a blur of stolen moments and whispered promises. Kenji, despite his outward stoicism, showed a vulnerability Aisha hadn't anticipated. He'd bring her small gifts – a single, perfect orchid, a hand-painted silk fan, a delicate jade pendant – each a silent testament to a tenderness that belied his dangerous profession. These small gestures were interspersed with the fiery intensity of their nights, a passionate dance between cultures, a fusion of their desires that transcended language and background. Yet, under the surface of their passionate encounters, a current of unease ran, a subtle tremor of doubt that cast long shadows over their burgeoning love.

Aisha found herself constantly looking over her shoulder, the memory of the attack fresh in her mind. The city, once her sanctuary, now felt like a stage for a play in which she was a reluctant actor, her every move scrutinized, her every breath monitored. Kenji's protection was a double-edged sword; it shielded her from danger, yet it also kept her tethered to a world she didn't fully understand, a world rife with secrets and betrayals. The weight of her secret, the accidental recording of the drug deal, pressed down on her, a constant reminder of the precariousness of her position.

One evening, as they sat on the balcony of Kenji's luxurious apartment, overlooking the glittering cityscape, Aisha broke the silence that had settled between them. "Kenji," she began, her voice barely a whisper, "There are things I need to tell you. Things you need to know." The words hung in the air, heavy with unspoken fears and unresolved anxieties. His eyes, usually alight with passion, held a flicker of apprehension. He knew, she realized, that something was wrong, that any doubt had fallen over their fragile peace.

She confessed her fear of his world, the Yakuza's code of silence, the ever-present threat of violence. She confessed her fear of betrayal, her fear of becoming another pawn in a game she didn't understand. His response was surprising, a mixture of understanding and a raw honesty Aisha hadn't expected.

He spoke of the betrayals he had witnessed, the sacrifices he had made, the weight of his family's expectations. He admitted that his life was a dangerous tightrope walk and that he, too, carried the burden of secrets, secrets that were inextricably linked to his heritage and his family's legacy.

"My world is not one of roses, Aisha," he confessed, his voice low and husky. "It's a world of shadows and secrets, of loyalty and betrayal. Trust is a currency that's easily spent and rarely earned. I want to make you trust me, but I know that's an awkward thing to ask for."

Their conversation stretched late into the night, fueled by honesty and shared vulnerabilities. They spoke of their pasts, their traumas, their dreams, and aspirations. He revealed snippets of his childhood, the strict discipline, the unwavering loyalty demanded by his family, the weight of tradition that he both embraced and fought against. He spoke of the women in his life, the expected submission, the unspoken rules, and the stifling expectations. He spoke of how he had always struggled with how to balance his family's expectations with his own desires. He spoke of the women that had been forced into his life by his father. He confessed his desire for genuine connection, his hunger for a love that transcended the constraints of his world.

Aisha, in turn, shared her own story – her escape from poverty, her harrowing relationship with her former lover, the scars that still lingered on her soul. She spoke of her longing for security, for a genuine connection, for a love that was not merely physical but profound. She spoke of how his acceptance and support had given her the strength she never thought she could find. His world might be one of danger and uncertainty, but for the first time in her life, she felt seen, truly seen, by someone who understood the complexities of her past and her aspirations for the future.

The trust between them, however, remained fragile. Whispers and insinuations, subtle shifts in the atmosphere, hinted at unspoken conflicts simmering beneath the surface. Aisha noticed Kenji's increasing irritability, the fleeting glances towards his phone, the hushed conversations he had in private. She began to question his loyalty, to wonder if he was hiding something from her, if their passionate connection was merely a distraction from a deeper, darker reality.

One day, she found a cryptic message on his phone – a series of numbers and symbols that seemed out of place, a coded communication that set off alarm bells in her mind. Her intuition, honed by years of navigating a treacherous life, told her that something was wrong, that she was being kept in the dark. Paranoia gnawed at her, feeding on her insecurities and her fear of betrayal. The trust she had carefully built began to crumble, replaced by doubt and suspicion.

The conflict escalated during a lavish Yakuza gathering, a display of wealth and power that both captivated and terrified Aisha. She found herself the center of attention, admired and coveted by men whose intentions were far from honorable. The simmering tensions between Kenji and his family members was plain to see. The constant vigilance of his family members, their watchful eyes, their subtle manipulations, sent shivers down her spine. Their words were laced with barbed remarks, thinly veiled threats.

She witnessed an intense argument between Kenji and his uncle, a powerful figure within the organization, a man whose gaze radiated cold calculation. The argument was about her, Aisha realized, a subtle clash between tradition and Kenji's undeniable affection for her. The air was thick with unspoken accusations, hidden alliances, and the ever-present threat of violence. She felt like a chess piece, her position on the board dictated by the desires and ambitions of others.

Amidst the opulent splendor, the subtle tension was almost palpable. The conversations, seemingly innocuous, held undercurrents of rivalry, power plays, and unspoken desires. She saw the way certain men looked at her, a predatory gleam in their eyes, the unspoken promises, the veiled threats. The realization hit her with the force of a physical blow: her relationship with Kenji was not just a matter of personal choice; it had become a political issue within the Yakuza, a strategic move in their internal power struggle.

Kenji, caught in the crossfire of family loyalty and forbidden love, attempted to assure her, to explain the complexities of his position. He insisted on his love, his loyalty. But his words seemed hollow in the face of the blatant disrespect and open hostility she faced from other members of his family. His attempts at reassurance felt strained and unconvincing.

The events of the night pushed her to the brink. She confronted Kenji, demanding honesty, demanding transparency. The ensuing argument was a heartbreaking collision of love, loyalty, and fear. He confessed his position, his inability to break free from his family's control without jeopardizing his safety, as well as hers. The weight of his past, his family's history, his obligations, proved overwhelming. He was caught between two worlds, two conflicting loyalties, a painful dichotomy that tested the limits of their love and their trust.

In the aftermath of their explosive argument, Aisha was left reeling, grappling with the complexities of their situation, the dangerous game of love and betrayal they were entangled in. The line between truth and deceit blurred, the boundaries between trust and suspicion became increasingly unstable. Their future together seemed as uncertain as the path ahead. The silk and shadows of their relationship had woven themselves into a tangled web of dangerous possibilities. Yet despite it all, a spark of hope still flickered. The depth of their connection, the raw intensity of their love, refused to be extinguished entirely. The battle for their trust, for their love, was far from over. The journey was only beginning.

The days that followed were a crucible, forging Aisha in the fires of uncertainty and fear. The opulent setting of Kenji's life, initially alluring, now felt like a gilded cage. The constant surveillance, the veiled threats, the subtle manipulations – they chipped away at her confidence, threatening to reduce her to a mere plaything in Kenji's dangerous game. Yet, instead of succumbing to fear, something unexpected happened. Aisha found a strength she hadn't known she possessed. It wasn't a sudden revelation, but a slow, steady burning, fueled by a deep well of self-respect and a quiet, unwavering courage.

It started with small acts of defiance. She refused to cower in the face of intimidating glares, holding her gaze steady, her posture unwavering. She questioned the assumptions of Kenji's associates, challenging their thinly veiled insults with sharp, witty retorts that left them momentarily speechless.

Her voice, once a whisper, now carried an edge of steel, a quiet determination that surprised even herself. She learned to navigate the intricate social dynamics of Kenji's world, picking up the subtle cues, deciphering the coded language, and skillfully maneuvering through the treacherous currents of the Yakuza.

One evening, during a particularly tense gathering at Kenji's family estate, a renowned geisha, elegant and sharp as a katana, offered Aisha a seemingly innocuous piece of advice: "Strength is not the absence of fear, but the ability to rise above it." The words resonated deeply within Aisha, solidifying her burgeoning self-assurance. She realized that her fear was not a weakness, but a compass guiding her towards self-preservation and empowerment. She recognized the power of self-awareness and self-belief as a stronger weapon than any physical defense.

She began to cultivate her own sources of strength. She rediscovered her passion for writing, finding solace and empowerment in the act of creating, of transforming her fear and anxieties into words of defiance and resilience. She started documenting her experiences, chronicling her journey through the dangerous world she found herself in. Each entry served as a testament to her growing strength, a record of her battles won and lessons learned. She filled notebooks with vivid descriptions of the people she met, the events she witnessed, and her own shifting emotions, her vulnerability, and her growing self-reliance. The act of writing itself felt like an act of rebellion, a claim of ownership over her own narrative.

She also reached out to her network of support. A trusted

childhood friend, a woman with a background in social work and years of experience supporting survivors of domestic violence, provided crucial emotional support and guidance. Their conversations provided Aisha with a safe space to process her fears, to dissect the complex dynamics of her relationship with Kenji, and to formulate strategies for protecting herself. She rediscovered the strength she had found years ago and realized that surviving her previous relationship had already equipped her with the tools and resources to face whatever the future held.

The connection with her friend was a lifeline, offering her both emotional sustenance and practical advice. Her friend helped her understand the dynamics of power, control, and manipulation, helping her discern genuine affection from strategic manipulation. Her advice wasn't solely focused on navigating the complex world of the Yakuza; it also empowered Aisha to understand her own needs, desires, and boundaries.

Aisha's newfound strength wasn't solely emotional. It manifested physically as well. Inspired by the graceful movements of the geishas she observed, she began practicing martial arts. She found a dojo run by a strong, independent woman who taught her self-defense techniques, empowering her with the physical capacity to protect herself should the need arise. The training was more than just self-defense; it was a pathway to self-discovery, a testament to her unwavering resolve. She found a sense of focus, discipline, and inner peace through these practices. She felt increasingly confident in her ability to take charge of her own physical safety and emotional well-being.

The change in Aisha was palpable. Kenji noticed it. He saw the newfound fire in her eyes, the quiet confidence in her demeanor, the way she carried herself with an air of self-assuredness that was both captivating and intimidating. Initially, he was wary, even slightly apprehensive. He was accustomed to the submissive women that his family had placed around him. Aisha's rebellion, however, was not directed at him; it was an assertion of her own self-worth, a declaration of her independence. It was a testament to the unwavering strength she had found within herself.

He understood that she was not merely reacting to his world; she was actively shaping her own experience within it. He began to respect her strength, admiring her resilience, her unwavering spirit. He saw how her strength didn't diminish their love; instead, it enhanced it, transforming their relationship into something deeper, more equitable, and more profound.

The turning point came during a tense standoff with Kenji's uncle. He had made a derogatory remark about Aisha, implying that she was nothing more than a temporary diversion, a plaything for Kenji's amusement. Aisha responded with a cutting remark that not only shut the uncle down but also earned her newfound respect from some unexpected corners of the Yakuza.

Her response wasn't a mere display of defiance but a carefully crafted statement, a calculated maneuver that exposed the uncle's hypocrisy and solidified her position within Kenji's world. She wielded her intelligence, her wit, and her newfound confidence as weapons, proving that her strength wasn't merely physical, but also intellectual and emotional.

The incident shifted the power dynamics within Kenji's family. They had underestimated Aisha's strength, her intelligence, and her will. She was no longer viewed as a mere prize to be acquired or a commodity to be traded; she became a force to be reckoned with, a woman who could not be easily controlled or dismissed. Her strength extended beyond her own resilience and impacted those around her.

This newfound empowerment did not magically erase the dangers that Aisha faced. The threats remained, the secrets still hung heavy in the air. However, the balance of power had shifted. Aisha was no longer merely a victim of circumstance, but an active participant in shaping her own destiny. She discovered a strength she never knew she possessed, a strength that transformed her from a woman battered by life into a woman empowered by it. The silk and shadows of Kenji's world remained, but now, Aisha stood tall, a woman who was now more than a match for the darkness that surrounded her, and a force to be reckoned with. The journey was far from over, but the path ahead was illuminated by the unwavering light of her newly discovered strength.

CHAPTER 4: THE PRICE OF LOYALTY

The air in Kenji's ancestral home hung heavy with the scent of incense and unspoken words. We sat on low cushions, the soft glow of paper lanterns casting long shadows across the tatami mats. Outside, the Tokyo night hummed with a vibrant energy, a stark contrast to the quiet intensity within. He'd poured us both sake, the amber liquid shimmering in the dim light. The silence stretched, punctuated only by the gentle clinking of our cups.

Then, he began to speak, his voice low and measured, each word carefully chosen. He spoke of a past I hadn't known, a past shrouded in secrets and shadows, a past that explained the steely glint in his eyes, the quiet intensity that simmered beneath his calm exterior.

He spoke of his grandfather, the patriarch who had built the beauty empire from the ground up, a man who had risen from humble beginnings to become a powerful figure within the Yakuza. He spoke of the unwavering loyalty demanded within the family, a loyalty that bordered on obsession, a loyalty that demanded absolute obedience and unwavering devotion. It was a loyalty forged in fire, tested by betrayal, and solidified by bloodshed. He painted a picture of a man who valued tradition more than anything else, a man who believed in the rigid code of honor, even if that code was often brutal and unforgiving.

He described the intricate web of alliances and rivalries that defined his family's existence within the Yakuza, a world of shifting allegiances and unspoken threats. He detailed the calculated risks, the strategic maneuvers, the constant vigilance required to survive in such a treacherous environment. He spoke of betrayals that echoed through generations, betrayals that had cost lives and fortunes, betrayals that had left deep scars on the family's soul. He spoke of his father, a man torn between the demands of tradition and his own yearning for a different life, a life free from the violence and intrigue that had defined his existence. His father's struggle, Kenji said, was the defining event in his own life.

He revealed a clandestine affair his father had engaged in, a love story hidden in the shadows, a love that defied the strictures of the Yakuza code. The woman, a beautiful geisha named Hana, was not of their world. Their clandestine meetings were fraught with peril. The risk of discovery carried dire consequences, both for his father and for Hana. Yet, their love persisted, a testament to the human spirit's capacity to transcend even the most restrictive societal norms.

Their clandestine relationship bore fruit—Kenji's younger sister, Akari. The existence of Akari threatened to unravel his father's position within the Yakuza, and as a consequence, the entire family's standing. Akari's existence was a carefully guarded secret, a silent witness to a dangerous love affair. This secret carried its own weight of vulnerability and risk.

The revelation of Akari's existence ultimately led to a violent confrontation, a brutal clash between tradition and forbidden love. Kenji's father, caught in the crossfire, made a choice that would shape the destinies of his children. He chose to protect Hana and Akari, to shield them from the wrath of the Yakuza. This act of defiance, while born from love, shattered the carefully constructed world around them. He made a choice, prioritizing his own bloodline above unwavering loyalty to his family and tradition.

The fallout was swift and brutal. Kenji's father was ostracized, his position within the Yakuza stripped away. Hana, forced to flee with Akari, disappeared into the shadows, leaving Kenji with the responsibility of protecting his younger sister. The price of his father's loyalty was steep— exile, poverty, and a life lived in fear and uncertainty. Kenji recounted his own childhood, a stark contrast to the opulent lifestyle he now leads. He painted vivid images of cramped living quarters and constant fear for his and his sister's well-being.

This was the origin of his ruthlessness, of his determination to succeed, to rebuild what had been lost. The memory of his father's sacrifice fueled his ambition, driving him to achieve a level of power and influence that would ensure his family's security and protect them from the threats that still haunted them. It was a burden he carried quietly, a secret sorrow hidden beneath a veneer of calm sophistication. His vulnerability was unexpected, startlingly genuine.

He spoke of the constant fear he lived with for his sister, a fear that shaped his decisions, influencing his every move. The loss of his father had left a deep void, a wound that would never truly heal. He sought solace in his work, his dedication to the family business providing an escape from the weight of his past. However, a deep-seated longing for his father remained.

This past, he admitted, was why he initially pursued me. The initial lust, the undeniable chemistry, was only one aspect of what had drawn him to me. I'd become a symbol of something he couldn't have before. I represented a new beginning, an escape from the constraints of his past, a chance to create a life different from the one he had always known. The intensity of our relationship, he explained, was born out of both desire and a deep-seated need for connection. The fear of betrayal, of repeating his father's mistakes, was very real.

He also spoke of Akari, his sister, who had grown into a strong, independent woman despite her unconventional upbringing. She had been a constant source of strength, a reminder of the family he had lost and the family he was now desperately trying to create. He spoke of his love for her, a love that bound them together in the face of adversity.

As the night deepened, the sake flowed, and the secrets spilled forth like a torrent. Kenji's revelations were not merely an exposition of his family history; they were an unveiling of his soul, a testament to his strength and vulnerability. The lines between loyalty and betrayal, between love and loss, were blurred, painting a complex portrait of a man caught in the turbulent currents of his heritage. It was a story of profound love and profound loss, and through his revelations, I began to understand the man I had fallen for, a man who carried the weight of generations on his shoulders, yet still found room in his heart for love. His story was a testament to the enduring power of family, even amidst violence and betrayal, a reminder that love could bloom even in the darkest corners of the world. He wasn't just the heir to a beauty empire; he was the heir to a complex legacy, a legacy that both haunted and defined him.

The weight of these confessions hung in the air long after the last drop of sake was consumed, long after he had finished telling his story. It illuminated his actions, his decisions, the way he moved through the world, the way he interacted with me. It explained the intensity of our connection, the fear and the longing that danced between us. It painted a picture of a man who was both fiercely protective and profoundly vulnerable, a man who was struggling to balance the demands of his family, his past, and his present. His confession was a turning point, a shift in the dynamic of our relationship. It forged a deeper understanding, a stronger bond built on shared vulnerability and a mutual understanding of the sacrifices and complexities that defined our lives. The silence that followed was more profound, more intimate, than any words could ever express. The secrets had been revealed, and the consequences of that revelation lay ahead, waiting to be faced.

The quiet intensity of Kenji's confession lingered, a palpable weight in the air even after the sake was gone and the lanterns dimmed. His vulnerability, so unexpected in a man of such power, had cracked open something within me, a sense of understanding that transcended the erotic pull that had initially drawn us together. But the revelation didn't erase the danger. My brush with death hadn't been a fluke; the drug deal I'd unwittingly recorded hadn't been a one-off. It was time to act, not just react.

Kenji's world was a minefield, and I wasn't about to wait passively for the explosion. My past with Marcus, a low-level drug dealer whose brutality had scarred me both physically and emotionally, had taught me one thing: survival depended on proactive defense. Kenji might be a powerful Yakuza, but

I had my own strengths, my own intelligence, and my own fierce determination to survive. I wouldn't be a passive player in his game.

My investigation began subtly. I started by re-examining the video footage I'd accidentally captured, the grainy images showing snippets of faces, hushed conversations, and the exchange of a package that could have easily cost me my life. I had downloaded it to my encrypted laptop, a precaution born of years spent dodging danger. The faces were mostly obscured, but there were details: tattoos, clothing styles, mannerisms. Details that spoke volumes to someone who understood the subtle codes of the street.

My childhood in South Central LA had been a crucible of hard lessons. Survival wasn't about passivity; it was about observation, analysis, and strategic thinking. I'd learned to read the unspoken cues, the subtle shifts in body language, the fleeting expressions that betrayed a person's true intentions. It was the same skill set that helped me navigate the complex social dynamics of my predominantly black neighborhood, and it was the same skill set I was now bringing to bear on Kenji's world. I had always felt a certain kinship with the resourcefulness and resilience of my people, our ability to rise above adversity. My intelligence and my analytical abilities were my weapons of choice.

My first step was finding someone who could help me decipher the visual data. I reached out to an old acquaintance, a tech wiz named Marcus – no relation to my ex – who owed me a favor. Marcus was brilliant, a self-taught programmer with a knack for decrypting and enhancing digital information. He lived outside the usual social circles of the Yakuza, making him the perfect ally. We met at a nondescript café in a quiet part of Tokyo, far removed from the city's neon-drenched pulse. His expertise was far more than simple technological prowess; he understood the underbelly of the city, too. The way in which certain details could be used, not just to tell a story but to weave a narrative that could eventually expose a criminal network.

He analyzed the footage, his nimble fingers flying across the keyboard. Hours melted away as he meticulously enhanced the images, isolating key features and searching for identifying markers. The tattoos, initially indistinct, slowly resolved into recognizable symbols: a dragon intertwined with a serpent, suggesting a possible affiliation with a specific Yakuza family. He found details in the clothes, the subtle nuances in the way they stood and moved. There were patterns, and he highlighted them all for me.

"This isn't just a one-off deal," he said, his voice low, grave. "These guys are organized, professional. The way they moved, the signals they sent. There's a hierarchy, a structure."

His analysis gave me the first pieces of a puzzle, small fragments of information that hinted at a much larger, more dangerous picture. It wasn't just Kenji's world; it was a complex network, and I had accidentally stumbled into its heart. I needed to understand the players involved, their connections, and their motives.

My next step involved reaching out to my contacts in the global intelligence community. My past experiences had given me access to individuals who, while operating outside the law, possessed invaluable information. These were people with intricate knowledge of international criminal networks, skilled at gathering intel and identifying patterns. They respected my abilities, my willingness to push boundaries while remaining cautiously self-reliant. They weren't about cheap thrills or superficial victories; they were all about the long game.

Through these channels, I unearthed information about the specific Yakuza family that appeared to be involved. It confirmed Marcus' findings and filled in critical gaps, illuminating a web of intricate relationships that extended far beyond Tokyo's borders. The family was known for their brutal efficiency, their ruthlessness, and their extensive network across the Asian black market. They were dealers of more than just drugs; they moved arms, laundered money, and dealt in human trafficking.

As the days turned into weeks, my investigation took on a life of its own. I was consumed by the pursuit of answers, poring over documents, following leads, and utilizing my skills to build a comprehensive understanding of the situation. I used all the skills that my black upbringing had taught me – a mixture of caution, resourcefulness, and intuitive understanding of human behavior – to navigate the dangerous terrain. The pursuit required tact, determination, and a steely resolve to avoid being discovered.

The investigation started to become intertwined with my relationship with Kenji. The more I learned, the more complex his world became. It wasn't just a family business; it was a network of power and influence, with shadowy figures and hidden agendas operating in the background. My own desires, my fascination with Kenji, now clashed with the ever-growing danger. The lines between personal involvement and professional investigation started to blur.

The closer I got to the truth, the more precarious my position became. I was walking a tightrope, balancing my desire to protect myself with my growing feelings for Kenji, who, despite his family's involvement, remained unaware of my investigation. The weight of my discovery pressed down on me, a heavy burden I had to carry alone. I knew that this investigation was not merely about my own survival, but could potentially unravel an international criminal empire.

Meanwhile, my growing understanding of the Yakuza's operations gave me a new perspective on Kenji's actions, his motivations, and the weight he carried on his shoulders. The price of loyalty, the constant struggle between tradition and personal desires, became crystal clear. He wasn't just a powerful man; he was a prisoner of his past, caught in a web of family obligations and societal expectations.

The investigation gave me a deeper understanding of the culture that shaped Kenji, a culture I had only glimpsed before. It allowed me to appreciate the depth of his dedication to his sister, his loyalty to her, and the sacrifices he had made. His ruthlessness was not simply born of inherent cruelty but from a deep-seated need to protect his family, to secure their future in a world where loyalty had a price.

My investigation wasn't about revenge; it was about survival, about protecting myself and those I cared about. I wanted to control my own narrative, to avoid becoming another victim in their brutal game. I was charting my own course, utilizing my skills, my intelligence, and my determination to navigate the dangerous waters of Kenji's world, a world where the price of loyalty was paid in blood, and where betrayal was always lurking just around the corner. The tension was building; my investigation was bringing me closer to the truth, but the closer I got, the more dangerous it became. The threat was real, and it was closing in.

The humid Tokyo air hung heavy, thick with the scent of rain and impending violence. We stood on the precipice of a forgotten shrine, its weathered stone torii gate a stark contrast to the glittering cityscape sprawling behind us. Kenji, usually radiating an aura of effortless control, was tense, his jaw clenched, his usually playful eyes narrowed with a fierce intensity that sent shivers down my spine. He was flanked by two imposing figures, their faces obscured by the shadows of their wide-brimmed hats, their presence radiating an aura of cold, calculated menace.

Across from us stood the leader of the opposing faction, a man known only as "Oni," his name a fitting moniker for the brutal, almost demonic aura he exuded. He was flanked by his own goons, their movements fluid and dangerous, like coiled vipers ready to strike. The air crackled with unspoken threats, a silent battle of wills waged between two powerful forces. The clash wasn't just about territory or power; it was a personal confrontation, a showdown born from years of simmering resentment and betrayal.

Kenji's hand rested lightly on the hilt of his katana, a subtle gesture that spoke volumes about the gravity of the situation. He hadn't drawn the sword yet, but the mere implication of its presence hung like a threat between us, a palpable reminder of the potential for bloodshed. The silence was broken only by the chirping of crickets and the distant hum of the city, a stark contrast to the lethal tension that filled the air.

"Kenji," Oni's voice rasped, cutting through the silence like a knife, "this ends tonight. You've overstepped your boundaries. The deal was simple. You were to stay out of our territory. You failed to uphold your end of the bargain."

Kenji didn't flinch, his gaze unwavering. "My loyalty is to my family, Oni. And you crossed a line. You threatened my sister. That was a mistake." His voice was calm, controlled, yet laced with an underlying fury that sent a jolt through me. The carefully constructed façade of polite indifference had shattered, revealing the fierce warrior beneath.

Oni laughed, a harsh, guttural sound. "Loyalty? In this world, loyalty is a luxury few can afford.
It's a commodity traded, bought, and sold. And you, Kenji, have become expendable."

He gestured to his men. "Take him."

The air exploded into motion. Kenji's men moved with balletic precision, their movements a blur of controlled violence. Oni's men retaliated, the clash of bodies and steel a symphony of controlled chaos. It was a dance of death, a deadly ballet where every move was calculated, every strike aimed to inflict maximum damage. Kenji, however, remained surprisingly calm in the storm. He moved with grace and power, a master of his craft, his blade a deadly extension of his will.

I stood frozen, caught between the two warring factions, my

heart pounding a frantic rhythm against my ribs. The violence was mesmerizing and terrifying at the same time. It reminded me of the chaotic energy of my own South Central upbringing, only amplified, intensified, and refined by centuries of tradition. I felt a strange sense of kinship with the intensity of it all; it was a fierce, almost primal struggle.

My initial instinct was to flee, to escape the brutal dance of death unfolding before me, but I knew I couldn't. Not yet. My investigation, my quest for answers, was tied to this confrontation. I had to witness it unfold to completely understand the dynamics of power in this world and how Kenji operated within it. My role was different from his; I had to observe.

The fight raged on for what seemed like an eternity, a blur of motion and sound. Kenji, despite being outnumbered, held his own, his skill and precision a testament to his years of training. His movements were economical, each blow perfectly placed, each parry calculated to disarm and disable. He was a master of strategy, a warrior who understood the rhythm of battle. His combat style showcased not just brute strength, but a deep understanding of leverage, momentum, and pressure points. I had to admit, there was a certain artistry in his movements, an almost balletic elegance that belied the deadly intent behind them.

But Oni's men were relentless, their numbers a significant advantage. Kenji was sustaining injuries, small cuts and bruises appearing on his arms and face. I caught a glimpse of a deep gash on his side as he disarmed one of his attackers. The blood was quickly soaked into his black clothing. The fight was shifting in Oni's favor.

Just as I feared Kenji was about to be overwhelmed, a sudden shift in the dynamics caught my attention. I had been analyzing the situation, not just from a physical standpoint, but also from the intelligence I had been collecting. My knowledge of the various factions and their underlying power structures seemed to provide me with a sudden insight.

I noticed a subtle hesitation in Oni's men, a flicker of uncertainty in their eyes. It was then I realized that I was looking at the situation through a completely wrong lens. It wasn't just a random brawl among rival Yakuza gangs; it was part of a larger, more complex strategy. The unexpected hesitation was a crucial element that tipped the scales.

Suddenly, the air was pierced by the sound of approaching sirens. It was a coordinated intervention, strategically timed to disrupt Oni's plans. The sirens were not accidental; they represented a shift in power dynamics. Someone else was involved, someone with the ability to influence events on a larger scale. This was not just a local conflict; it was a move on the international chessboard.

Oni's men, momentarily paralyzed by the unexpected disruption, hesitated, their carefully planned attack dissolving into chaos. They began to retreat, their leader giving a disgruntled growl. The carefully constructed façade of power crumbled before the sudden intervention.

Their meticulously coordinated assault had fallen apart in the face of unexpected external pressure.

Kenji, seeing his opportunity, swiftly disengaged from his attackers and moved to protect me from being caught in the crossfire. He pulled me close, his embrace both protective and intensely intimate. The confrontation had ended not with a decisive victory, but with a strategic retreat. We had survived, but the underlying tensions were far from resolved. The events of that night were a stark reminder of the precarious nature of power, the ever-shifting alliances, and the high price of loyalty in a world ruled by violence and intrigue. The price of loyalty, in this dangerous dance of power, was not just physical wounds, but a constant state of precarious balance, where survival hinged on strategy, anticipation, and the ability to anticipate the unforeseen.

The aftermath left us reeling, both physically and emotionally. Kenji's injuries were severe, though not life-threatening. The encounter had reinforced the complex web of loyalties and betrayals that characterized his world. The confrontation hadn't resolved the conflict, rather it had intensified the stakes.

The unexpected intervention, the appearance of the police sirens, hinted at a deeper conspiracy, a network of hidden players and shifting alliances that I was only beginning to understand. It was a subtle reminder that the fight was far from over. The victory, if it could even be called that, was pyrrhic, a momentary reprieve in a prolonged war. Kenji's world, it seemed, would continue to be a dangerous place, a world where loyalty had a price, and where betrayal lurked around every corner. The night at the shrine had only served to deepen the mystery, escalating the stakes, and making me realize that my investigation had only just begun.

The sterile white of the hospital room felt jarring after the raw, visceral energy of the shrine. Kenji lay in the bed, his face pale, his breathing shallow, but his eyes, those captivating dark pools, held a spark of defiance. The bandages wrapped around his torso spoke of a deeper injury than I had initially perceived, a stark reminder of the night's brutality. He looked like a fallen warrior, but the glint in his eye refused to be extinguished. He was resilient, stubborn, and deeply wounded, both physically and emotionally.

"They were expecting a fight," Kenji rasped, his voice hoarse. "Oni wanted a public display of power, a clear message to the other factions. He underestimated the reach of my family. But he overestimated his own." He paused, wincing as he shifted slightly. "The sirens… that wasn't the police."

My breath hitched. "You mean…?"

He nodded, a subtle movement. "My family has its own network of informants, its own way of dealing with threats. The sirens were a distraction, a way to create chaos and allow for a strategic retreat. It was a calculated move, a show of power designed to send a message to Oni, and to anyone else watching."

A new understanding washed over me. The seemingly random appearance of the sirens, the sudden shift in Oni's demeanor, it had all been orchestrated. It wasn't just Kenji and his family; there was a larger game at play, a network of alliances and betrayals far more intricate than I had initially imagined. This wasn't just a struggle for territory; it was a war for control, a fight for supremacy in a world steeped in ancient traditions and modern ambition.

But the most unexpected twist came a few hours later. A woman entered the room, her appearance as striking as the contrast between the sterile hospital environment and the vibrant tapestry of her traditional Korean hanbok. Her name was Sun-hee, and she was introduced as Kenji's aunt – a formidable woman with a sharp intellect and an even sharper gaze. She spoke little, her words precise, her movements economical. She was a woman of quiet power, a force to be reckoned with. There was a gravity about her, an aura of experience and wisdom that commanded respect.

Sun-hee and Kenji exchanged a few words in Japanese, a rapid exchange of precise and efficient communication, their closeness palpable despite the presence of others. She spoke very little to me; and I only learned of their conversation during a much later time. Sun-hee's presence served as an unspoken acknowledgment of the precariousness of Kenji's position, a tacit understanding of the ever-shifting tides of power. She had come not merely as a concerned relative, but as a strategic player, a key figure in this intricate game of dominance.

My shock was profound. I expected allies to be loyal companions, not distant relatives of those at the center of organized crime.

"I owe you a debt," Kenji said, his voice stronger now, "and my aunt recognizes that. She sees the value in an unexpected ally."

"An unexpected ally? What does that even mean?" I asked, my confusion evident. I was a pawn, and I did not know the rules of the game.

"Your recording… it's far more valuable than you realize," Sun-hee explained, her voice a low, melodious tone that carried an underlying strength. "It's a bargaining chip, a piece in a larger game."

Suddenly, everything clicked into place. My accidental recording of the drug deal, the one that had nearly cost me my life, was not just a piece of evidence; it was a weapon. Sun-hee's interest wasn't in me personally, but in what I held in my possession, in the information I unwittingly acquired. I was a strategic asset, a pawn in a game I didn't even know I was playing. My background, my independent investigation, and the intelligence I possessed gave me an unfamiliar perspective.

The following days were a whirlwind of activity. Sun-hee introduced me to a network of contacts I never knew existed; individuals from various spheres of influence in Tokyo's underbelly. These individuals, often operating outside the law, were as diverse as the city itself, their allegiances as fluid as the currents of the Sumida River. There was a quiet dignity among them, a respect for tradition and hierarchy. But underneath it all, there was a simmering undercurrent of ambition, of a desire to rise above, a hunger for more power, more influence.

I was surprised to see that the majority of those working in the network were Asian women, often overlooked and underestimated in the male-dominated world of the Yakuza. These were individuals who had learned to maneuver the treacherous waters of this underworld, leveraging their skills and intelligence to achieve their goals. They did not shy away from power, recognizing it as a tool to be wielded, to be used for their own advantage. Their knowledge and strength challenged my assumptions about gender roles and power dynamics within these communities.

Their world, I quickly learned, was a complex tapestry of alliances and rivalries. It was a world where loyalty could be bought, sold, and betrayed in a heartbeat. And they were masters of the game, playing the various factions against each other, creating, and exploiting opportunities for their own gain. They were shrewd, strategic, and incredibly resourceful, operating in the shadows with expertise and skill. The women in this network displayed incredible resilience, and their resourcefulness challenged my notions of societal roles and expectations. They were more than just victims or pawns; they were players in this dangerous game, their own agency shaping the narrative. And I, an outsider, found myself becoming a pivotal part of their game.

Sun-hee explained that my skills were an asset, that my independent nature and my capacity to view things from an outsider's perspective were unique. My ability to analyze patterns, to see connections others missed, made me valuable.

Kenji, despite his injuries, played a key role in guiding me. His knowledge of the Yakuza, his understanding of the intricate power dynamics, and his connections within this world provided the foundation on which we built our strategy.

We started piecing together fragments of information, connecting seemingly disparate events. I discovered that Oni's operation was more extensive than it appeared, his reach extending far beyond the local drug trade. His actions, we learned, were linked to a much larger criminal network, one that was involved in international arms trafficking.

Our strategy involved a slow, calculated approach, a game of deception that involved leaking carefully chosen bits of information to various factions. It was a high-stakes gambit that played on the various rivalries and ambitions within the Yakuza. It required precise timing, strategic maneuvers, and a thorough understanding of the subtle power plays and the complexities of the relationships within this world. The unexpected alliance created a new dynamics that no one had predicted.

This unexpected partnership—a Black American woman and a member of the Yakuza, working alongside his formidable aunt—was a bold stroke. It was a testament to the inherent unpredictability of life, the way seemingly disparate elements can converge to create unforeseen opportunities. It was also a reflection of the resilience of those who find themselves on the fringes, those who have been marginalized and overlooked, rising to become crucial players in this dangerous game. Our alliance was a powerful symbol of the unexpected power of collaboration and understanding amidst the chaos. This partnership, born from a chance encounter and a shared need for survival, was now the key to unraveling a web of deceit and uncovering the truth behind Oni's operation. The risks were substantial, but the potential rewards, in terms of exposing a far-reaching criminal enterprise, were even greater. The stakes were high, the outcome uncertain, but the game was afoot. The unpredictable dance of power continued, and with each step, we moved closer to the truth, yet further into the heart of a world where loyalty came at a steep price, and betrayal was always just a heartbeat away. The path ahead remained treacherous, filled with potential dangers, but armed with our unlikely alliance and a shared determination to prevail, we were ready to face whatever came next. The unexpected alliance had not only changed the game but also transformed our lives forever.

The days that followed were a blur of clandestine meetings, hushed conversations, and the constant pressure of the looming threat. Kenji, still recovering from his injuries, remained a vital source of information, his insights into the Yakuza's intricate web of power proving invaluable. Sun-hee, ever watchful, orchestrated our moves with precision, her calm demeanor belying the gravity of the situation. I, the accidental pawn in their high-stakes game, found myself becoming an increasingly important player. My outsider's perspective, coupled with my analytical skills, allowed me to see connections that even the seasoned Yakuza members overlooked.

My role was to analyze the data we gathered: intercepted communications, financial records, coded messages – a chaotic jumble of information that only started to reveal its significance once I pieced it together. The longer I worked with Sun-hee and Kenji, the more I appreciated their expertise. Sun-hee, a woman who moved with the silent grace of a predator, possessed a keen strategic mind. Her knowledge of the Yakuza's inner workings, their rituals, and their unspoken rules, was as vast as the Tokyo skyline at night. Kenji, despite his physical limitations, remained a crucial link, his intimate knowledge of the rival factions providing a critical advantage.

One evening, amidst the tension and uncertainty, Kenji revealed a secret that shook me to my core. Oni wasn't just a rival gang leader; he was someone from his own family, a distant cousin with a long-standing grudge against Kenji's father. This internal conflict, this betrayal within the family, threatened to shatter the delicate balance of power that held the Yakuza together. The revelation added a layer of personal stakes to our already perilous mission. It was no longer simply about stopping a drug operation; it was about preventing a devastating family feud that could plunge the entire organization into chaos.

As we delved deeper, the risks escalated. We learned that Oni had informants within Kenji's own family. The whispers of betrayal echoed through the hushed conversations and furtive glances. The lines between loyalty and treachery blurred, making it impossible to discern who was a friend and who was a foe.

Then came the ultimatum. Sun-hee informed me that Oni was demanding a sacrifice – a symbolic gesture to appease his anger and prevent an all-out war. The sacrifice: me. He wanted me, not just as a prize, but as a means to humiliate Kenji and his family, a public display of his power.

The weight of the decision crushed me. My initial reaction was terror, a primal fear for my own safety. But then, a different feeling emerged – a fierce protectiveness towards Kenji. My love for him, initially fueled by passion and mutual attraction, had deepened into something far more profound – a selfless love that transcended my own fears and desires. I saw in his eyes not just his pain, but the weight of the responsibility he carried for his family.

I knew what I had to do. The thought of surrendering myself to Oni, a man who embodied brutality and cruelty, filled me with dread. Yet, the alternative—a devastating war that would claim countless lives—was unthinkable. I looked at Kenji, his face etched with worry, and saw the courage and strength he held, even as he battled his own pain. This man had risked everything for me, and now it was my turn to sacrifice for him.

My decision to sacrifice myself wasn't merely an act of bravery; it was a testament to the depth of my love and loyalty. It was a recognition of the intricate tapestry of my own desires against the backdrop of his dangerous life. The knowledge that I was making a choice born not out of weakness but out of unwavering commitment strengthened my resolve.

The ensuing events were a whirlwind of calculated movements. Sun-hee, with her intricate network of contacts, orchestrated a meticulously planned surrender. It wasn't a straightforward submission; it was a strategic maneuver, designed to expose Oni's weaknesses and destabilize his power base. I wouldn't simply be handed over; I would be used as bait to trap him.

The day of the "surrender" arrived, heavy with anticipation and uncertainty. I dressed in simple clothing, removing all jewelry and discarding anything that could be identified as mine. I wanted to be anonymous, an unremarkable figure swallowed by the shadows of the Yakuza world. Kenji stood beside me, his gaze steady, his hand gently gripping mine. He spoke little, but the strength in his touch assured me he knew the risks we were both taking.

As we approached Oni's territory, I felt a strange mixture of fear and resolve. The streets were eerily silent, the usual cacophony of Tokyo replaced by an unnerving quiet. It was a city holding its breath, waiting for the fallout of our actions.

The meeting took place in a dilapidated warehouse, the air thick with tension. Oni and his men waited. Their faces, hard and emotionless, betrayed their true intentions. Oni's eyes, however, held a glint of arrogance, a belief in his own invincibility. He underestimated our plan, our strategy. He was blind to the truth, the trap that was being laid around him.

The "surrender" unfolded as planned. I played my role, showcasing a facade of vulnerability and fear. But beneath the surface, I was alert, my senses heightened, anticipating the moment of action. The moment where the trap would spring. The moment of revelation.

What happened next was a cascade of events, a chaotic ballet of deceit and counter-deceit. The seemingly simple surrender transformed into a calculated ambush. Sun-hee's network sprang into action, creating a diversion that allowed Kenji and his forces to move undetected. They captured Oni and most of his trusted associates. It was a stunning victory, a testament to the careful planning and unwavering bravery of those involved.

But even in victory, the price of loyalty remained. My sacrifice, the decision to offer myself as bait, left an indelible mark, a scar that would run deeper than any physical wound. The experience transformed me, shaping my understanding of love, loss, and the devastating consequences of loyalty. The cost was high, but the victory was sweet, the outcome worth the pain. The aftermath was long and arduous, with the Yakuza world undergoing a significant reshaping. The delicate balance of power had been irrevocably altered. My role in this upheaval transformed my standing. I was no longer merely a pawn, but a player, one who was deeply entwined with the lives and fate of these powerful individuals.

My relationship with Kenji had been forged in the crucible of danger and sacrifice, and its intensity deepened with each shared trial. Our love was a fierce and unwavering commitment, built on mutual respect and trust. It was a love that transcended cultural boundaries and societal expectations, a testament to the extraordinary connection we shared.

The scars remained, but so did the love, even stronger and deeper than before. The price of loyalty had been paid, but the rewards, though hard-earned, were immeasurable. The future remained uncertain, the path ahead still treacherous, but we faced it together, united by our love and a shared determination to build a future free from the shadows of the Yakuza's dangerous world.

CHAPTER 5:
BURNING BRIDGES

The aftermath of Oni's capture was a whirlwind of activity. The Yakuza world, already teetering on the edge of chaos, now faced a seismic shift in power. Kenji, despite his victory, bore the weight of his family's internal struggle. The betrayal by Oni, a blood relative, had exposed deep fissures within the organization, cracks that threatened to fracture its foundations. The whispers of dissent, previously muffled, now grew louder, echoing through the dimly lit backrooms and hushed gatherings of the Yakuza.

My own position was precarious. I had been instrumental in Oni's downfall, but my status remained ambiguous. I was an outsider, an African American woman thrust into the heart of a Japanese criminal underworld, my life intertwined with the fates of these powerful, often ruthless, men and women. My relationship with Kenji, forged in the fires of danger and sacrifice, was a beacon of hope amidst the swirling storm of betrayal and uncertainty. Yet, it was a love that existed in the shadows, constantly vulnerable to the capricious whims of fate and the relentless machinations of the Yakuza.

Kenji's father, the head of the family, summoned me to his office, a stark, minimalist space that belied the immense power it represented. He was a man of few words, his expression unreadable, his gaze piercing. He offered me neither gratitude nor apology, but a simple acknowledgment of my contribution to the family's survival. The unspoken understanding hung heavy in the air: my life was now inextricably linked to his family's destiny. There was no escaping the complexities of the situation, no simple solutions to the intricate web of loyalties and betrayals.

The ensuing days were filled with tense negotiations, strategic alliances being forged and broken with the same ruthless efficiency that characterized the Yakuza's operations. The fallout from Oni's betrayal extended beyond the immediate family, affecting the balance of power within the entire network. Rival factions sensed weakness and exploited it, vying for dominance in the power vacuum left by Oni's arrest.

During this period, Sun-hee's role proved invaluable. Her network, a vast and intricate system of informants and operatives, ensured that we remained one step ahead of the shifting tides. She moved like a phantom, gathering intelligence, identifying threats, and orchestrating countermeasures with a precision that was both terrifying and awe-inspiring. Her understanding of the Yakuza's intricate social structure and unspoken codes of conduct was unmatched, her loyalty unwavering despite the immense risk to her own life. She was, in her own way, a force of nature, a woman who had carved out her place in this male-dominated world with ruthless efficiency and steely determination.

My relationship with Kenji deepened, evolving beyond the initial spark of attraction into something more profound. We found solace in each other, sharing unspoken anxieties and celebrating small victories amidst the chaos. The shared trauma we had endured had forged an unbreakable bond, a testament to our resilience and the strength of our love. But our intimacy was always tinged with a shadow of apprehension, the ever-present awareness that our love story unfolded within a world where betrayal was as commonplace as breathing.

The cultural differences between us added another layer of complexity to our bond. My upbringing in the African American community, with its history of struggle and resilience, contrasted sharply with Kenji's background in the traditional Japanese Yakuza. We navigated these differences with a mixture of humor and sensitivity, appreciating the rich tapestry of our respective cultures. Our physical intimacy, often a refuge from the harsh realities of our lives, reflected this blending of cultures, each sensual encounter a unique exploration of our combined experiences. Our love was a testament to the universality of human connection, transcending boundaries of race, culture, and societal expectations.

But even amidst the turbulent waters of the Yakuza's power struggles, there were moments of tranquility. Stolen moments of intimacy, whispered secrets shared in the quiet corners of a bustling city, quiet evenings spent in Kenji's family's opulent but understated home. These moments, fleeting as they often were, were precious reminders of the simple joys and the profound love that sustained us amidst the storm.

The investigation into Oni's network continued, revealing a deeper conspiracy that extended far beyond the initial drug operation. It was a network of corruption that reached into the highest levels of the Yakuza, implicating key figures who had long been considered untouchable. The revelations were shocking, uncovering a web of deceit and betrayal that had been woven over decades. The investigation unearthed hidden alliances, secret deals, and long-forgotten grudges, revealing the true extent of the power struggles within the Yakuza.

As we delved deeper into the heart of the conspiracy, the risks increased exponentially. The lines between allies and enemies blurred, making it impossible to discern who could be trusted. We found ourselves facing threats not only from within the Yakuza, but from outside forces who sought to exploit the resulting instability. The fight for survival became a desperate struggle against overwhelming odds, a battle against a network of corruption so deeply entrenched that it seemed insurmountable.

The tensions within Kenji's family escalated. The cracks that had appeared after Oni's betrayal widened, threatening to fracture the family's unity. Old grudges resurfaced, simmering beneath the surface, fueled by ambition and the intoxicating power the Yakuza wielded. The family's internal struggle mirrored the larger conflict within the organization, a microcosm of the chaos and betrayal engulfing the Yakuza world.

Throughout this tumultuous period, my relationship with Kenji served as an anchor in the storm. We faced each challenge together, supporting each other, finding strength in our shared love. My outsider's perspective, my ability to think outside the constraints of Yakuza tradition, proved to be an unexpected asset in navigating the complexities of their internal conflicts.

The final confrontation was inevitable. A showdown between

the remaining factions vying for control of the Yakuza. It was a battle not just for power, but for survival, a clash between forces steeped in tradition and ambition. The fight was brutal, a stark reminder of the violence and brutality inherent within the Yakuza's world. I found myself playing a pivotal role, using my analytical skills and knowledge of the opposing factions to assist Kenji and his allies in achieving victory.

The aftermath of the battle left a trail of destruction. Many lives were lost, and the Yakuza landscape was forever altered. Kenji emerged as a powerful figure, his position secured but his heart heavy with the cost of victory. The scars of betrayal ran deep, both within the organization and within his family. My role in the events had elevated my standing, but at a steep price.

My future remained uncertain. My life with Kenji was inextricably linked to the dangers inherent within the Yakuza world, but our love had weathered the storm. It had grown stronger, more resilient, through the trials we had faced together. The future held both promise and peril, but we would face it together, united by a love that transcended the complexities and dangers of the world around us. Our love was a testament to the strength of the human spirit, a beacon of hope in a world defined by violence and betrayal.

The air hung thick with the scent of rain and fear. We were trapped. The warehouse, once a clandestine meeting place for Kenji's family, now echoed with the sounds of pursuing footsteps and shattering glass. Oni's loyalists, emboldened by the chaos following his arrest, had launched a desperate attempt to regain control, and we were caught in the crossfire. Kenji had underestimated the depth of their loyalty, the ferocity of their desperation. We'd barely escaped the initial ambush, a hail of bullets narrowly missing us as we scrambled through the labyrinthine corridors. My heart hammered against my ribs, a frantic drumbeat against the backdrop of the escalating violence.

The adrenaline coursed through my veins, a potent cocktail of terror and exhilaration. Kenji's hand, strong and reassuring, gripped mine, his touch grounding me amidst the chaos. He moved with a practiced efficiency, his years of experience in the Yakuza evident in every calculated maneuver, every decisive action. He was a whirlwind of controlled aggression, a lethal force navigating the treacherous landscape of the warehouse with unwavering focus.

We navigated the maze-like interior of the warehouse, our senses heightened, our movements fluid and silent. Each shadow seemed to conceal a lurking danger, each creak of the floorboards a potential threat. The air throbbed with tension, the silence punctuated only by the rhythmic thud of our running feet and the distant shouts of our pursuers. Kenji's eyes, usually warm and expressive, were narrowed, focused, and intensely serious. His face, usually etched with a playful charm, was set in grim determination.

We reached a dead end. A heavy metal door, reinforced with steel bars, blocked our path. The sound of footsteps grew closer, echoing ominously down the corridor. We were cornered. Kenji's gaze met mine, a silent acknowledgment of our desperate situation. There was no room for hesitation, no time for fear. We had to find another way out.

He swiftly assessed the situation, his eyes scanning the

surroundings with a practiced keenness.

His gaze fell upon a small, almost invisible ventilation shaft high up on the wall. It was a slim chance, a risky gamble, but it was our only option.

"Aisha," he whispered, his voice barely audible above the rising din of the approaching pursuers. "Trust me."

He hefted me onto his shoulders, his grip firm and steady. Using his strength and agility, he scaled the wall, his movements as smooth and effortless as a seasoned climber. The ascent was grueling, my body trembling with a mixture of exertion and fear. The air grew thin, the smell of dust and rust filling my nostrils.

Once we reached the ventilation shaft, Kenji carefully maneuvered us into its narrow confines. The space was claustrophobic, the air stale and heavy. We inched our way through the dark, cramped passage, the metallic grating digging into our skin. Every rustle, every creak of the metal, sent shivers down my spine. The sounds of our pursuers faded, replaced by the rhythmic thump of our own hearts.

The journey through the ventilation shaft was a test of endurance, a grueling crawl through the bowels of the building. We navigated tight corners, avoided obstacles, and pressed onward, propelled by adrenaline and the sheer will to survive. Kenji's presence, his strength, and his calm demeanor provided me with the strength I needed to continue, even as despair threatened to consume me.

Finally, after what felt like an eternity, we emerged from the ventilation shaft onto the roof of the warehouse. The cool night air washed over us, a welcome relief from the stifling confines of the duct. Below us, the city lights twinkled like a million fallen stars, a breathtaking panorama that offered a stark contrast to the chaos we had just escaped. We were safe, for now.

But our escape was far from over. The warehouse was surrounded, a sea of flashing lights and sirens adding a cacophony to the already tense atmosphere. We had to reach Kenji's car, parked several blocks away, across a network of crowded city streets. It was a perilous journey, a highstakes game of cat and mouse played against the backdrop of a sprawling metropolis.

Kenji's knowledge of the city's back alleys and hidden passageways proved invaluable. He expertly navigated the labyrinthine streets, his movements swift and decisive, his awareness of our surroundings sharp and focused. He led me through narrow side streets, across rooftops, and through dimly lit alleyways, each step a calculated risk, each turn a gamble with fate.

We moved like shadows, blending into the urban landscape, our presence almost imperceptible amidst the city's bustling night life. The chase was relentless, punctuated by the distant wail of sirens and the occasional shout of a pursuing officer. The threat was ever-present, a shadow that hung over us, a constant reminder of the danger that stalked us.

The tension was palpable, the air thick with the anticipation of capture. Each rustling leaf, each passing car, could have been our pursuers. We pressed on, our determination fueled by the sheer will to survive, our bond strengthened by the shared peril we faced. We were a team, united in our fight for freedom, our love a potent force that sustained us amidst the chaos.

Finally, we reached Kenji's car, a sleek, black sedan that stood out amidst the city's ordinary vehicles. We jumped in, Kenji fumbling with the ignition as the sounds of pursuit drew closer. The engine roared to life, and with a screech of tires, we sped away, leaving the warehouse and our pursuers behind.

The city lights blurred into streaks of color as we sped through the streets, a thrilling escape from the clutches of death. We were free, for now. But the shadow of Oni's betrayal, the threat of his remaining loyalists, still loomed large, casting a long and ominous shadow over our future. Our journey, our fight for survival, was far from over. The escape from the warehouse was just the beginning of a long and dangerous road ahead. A road we would have to travel together. The journey ahead would be challenging, but our bond, forged in the fires of danger and escape, would be our guide and strength. Our love, a beacon in the darkness, would light the path. Our future was uncertain, but we faced it united and resolute, our hearts beating as one against the odds.

The adrenaline faded, leaving behind a bone-deep exhaustion that clung to me like a second skin. The escape had been exhilarating, terrifying, and utterly exhausting. We sat in Kenji's car, the engine still humming, the city lights a swirling kaleidoscope outside the window. Silence stretched between us, heavy with unspoken anxieties. Kenji's hand found mine, his touch a grounding presence amidst the lingering chaos.

"We need to get you somewhere safe," he finally said, his voice low and husky, the usual playful lilt absent. His eyes, usually sparkling with mischief, were shadowed with concern. The Kenji I knew, the man who could charm the birds from the trees, was replaced by a man hardened by the brutal realities of his world. A man who bore the weight of responsibility, of family, of loyalty, a weight he carried with stoic grace.

"Safe?" I echoed, the word tasting like ash in my mouth. "Where is safe anymore?" The question hung in the air, unanswered, a stark testament to the precariousness of our situation. The warehouse had been a symbol of his world, a world I had now stumbled into, a world where danger lurked around every corner, where loyalty was a double-edged sword, and where the line between life and death was as thin as a whisper.

We drove for what felt like hours, the city morphing into a blur of lights and shadows. Kenji's silence was punctuated only by the occasional terse instruction to the driver, a young man whose face was etched with a mixture of fear and unwavering loyalty. Kenji's world, I was realizing, wasn't just about opulent beauty stores and lavish parties. It was a world of shadows and secrets, of power struggles and betrayals, a world where the slightest misstep could have devastating consequences.

He finally pulled up to a small, unassuming house nestled in a quiet, residential neighborhood, a stark contrast to the opulent luxury of his usual surroundings. It felt strangely out of place, a quiet refuge in the midst of the city's relentless energy. The house held a sense of tranquility, a sanctuary from the storm that raged outside.

Inside, the atmosphere was calm and reassuring. The air was filled with the scent of incense and something subtly sweet, a comforting contrast to the metallic tang of fear that still clung to me. A woman, her face etched with kindness and warmth, greeted us. Kenji introduced her as Hana, his aunt. She moved with a quiet grace, her movements fluid and calming, her presence a soothing balm on my frayed nerves.

Hana prepared tea, the gentle clinking of cups a counterpoint to the turmoil swirling within me. As I sipped the warm liquid, the tension slowly began to ease. Hana's quiet presence, the comforting scent of the incense, the gentle warmth of the tea, all contributed to a sense of peace that I hadn't felt since before the warehouse incident. The fear remained, a low hum beneath the surface, but it was tempered by a newfound sense of security.

Kenji finally broke the silence, his voice soft but serious. "Oni's arrest has shaken things up. His loyalists are desperate, and they're unpredictable." He paused, his gaze locking with mine. "This recording...it's more dangerous than we initially thought."

The recording. The accidental capture of a drug deal, a moment of carelessness that now held the power to destroy us both. It was a constant reminder of the precariousness of our situation, a ticking time bomb waiting to explode.

"The police are already investigating. They're looking for the people involved, and that includes us, even indirectly. The fact you were there...it links you to Kenji, and by extension, his family," he continued, his voice laced with a mixture of concern and regret. His confession was a heavy burden, adding another layer of complexity to our already complicated relationship.

"We're not just dealing with Oni's loyalists now. The police are a factor. We need to be careful. Much more careful." He studied my face, searching for any sign of fear or panic. "We need to lay low. For a while."

The weight of his words settled heavily on my shoulders. Our escape had merely postponed the inevitable confrontation. We had bought ourselves time, but the ticking clock of our predicament hadn't stopped. It had merely been slowed. Our love, our connection, had saved us, had gotten us out, but it was also inextricably linked to the danger we now faced.

The following days were a blur of hushed conversations, furtive glances, and a constant sense of unease. Kenji's world, already shrouded in secrecy, was now cloaked in an even thicker veil of caution. The opulent parties and lavish dinners were replaced by quiet evenings spent in Hana's house, the days filled with a simmering tension that hung in the air.

Kenji was constantly on edge, his phone glued to his ear, his eyes darting to every shadow, every passing car. His normally playful demeanor was replaced by a grim determination, his usual charm veiled by a palpable seriousness. The man I had fallen for, the man who had ignited a flame within me, was changing, his personality morphing under the weight of his circumstances.

Our relationship, forged in the heat of passion and the thrill of danger, now faced a new and unexpected test. The intensity of our physical connection remained, but the intimacy was laced with a new layer of vulnerability, a shared understanding of the fragility of our situation. Our love, once a source of joy and excitement, was now a beacon of hope in the face of adversity, a shared bond that would determine our survival.

The weight of our actions—my accidental recording, Kenji's involvement in the Yakuza, our escape from the warehouse—pressed down on us, altering the dynamics of our relationship. The playful banter, the tender moments, were overshadowed by the constant threat of exposure, the ever-present danger of discovery. The erotic passion that had once defined our connection was now laced with the bitter taste of fear, the shared knowledge of the consequences that awaited us.

Each stolen moment together felt precious, fragile, like a butterfly's wing, easily crushed. The intimacy, while still potent, was charged with a raw vulnerability, a shared understanding of the potential cost of our love. Our lives, once seemingly separate, were now inextricably intertwined, bound by a shared fate. The consequences of our actions weren't simply external threats; they were shaping the very core of our relationship, testing its resilience, its strength, and its capacity for endurance.

The unspoken question hung between us, heavy with

unspoken implications: How long could we outrun our past? How long could we hide from the consequences of our actions? How long before the shadow of the warehouse caught up with us, engulfing us in its darkness? The answer remained elusive, a daunting challenge we would have to face together, our love a flickering candle in the face of an encroaching storm. The burning bridges behind us were a stark reminder of the perilous path we had chosen, a path that led through darkness and uncertainty, towards a future still shrouded in mystery. The journey was far from over, but with each other's hand in ours, we would face whatever lay ahead, ready to fight for our love, our lives, and our future. The consequences of our actions were undeniable, but our love, strong and resilient, was our compass, guiding us through the storm.

The quiet house, a haven from the storm, became our sanctuary. Days bled into weeks, each sunrise bringing a fragile hope, a cautious optimism that felt as tenuous as a spider's silk. Hana, Kenji's aunt, became a silent guardian, her presence a calming force in the midst of our turmoil. She understood the unspoken language of fear and apprehension, her eyes reflecting a quiet strength that reassured me. She cooked us meals, her culinary skills a testament to the warmth and generosity of her spirit. The scent of simmering spices, the gentle hum of conversation in Japanese, created a bubble of normalcy in the chaos of our lives.

Kenji, however, remained restless. His usual playful charm was replaced by a quiet intensity, his every movement calculated, his gaze ever watchful. The weight of his family's legacy, the shadow of the Yakuza, pressed upon him, etching lines of worry onto his normally smooth features. He spent hours on the phone, his conversations hushed, his words clipped and urgent. He meticulously planned our days, ensuring our movements were discreet, our whereabouts unknown. The man I loved, the man who had once swept me off my feet with his irresistible charm, was now a warrior, fighting to protect us both.

Our intimacy, once a fiery explosion of passion, became a slow burn, a quiet intensity that mirrored the delicate balance of our lives. Our lovemaking was punctuated by long, silent moments, our bodies intertwined, our hearts beating in unison against the backdrop of our shared anxieties. The fear, though ever-present, did not extinguish the flame between us. Instead, it forged a new intimacy, a deeper connection forged in the crucible of adversity. It was a love tempered by the knowledge of our precarious situation, a love that whispered promises of a future we weren't sure we would reach.

One evening, as we sat on the porch, watching the city lights twinkle in the distance, Kenji took my hand. His touch was gentle, reassuring. The city noises seemed to fade, leaving only the rhythmic sound of our breaths and the gentle rustling of leaves.

"Aisha," he began, his voice husky with emotion. "We can't stay here forever. This isn't a life, it's an existence." His eyes were filled with a mixture of determination and apprehension. "We need to plan our escape. We need a new beginning."

Escape. The word hung in the air, heavy with the weight of our situation. Escape from the Yakuza, escape from the police, escape from the shadows of our past. It was a daunting task, fraught with peril, but it was also the only path to a future worth living.

The planning was meticulous, each detail carefully considered. Kenji, with his connections and resources, was able to arrange for us to leave the country, to start anew in a place where our past wouldn't follow us. It was a complex operation, involving forged documents, secret routes, and a carefully orchestrated departure. The fear was constant, but it was tempered by a shared determination, a mutual desire for a life free from the constraints of our past.

We sold some of Kenji's less conspicuous assets, ensuring a modest financial foundation for our future. There were moments of doubt, of fear, of wondering if we were making the right decision. But Kenji's unwavering determination, his love for me, fueled my own resolve. We were a team, bound by our love, our shared experiences, and our shared vision of a future free from the dangers that had haunted us.

The day we left felt surreal. We drove away from Hana's house, leaving behind the sanctuary that had protected us, a bittersweet goodbye to a temporary refuge. The city lights receded into the distance, our faces turned towards an uncertain future. As we drove, I felt a mix of apprehension and exhilaration. The weight of our past, the ever-present danger, was still with us, but now it felt lighter, less oppressive. We had taken a leap of faith, a leap into the unknown, driven by hope and a love that refused to be extinguished.

Our journey was long and arduous. There were moments of fear, of uncertainty, of second-guessing our decisions. But with each passing mile, with each new sunrise, our determination grew stronger. We learned to rely on each other, our love becoming a beacon in the darkness. We found ourselves laughing, sharing stories, dreaming of our new life. The weight of our shared past remained, but it no longer dominated our present.

We eventually arrived in a small coastal town nestled in the quiet beauty of East Asia. Here, away from the shadows of our past, we began to build a life together. The transition wasn't easy. There were moments of homesickness, of loneliness, of adjusting to a new culture, a new language, a new way of life. But we were together, and that was all that mattered.

Kenji, far from the constraints of his family's expectations, shed the grim determination that had weighed him down. His playful charm returned, his smile brightening his face, his eyes twinkling with mischief once more. He opened a small, unassuming beauty store, very different from the opulent establishments of his family's empire, but it was his own, a testament to his resilience and his determination to create a life outside the shadow of his past. He was no longer a Yakuza heir; he was Kenji, a man who found peace and happiness in the simple act of creating something beautiful.

I, too, found my place, my purpose. I used my experiences, both good and bad, to help others, becoming a support group facilitator for women escaping abusive relationships. It was my way of making sense of my past, of finding meaning in my pain, of turning a negative into a positive. I found a sense of fulfillment, a purpose beyond the chaos and trauma I had endured. Our love sustained us. It was our anchor in the stormy seas of our past, our guide through the uncharted waters of our future.

Our new life wasn't without its challenges. There were moments of doubt, of fear, of wondering if we had made the right choices. But our love, strong and unwavering, was the foundation upon which we built our new life. It was a testament to the enduring power of the human spirit, a celebration of our resilience, our determination, and the transformative power of love. We learned to appreciate the trivial things, the quiet moments, the shared laughter. We celebrated our differences, our unique cultural heritages, weaving them together to create a new tapestry, a testament to our love and our future.

Our new beginning was not an erasure of our past but a conscious choice to shape a different future, one built on love, resilience, and a shared desire for a life filled with peace, joy, and unwavering commitment. It was a testament to our courage, our determination, and the enduring strength of our love. It was a fresh start, a chance to build something beautiful, something lasting, something truly our own, a love story etched not just in passion but also in resilience, in hope, and in the quiet determination to forge a future free from the shadows of the past. Our love story had many chapters, but this new beginning promised to be the most beautiful one yet. The journey had been long and arduous, filled with danger and uncertainty, but as we looked out at the vast ocean, at the endless horizon before us, we knew we had finally found our haven, our home, our forever.

The coastal town, nestled between the sapphire sea and emerald hills, offered a deceptive tranquility. The air, scented with salty breezes and blooming jasmine, was a stark contrast to the suffocating atmosphere of Kenji's past. Yet, beneath the surface of this idyllic setting, a quiet anxiety simmered. Our escape had been meticulously planned, a carefully orchestrated dance around the long arm of the Yakuza and the watchful eyes of the law, but the future remained a vast, uncharted ocean.

Kenji, despite the outward calm he projected, wore a subtle tension. His smile, though genuine, held a flicker of apprehension. He would often stare out at the horizon, his gaze lost in the vast expanse of the sea, as if searching for answers to questions he couldn't articulate. His small beauty store, a testament to his desire for independence, was thriving, but success felt bittersweet, tainted by the knowledge that we were still living under an assumed identity, still looking over our shoulders.

My own anxieties mirrored his. The support group, a haven for women escaping similar traumas, provided a sense of purpose, but it also served as a constant reminder of the darkness we had left behind. The faces of my clients, etched with the scars of abuse and betrayal, reflected my own past, a haunting echo of a life I was desperate to outrun. The quiet moments, once filled with the blissful intimacy of our newfound freedom, now held a subtle undercurrent of fear.

The initial euphoria of escape had begun to fade, replaced by the quiet hum of uncertainty. We were building a life, brick by brick, but the foundation felt shaky, vulnerable. The fear wasn't as sharp, as immediate as it had been in the city, but it was a persistent presence, a shadow lurking at the edges of our happiness. Our nights, once filled with enthusiastic embraces, were sometimes punctuated by restless sleep, by whispered fears shared in the darkness.

One evening, as we sat on our small porch, listening to the gentle rhythm of the waves, Kenji broke the comfortable silence. "Do you ever feel it, Aisha?" he asked, his voice low, barely a whisper.

I nodded, understanding the unspoken question. "The weight," I said, my own voice trembling slightly. "It's always there, a low hum beneath the surface."

"The Yakuza... they won't simply forget," he said, his gaze fixed on the darkening horizon. "They have long memories, long arms. And the debt... it's not easily erased."

His words were a cold splash of reality, shattering the fragile illusion of safety we had carefully constructed. The debt he spoke of wasn't merely financial; it was a debt of blood, of loyalty, of family. Leaving the Yakuza was not simply walking away; it was an act of rebellion, an act that carried immense consequences.

Our conversations became increasingly cautious, our words carefully chosen, our expressions guarded. We spoke in hushed tones, avoiding specific names, using coded phrases to refer to the past. The air between us, once charged with passion and playful banter, was now thick with unspoken fears and anxieties.

The small coastal town, initially a sanctuary, began to feel like a cage, a beautiful prison of our own making. The isolation, while initially peaceful, now felt stifling, amplifying our fears. The vibrant culture of the region, initially a source of wonder and fascination, was now viewed with a wary eye, each new face a potential threat, each casual conversation a potential risk.

Our dreams, once vivid and hopeful, became clouded with uncertainty. The vision of our future, once a bright, shining beacon, was now obscured by the looming shadows of the past. The question of whether we would be able to build a lasting future, a future free from fear and paranoia, became a daily struggle.

One day, a plain, unmarked envelope arrived, bearing no return address. Inside, a single, crisp photograph: a picture of our previous home, Kenji's aunt Hana's house, seemingly innocuous, yet carrying a chilling message. Beneath the photo, a single word, written in elegant calligraphy: "Found."

The chilling simplicity of the word sent a jolt of icy fear through my veins. It wasn't a threat, not explicitly, but it was a clear signal: they were still watching, still tracking our movements. Our carefully constructed anonymity was crumbling, the walls of our sanctuary beginning to crack.

The uncertainty of our future became a palpable presence, a suffocating weight in the air. Every shadow seemed to hold a threat, every unfamiliar face a potential enemy. The vibrant colors of our new life began to fade, replaced by a muted palette of fear and apprehension. The laughter that had once filled our small home was now replaced by a tense silence, broken only by the quiet rustle of leaves and the distant cry of seagulls.

Kenji, ever the stoic, remained outwardly calm, but I could see the turmoil brewing beneath the surface. His hands trembled slightly as he reread the chilling message, his eyes dark with a grim determination. The playful charm that had once captivated me was now replaced by a guarded intensity, a silent battle waged within his soul.

We were at a crossroads, our carefully constructed future teetering on the brink of collapse. The escape, once a symbol of hope and freedom, had transformed into a desperate game of cat and mouse, a relentless chase against an unseen enemy. Our love, once our anchor, now felt like a fragile raft in a raging storm, tossed about by the unpredictable currents of fate.

The quiet serenity of our coastal haven had become a deceptive façade, masking the underlying tension, the palpable fear that haunted our every waking moment. The question lingered, unspoken yet ever-present: could we truly escape our past, or were we destined to forever live in its shadow? Our future, once a canvas painted with vibrant hues of hope and promise, had become a stark, uncertain landscape, shrouded in mystery and apprehension. The journey ahead was fraught with peril, a path paved with both immense challenges and the faint, flickering flame of hope. And as we stood on the precipice of the unknown, hand in hand, our love story remained unwritten, its future as unpredictable as the vast, turbulent ocean that stretched before us. The cliffhanger hung heavy in the air, a silent question mark that resonated with the reader's anticipation of the next chapter, a chapter where our fate hung precariously in the balance.

CHAPTER 7: WHISPERS OF THE PAST

The flickering gaslight cast long shadows across his face, highlighting the sharp angles of his cheekbones and the subtle lines etched around his eyes – lines that spoke not only of age, but of the weight of unspoken burdens. He sat silently for a long time, the clinking of ice in his glass the only sound in the otherwise quiet room. He wasn't nursing a drink; he was nursing a memory, a ghost of a past that he rarely allowed himself to revisit.

"My grandfather," he finally began, his voice low, a husky murmur that carried the weight of years. "He was... a force of nature. The head of the family, a man whose name commanded respect, even fear. He built the empire, brick by painful brick. He wasn't a man of sentiment, not outwardly, but his love for his family, for his traditions, was fierce, unwavering. It was a love carved in iron, as unforgiving as it was absolute."

He paused, swirling the ice in his glass, the amber liquid catching the light. "The Yakuza... it's not just a criminal enterprise, Aisha. It's a family. A brotherhood. A way of life. It's ingrained in our blood, passed down through generations. Loyalty, honor, duty – these are not mere words, but the very air we breathe. But there's a price, a steep price for belonging. A price paid in sacrifices, in compromises, in lives given and taken."

He spoke of his childhood, a world of stark contrasts: the opulent beauty of his family's homes, the sheer power wielded by his grandfather, juxtaposed against the harsh realities of the streets, the ever-present shadow of violence that lurked just beneath the surface. He recalled clandestine meetings in dimly lit backrooms, hushed whispers carried on the smoke-filled air, the chilling weight of unspoken threats. He spoke of the rigid discipline, the endless training, the relentless pursuit of perfection, a relentless molding into the image of a Yakuza heir.

He wasn't just learning business tactics; he was learning how to fight, how to kill, how to manipulate, how to disappear. It was a brutal education, a baptism by fire, one that left him scarred, but also forged him into the man he was today. He described the rigorous training regimen – the grueling physical exercises, the relentless sparring sessions, the constant honing of his skills. Every scar, every bruise, every ache was a testament to his dedication, a hard earned badge of honor in a world where weakness was a liability, a death sentence. He learned to fight with his hands, his feet, his mind. He learned to use weapons, to wield them with lethal efficiency.

But within this harsh environment, there were moments of unexpected tenderness. He spoke of his grandmother, a woman of quiet strength, who found subtle ways to counterbalance the harshness of his grandfather's rule. She taught him the art of the tea ceremony, a ritualistic practice that offered moments of serenity, a refuge from the storms of his daily life. She instilled in him a profound respect for tradition, for cultural heritage, for the beauty of simplicity amidst the relentless chaos of his world. She was his anchor, his connection to a gentler side of his heritage. Her quiet influence tempered the harsh edges of his upbringing, adding nuances to his character that made him more than just a ruthless Yakuza heir.

He described the internal conflicts that plagued him, the moral dilemmas he faced, the constant struggle between loyalty to his family and his own sense of right and wrong. He spoke of brothers who had fallen, of betrayals and broken promises, of rivals and enemies who were eliminated without a second thought. The world of the Yakuza was one of shifting alliances, brutal betrayals, and constant threats. Yet amidst the violence and brutality, he found an unexpected sense of camaraderie, a brotherhood forged in the fires of shared adversity. The shared experiences, the unspoken codes, the unwavering loyalty – these bound him to his brothers tighter than any blood tie ever could. There was a code, a deeply ingrained moral compass, even amidst the moral gray areas.

He confided in me about his father, a figure that loomed large in his life, yet remained largely elusive. His father, consumed by ambition and power, had been a complex enigma. His father's influence had shaped him profoundly, fueling his ambition while simultaneously breeding a sense of uncertainty and a desire to define his own path, separate from his father's shadow. He struggled to reconcile the man he had become with the influence of his father's actions. It was a struggle that constantly played out in his subconscious, a lingering conflict that colored his present actions and fueled his desires.

The story of his past was a tapestry woven from threads of violence, loyalty, tradition, and unexpected tenderness. It was a journey of self-discovery, a continuous struggle to balance the weight of his heritage with his own evolving sense of morality. He revealed a carefully guarded vulnerability, an acknowledgement of the scars that shaped him, the wounds that still ached beneath the surface of his stoic exterior. His story was not just a narrative of a life within the Yakuza; it was a testament to the human spirit's capacity for resilience, for transformation, for finding moments of peace amidst unrelenting chaos.

He spoke of moments of rebellion, quiet acts of defiance against the rigid structure of his family. These weren't overt acts of revolution, but small, carefully calculated steps towards forging his own path. They were subtle, almost imperceptible acts, yet they spoke volumes about the man he was becoming – a man who was starting to question the traditions, the structures, the inherent violence of the life he had been born into. He wasn't merely playing a role; he was shaping his own destiny, carving out a space for himself, free from the stifling grip of his heritage.

He spoke of his love for his mother, a woman who, despite the inherent dangers of his world, had always offered him a haven of quiet comfort and unconditional love. He had witnessed firsthand the sacrifices she had made, the subtle ways she had navigated the complexities of the Yakuza world to protect him and his siblings. Her influence on his life had been profound, a constant reminder of the importance of compassion, family, and the essential human need for connection, amidst the relentless struggles of the world they lived in. Her quiet strength had served as a counterpoint to the harsh realities of the Yakuza, helping him to balance the scales.

He revealed a softer side, a vulnerability he had carefully concealed from the world. He spoke of the moments of doubt, the weight of responsibility, the fear of failure. These confessions were not admissions of weakness, but rather expressions of his capacity for empathy and his recognition that even the most powerful individuals have moments of uncertainty. He spoke of the burden of leadership, of the constant vigilance required to maintain his position and protect his family. The weight of his heritage was immense, and the pressure to live up to the expectations placed upon him was a constant companion. He acknowledged the sacrifices he had made, the price he had paid, and the continuing weight he carried.

He looked at me, his eyes searching, questioning, as if seeking understanding and reassurance. It was a moment of profound intimacy, a glimpse into the depths of his soul, a revelation of the complex and contradictory nature of a man caught between his past and his future. He sought not forgiveness, but acceptance; not absolution, but understanding. It was a silent plea, a profound confession. His story, in its totality, was a testimony to the intricate balance between loyalty, duty, ambition, and the enduring pursuit of self-discovery, a testament to a man who was not merely a product of his environment, but a conscious creator of his destiny. And it was in these revelations that I saw not just the man I loved, but the person he was striving to become.

The silence that followed his confession hung heavy in the air, thick and suffocating like the humidity of a summer night in Tokyo. I reached out, my hand finding his, his fingers long and slender, surprisingly delicate against my own. His skin, usually cool and smooth, felt strangely warm, the pulse in his wrist a frantic tattoo against my palm. The vulnerability he had displayed, the raw honesty of his confession, had left me breathless, mesmerized. But it also stirred a sense of unease, a premonition of shadows yet to be revealed.

He shifted, a subtle movement that broke the spell, and the mask of his usual composure slipped back into place, though the undercurrent of tension remained. "There are things," he said, his voice low, barely a whisper, "things I haven't told you. Things that… complicate things."

He spoke then of a betrayal, a shattering incident from his youth that had left a gaping wound in his soul, a wound that even time and the brutal training of the Yakuza hadn't been able to fully heal. It involved a close childhood friend, a brother-in-arms who had pledged unwavering loyalty, only to betray him in the most devastating way imaginable. The details were sparse, shrouded in the careful ambiguity that was a hallmark of the Yakuza culture, but the pain was palpable, radiating from him like heat waves from the summer pavement. The friend's motivations remained mysterious, but the act itself had shattered Kenji's faith in loyalty, in brotherhood, in the very foundations of the world he knew. He spoke of the agonizing decision he'd had to make, a choice between the unforgiving code of the Yakuza and his own sense of justice, a conflict that continues to haunt his conscience.

This betrayal, he explained, wasn't just a personal tragedy; it had far-reaching repercussions. It had exposed vulnerabilities within the family, cracks in the carefully constructed façade of power. It had brought shame, not just to Kenji himself, but to his family, causing friction and mistrust among his own kin. This internal conflict, he revealed, had fueled some of his grandfather's ruthless decisions, decisions that had resulted in violence and death. The repercussions, a ripple effect of consequences, reached far beyond Kenji's initial personal pain, affecting the entire family dynamic. His grandfather's rigid approach to quelling the internal dissent had further hardened his heart and impacted his relationship with his own son, Kenji's father. The family was fractured, the wounds both deep and festering.

His father, he continued, had been deeply affected by this betrayal as well, the repercussions resonating through his own ambition and driving him towards even more ruthless acts. He felt the weight of the past on his shoulders, the unspoken expectations, the legacy of violence and betrayal that had been passed down through the generations. The cycle of violence, fueled by betrayal and a thirst for power, had created a deep chasm within his family. He had learned early that the lines between right and wrong were constantly blurred, where vengeance was as vital as loyalty, and the pursuit of power eclipsed all other concerns.

He spoke of his own struggles with this legacy. He'd inherited a seat on a throne built on the backs of broken loyalties and bloodshed, and even his own acts of rebellion were often tempered by the necessity to maintain power and protect his family. He wasn't sure if he could truly escape the shadow of his past, even as he yearned for a future free of violence. This realization intensified the conflict between his own values and the expectations placed upon him by his family, a conflict that threatened to tear him apart. The struggle was not just a personal one, but one intertwined with the historical legacy of the Yakuza and the intricate web of relationships within the family.

The unspoken question hung between us, heavy and suffocating: Could he ever truly escape the weight of his past? Could their relationship survive the unresolved conflicts that threatened to consume him?

As the night deepened, he spoke of other, more personal conflicts. The internal battles waged within him, not just against the ghosts of his past, but against his own desires, his own evolving sense of self. The rigid structure of the Yakuza, the ironclad rules and traditions, were constantly at odds with his own desires for something more, something gentler, something free from the constant threat of violence. He loved me, he admitted, but was uncertain if he could ever fully commit to a life outside the one he had always known. The conflict between loyalty to his family and his love for me was a constant struggle, a wrenching internal conflict that threatened to tear him apart.

He spoke of the fear of betraying his family, the potential consequences of stepping outside the established order. The Yakuza was a family, a brotherhood, and betrayal was unthinkable. Yet, the very act of loving me, of cherishing our relationship, felt like an act of rebellion, a silent defiance against the very fabric of his existence. His past had taught him the painful consequences of misplaced trust and loyalty, leaving him deeply scarred and wary of vulnerability. He loved me, he admitted, but he struggled with the notion of sharing the delicate intimacy that is a genuine love and commitment in the face of his family's inherent threats.

He described the almost unbearable pressure to uphold

the family name, the immense responsibility that weighed heavily on his shoulders. His lineage demanded strength, ruthlessness, and unwavering loyalty. But in his heart, he craved gentleness, understanding, a life that was something other than a never-ending succession of strategic maneuvers and violent acts. This was the internal battle, the conflict that gnawed at his soul, leaving him perpetually on edge, perpetually uncertain.

The conversation stretched into the early hours of the morning. He revealed layers of his past, each revelation adding a new dimension to the complex tapestry of his life. The story unfolded in fits and starts, punctuated by long silences, during which the weight of his unspoken anxieties seemed to press down on us, stifling the breath in the room. He revealed a past love, a woman he had lost under tragic circumstances, a loss that continues to haunt him, a pain that is rarely visible, but that deeply impacts his behavior and his choices.

The unresolved conflict between his family's demands and his personal desires continued to define his present and to affect the future of our relationship. The internal conflict within him continues to play out as he struggles to reconcile the life he was born into with the love that had unexpectedly blossomed with me, and how to navigate his personal journey within a world where love and loyalty do not always coincide, but often clash in dramatic fashion.

He revealed instances where his loyalty to his family had been tested, where he'd had to make difficult choices between personal convictions and the rigid expectations of the Yakuza. The past was inextricably linked to his present actions. The weight of those choices, the lingering moral ambiguity, created new layers of unresolved conflict and tensions in his already precarious world. These conflicts were not simply issues of personal betrayal, but also reflected conflicts of cultural values and traditions. The Yakuza's code of conduct and family loyalty directly clashed with the more individualistic ideals of the Western world.

He talked about the sacrifices he'd made, and the sacrifices he anticipated having to make. His confession touched upon moments of quiet rebellion, acts of defiance against the violent traditions of the Yakuza. But even in these acts, he revealed a persistent sense of guilt, a fear that he was betraying something vital within him. He wasn't sure if these acts of rebellion were truly sufficient to escape the long shadow of his heritage. This added layer of uncertainty heightened the already considerable tension between his past and his future, his family, and his love for me.

His words hung in the air like smoke, lingering long after he had stopped speaking, and a chilling awareness settles in – the path ahead for us is far from clear, the weight of his past and the uncertainty of the future creating a formidable barrier to overcome. The unresolved conflicts from Kenji's past were not just historical events, but active forces shaping his present and casting a long shadow over our future. The tension between his loyalty to his family and his love for me threatened to become a precipice that could break us apart. The question is not simply if we can survive, but how. And as the first rays of dawn painted the sky, we were left facing the daunting task of navigating a future shrouded in uncertainty and the lingering weight of unresolved conflicts.

The dawn light, a pale wash of apricot and rose, painted the Tokyo skyline as Kenji finally fell silent. The confession, a torrent unleashed in the dead of night, had left him drained, the weight of his past seeming to physically press down on his shoulders. He looked at me, his dark eyes shadowed with a weariness that went beyond simple exhaustion. It was the weariness of a soul burdened by years of guilt, years of carrying a weight too heavy for any one man to bear.

He hadn't just confessed to a betrayal; he had confessed to a lifetime of compromises, of choices made in the suffocating grip of family expectations and the unforgiving code of the Yakuza. He spoke of a specific incident, a mission gone wrong, a civilian caught in the crossfire. A young woman, innocent and vibrant, who died because of his actions, a mistake he made years ago, a mistake that haunted him to this day. The memory, he said, was a constant companion, a shadow clinging to him, whispering doubts and fueling his nightly terrors. He carried the image of her face, young and filled with life, in his memory, a constant reminder of the price of violence and the unforgiving nature of his chosen path.

He hadn't intended to kill her. It was a reckless act, a moment of carelessness amidst the adrenaline-fueled chaos of a clandestine operation. Yet, the consequences were irreversible, the guilt a heavy cloak he had been forced to wear ever since. He spoke of the rituals of apology he'd undertaken, the silent prayers he whispered to ancestors he hoped would understand the weight of his remorse. He had sought forgiveness from his family, but it felt hollow, a gesture demanded by tradition rather than a true cleansing of his soul. He was searching for redemption not just in the eyes of others, but more importantly, within himself. He sought that quiet inner peace, a peace that had eluded him for years. He was trying to understand the depths of his pain and to accept the responsibility for his actions, to find a path toward genuine atonement and self-forgiveness.

His journey toward redemption wasn't a simple path of confession and penance. It was a complex and winding road, fraught with obstacles and internal conflicts. He spoke of the difficulty in reconciling his actions with the values he secretly held dear, values that seemed at odds with the brutal realities of his world. He talked of his attempts to use his power and influence for good, quietly supporting charities, providing aid to those in need, seeking some measure of balance to counter the darkness in his past. These acts of kindness were not born out of a desire for public recognition but from a deep-seated need to atone, to make amends for the harm he had caused. His quiet philanthropy, the small acts of generosity he carried out in the shadows, provided a small measure of comfort, a tiny crack of light in the darkness.

The weight of his past wasn't something he could simply shed, like a worn-out garment. It was woven into the fabric of his being, a permanent part of his identity. But he was striving to transform that weight, to use it as fuel for positive change, to find a way to channel his remorse into something constructive. He was trying to reconcile his violent past with his desire for a peaceful future, a future he envisioned not just for himself, but for his family and for the world he inhabited.

He spoke of the cultural conflicts that intensified his internal struggle. His upbringing within the Yakuza had instilled in him a strict code of loyalty, a deep-seated respect for tradition, and a belief in the necessity of violence to maintain order and power. Yet, his relationship with me, a woman from a vastly different culture, had challenged those ingrained beliefs. He struggled to reconcile the rigid hierarchy and unwavering loyalty demanded by his family with the open communication and mutual respect that characterized our bond. He found himself drawn to a more Western concept of individual expression and personal choice, a stark contrast to the collectivist mindset of the Yakuza.

This cultural clash fueled his desire for redemption. He wasn't merely seeking forgiveness for past transgressions, but also seeking a way to bridge the gap between two vastly different worlds, to create a space where his personal values could coexist with his family obligations. It was a challenging path, a constant negotiation between tradition and modernity, East and West, loyalty, and love. He was attempting to create his own path, a path of moral complexity, one that did not fit neatly into any established categories. He was navigating a dangerous path. His quest for redemption wasn't just a personal journey; it was a cultural one.

He described the subtle shifts in his family's dynamics, the gradual erosion of the rigid hierarchical structure of the Yakuza. He spoke of a growing awareness within his family, an increasing understanding of the human cost of their chosen path. He described his own role in this shift, his attempts to influence his family towards a more compassionate and less violent approach. He wasn't advocating for a complete dismantling of the Yakuza, but he was pushing for a reform, a gradual evolution toward a system that valued human life more than the pursuit of power. His actions were often small, almost imperceptible shifts, but their cumulative effect was undeniable. He was working within the system to change it from within, to make it more just and less violent.

His journey toward redemption was inextricably linked to his love for me. Our relationship had become a catalyst for his personal growth, a source of strength and inspiration.

My presence challenged his ingrained beliefs, forcing him to confront his past and to reconsider his future. I didn't just represent a different culture; I represented a different way of being in the world, a way of being that was gentler, more open, and less focused on violence. My love for him was not simply a romantic attachment but also a profound act of faith in his capacity for change. My acceptance of him, regardless of his past, gave him the strength to face the difficult choices ahead.

Our love story wasn't simply a tale of passion and desire; it was a story of transformation and growth. It was a story of a man wrestling with his past, searching for forgiveness, and striving to create a better future for himself and for those around him. His redemption wasn't a destination but a journey, an ongoing process of self-reflection, self-improvement, and atonement. And it was a journey I was privileged to share with him, a journey filled with challenges, uncertainties, and a love that transcended cultural boundaries and the weight of the past.

The weight of his past, however, still cast a long shadow. The threat of violence, the potential for betrayal, and the inherent dangers of his world still loomed large. He remained vigilant, always aware of the potential consequences of his actions, always alert to the dangers lurking in the shadows. His redemption was not a guarantee, but a fragile hope, a commitment to a path of constant striving and self-improvement. He was constantly navigating a treacherous path, balancing his loyalty to his family with his newfound values and the profound love he felt for me.

As the sun climbed higher in the sky, casting long shadows across the city, Kenji took my hand. His touch was still tentative, still carrying the weight of his past, but there was also a newfound strength, a sense of resolve. He knew the road ahead would be long and arduous, but he was ready to walk it, ready to face the challenges that lay before him. He was prepared to face the ghosts of his past, to confront the unresolved conflicts within his family, and to fight for a future where love, loyalty, and justice could coexist. The path to redemption was long and difficult, but with me by his side, he believed he could make it. He believed, finally, that a future free of violence, free of the shadow of his past, was within reach. His journey was not only about seeking forgiveness for his past actions, but also about creating a better future, a better version of himself. The quest for redemption was, in many ways, a quest for a new identity, a new beginning.

The quiet strength in Kenji's confession had shaken me to my core. His vulnerability, so starkly different from the hardened exterior he presented to the world, had pierced through my defenses, leaving me both awestruck and deeply moved. His story wasn't just about a single act of violence, but about the insidious nature of a life lived under the shadow of the Yakuza, a life where loyalty and tradition often clashed with conscience and compassion. I knew then that my role wasn't just to be his lover, but to be his anchor, a steadfast presence in the tempest of his soul.

My support didn't come in grand gestures or dramatic pronouncements. It was woven into the fabric of our daily lives, the small acts of kindness and understanding that spoke volumes more than words ever could. I listened patiently as he recounted the details of his past, offering no judgment, only empathy and unwavering support. His confessions weren't always easy to hear; the images he painted were often brutal and disturbing. But I held his gaze, my hand resting on his, offering a silent promise of unwavering love and steadfast support. My presence was a silent acknowledgment that he wasn't alone in his struggle, that he didn't have to carry the burden of his past by himself.

I learned to understand the nuances of his culture, the intricate web of family obligations and the unforgiving code of honor that governed his life. I spent hours researching the Yakuza, delving into their history and traditions, not to condemn but to understand the forces that had shaped him. My understanding wasn't about condoning his past actions, but about contextualizing them, about seeing him as a complex individual caught in a complicated web of circumstance and cultural pressures.

My love for Kenji wasn't simply a romantic entanglement; it was a deep, profound connection that transcended cultural differences and the weight of his past. It was a love that embraced his flaws and celebrated his strengths, a love that saw past the hardened exterior to the vulnerable soul within. Our physical intimacy was a testament to this connection, a way of communicating our love and support beyond words. Our lovemaking wasn't just about passion, but a profound act of healing, a way of forging a stronger bond amidst the chaos of his life. It was about physical comfort and emotional support, a dance between two souls seeking solace and understanding.

I understood the delicate balance he had to maintain. His loyalty to his family was profound, a deep-seated commitment forged through years of tradition and unquestioning obedience. But his love for me was equally strong, a powerful force that challenged the rigid structures of his world. He often walked a tightrope, struggling to balance his familial obligations with his personal desires, a constant negotiation between tradition and modernity, loyalty, and love. I respected his loyalty to his family but also encouraged him to find a path where his personal happiness and his family's expectations could coexist. I supported his efforts to reform the organization, to make it a more just and less violent entity.

I also helped him navigate his relationships with his family. I learned to speak some Japanese, not fluently but enough to engage in basic conversations and to show respect for his elders. I attended family gatherings, learning the subtle nuances of their customs and traditions. My presence wasn't always met with open arms, but my consistent warmth and respect gradually eroded some of the initial suspicion and apprehension. I became a silent observer, a careful listener, seeking to understand the complexities of his family dynamics, the unspoken rules, and the subtle power plays.

Through it all, I reminded him of his inherent goodness, of the compassion that shone through even the darkest moments of his past. I celebrated his quiet acts of philanthropy, the ways in which he used his influence to help those in need. I encouraged his efforts to make amends, not just for his past actions but for the systemic injustices he saw within the Yakuza. My love for him fueled his desire to change, to seek redemption, not just in the eyes of others, but more importantly, in his own.

My support wasn't passive. I actively encouraged him to seek therapy, to process his trauma and to find healthy ways to cope with the weight of his past. I became his confidante, his rock, someone he could turn to in moments of doubt and despair. My love was a refuge, a safe haven where he could be himself, without judgment or fear. It was a love that nourished his soul, helped him heal, and gave him the strength to face the challenges that lay ahead.

The path to redemption was not linear. There were moments of doubt, of setbacks, of intense emotional turmoil. But through it all, my love remained a constant presence, a source of strength and unwavering support. I didn't promise easy answers or painless solutions; I simply offered my unwavering love and my steadfast commitment to journey alongside him. My presence was a silent testament to my faith in him, in his capacity for change, and in the enduring power of love to heal even the deepest wounds.

Our relationship wasn't devoid of conflict. The cultural differences between us sometimes created friction, misunderstandings, and moments of frustration. But even in conflict, our love persisted, deepening and strengthening our bond. We learned to navigate these differences, to find common ground, to respect each other's values and perspectives. Our intimacy grew richer, incorporating elements of both our cultures, bridging the gap between East and West, tradition, and modernity.

Our love became a testament to the resilience of the human spirit, a powerful narrative that transcended cultural boundaries and the weight of the past. It was a love story not just about passion and desire, but about healing, forgiveness, and redemption. It was a story of transformation and growth, a journey of self-discovery and mutual support. And it was a story that I was privileged to share with Kenji, a man whose journey had profoundly changed my life as well. His redemption was not simply his own; it was a testament to the transformative power of love, compassion, and the unwavering support of someone who believed in him, flaws, and all.

The journey continued, filled with challenges and triumphs, moments of profound connection and periods of painful introspection. But through it all, our love remained the North Star, guiding us through the darkest nights and celebrating the brightest dawns. His past was a part of him, a significant part of his history, but it didn't define him. It was a part of our story, a testament to the resilience of the human spirit, and the enduring power of love to conquer even the deepest wounds and the most difficult challenges. His journey, and ours, was far from over, but with each passing day, the path towards redemption became clearer, stronger, and more defined by the unbreakable bond that we shared. Our love story was far from a fairy tale, but it was a powerful testament to the healing power of true, unconditional love. And that, more than anything, was what truly mattered.

The aftermath of Kenji's confession hung heavy in the air, a silent testament to the vulnerability he'd bravely exposed. It wasn't just the violence he'd witnessed and participated in; it was the weight of a life lived under the Yakuza's shadow, a life where family loyalty often clashed with his own burgeoning conscience. The unspoken questions danced between us, a silent ballet of apprehension and hope. Could we, two souls from such different worlds, truly build a future together? Could trust blossom from the ashes of his past?

The rebuilding of trust wasn't a sudden event, a grand declaration of faith. It was a slow, deliberate process, painstakingly crafted in the quiet moments between passionate nights and the hushed anxieties of daylight hours. It began with simple acts: a shared cup of tea in the morning light, a hand squeezed in silent reassurance during a stressful phone call, the gentle brush of his fingers against my skin as we fell asleep. These small gestures, seemingly insignificant on their own, woven together, created a tapestry of affection and support.

I delved deeper into understanding his culture, not just the superficial aspects, but the intricate web of tradition and obligation that shaped his identity. I spent countless hours reading books on Japanese history and culture, learning about the complex social structures and the unwavering emphasis on family honor. I wasn't trying to condone his past actions, but to understand the context, the forces that had shaped the man before me, the man I loved. I even started taking Japanese lessons, a small step towards bridging the vast cultural chasm between us. The language was difficult, the grammar frustrating, but each novel word learned was a victory, a small step towards a deeper understanding and connection.

Our conversations became more open, less guarded. He spoke of his childhood, his relationship with his father, the expectations placed upon him from a youthful age. He shared stories of his friends, of the men he'd considered brothers, of the complexities of loyalty within the Yakuza's hierarchical structure. His voice was often strained with emotion, his eyes brimming with unshed tears, but he spoke, unburdening himself, trusting me to hold his pain without judgment. It was a slow, painful process, but with each shared memory, each revealed vulnerability, a fragile trust began to take root.

I, in turn, opened myself up to him, sharing fragments of my own past, the scars left by my previous relationship, the trauma that had shaped my perceptions of love and trust. It wasn't easy to expose my vulnerabilities, to admit my fears and insecurities. But in Kenji's quiet strength, in his unwavering support, I found the courage to be honest, to be vulnerable, to let him see the real me, not the carefully constructed facade I had presented to the world.

We explored new ways to connect, to celebrate the differences that enriched our relationship. He introduced me to traditional Japanese ceremonies, to the art of flower arranging, to the quiet beauty of a Zen garden. I, in turn, shared my love for soul music, my passion for cooking, my appreciation for the vibrant energy of African American culture. We found joy in these shared experiences, building a common ground between two vastly different worlds.

The sexual intimacy between us deepened, becoming a testament to our growing trust and understanding. It was more than just physical pleasure; it was a powerful act of communication, a way of expressing our love, our support, our shared vulnerability. We explored different aspects of our cultures, blending the sensuality of Western practices with the traditions of the East, creating a unique tapestry of intimacy that was uniquely ours.

But the path wasn't always smooth. There were moments of doubt, moments of fear, moments when the weight of Kenji's past threatened to overshadow our present happiness. There were times when the cultural differences between us caused misunderstandings, friction, and conflict. But through it all, our commitment to each other remained unwavering. We learned to communicate openly and honestly, to express our feelings without fear of judgment, to navigate the complexities of our relationship with patience and understanding.

Kenji's family remained a significant challenge. While some members of his family had gradually warmed to me, others remained deeply skeptical, suspicious of my intentions. I knew that gaining their acceptance would be a long and arduous process, but I persevered, showing consistent respect and warmth, attempting to understand their traditions and their concerns. My efforts were not always met with success, but Kenji's love and support were my constant anchors. He navigated the complex dynamics of his family with grace and patience, explaining my actions and intentions to those he felt I needed to connect with. His subtle interventions, alongside my own attempts, slowly began to chip away at the initial resistance, fostering a sense of cautious acceptance.

We faced external threats as well. The lingering consequences of the drug deal I'd accidentally recorded still cast a long shadow, a constant reminder of the dangers inherent in Kenji's world. We had to be cautious, to protect ourselves, to navigate the treacherous waters of the Yakuza's underworld with careful deliberation. Yet, the danger only served to strengthen our bond, our mutual reliance becoming a source of comfort and strength.

Through it all, our love for each other became a sanctuary, a refuge from the storms of life. It was a love that didn't shy away from the difficult conversations, the uncomfortable truths, the challenges that threatened to tear us apart. It was a love that embraced vulnerability, that celebrated our differences, that acknowledged our flaws, and that ultimately strengthened our bond.

The process of building trust between us wasn't just about overcoming Kenji's past; it was about building a future together, a future rooted in mutual respect, understanding, and unwavering commitment. It was about weaving together the threads of two distinct cultures, two unique personalities, into a strong, resilient tapestry of love. The journey was long, often arduous, but the destination – a love forged in the fires of adversity and nurtured in the warmth of mutual trust – was worth every single step of the way. The whispers of the past remained, but they were now overshadowed by the resounding strength of our present, a love story written not just in passion, but in the quiet resilience of two hearts beating as one. And in that rhythm, I found solace, a peaceful understanding that our love story, though unconventional, was as real and enduring as any other.

CHAPTER 6:
HARLEM NIGHTS

The plane descended, the city lights of New York sprawling beneath us like a glittering tapestry woven with shadows and brilliance. Harlem, my Harlem, awaited us. The coastal haven, though beautiful, had been a gilded cage, its tranquility a deceptive balm on wounds that refused to fully heal. Kenji held my hand, his touch a grounding force against the familiar tremor of anxiety that coiled in my stomach. He knew what this return meant to me, not just geographically, but emotionally. This wasn't simply a return to a place; it was a return to a part of myself I'd almost lost.

The taxi navigated the familiar streets, a symphony of honking horns and vibrant chatter filling the air. The scent of fried chicken and jerk spice hung heavy in the humid night, a comforting perfume of home. The buildings, a mix of crumbling grandeur and newly renovated brownstones, were witnesses to generations of stories, tales of struggle and resilience woven into the very fabric of the neighborhood. It was a place of both deep-seated pain and unwavering strength, a place that had shaped me, scarred me, and ultimately, held me.

Kenji watched me intently, his gaze mirroring the complex emotions swirling within me. He hadn't grown up in this environment, yet he seemed to grasp its intrinsic power, its ability to both nurture and wound. His silence was not judgmental, but rather a quiet respect for the significance of this homecoming. He knew this was where I needed to be, to reconnect with the strength of my roots, to find solace amidst the chaos, to heal in a way the isolated serenity of the coast could never provide.

My apartment, small but familiar, felt like a welcoming embrace. It was a haven, meticulously maintained by my aunt, a testament to the enduring support of my community. It was a place where I could finally shed the layers of assumed identity, the masks I'd worn for protection, and simply be Aisha. The worn armchair, the scent of lavender from the potpourri on the table, the faded family photographs adorning the walls – each object pulsed with a comforting sense of continuity. It was a reminder of who I was, of where I came from, a solid foundation upon which to rebuild.

The next few days were a blur of reunions and reconnections. I found myself surrounded by the warm embrace of family and friends – my Aunt Vivian's ever-present laughter, the reassuring hugs from my cousins, the knowing glances from old friends who had witnessed my journey, both the triumphs and the tribulations. They didn't pry; they simply offered their unwavering support, their understanding, and their love. Their acceptance of Kenji, despite the cultural differences and the enigmatic nature of his past, was a testament to their open hearts and minds.

They saw past the Yakuza, past the whispers of his dangerous family, and saw the man I loved, the man who had rescued me from the darkness, the man who was fiercely loyal and deeply devoted. They recognized the love in his eyes, a love that was as genuine and as powerful as any they had ever known. The initial hesitation, the subtle curiosity regarding his background, quickly faded, replaced by genuine warmth and acceptance. This was the power of Harlem, the strength of its community, its ability to embrace those who showed compassion and respect.

My support group meetings became a lifeline. Sharing my story, not as a victim but as a survivor, empowered me. Hearing the stories of other women, their resilience in the face of adversity, reinforced my own strength, my determination to build a future free from fear. The shared experiences forged a bond of sisterhood, a network of support that extended beyond the confines of the group, a reminder that I wasn't alone, that my journey was shared by others. Kenji attended some of the meetings with me, and although initially hesitant, he became an active listener, offering quiet support to the women who shared their own vulnerabilities. His presence was a silent testament to his commitment, to his understanding of the importance of community healing, and to his willingness to navigate the cultural nuances of my world.

Evenings were spent exploring the familiar streets of Harlem, rediscovering the vibrant culture I had almost forgotten. The live music spilling from the clubs, the aroma of soul food wafting from the restaurants, the lively conversations on the street corners – it was a sensory explosion, a reminder of the rich tapestry of life that pulsed through the heart of Harlem. Kenji, ever observant, soaked in the atmosphere, his curiosity evident in his questions and his attentiveness to detail. He learned about the history of the neighborhood, the struggles of its people, and the indomitable spirit that continued to thrive.

One evening, we found ourselves at the Apollo Theater, a sacred space in Harlem's cultural landscape. The energy was electric, the performances captivating. Kenji was mesmerized, completely enchanted by the raw talent and emotional depth of the music and the performers. He saw beyond the surface, recognizing the same resilience and strength he had come to admire in me. He understood, on a deeper level, the power of this community, its ability to create beauty and inspiration even in the face of adversity.

Our nights were filled with a profound intimacy, a mixture of passionate embraces and quiet conversations. The shared anxieties of the past still lingered, the shadows of the Yakuza's reach still loomed large, but our love was a constant, a beacon in the darkness. His love was a grounding force, a solid rock against the persistent waves of fear. He held me close, whispering words of reassurance and hope, and in his arms, I found a sanctuary against the uncertainties of the future.

Harlem wasn't just a refuge; it was a catalyst for growth and healing. It allowed me to connect with the strength of my roots, to reclaim my identity, and to build a new foundation for a future where hope outweighed fear. It was a place where I could be both vulnerable and powerful, both cherished and empowered. And amidst the chaos and vibrancy of Harlem, our love story continued, its narrative unfolding against the backdrop of a city that held both our past and our potential. The comforting familiarity of Harlem was more than just a physical place; it was a spiritual homecoming, a place where I could nurture the resilience that had carried me through the darkest moments and embrace a future where love, healing and hope could thrive. The uncertainty of the Yakuza's pursuit remained, but in Harlem, I found a strength I didn't know I possessed, and the power of community fortified our love in a way that made the challenges ahead seem, perhaps, just a little bit less daunting.

The days that followed were a tapestry woven with threads of vulnerability and strength. The initial euphoria of returning home had subsided, leaving behind a quiet intensity, a space for deeper introspection. Harlem, with its vibrant energy, became the backdrop for our journey of healing and reconciliation. Kenji, ever the observant student of my world, began to understand the subtle nuances of my emotional landscape. He learned to recognize the subtle tightening of my jaw, the fleeting shadows that crossed my eyes, the way my breathing would quicken when a memory, sharp and painful, pierced the surface of my composure. He learned the language of my silence, a language born from years of protecting myself from the harsh realities of my past.

He didn't attempt to rush the process; he patiently waited, his love a quiet presence, a steady hand in the storm. He learned to offer comfort not through words, but through the gentle caress of his fingertips on my skin, the warm embrace of his arms, the quiet strength of his presence. He understood that healing wasn't a linear path, but a meandering journey, filled with unexpected detours and moments of profound vulnerability.

One evening, as we sat on the stoop of my Aunt Vivian's brownstone, the warm night air heavy with the scent of honeysuckle, I finally allowed myself to speak of the man who had left such a deep scar on my soul. The words came in broken whispers, punctuated by tears that streamed down my face, each tear a testament to the pain that had haunted me for so long. It wasn't a dramatic confession, but a quiet unraveling, a gentle release of the burdens I had carried for so many years.

Kenji listened, his gaze unwavering, his presence a comforting anchor in the emotional tempest that raged within me. He didn't interrupt, didn't offer platitudes or empty reassurances. His silence was not indifferent; it was a profound act of respect, a recognition of the deep-seated pain I was finally confronting. He simply held my hand, his touch a steady pulse of strength against the tremors of my memories.

When I was finished, the silence that followed wasn't awkward or uncomfortable; it was a shared space of understanding, a quiet acknowledgment of the weight of my past. Then, softly, he spoke, his words a balm on my wounded spirit. He spoke not of judgment or blame, but of empathy and compassion. He shared his own experiences of loss and betrayal, of the scars that had shaped him, the vulnerabilities he had learned to embrace.

His words weren't meant to diminish my pain, but to normalize it, to remind me that I was not alone in my struggle, that the scars I carried were a testament to my resilience, not my weakness. He spoke of his own family, the complexities of their world, the traditions and expectations that sometimes felt suffocating. He admitted to his own vulnerabilities, his own struggles with balancing his loyalty to his family with his love for me.

That night, as we held each other close, a new level of intimacy was forged, an intimacy that extended beyond the physical realm, an understanding that transcended the cultural differences that once seemed insurmountable. It was the beginning of a true partnership, a shared journey toward emotional wholeness.

Our journey of healing was not always easy. There were moments of regression, moments of doubt, moments when the shadows of the past threatened to engulf us. But each time, we found our way back to each other, our love a beacon in the darkness. We learned to communicate not just through words, but through touch, through gestures, through shared silences.

Kenji's presence in my support group meetings became increasingly impactful. He listened intently to the stories of other women, their pain resonating deeply with his own understanding of vulnerability and strength. He began to offer a unique perspective, one that bridged cultural divides and fostered a sense of shared humanity. His empathy and respect earned him the trust of the women in the group, solidifying his place in my world, not just as my lover, but as an ally in my fight for healing.

We explored Harlem together, rediscovering its rich history and vibrant culture. We visited the Studio Museum in Harlem, immersing ourselves in the art that reflected the struggles and triumphs of the African American community. Kenji's genuine interest in my heritage, his willingness to learn and understand, was a constant source of comfort and reassurance. He was not merely an observer; he was an active participant in my journey of self-discovery.

We spent evenings at the Apollo, where the raw energy and emotional depth of the performances resonated deeply with our shared journey of healing. We discovered a shared love of jazz, the improvisational nature of the music reflecting the fluidity of our own emotional landscapes. The music became a soundtrack to our journey, a tapestry of notes that expressed the complexities of our love story.

Our intimacy deepened, evolving from passionate encounters to moments of quiet tenderness. We learned to communicate not just through words, but through touch, through shared silences, through a mutual understanding that transcended language and culture. The physical connection remained vital, a testament to our mutual desire and a source of strength and comfort. But it was the emotional intimacy, the shared vulnerability, that truly cemented our bond.

The threat of the Yakuza still lingered, a dark shadow that occasionally clouded our happiness.
But our shared journey of healing gave us strength, a resilience that allowed us to face the future together. We were not just two individuals; we were a united front, a team navigating the complexities of our lives with unwavering commitment and mutual support. Harlem became our sanctuary, a place where we could heal, grow, and build a future where our love could flourish, unburdened by the weight of the past. It was a journey of self-discovery, of reconciliation, not just with each other, but with ourselves. The vibrant pulse of Harlem, its resilience, its capacity for both pain and joy, mirrored our own journey towards wholeness, and in that resonance, we found a profound sense of belonging, a powerful and enduring love that would guide us through the uncertainties that lay ahead. The city that held the shadows of my past also held the promise of our future, a future painted with the vibrant hues of love, healing, and hope.

The warmth of Harlem enveloped me, a comforting embrace against the chilling realities of Kenji's world. It wasn't just the physical warmth of the summer nights, but the warmth of community, the comforting presence of familiar faces and voices that had anchored me through storms before. Aunt Vivian, her face etched with the wisdom of years, became my unwavering rock. Her kitchen, always filled with the aroma of simmering collard greens and sweet potato pie, became a sanctuary, a space where worries could melt away amidst the laughter and stories shared over steaming mugs of sweet tea. Her quiet strength, her unwavering faith, became a balm on my soul, a constant reminder that I was loved, supported, and cherished.

My childhood friends, a vibrant tapestry of personalities and experiences, rallied around me. There was Simone, the pragmatic lawyer, ever-ready with sound advice and a shoulder to cry on. Then there was Marcus, the gentle artist, whose paintings captured the soulful essence of Harlem and offered a visual balm to my troubled spirit. And Leslie, the vibrant entrepreneur, who kept our spirits high with her infectious laughter and unwavering belief in our ability to overcome any obstacle. Their presence, their willingness to listen without judgment, to offer a helping hand without expectation, created a safety net, a feeling of belonging that deepened my resolve to face whatever challenges lay ahead.

Beyond my immediate circle, the wider Harlem community extended its embrace. The women at my support group, a diverse collection of souls navigating their own journeys of trauma and healing, provided a sense of shared understanding and camaraderie. Their stories, their struggles, mirrored my own, creating a space where vulnerability was not weakness but a shared strength. Sharing my experiences with them, hearing their experiences in return, created a tapestry of resilience, a testament to the power of human connection and collective healing. Kenji's presence in these meetings, initially a source of nervous energy, had become a source of unexpected comfort. He listened with a respectful attention that transcended cultural barriers, his empathy a silent testament to his growing understanding of the complexities of the human spirit.

The church, a cornerstone of the Harlem community, became another refuge. The soulful hymns, the uplifting sermons, and the comforting embrace of fellow parishioners offered a spiritual respite, a space where faith and hope could intertwine to offer solace and strength. Pastor Thompson, a wise and compassionate man, offered guidance and support, reminding me of the enduring power of faith and resilience. His words were not mere platitudes but a testament to the enduring strength of the human spirit, a reminder that even in the darkest of times, hope remains a beacon in the distance.

One Sunday, after a particularly emotional service, I found myself walking through the streets of Harlem, the weight of my past momentarily lifted by the warmth of the community. The vibrant colors of the buildings, the rhythmic beat of gospel music spilling from open windows, the laughter of children playing in the streets – all these elements combined to create a symphony of life, a testament to the resilience and enduring spirit of Harlem.

It was in this vibrant setting that I began to understand the power of community, the profound impact of shared experiences and mutual support. Harlem was more than just a neighborhood; it was a sanctuary, a nurturing environment where healing could flourish. The bonds of friendship, of family, of shared faith, became my armor, my shield against the darkness. They provided a sense of belonging, a reminder that I was not alone, that I was surrounded by love, support, and unwavering faith.

My relationship with Kenji, once a source of intense and conflicted emotions, began to take on a new dimension. His initial apprehension about the African American community melted away as he witnessed its warmth, its resilience, its unwavering capacity for love and support. He was welcomed, not as an outsider, but as a member of the community. He began to participate in community events, attending the annual Juneteenth celebration and joining us for the lively Thanksgiving dinners at Aunt Vivian's. His willingness to engage, to learn, to understand, deepened his bond with me and expanded his own understanding of what it meant to belong.

The support extended beyond social gatherings. Simone helped me navigate the legal intricacies of my situation, ensuring that I was protected from further harm. Marcus created a series of portraits that captured the strength and resilience of the women in my support group. Leslie offered business advice, encouraging me to pursue my entrepreneurial dreams, a path I'd long abandoned due to past trauma. Even the smallest acts of kindness – a friendly wave, a shared smile, a helping hand – became powerful symbols of the enduring strength of community.

The women in my support group became more than just fellow travelers on a journey of healing. They became a sisterhood, offering emotional support, practical assistance, and a sense of shared purpose. We celebrated each other's victories, big and small, and offered comfort during times of setbacks. We created a safe space where vulnerabilities could be shared without fear of judgment, where laughter and tears could coexist, and where the power of collective resilience was palpable. Kenji, observing this dynamic, expressed his admiration for the women's strength and the bond that united them.

Kenji's integration into this community wasn't without its initial challenges. The cultural differences were undeniable, but the shared values of love, loyalty, and mutual respect formed a common ground. He participated in community events, not as a mere observer but as an active participant. His interactions with the elders of the community, initially hesitant, blossomed into genuine respect. His willingness to learn and embrace the cultural nuances showed not just respect, but a genuine desire to be part of the fabric of Harlem. He learned to appreciate the richness of our history, the vibrancy of our culture, and the enduring strength of our community spirit.

The support system I found in Harlem wasn't just a temporary respite; it became an integral part of my healing journey, strengthening my resolve to face the challenges that lay ahead. It wasn't just a collection of individuals; it was a community, a web of interconnected lives, where every thread played a crucial role in providing strength, support, and unwavering love. The energy of Harlem, its resilience, its capacity for both pain and joy, became a mirror reflecting my own journey toward wholeness. And in that reflection, in that community, I found a sense of belonging that would forever anchor my spirit. The love I found in Harlem, the support of my community, and the deepening bond with Kenji became a powerful force propelling me forward, a constant reminder that even in the face of adversity, love, community, and resilience can prevail. This support, this bedrock of community, would sustain me as I navigated the complexities of Kenji's world, the looming threat of the Yakuza, and the enduring shadows of my past. It was a testament to the enduring power of human connection and the unwavering strength of the human spirit.

The Harlem nights, once a comforting balm, now felt charged with a different kind of energy. The warmth remained, the laughter and the camaraderie still present, but beneath it all lay a simmering tension, a quiet anticipation of the confrontation I knew I had to face. The past, like a persistent shadow, had followed me from the opulent world of Kenji's family into the familiar embrace of my community, but here, in the heart of Harlem, I felt empowered to finally confront it.

It wasn't a decision made lightly. For years, I'd built walls around my past, brick by painful brick, shielding myself from the memories that still threatened to consume me. The memories of betrayal, of violence, of the man who had stolen not just my innocence, but my sense of security and self-worth. He had left me shattered, a vessel adrift in a sea of pain and self-doubt. The scars, both visible and invisible, were a constant reminder of the darkness I had endured. But Harlem, with its unwavering embrace, had provided me with the strength and the courage to finally confront those demons.

The process began subtly. It wasn't a grand, dramatic unveiling, but a slow, deliberate peeling away of layers, a gradual uncovering of buried emotions. It started with small conversations, shared moments of vulnerability with the women in my support group. Their stories, their shared experiences of overcoming adversity, gave me the permission to finally share my own truth, to voice the pain I had carried for so long in silence. Their empathy, their understanding, created a safe space where I could begin to process my trauma without judgment or condemnation.

Each shared story, each whispered confession, was a small step forward, a gradual chipping away at the walls I had so painstakingly constructed. It was like excavating a buried treasure, each unearthed fragment revealing a piece of the puzzle, a piece of myself I had long forgotten. The pain was intense, raw, but it was also cathartic, a necessary release of pent-up emotions that had been bottled up for far too long.

Simone, with her sharp legal mind, helped me frame my experiences, helping me to see the pattern of abuse, the cycle of violence I had unknowingly allowed myself to be trapped in. Her analytical approach, her ability to detach emotion from the facts, helped me gain a clearer perspective on my past, to see it not as a defining characteristic, but as a chapter in my life, a difficult chapter, but one that did not have to dictate my future.

Marcus, with his artistic sensitivity, captured the essence of my struggle in his paintings. His canvases became a visual representation of my healing journey, transforming the raw pain into something beautiful, something that could be contemplated and understood. His art gave voice to the emotions I struggled to articulate, bridging the gap between the chaos within and the quiet strength I was beginning to cultivate.

Leslie's entrepreneurial spirit reminded me of my own potential, my own capacity for resilience. She encouraged me to see my past trauma not as a limitation, but as a catalyst for growth, a source of strength that could propel me toward my goals. Her belief in me, her unwavering support, fueled my determination to reclaim my life, to create a future unburdened by the shadows of the past.

Pastor Thompson, with his wisdom and compassion, offered spiritual guidance, reminding me of the power of forgiveness, both for myself and for those who had hurt me. His sermons resonated deeply, offering solace and strength, reaffirming the idea that healing was not just about confronting the past, but also about embracing the possibility of a brighter future. His words were not platitudes, but a genuine expression of faith in my ability to overcome.

The process was not linear. There were days when the pain threatened to overwhelm me, days when the memories felt too vivid, too raw. There were moments of doubt, moments when I questioned my ability to move forward, moments when the weight of the past felt too heavy to bear. But the unwavering support of my community, the strength of my friends and family, the guidance of my spiritual advisor, kept me grounded, kept me moving forward, one step at a time.

Kenji, initially an outsider to this deeply personal journey, became an unexpected source of strength. He listened patiently, attentively, never judging, never pushing. His presence, his quiet empathy, became a silent testament to his growing understanding of the complexities of the human spirit. He observed the resilience of the Harlem community, the strength of the women in my support group, and he learned to appreciate the profound impact of shared experiences and mutual support.

His respect grew not only for me, but for my community, its culture, and its unwavering spirit. He began to understand that my past was not merely a personal narrative but a reflection of the broader social injustices that affected many in the African American community. His respect transcended cultural boundaries, a silent acknowledgment of the shared human experience of trauma and resilience.

As I confronted my past, I realized that true healing was not about erasing the pain, but about integrating it into the narrative of my life, transforming it from a source of weakness into a source of strength. The scars remained, but they no longer defined me. They were reminders of the battles I had fought and won, testaments to my resilience and the enduring power of the human spirit.

The night air in Harlem felt different now, lighter, fresher. The weight I had carried for so long had begun to lift, replaced by a growing sense of hope, of possibility. The past was still present, but it no longer held me captive. I had faced it, confronted it, and emerged stronger, more resilient, more determined to create the future I deserved. Harlem, my community, had been my sanctuary, my refuge, my source of strength. And in the heart of that vibrant, resilient community, I found not only healing, but a newfound sense of self, a sense of purpose, and a profound understanding of my own unwavering strength. The journey wasn't over, but I knew, with absolute certainty, that I was finally ready to embrace whatever lay ahead. The future remained uncertain, but the past, once a crippling weight, had become a stepping stone on my path towards wholeness. The embrace of Harlem, the unwavering support of my community, and the deepening bond with Kenji—all these forces coalesced into a powerful current, propelling me forward into a future brimming with both possibility and hope. The shadows remained, but now, they were merely a backdrop to the vibrant tapestry of my life.

The quiet intimacy of our shared apartment in Kenji's building, a stark contrast to the vibrant chaos of Harlem, became a sanctuary. It wasn't just the physical space, but the unspoken understanding that bloomed between us, a silent acknowledgment of the vulnerabilities we each guarded. He saw the lingering shadows in my eyes, the subtle flinches when a loud noise startled me, the way I instinctively recoiled from sudden touches. He didn't pry; he simply offered a hand, a reassuring presence, a quiet strength that allowed me to relax, to breathe.

We spent hours in companionable silence, the rhythmic hum of the city a soothing backdrop to our shared space. He'd brew strong, fragrant Japanese tea, the steam swirling in the air like a silent conversation. We'd trace each other's hands, finding solace in the simple act of physical closeness, a language far more eloquent than words. These moments were a balm, a softening of the harsh edges of our lives. My past, still a raw wound, slowly began to heal under the gentle touch of his presence. His world, with its complexities and hidden dangers, became less daunting, less intimidating when shared with me.

His family, initially a source of both fascination and apprehension, became less forbidding as I learned to navigate their intricate social dynamics. The initial formality gave way to a grudging respect, earned not through subservience but through an unwavering sense of self. I learned to appreciate the traditions, the unspoken codes of conduct, understanding that beneath the rigid exterior lay a deep-rooted sense of loyalty and family devotion – a mirror image, in many ways, of the strength and resilience I witnessed in my own Harlem community. Kenji's mother, initially wary, started to see past the superficial differences, recognizing a shared strength and determination in our relationship. Her acceptance, though slow, was profound and ultimately, deeply satisfying.

One evening, while sharing stories, Kenji recounted a childhood memory, a moment of vulnerability that revealed a softer side to the man I knew as the composed, enigmatic heir to a Yakuza empire. He spoke of a cherished grandfather, a man of immense power, yet also incredibly gentle and kind. The story highlighted the cultural duality of his upbringing —a mix of old-world traditions and the complexities of the modern world. It was a moment of shared intimacy, a glimpse into his soul. In that moment, I saw not just the powerful Yakuza leader, but the boy who had once needed comfort and assurance, a vulnerability that resonated deeply within me.

In turn, I shared more of my own story, not just the broad strokes of my past, but the painful specifics. The fear, the betrayal, the lingering trauma. He listened without judgment, his hand a comforting presence on my back as I spoke, his eyes conveying an empathy that transcended cultural barriers. His quiet strength, his unwavering support, became the bedrock upon which our love flourished. It wasn't a fairytale romance, but a deep and enduring connection forged in the crucible of shared experience.

Our intimacy deepened, evolving beyond mere physical attraction into a profound spiritual and emotional connection. Our lovemaking became a sacred ritual, a way of expressing the vulnerability and trust that had grown between us. We explored the nuances of both our cultures, blending Western passion with Eastern traditions, creating a unique intimacy that reflected the richness of our shared heritage. It was a dance, a symphony of touch and sensation, where our bodies spoke a language that words could never fully capture.

However, our bond wasn't without its challenges. The inherent dangers associated with Kenji's world cast a long shadow, a constant reminder of the precariousness of our situation. Threats, both implicit and explicit, loomed large, assessing the strength of our connection. We navigated these challenges not as individuals, but as a team, facing the storm hand in hand. It wasn't always easy, but facing those uncertainties together strengthened our resolve, further deepening our love and commitment.

One particular incident involved a confrontation with a rival faction within the Yakuza. The tension was palpable, the air thick with the threat of violence. But in the midst of the chaos, Kenji's unwavering gaze reassured me, a silent promise of protection, a testament to the strength of our bond. It was in these moments of crisis that the true depth of our commitment was revealed. We emerged from this crisis stronger, our love tempered by the fires of adversity, and our relationship forged anew in the crucible of shared peril.

The recording of the drug deal, a constant threat looming over my head, became another test. Kenji, utilizing the resources and influence of his family, ensured my safety, yet he did so in a way that honored my autonomy, never diminishing my agency or my independence. His support was crucial, yet it was coupled with a deep respect for my right to choose my path, making our relationship stronger than ever.

Our love was not merely a refuge from the chaos of our individual worlds; it was a transformative force, a shared journey toward self-discovery and healing. We learned from each other's cultures, acknowledging and celebrating our differences. We supported each other's growth, challenging each other to become better versions of ourselves. The complexities of our respective backgrounds, initially a source of potential conflict, instead became a tapestry upon which we wove a love story unlike any other. It was a love built on trust, respect, and a shared commitment to navigate the world, hand in hand, through storms and sunshine, together. The bond we shared was resilient, a testament to the enduring power of love in a world often defined by adversity.

The cultural exchange became a fascinating journey, a blend of Harlem nights and the quiet elegance of a Japanese tea ceremony. We found common ground in the simple pleasures —a shared meal, a quiet evening spent side by side, the warmth of physical affection—moments that transcended cultural differences and highlighted the universal language of human connection. Kenji learned to appreciate the vibrant energy and cultural richness of Harlem, discovering a different perspective on the world and on himself. He witnessed the resilience of my community, the strength of its people, and developed a deep respect for the cultural heritage that had shaped me.

My own perspective expanded as well, broadening beyond the confines of my immediate experience. I began to see the universality of human experience—the shared struggles, the triumphs, the common threads of love, loss, and resilience that connected people across cultures and continents. Kenji's introduction to the vibrant tapestry of Harlem broadened his understanding of the African-American experience, a cultural landscape far removed from his own. The cross-cultural pollination enriched us both, creating a deeper appreciation for the beauty and diversity of the human experience.

Through all the challenges and triumphs, through the shared laughter and quiet tears, our love blossomed into something profound and enduring. It was a love that tested us, strengthened us, and ultimately transformed us, becoming the foundation upon which we built a future as uncertain as it was promising. Our bond was a testament to the human capacity for connection, a powerful force that transcended cultural barriers and personal traumas, a love story woven in the heart of Harlem and strengthened by the resilience of two souls from vastly different worlds. The vibrant energy of Harlem and the serene beauty of Kenji's world coalesced, creating a unique space where our love could flourish, a testament to the enduring strength of a bond forged in the fires of adversity and nurtured by the delicate tendrils of shared hope.

AUREALIA NELSON

CHAPTER 8:
EASTERN PROMISES

The initial resistance from Kenji's family felt like an insurmountable wall. His older brother, Hiroki, a man whose face seemed permanently etched with disapproval, was the most vocal in his opposition. His thinly veiled disdain was palpable, his silences more damning than any outright rejection. He saw me as an outsider, a threat to the carefully constructed order of their world, a world built on generations of tradition and fiercely guarded honor. He questioned my motives, my background, my very essence. His suspicion was a constant, icy presence, chilling even the warmest moments shared with Kenji.

His mother, however, presented a different challenge. While not openly hostile, her quiet disapproval spoke volumes. Her silence was a form of passive resistance, a subtle rejection disguised as polite indifference. She would offer me tea, but her gaze never truly connected. She would nod politely to my greetings, but her touch lacked warmth, her smiles felt strained and artificial. She was a woman of subtle gestures, and her disapproval was expertly communicated through the delicate dance of her unspoken words.

Kenji's father, the patriarch of the family, remained an enigma. He seldom spoke, his presence a looming shadow of power and authority. His silence was a heavy cloak, shielding his true feelings, making it impossible to decipher his acceptance or rejection. He observed, he assessed, his gaze sharp and piercing, making me feel perpetually under scrutiny. His approval was the ultimate prize, a summit I yearned to reach, yet felt increasingly impossible to attain.

Breaking through this wall of resistance required patience, understanding, and a deep commitment to bridging the cultural divide. I started small. I learned to bow appropriately, mastering the nuances of respect embedded within the gesture. I studied their customs, from the elaborate tea ceremonies to the intricate art of calligraphy. I embraced their traditions, not out of obligation, but out of a genuine desire to understand and connect with them on their terms.

I spent hours with Kenji's mother, learning the art of flower arranging, ikebana. The delicate process, the precise placement of each bloom, mirrored the delicate dance of building a relationship with her. We found common ground in our shared appreciation for beauty, for the subtle artistry of creating something meaningful and lasting. It wasn't a sudden breakthrough, but a slow, gradual thawing of her reserved nature, a subtle softening of her initially rigid demeanor.

I also made an effort to understand the complexities of the Yakuza's traditions and their rigid family structures. I learned about their code of honor, their unwavering loyalty, their deep seated sense of family obligation. I understood that their skepticism wasn't solely directed at me, but was rooted in a deep-seated fear of the unknown, of the disruption that an outsider could bring. I attempted to showcase respect for their way of life, demonstrating that I wasn't attempting to undermine their culture but rather to respectfully enter it.

My efforts weren't always met with immediate success. There were tense family dinners, fraught with silences and awkward conversations. There were moments when I felt like an outsider looking in, a constant reminder of the cultural gulf that separated me from them. But Kenji remained my steadfast support, translating, mediating, patiently explaining my actions and intentions. He navigated the complex dynamics within his family with grace and understanding, softening the edges of their resistance. He was the bridge between our worlds, the unwavering support that kept me from giving up.

I also sought to connect with his family on a personal level, learning about their individual stories, their triumphs, and their struggles. I discovered that Hiroki, despite his outward hostility, was fiercely protective of his family, driven by a deep-seated loyalty that mirrored the same dedication I had for Kenji. His skepticism wasn't about me; it was a defensive mechanism, a shield protecting his brother from potential hurt. Once I understood this, my approach shifted. I showed him my respect for his loyalty, highlighting the depth of my own love for Kenji.

Slowly, subtly, the ice began to melt. Hiroki's harsh words became less frequent, his silences less condemning. His mother's touch became warmer, her smiles more genuine. Even his father's gaze softened slightly, a subtle shift that signaled a tentative acceptance. It wasn't a complete transformation, but a crucial step, a sign that I was gradually gaining a foothold in their world. They started inviting me to more family gatherings, subtly including me in their conversations, their lives. This gradual integration was a testament to the power of patience, understanding, and unwavering respect.

One evening, during a quiet family dinner, Kenji's father finally spoke to me directly, acknowledging my presence with an unexpected warmth. He spoke not in flowery compliments, but in a quiet observation, acknowledging my efforts to learn their culture, my commitment to their family, my love for his son. His words were few, but they held the weight of generations, the unspoken acceptance that had been slowly building within him. His silent observation throughout the previous months proved more than just passive judgment. It was a deep assessment of character and a respect for the path I had taken.

The acceptance wasn't complete, nor was it unconditional. There would be moments of lingering skepticism, moments when the cultural differences would still create friction. But the wall had crumbled, replaced by a tentative bridge of understanding and mutual respect. It was a testament to the power of love, of persistence, of bridging cultural divides, a powerful symbol of acceptance in a world often defined by differences and prejudice. The journey had been long and arduous, filled with challenges and moments of doubt. But the arrival at this point, this fragile but real acceptance, felt like a victory, a milestone reached only through unwavering commitment and the strength of love's transformative power. It was the promise of a future built on mutual respect, understanding and the shared hope of a family bound by love, transcending cultural boundaries and ancestral differences. The path ahead remained uncertain, but the future felt brighter, infused with the hope of a genuine family acceptance, a family that transcended cultural boundaries and prejudice.

The tentative acceptance from Kenji's family wasn't a sudden blossoming of warmth but a slow, painstaking process of sowing seeds of understanding. It required patience, a quality I hadn't always possessed, especially after the trauma of my past. But Kenji's unwavering support, his constant translations and explanations, his quiet acts of reassurance, helped me navigate the treacherous waters of his family's traditions.

My efforts to learn Japanese extended beyond simple phrases. I enrolled in evening classes, immersing myself in the language's nuances, its subtle inflections and complex grammar. It wasn't merely about communication; it was about understanding the cultural context behind the words, the unspoken rules and conventions that governed their interactions. I discovered that the language itself reflected the Japanese emphasis on indirect communication, on politeness and deference, aspects that often clashed with the more direct, assertive style of communication prevalent in my own culture. Bridging this gap became a crucial part of my personal journey.

Beyond language, I dove deeper into understanding Japanese culture. I studied the art of calligraphy, the precise strokes and the delicate balance required to create elegant characters.

The discipline and focus demanded by calligraphy were a welcome contrast to the chaos of my past, offering a sanctuary of peace and focus. I even attempted to learn the intricate art of tea ceremony, Chado, a ritual steeped in tradition and symbolism. The meticulous preparation, the careful pouring, the quiet contemplation – it was a meditative practice that fostered a sense of calm and respect for the details, the rituals that held their culture together.

My culinary explorations also played a significant role. I started small, carefully following recipes for traditional Japanese dishes, meticulously measuring ingredients, and mastering the subtle art of Japanese flavors. Kenji's mother, though initially reserved, took a quiet interest in my attempts. We would spend hours in the kitchen together, the rhythmic chopping of vegetables a silent language of shared purpose. She taught me the secrets of making perfect sushi rice, the delicate art of preparing tempura, and the nuanced flavors of miso soup. These weren't just cooking lessons; they were intimate exchanges, opportunities to connect on a personal level, to find common ground beyond the cultural differences.

One particularly memorable evening, we spent hours making mochi, the sweet rice cakes. The process was labor-intensive, requiring patience and precision. As we pounded the sticky rice mixture, a rhythmic thud filling the kitchen, we talked. She spoke about her own life, her childhood in a small village, the challenges she faced as a young woman in a patriarchal society. She shared stories of her own mother, her own struggles to balance tradition and modernity. It was in these shared moments, in the quiet intimacy of the kitchen, that the walls between us began to crumble, replaced by a growing sense of understanding and shared experience.

My understanding of the Yakuza's cultural context also deepened. I learned that their strict code of honor, while seemingly brutal at times, stemmed from a deep-seated sense of loyalty and responsibility. I started to comprehend the complex power dynamics within the family, the intricate web of alliances and rivalries that shaped their relationships. I understood that their skepticism toward me wasn't born out of malice, but rather out of a protective instinct, a fear of jeopardizing their stability.

I spent time researching the history of the Yakuza, delving into their origins and their evolution over the centuries. This wasn't about condoning their actions, but about understanding the context within which their traditions existed, the socio-economic forces that had shaped their values and beliefs. I learned that the Yakuza wasn't a monolithic entity; it was a complex organization with internal conflicts, divisions, and shifting alliances. This understanding helped me approach my interactions with Kenji's family with a greater degree of empathy and nuance.

There were still moments of tension, moments of misunderstanding. Language barriers occasionally created frustration, cultural clashes sparked misunderstandings, and the lingering suspicion from some family members never fully dissipated. But these moments were now peppered with genuine moments of connection, laughter, and shared experience. Kenji, ever the patient bridge, skillfully navigated these moments, his understanding of both cultures making him an invaluable mediator.

Kenji's younger sister, Hana, was a surprisingly important ally. Initially shy and hesitant, she became a curious observer of our intercultural dance. She proved to be a key connector, her youthful perspective often providing insights into the family dynamics that even Kenji overlooked. She helped me understand the subtleties of Japanese humor, the understated wit, the playful teasing that often passed over my head. Through Hana, I gained access to a different side of the family, a more informal, less structured view of their lives.

One significant turning point occurred during Obon, the Buddhist festival honoring ancestors. The family gathered at their ancestral home, a beautiful traditional house nestled in the countryside. The ceremony was filled with rituals I didn't fully understand, yet I participated respectfully, offering incense and bowing with reverence. The shared experience, the common act of remembering their ancestors, created a sense of unity, a bond that transcended cultural differences. Later that evening, around a bonfire, we shared stories, laughed, and sang traditional songs. In that shared warmth, in the glow of the flames, I felt a profound sense of belonging, a sense that I was, against all odds, becoming part of their family.

It wasn't just about my efforts, however. Kenji's family, too, made an effort to bridge the gap. They tried to understand my background, my culture, my perspectives. They asked questions, listened attentively, and showed a willingness to learn. They made an effort to adapt, to make me feel welcome and included. This reciprocal effort was vital to the success of our bridging cultural divide.

The journey wasn't always smooth. There were moments of frustration, of feeling utterly lost and out of place. There were times when I questioned whether it was worth the effort, whether this intense emotional investment was sustainable. There were moments when my own cultural background was a source of both pride and pain, a painful reminder of past traumas and social inequalities. My experiences had shaped me, leaving me wary of trust, always alert to the potential for betrayal. But my love for Kenji, the unwavering bond we shared, provided the strength to continue, to persist through the challenges.

The process of bridging our cultures was an ongoing dialogue, a continuous learning experience for both of us and both our families. It wasn't a matter of assimilation or abandoning my own identity. Instead, it was about creating a space where both our cultures could coexist, enriching and complementing each other. It was about finding common ground, celebrating our differences, and building a relationship founded on mutual respect, understanding, and unwavering love. The path was still not without obstacles; there was much more to be learned and understood. But with each passing day, the bridge between our worlds became stronger, a testament to the power of love in the face of cultural differences and a powerful example of the enduring capacity for human connection.

The scent of black pepper and ginger hung in the air, a fragrant bridge between our worlds. Kenji, ever the culinary adventurer, had decided to experiment with a fusion dish – a spicy shrimp stir-fry with a subtle hint of wasabi, a nod to his heritage, paired with collard greens, a soulful tribute to mine. It was a small gesture, a culinary metaphor for our evolving relationship, a testament to the beautiful blending of our cultures.

This wasn't a mere blending of flavors; it was a conscious effort to create something new, something uniquely ours. We started with simple things. We'd celebrate Kenji's family's traditional festivals like Obon, honoring their ancestors with offerings of incense and quiet reflection, while also incorporating elements of my own cultural celebrations – a joyous blend of African drumming and traditional Japanese koto music echoing through the night. The fusion of our musical celebrations was an unexpected masterpiece of rhythm and harmony, a sonic embodiment of our unconventional romance.

Our anniversaries became occasions for creative culinary experimentation. One year, it was a Kentucky Derby-themed feast with sushi and bourbon. Another year, we celebrated with a lavish spread of soul food prepared with a Japanese twist, incorporating seaweed salad and pickled ginger alongside the mac and cheese and fried chicken. These celebrations weren't merely about the food; they were about the act of creation, the shared joy of bringing together disparate elements to form something unique and meaningful. Each dish was a miniature canvas, reflecting the vibrant colors of our relationship.

Our bedroom became a sanctuary of cultural exploration. Kenji's patience in teaching me the nuances of Japanese intimacy, the subtle art of touch, the quiet intensity of their approach, contrasted beautifully with my own fiery passion and more expressive style of lovemaking. The differences weren't just tolerated, they were embraced, each act of intimacy a lesson in mutual discovery. The bedroom wasn't just a place for physical connection; it was a laboratory of intimacy, a space where we explored the boundaries of our desires, bridging the gap between our cultural differences with every touch and kiss. We intertwined our cultural expressions of love, creating a unique and deeply satisfying tapestry of physical affection.

These weren't merely imitations; they were re-interpretations, imbued with our own personalities and experiences. We didn't erase our individual identities; instead, we woven them together, creating something richer, more complex, and more beautiful than either of us could have imagined alone. This weaving wasn't just in our physical love; it expanded into our everyday lives. We celebrated each other's holidays, learning the significance of each tradition and integrating them into our lives with mutual respect and understanding.

Kenji's family, initially wary, began to see the beauty in this intercultural fusion. They saw in our blending of traditions a reflection of their own willingness to adapt and evolve. Hana, Kenji's younger sister, became a key player in this evolution. Her enthusiasm for our unique blend of cultures was infectious, bridging any lingering gaps in understanding within the family. She became the translator not just of words, but of hearts, helping her family understand the depth and sincerity of our relationship.

One evening, while preparing for a family gathering, Kenji's mother shared a precious family heirloom – a hand-painted kimono, its vibrant colors depicting a blossoming cherry tree amidst a field of wildflowers. It represented a turning point in their acceptance of our relationship and was a symbol of their willingness to embrace change. The kimono wasn't merely a garment; it was a symbol of their growing acceptance and the testament of the power of our love to overcome cultural barriers.

Kenji's father, initially the most resistant, softened over time. He saw in our efforts to bridge our cultures a parallel to his own business ventures, the successful collaborations that brought together Eastern and Western markets. He recognized that the strength of our relationship wasn't in its uniformity but in its diversity, in the richness and depth that came from our combined experiences. His silent approval was more meaningful than any vocal declaration.

My own family, while initially curious and somewhat skeptical of Kenji's world, also started to appreciate the richness and depth of Japanese culture. They began to understand that Kenji's family, despite their involvement in the Yakuza, was deeply rooted in their traditions, their commitment to family unyielding. This understanding came from shared experiences, from the simple act of sharing a meal, from listening to stories, and from witnessing the unwavering support of Kenji's family towards each other.

Our blended traditions weren't without challenges. Misunderstandings still occurred, particularly in navigating the complex power dynamics within Kenji's family. But these moments were now approached with a greater sense of understanding, a shared commitment to communication and mutual respect. We learned to listen, to ask questions, and to find common ground, even in moments of disagreement.

Our fusion extended beyond our immediate relationship, influencing our circle of friends. We hosted gatherings that celebrated both African American and Japanese culture, blending cuisines, music, and traditions into a vibrant tapestry of shared experience. Our home became a haven for cross-cultural exchange, a testament to the beauty of diversity and the power of love in bridging divides. These gatherings were more than parties; they were cultural exchanges, where friendships bloomed, fueled by our shared experience.

The fusion of our cultures extended beyond the superficial; it became an integral part of our identity, shaping our perspectives, our values, and the way we navigated the world. We didn't erase our pasts; instead, we carried them with us, blending our experiences into a richer, more complex narrative. Our relationship was a continuous journey of discovery, a testament to the transformative power of love and the beauty of bridging cultural divides.

We even started a tradition of writing letters to each other, each letter written in the other's language, a symbol of our ongoing commitment to learning and understanding. These letters were more than just words on paper; they were love letters, histories of our relationship, capturing the nuances of our evolving bond. They chronicled our journey, the triumphs and challenges, the moments of laughter and the moments of quiet contemplation. They were a unique way to celebrate our cultural fusion, a testament to our enduring love.

The fusion wasn't always easy. There were moments of conflict, of misunderstanding, where the weight of cultural differences threatened to overwhelm us. But these were moments of growth, opportunities to learn and adapt, to deepen our understanding of each other and our respective cultures. It was in these moments that our love was tested and ultimately strengthened.

The creation of new traditions wasn't a passive act; it was a continuous process, a dialogue, a negotiation between two distinct cultures. It was a dance, a rhythmic interplay of give and take, a testament to the enduring power of love and the beauty of forging something new from the ashes of the past. Our love story wasn't a simple narrative; it was a complex tapestry, interwoven with threads of passion, respect, and a commitment to creating something uniquely and beautifully our own. It was a testament to the enduring capacity of love to overcome obstacles, to transcend boundaries, and to create a future where differences are celebrated, not feared. And in this new tradition, in the fusion of our lives, we found a love unlike any other, a love that blossomed from the unlikely soil of two cultures, a testament to the unifying power of love's enduring flame.

The rhythmic clang of the kitchen knives, a familiar symphony in Kenji's family home, was a stark contrast to the quiet hum of my own kitchen back in Atlanta. Here, the preparation of food was a ritual, a carefully choreographed dance passed down through generations. Each slice, each chop, was imbued with meaning, a silent testament to the family's history and traditions. I watched Kenji's mother, her hands moving with practiced grace, and felt a deep respect for the artistry she poured into every dish. It wasn't merely about sustenance; it was an expression of love, a way of connecting with those who came before and those who would follow.

It wasn't always easy to navigate the intricate social dynamics of Kenji's family. The Yakuza's influence cast a long shadow, a constant reminder of the dangers inherent in their world. But beyond the organized crime, there existed a deep-seated loyalty, a powerful sense of family, and unwavering traditions that transcended the illegal activities. It was a complex tapestry, interwoven with threads of darkness and light, loyalty and betrayal, respect, and fear. My initial apprehension gradually gave way to a deeper understanding, a recognition that the family's internal structure, though unconventional, was as intricate and powerful as the delicate floral arrangements adorning their ancestral home.

One of the biggest challenges was the language barrier. While

Kenji spoke fluent English, the subtle nuances of Japanese conversation often escaped me. His family, for the most part, relied heavily on Kenji to translate, leaving me feeling isolated, like a spectator rather than a participant in their conversations. I began studying Japanese, diligently working through textbooks and language apps, eager to connect with them on a deeper level. The struggle wasn't just about learning a language; it was about gaining access to their hearts and minds, to fully understand their world.

My efforts weren't met with immediate acceptance; there was a palpable hesitation, a certain guardedness in their initial interactions with me. But slowly, through small gestures of kindness, acts of shared effort and patient understanding, I started to break down the walls. I learned to appreciate the significance of bowing as a greeting, the beauty of calligraphy, the importance of tea ceremonies, the meticulous attention to detail in the preparation of traditional meals. These were not merely cultural practices; they were expressions of respect, harmony, and deep-rooted traditions.

The concept of "face," so crucial in Japanese culture, was particularly challenging. The preservation of honor and reputation was paramount, demanding a level of sensitivity and awareness that I hadn't previously encountered. A single misplaced word, a careless gesture, could cause irreparable damage to relationships and social standing. I learned to tread carefully, to choose my words wisely, to pay close attention to nonverbal cues, and to observe the intricate social dynamics before responding or acting. I learned that silence, when carefully chosen, could be more eloquent than words, a testament to the power of observation and mindful interaction. It was a constant learning curve, a testament to the beauty and complexity of Japanese etiquette.

There were times when cultural differences led to misunderstandings and friction. My own direct, sometimes blunt communication style, a hallmark of my upbringing, often clashed with the more indirect and subtle approach favored by Kenji's family. I learned to temper my directness, to soften my language, to rely more on nonverbal cues to convey my meaning. It was a challenging, yet rewarding, process. The result was a gradual easing of tension and a growing comfort in navigating the subtleties of their communicative norms.

Conversely, Kenji had to adapt to my more outwardly expressive personality. My enthusiasm, my passionate displays of affection, sometimes felt overwhelming to him, at odds with the more reserved expression of love in his culture. We learned to meet in the middle, to find a balance between his quiet intensity and my effusive displays of affection, bridging the gap between our cultural norms and creating a unique language of love that was both ours.

The intimate aspects of our relationship were equally impacted by our cultural differences. Kenji's approach to intimacy was subtle, focused on building emotional intimacy first, a quiet intensity that contrasted sharply with my own more passionate and direct style. Learning to understand and appreciate these distinctions was a journey of mutual discovery and exploration, a merging of intimate styles that ultimately created a richer, more complex, and profoundly satisfying sexual experience. Our intimacy wasn't just physical; it was a profound merging of cultural sensibilities, a lovemaking that was as beautifully intricate and complex as our cultural backgrounds.

The challenge wasn't to erase our cultural identities but to integrate them, to create a space where our unique perspectives could coexist and complement each other. This wasn't always easy. Navigating these cultural complexities required patience, understanding, a willingness to compromise, and an unwavering commitment to mutual respect. It demanded a degree of self-awareness, a willingness to step outside of one's own cultural comfort zone, and embrace the enriching aspects of a unique intercultural exchange.

One evening, during a family dinner, Kenji's grandmother, a formidable woman whose wisdom was evident in every word she uttered, spoke to me in broken English, her eyes twinkling with amusement. She said something about the "beautiful chaos" of our relationship, a testament to the power of love to transcend cultural boundaries and create something beautiful and enduring. Her words resonated deeply, capturing the essence of our journey, the challenges overcome, and the rewarding tapestry of our blended cultural backgrounds.

Kenji's family's involvement in the Yakuza remained a constant, albeit unspoken, undercurrent in our lives. The potential dangers were ever-present, a silent threat that hovered in the background. But amidst the uncertainty and apprehension, I found a deeper appreciation for their unwavering loyalty, their strong family bonds, and the complexity of their traditions. My growing understanding of their culture helped me navigate the complexities of their world, allowing me to find a place within their family, a place of respect and acceptance, despite the obvious risks and challenges.

My own family, initially hesitant and apprehensive about my relationship with Kenji, gradually came to appreciate the richness and depth of his culture and the sincerity of our love. The initial skepticism and apprehension were replaced by curiosity and a genuine interest in the intricacies of Japanese culture and traditions. Shared meals, stories exchanged, and a willingness to learn and understand helped bridge the gap between two very different worlds, creating a stronger and more supportive bond between both families.

This journey of cultural understanding wasn't without its setbacks. There were still moments of misunderstanding, times when cultural differences threatened to overwhelm us. But these moments of conflict became opportunities for growth, chances to learn and adapt, to deepen our understanding of each other and our respective cultures. Each obstacle surmounted strengthened our relationship, forging a bond that was resilient, compassionate, and deeply rooted in mutual respect. The fusion of our cultures wasn't a passive blending; it was a dynamic exchange, an ongoing conversation that continually enriched our lives.

The vibrant tapestry of our lives together was woven with threads of two distinct cultures, a testament to the beauty of diversity. It wasn't always easy. There were moments of jarring dissonance, clashes of communication styles, and misunderstandings fueled by cultural differences. Yet, these very clashes became the fertile ground where our love bloomed, stronger and more resilient for having navigated the complex terrain of our contrasting worlds.

Kenji's world, steeped in the traditions and complexities of Japanese culture, was a stark contrast to my own upbringing in the vibrant, soulful heart of the African American community. His family's reverence for tradition, their emphasis on honor and "face," their subtle, nuanced communication, all felt worlds away from my more direct, expressive, and often boisterous family gatherings. Yet, within these differences lay a richness, a depth of experience that continually enriched our relationship.

One particular incident stands out. During a family gathering at my grandmother's house in Atlanta, the aroma of collard greens, fried chicken, and sweet potato pie filled the air – a familiar comfort to me, a sensory experience deeply rooted in my heritage. Kenji, ever the observant student of culture, watched with fascination as my family engaged in lively conversations, their laughter echoing through the house. He tasted the food, marveling at the bold flavors, the comforting warmth of the dishes. Yet, he also noticed the subtle nuances – the way my grandmother's eyes twinkled as she shared stories of her life, the unspoken communication between my aunts and uncles, the subtle dance of respect and affection that flowed between family members.

Later, as we strolled through the park near my grandmother's house, Kenji confessed his fascination with the way my family interacted, the warmth and affection that permeated our gatherings. He observed the subtle differences in our style of communication – the expressive body language, the shared laughter, the open display of affection, all so different from the often reserved demeanor he was accustomed to within his own family. It was a moment of mutual understanding, a recognition of the beauty and richness that each culture possessed.

His observations prompted me to consider the subtle,

unspoken rituals within his family. The intricate tea ceremonies, the graceful bowing, the hushed reverence during family discussions – these elements weren't simply cultural practices; they were manifestations of deep-seated values, expressions of respect and harmony. I found myself appreciating the quiet intensity of their interactions, the nuanced communication that transcended words.

We started exchanging cultural experiences, sharing stories and perspectives. I introduced Kenji to the rhythms of gospel music, the vibrant energy of African American dance, the rich tapestry of Black literature. He, in turn, shared the beauty of Japanese calligraphy, the serenity of Zen gardens, the elegance of traditional Japanese music. These exchanges were not merely acts of sharing; they were bridges, pathways that connected our worlds, strengthening the bond between us.

My family, initially hesitant and even somewhat apprehensive about our relationship, slowly came to understand and appreciate the beauty of Kenji's culture. My grandmother, a woman of unwavering faith and profound wisdom, embraced Kenji with open arms, acknowledging the love we shared and the richness of his background. She saw not a threat, but an enriching addition to our family, a testament to the universality of love that transcended cultural barriers.

The challenges, however, didn't vanish overnight. Navigating the complexities of two vastly different cultures required constant adaptation, a continuous effort to understand and appreciate each other's perspectives. There were times when our communication styles clashed, when misunderstandings arose, when cultural nuances led to friction. But each of these hurdles served as opportunities for growth, reinforcing our commitment to understanding and mutual respect.

Our intimate life also reflected this cultural fusion. The passionate intensity that was natural to me met Kenji's quieter, more emotionally nuanced approach to intimacy. We learned to bridge this gap, creating a space where both our styles could coexist, complementing each other, enriching the experience. Our lovemaking became a dance, a delicate choreography of contrasting rhythms, a fusion of two distinct styles.

The exploration of our differences extended beyond our personal relationship. We actively sought out opportunities to learn more about each other's cultures. I enrolled in a Japanese language class, while Kenji attended a series of lectures on African American history and culture. These efforts weren't merely academic pursuits; they were expressions of our commitment to bridging the gap between our worlds, to building a shared understanding. We attended cultural festivals, celebrated each other's holidays, and immersed ourselves in the richness of both cultures.

The diversity of our shared experiences expanded to include our friends and families. Kenji's family, despite their initial reservations, gradually welcomed me into their fold. They saw not just a Western woman, but a person who genuinely respected their traditions and was willing to learn and adapt. The family dinners became occasions of cultural exchange, moments of shared laughter and understanding. Similarly, my family embraced Kenji, recognizing the depth of his character and the sincere affection he held for me.

Our shared experiences expanded beyond personal

relationships, affecting our professional lives. My work as a writer allowed me to explore themes of cultural diversity and intercultural relationships. The stories I wrote became reflections of our journey, a celebration of the richness of our lives together. Similarly, Kenji's involvement in his family's business offered opportunities to integrate aspects of both our cultures.

The celebration of diversity wasn't simply a theme in our relationship; it was the very foundation upon which our love was built. It was a dynamic process, a continuous journey of learning, adaptation, and understanding. It involved accepting our differences, appreciating our unique perspectives, and creating a space where both cultures could coexist and flourish.

Our relationship became a powerful testament to the unifying power of love. It challenged preconceived notions, expanded our horizons, and enriched our lives in ways we could never have imagined. The challenges we faced, the cultural differences we navigated, only served to deepen our bond, to create a love story as unique and beautiful as the tapestry of our cultural backgrounds. It was, and remains, a testament to the power of diversity, a celebration of two distinct worlds coming together in perfect, imperfect harmony. It was a love that blossomed amidst the differences, a love that embraced the beauty of our contrasting cultural heritage, proving that true love knows no bounds, no cultural barriers, only the shared human experience of love, loss, acceptance, and growth. The risks, the challenges, the journey – they all contributed to the strength and depth of our love. It was a love forged in the fires of cultural understanding, a love story for the ages, a story of two souls entwined, bound not just by passion, but by the unwavering respect and appreciation for the rich tapestry of our diverse heritages. And that, my dear readers, is a love story worth celebrating.

CHAPTER 9:
AISHA'S CHOICE

The humid Atlanta air hung heavy, thick with the scent of jasmine and the unspoken tension simmering between Kenji and me. We sat on the porch swing of my grandmother's house, the rhythmic creak a counterpoint to the frantic beat of my heart. The idyllic scene belied the storm raging within me. The choice before me felt like a chasm, a gaping divide between the life I knew and the life I craved, between safety and danger, between the familiar comfort of home and the intoxicating allure of Kenji's world.

It had started subtly, a whisper of unease that gradually grew into a roar. The drug deal I'd inadvertently recorded, a fleeting moment caught on my phone, had cast a long shadow over our lives. The grainy video, a fleeting glimpse of masked faces and hushed transactions, had become a dangerous secret, a ticking time bomb threatening to explode in our faces. Kenji, with his Yakuza connections, had initially dismissed it as inconsequential, a minor incident easily handled within his network. But a growing unease gnawed at me, a feeling that the consequences were far more significant than he let on. The threat, once distant, now felt palpable, close enough to touch.

The Yakuza, with their intricate web of power and influence, weren't merely a criminal organization; they were a deeply ingrained part of Japanese society, a force that operated both within and outside the law. Their code of honor, their unspoken rules, were a world I was only beginning to understand, a world both fascinating and terrifying. Kenji's family, despite their outward affluence and sophistication, were intrinsically linked to this complex network, a reality that now seemed to loom over our relationship like a dark cloud.

Kenji, sensing my apprehension, reached for my hand, his touch both comforting and unsettling. His eyes, usually sparkling with mischief and passion, were clouded with a deep concern. He understood the weight of my dilemma, the agonizing choice that lay before me. He'd explained the risks, the potential dangers, in his quiet, measured way, but his words offered little solace. The decision wasn't simply about our relationship; it was about my life, my future, my very existence.

"Aisha," he began, his voice low and husky, "you need to understand… this isn't just about me.
It's about your safety. They won't hesitate."

His words, though laced with concern, didn't lessen the weight of the decision. The "they" he referred to represented a world far removed from my own, a world where loyalty and betrayal were intertwined, where honor and violence danced a precarious waltz. The choices I faced were stark, each with potentially devastating consequences. I could hand over the recording, potentially implicating Kenji, and his family, risking their wrath and jeopardizing our relationship, perhaps even their lives. Or, I could keep the recording, burying the secret, hoping it would remain hidden, but risking my own safety, and living in constant fear of discovery. Neither option offered peace, neither promised a happy conclusion.

The weight of the decision pressed down on me, suffocating me with its gravity. I thought of my family, their unwavering support, their love, a constant source of strength in my life. I pictured my grandmother, her gentle smile and comforting presence, a woman who had weathered countless storms with unwavering grace. The thought of jeopardizing their safety, of bringing this danger into their world, filled me with a sense of profound guilt.

Then I thought of Kenji, his unwavering love, his quiet strength, his fierce loyalty. He was a world away from the life I'd known, yet he'd opened my heart in ways I never thought possible. He'd shown me a separate way of loving, a different way of life, a world of intricate rituals and unspoken codes. The thought of losing him, of sacrificing our love for the sake of safety, felt like a physical wound, a searing pain that threatened to consume me.

The night stretched out before us, an endless expanse of uncertainty. The crickets chirped their monotonous song, a soundtrack to my internal turmoil. I paced the porch, my mind racing, wrestling with the myriad possibilities, the potential outcomes. Each choice seemed to lead to a different kind of devastation. The conflict within me was a battlefield, a war between my head and my heart, between reason and emotion, between safety and love.

Kenji remained silent, watching me, his eyes mirroring my internal struggle. He didn't press, didn't try to influence my decision. He understood the magnitude of the choice, the profound impact it would have on our lives. He knew that this decision, more than any other, would define the future of our relationship, the future of us.

As dawn approached, painting the sky with hues of pink and orange, I finally spoke, my voice barely a whisper. My words, carefully chosen, reflected the complexity of my decision, the weight of the responsibility I bore. My choice, though difficult, was resolute. It was a choice born of both love and necessity, a blend of courage and vulnerability.

My decision wasn't a simple yes or no; it was a complex tapestry woven from fear and hope, loyalty, and self-preservation. It was a testament to the strength I'd found within myself, a strength nurtured by my heritage, by my love for Kenji, and by the unshakeable bond I shared with my family. It was a decision that would forever shape the course of my life, a decision that would test the limits of my courage and the depth of my love. The sun rose, casting its golden rays upon us, a silent witness to my difficult choice, a choice that would forever alter the trajectory of our lives. The choice I made that morning was not just about the video, or Kenji, or even my safety; it was about claiming my agency, my power, in a world that often sought to diminish it. It was about choosing my own path, carving my own destiny, even amidst the shadows and uncertainties that surrounded me. It was a decision that, in its complexity, reflected the rich tapestry of my own identity, the blend of strength and vulnerability that defined me as an African American woman navigating a world both familiar and foreign. And in the quiet stillness of that dawn, I found a strength I hadn't known I possessed, a strength that would carry me through whatever lay ahead. The journey would be long and arduous, but I knew, with unwavering certainty, that I was ready to face it, together with Kenji, side-by-side, forging our future in the face of adversity, our love a beacon in the darkness. The path ahead remained unclear, fraught with uncertainty, but with each sunrise, I would embrace the challenges, the risks, the uncertainties, and continue to forge my own destiny, a destiny shaped by love, courage, and the unwavering spirit of a woman who refused to be defined by her circumstances. My choice was a testament to the strength I found within myself, a strength that was not only mine but also a reflection of my heritage, my culture, and the love that bound me to Kenji. The future remained uncertain, a vast expanse of possibilities and uncertainties, but I stepped forward with a quiet determination, ready to face whatever challenges lay ahead, my hand firmly in Kenji's, my heart filled with a love that transcended cultural boundaries, a love that gave me the strength to confront the uncertainties of our future together. It was a love story still unfolding, a story written in the language of courage, resilience, and unwavering faith in the power of love to overcome even the most daunting of obstacles.

The sun climbed higher, painting the sky in vibrant hues, a stark contrast to the storm raging within me. Kenji's hand, warm and reassuring, remained clasped in mine, a silent promise of support in the face of the unknown. But the silence itself was heavy, laden with the unspoken weight of the decision that hung between us, a tangible barrier threatening to shatter the fragile peace we'd found.

My mind raced, replaying every detail of the past few weeks – the accidental recording, the hushed conversations, Kenji's controlled demeanor, the subtle shifts in his behavior that hinted at a deeper, more dangerous reality. The Yakuza weren't just a group of criminals; they were a family, a deeply entrenched part of Japanese society, with their own complex code of honor, their own unwritten rules. Kenji, with his quiet strength and effortless charm, had been the key that unlocked a world both alluring and terrifying. But now, that same key seemed to be leading me into a labyrinth of danger, a precarious dance with fate.

The choice wasn't simply between handing over the recording and keeping it hidden. It was a far more complex equation, a tangled web of loyalties and betrayals, of love and self-preservation. Handing over the recording meant potentially implicating Kenji and his family, exposing them to the wrath of their enemies, and bringing down a world that had both captivated and frightened me. The consequences could be devastating, reaching far beyond the immediate consequences. It meant risking his life, his family's lives, potentially unleashing a war I wasn't prepared for. It meant betraying the trust he'd placed in me, shattering the bond we'd so carefully built.

But keeping the recording meant living with a constant weight of fear, a gnawing uncertainty that threatened to consume me. It meant living in the shadows, constantly looking over my shoulder, wondering when the other shoe would drop. It meant risking my own life, and the lives of my family, the people I loved most in the world. My grandmother, with her unwavering faith and gentle wisdom, had always been my anchor, my safe harbor. The thought of jeopardizing her safety, bringing this darkness into her world, filled me with a profound sense of guilt.

The cultural clash added another layer of complexity to my dilemma. My African American heritage, with its strong emphasis on family and community, contrasted sharply with the rigid hierarchy and unspoken codes of the Yakuza. The values I'd grown up with, the lessons my grandmother had instilled in me, clashed with the realities of Kenji's world. Navigating these conflicting cultures felt like walking a tightrope, one false step away from a devastating fall.

I thought of the countless conversations I'd had with my grandmother about making tough choices, about navigating difficult situations with grace and strength. Her words echoed in my mind, a guiding force in the storm. She'd always stressed the importance of integrity, of standing up for what's right, even when it was difficult. But she'd also emphasized the importance of protecting oneself, of knowing when to fight and when to retreat. Finding the balance between these two principles was the heart of my dilemma.

Then there was Kenji himself. His love, fierce and unwavering, had shaken me to my core. He was a man of contradictions, a mixture of violence and gentleness, of power and vulnerability. He was both a protector and a danger, a man who could both soothe my anxieties and ignite my fears. He was a world away from everything I knew, yet he was the person who had truly seen me, understood me, in a way no one else had before. Losing him would be a profound loss, a wound that might never heal.

The hours stretched on, the silence broken only by the chirping of crickets and the gentle sway of the porch swing. The rising sun cast long shadows across the yard, highlighting the deep creases of concern etched on Kenji's face. He didn't press me, didn't try to influence my decision, respecting the magnitude of the choice I was grappling with. He understood that this decision, more than any other, would shape the future of our relationship, the future of us. He waited patiently, his silence a testament to his love, his trust in my judgment, his unwavering belief in my strength.

As the day wore on, I began to see the decision not simply as a choice between two paths, but as a forging of my own identity, a declaration of my own agency. It wasn't about choosing one path over the other, but about defining the path I would create for myself. It was a reflection of my past, my present, and the future I hoped to build. The essence of this choice was not a simple yes or no, but an affirmation of self, a declaration of my agency in a world that often tried to diminish or silence women of color.

I thought about the strength of my ancestors, the women who had endured unimaginable hardship and oppression, who had fought for their rights and for the rights of their children. Their resilience, their unwavering spirit, flowed through my veins, a source of strength I could draw upon in this moment of crisis. I was not just a woman in love; I was a daughter, a granddaughter, a woman shaped by generations of struggle and triumph. My choice had to reflect that legacy, had to honor the sacrifices made by those who came before me.

With newfound clarity, I understood that my choice wasn't just about the recording, or Kenji, or even my safety. It was about reclaiming my narrative, asserting my control in a situation that seemed designed to strip me of it. It was about choosing my own path, even if that path led me through darkness and uncertainty. It was about the strength I found within myself, a blend of courage and vulnerability that defined who I was as an African American woman navigating a world both familiar and alien.

And so, as the sun finally broke through the clouds, casting its golden light upon us, I spoke, my voice clear and steady. My decision was not one of simple compliance, or passive acceptance; it was a carefully considered path forged through introspection and a resolute understanding of the stakes involved. My decision was a testament to the complex tapestry of my identity, a culmination of everything I had lived and learned. It was a choice that embodied the strength of my heritage, the depth of my love, and the unwavering determination of a woman who would not be silenced or controlled.

The weight of my decision settled, a tangible presence in the quiet space between Kenji and me. It wasn't the lightness of relief, nor the crushing weight of despair, but something in between – a quiet understanding that had settled deep within my soul. The decision itself, the act of choosing, had been a journey in itself, a process of self-discovery that had unveiled facets of myself I hadn't known existed.

The sun, now high in the sky, cast a warm glow on Kenji's face, highlighting the delicate lines around his eyes, a testament to the quiet battles he'd fought, the burdens he carried. He watched me, his expression a mixture of anticipation and apprehension, a silent acknowledgement of the seismic shift occurring within me. This wasn't just a choice concerning a recording, a drug deal, or the Yakuza; it was a choice about my life, my future, my very essence.

The days following my decision were a blur of activity, a whirlwind of emotions. I found myself delving deeper into my own history, exploring the narratives of my ancestors, the women who had paved the way for me. My grandmother's stories, once familiar tales, took on a new significance, revealing a lineage of resilience, of courage in the face of adversity. I saw in them reflections of my own strength, a strength I hadn't fully recognized until now.

My research into African American history wasn't just an academic exercise; it was a personal pilgrimage, a journey of self-discovery. I learned about the struggles of women who had defied expectations, who had fought for their rights and their dignity, even in the face of overwhelming odds. I read about their triumphs, their resilience, their unwavering belief in the power of their own voices. These stories, woven into the fabric of my being, empowered me, strengthened my resolve, and illuminated the path forward.

The experience of connecting with my heritage gave me a powerful sense of belonging, a grounding in my identity as an African American woman. It reaffirmed my connection to a community that had nurtured and supported me, a community that had shaped my values and beliefs. This sense of belonging, this profound connection to my roots, gave me the courage to face the challenges ahead, the confidence to navigate the complexities of my situation. It solidified my resolve to forge my own path, to define my own destiny.

Parallel to this internal journey, my understanding of East Asian culture deepened. My initial perception of the Yakuza, rooted in stereotypical portrayals and media representations, had been challenged and reshaped by my experiences with Kenji and his family. I began to appreciate the nuances of their culture, the intricacies of their traditions, and the complex web of relationships that bound them together. I saw beyond the surface, recognizing the strength and resilience embedded within their societal structures.

Learning about their history, their values, and their perspectives helped me to bridge the cultural gap, to understand Kenji on a deeper level. It was a process of mutual understanding, a reciprocal journey of discovery that enhanced our connection. We began to discuss our respective cultures, sharing stories, perspectives, and values. This process of mutual exchange enriched our relationship, strengthening our bond and deepening our understanding of each other. The cultural differences, initially a source of conflict, now served as a bridge, connecting us in unexpected ways.

The intimacy we shared, both physical and emotional, became a sacred space, a sanctuary where our differences melded together, creating something new, something uniquely ours. Our love, once a source of conflict due to cultural differences, now became a powerful force that united us, transcending boundaries and preconceptions. Our shared experiences strengthened our bond, weaving a unique tapestry of love, understanding, and mutual respect.

Our sexual encounters, once marked by the intensity of our passionate connection, now included a layer of mutual exploration and respect. We learned to communicate our desires and boundaries, navigating our different cultural approaches to intimacy with greater sensitivity and understanding. The exploration of different sexual practices, initially driven by curiosity, now deepened our intimacy, fostering a greater level of trust and emotional connection.

The physical aspects of our relationship were intertwined with a growing emotional intimacy. It wasn't just about physical pleasure, but about exploring emotional vulnerabilities and building trust. The emotional intimacy that developed enhanced the physical aspects of our relationship, transforming our encounters into acts of profound connection and emotional expression.

Kenji's support during this period was unwavering. He never tried to control my decisions, instead providing a space for me to explore my feelings and come to my own conclusions. His patience and respect for my journey of self-discovery strengthened our bond, highlighting the genuine depth of his love and commitment. He recognized the importance of my self-discovery journey, understanding that this was crucial for my self-actualization. His understanding and support were essential in this journey.

Through this transformative process, I discovered a strength I never knew I possessed. I learned to embrace my complexities, to accept my vulnerabilities, and to stand firmly in my own truth. The self-discovery wasn't merely about understanding my African American identity or learning about Kenji's world; it was about understanding the entirety of my being, the intricate tapestry of my experiences, and the profound power of self-acceptance.

This newfound strength enabled me to confront the challenges ahead with unwavering determination. The decision made concerning the recording was not just a choice; it was a defining moment that shaped my future. It was a testament to the resilience I had discovered within myself, the power of self-discovery, and the depth of my own character. The weight of the decision was not merely a burden but a catalyst for self-discovery and personal growth. It was the defining moment that shaped my future.

The future remained uncertain, a vast landscape of possibilities, both exciting and daunting. But I faced it with a newfound confidence, a strength born from the crucible of self-discovery. The path ahead would undoubtedly present further challenges, but I knew, deep in my heart, that I had the strength, the resilience, and the clarity to navigate them, to create the future I desired, a future defined by my own agency and the unwavering power of my spirit. This was not merely a new chapter in my life, but a new beginning, a testament to the transformative power of self-discovery.

The air in the dojo hung heavy with the scent of incense and sweat. Kenji, his gi pristine white against the dark wood floor, moved with a fluid grace that belied the underlying power he possessed. He was a master of his art, his movements precise, deliberate, each strike imbued with a quiet intensity. Watching him, I felt a surge of admiration, not just for his skill, but for the discipline and self-control he embodied. It was a stark contrast to the chaotic world I had known before, the world of impulsive decisions and reckless abandon.

My own journey, however, was far from over. The decision I had made, though momentous, was only the first step on a long and winding path. The recording, the threat of the Yakuza's enemies, the potential for betrayal – these were still looming shadows, casting their long arms across my future. But now, armed with a newfound understanding of myself and the strength I possessed, I felt a sense of calm I hadn't experienced before. This wasn't the blind optimism of ignorance; it was the quiet confidence of someone who had faced their demons and emerged victorious.

The following weeks were a whirlwind of activity. I immersed myself in work, finding solace in the structure and routine. The beauty store, with its polished surfaces and calming aromas, was a sanctuary from the storm brewing outside. I focused on my tasks, meticulously organizing inventories, assisting customers, and learning the intricacies of the business. It was a grounding force, a tangible connection to a world separate from the shadows that pursued me.

Kenji, understanding my need for stability, provided unwavering support. He wasn't possessive, never trying to restrict my independence. Instead, he offered his strength, a silent presence that reassured me. He listened patiently to my anxieties, offering words of encouragement and understanding without judgment. His touch, gentle and reassuring, often brought a sense of peace. His quiet strength was a comforting anchor in the turbulent sea of uncertainty.

One evening, as we sat together on the balcony overlooking the city, the cityscape twinkling like a million fallen stars, he spoke of his own path, his own struggles. He spoke of the pressure to uphold the family name, the weight of tradition and expectation that pressed upon him. It was a vulnerability I hadn't seen before, a glimpse into the man behind the mask of the Yakuza. His confession surprised me; I found a depth in his words that challenged my pre-conceived notions of his world.

"There are things I would change," he confessed, his voice barely a whisper, "But some things are beyond my control. It's a complex web, Aisha. Family, honor, loyalty...they are intertwined, sometimes in ways that are difficult to understand."

His words resonated with me deeply. My own past, with its scars and broken promises, echoed his sentiment. The complexities of family, of loyalty, of the burden of tradition – these were themes that transcended cultural boundaries, weaving a common thread between our disparate experiences. In that shared understanding, a deeper connection blossomed.

I shared my own story with him, not just the highlights, but the details, the darkness, the moments of profound despair. I spoke of my past relationship, the violence, the betrayal, the lingering wounds. He listened patiently, his gaze unwavering, his touch soothing my anxieties. It was in that shared vulnerability that a true intimacy emerged, a bond forged in the crucible of mutual understanding and acceptance.

In the quiet moments, as we lay entwined, our bodies a testament to our passionate connection, I felt a sense of profound peace. The physical intimacy was more than just sensual pleasure; it was a profound expression of trust, of acceptance, of shared vulnerability. It was a testament to the strength of our bond, a sanctuary from the turbulent world outside. The sensual exploration intertwined with our emotional intimacy, creating an experience that transcended simple physical gratification. It was a deep dance of emotions and desires, a shared exploration of passion.

Our cultural differences, once a source of apprehension, became a springboard for exploration.
We spent hours discussing our respective heritages, our traditions, our values. His knowledge of Japanese culture,

history, and art provided me with a new perspective, broadening my understanding of the world. Conversely, my background and education in African American history and culture intrigued him, introducing him to a new world of artistic expression, social movements, and resilience. This exchange of knowledge enriched our relationship, creating a beautiful blend of cultures that transcended boundaries and differences.

One of the most impactful aspects of our journey together involved visiting my family. Introducing Kenji to my mother and sisters was a pivotal moment. Initially, they were wary. My mother, a woman of unwavering faith and strong morals, was particularly cautious. But Kenji's genuine respect, his quiet dignity, and his genuine love for me gradually eased their concerns. The cultural exchange and the mutual respect shown were key in bridging the initial gap. Through thoughtful conversations and honest exchange, we all came to understand and appreciate each other's perspectives.

The encounter highlighted the beauty of cultural exchange and the importance of communication. The initial hesitation transformed into a warm acceptance, a testament to the strength of our love and the power of understanding. My family's eventual blessing further cemented the strength of our bond, transforming their initial hesitation into support. The mutual respect we demonstrated was transformative.

My personal growth wasn't limited to understanding Kenji and his world. It also involved a deeper exploration of my own identity as an African American woman. I dedicated time to researching the history and contributions of Black women in various fields. I discovered role models whose resilience and strength resonated deeply with my own experiences. I found parallels in their journeys, their struggles, and their triumphs. This research empowered me further and helped shape my vision for the future. The sense of community and connection it provided strengthened my resolve. It was a vital component of my self-discovery and personal growth.

The threats remained, the shadows still lingered, but they no longer held the same power over me. I carried a strength within me, a resilience forged in the crucible of hardship and strengthened by love and self-discovery. The path ahead was uncertain, but I faced it with a quiet confidence, knowing that whatever challenges lay ahead, I had the strength to overcome them. The future was a blank canvas, ready for me to paint my own masterpiece, a masterpiece born from resilience, love, and the unwavering power of my spirit. The challenges had transformed me, making me stronger, more resilient, and more confident in my ability to shape my destiny. This was not just survival; it was thriving.

The humid Atlanta air hung heavy as I sat on my porch, the rhythmic chirping of crickets a counterpoint to the turmoil within me. Kenji's world, with its glittering facade and dangerous undercurrents, had exposed me to a level of intensity I'd never known. The adrenaline-fueled nights, the whispered secrets, the breathtaking intimacy—it all felt intoxicating, yet deeply unsettling. My past, a tapestry woven with threads of trauma and shattered trust, had left its mark. I carried the scars, both visible and invisible, like ancient hieroglyphs etched onto my soul. And yet, here I was, entangled in a relationship that challenged every preconceived notion I had about love, loyalty, and myself.

For so long, I had strived for perfection—a flawless exterior, a carefully crafted persona that shielded the vulnerabilities

I desperately tried to conceal. The image of the successful, independent woman, untouchable and unbreakable, was a mask I wore with increasing fatigue. It was a defense mechanism, built from necessity, a way to protect myself from the world's harsh realities. But the façade was crumbling, the weight of its artifice becoming unbearable. Kenji, with his quiet strength and unwavering acceptance, had slowly chipped away at the carefully constructed walls, revealing the cracks and imperfections beneath.

He didn't flinch at my past, didn't shy away from the darkness I carried within. Instead, he embraced it, acknowledging the scars without judgment, seeing the strength in my vulnerability. His love wasn't a conditional acceptance; it was a profound understanding, a recognition of my inherent worth, irrespective of my imperfections. It was a love that didn't demand perfection, but celebrated the mosaic of my experiences, the intricate details of my journey.

One evening, as the city lights shimmered like scattered diamonds across the Atlanta skyline, Kenji and I sat side-by-side, a comfortable silence settling between us. I confessed my fear of being judged, my persistent worry about the way others perceived me. The lingering anxieties that stemmed from my past relationship still haunted me, often manifesting as self-doubt and insecurity.

"Aisha," he said, his voice soft, his hand gently covering mine, "Your imperfections are what make you beautiful. They are part of your story, your strength. They are what have shaped you into the woman you are today." His words resonated deeply, dismantling the carefully constructed walls I had spent years building.

His acceptance wasn't just about overlooking my flaws; it was about celebrating them, appreciating the complexities that made me unique. He saw beyond the superficial, delving into the depths of my being, acknowledging the resilience that lay beneath the surface of my insecurities. This recognition liberated me from the shackles of perfectionism, allowing me to embrace my vulnerabilities, to own my story, flaws, and all.

This newfound acceptance extended beyond my relationship with Kenji. It seeped into every aspect of my life, transforming my perception of myself and my capabilities. I began to approach challenges with a newfound grace, acknowledging my limitations without self-criticism. I learned to forgive myself for past mistakes, to celebrate small victories, and to approach setbacks with a renewed sense of perspective.

My work at the beauty store, once a refuge from the chaos of my life, became a source of personal growth. I was no longer striving for unattainable standards of perfection but focusing on the joy and fulfillment derived from my work. The interactions with clients, the meticulous application of makeup, the transformation of each individual—it was all deeply satisfying. I discovered a passion for helping others, for empowering them through self-acceptance and selflove.

My relationship with my family also flourished. They had witnessed my struggles, my vulnerabilities, and my transformation. My mother, once wary of Kenji's Yakuza connections, now saw the depth of his character, the genuine love he held for me. Her acceptance, her unwavering support, was a testament to the power of love, understanding, and forgiveness. The family dinners, once strained with tension and unspoken anxieties, were now filled with laughter, warmth, and genuine connection.

My personal journey of self-acceptance wasn't always smooth; there were moments of self-doubt, setbacks that threatened to derail my progress. But each time, I found the strength to rise above, to learn from my mistakes, and to emerge stronger, wiser, and more empowered. The fear of judgment, once an insurmountable obstacle, gradually dissipated. I discovered the strength within myself, a resilient spirit fueled by self-love and the unwavering support of the people who mattered most.

Kenji's world, once a source of apprehension, had become a source of growth and understanding. I had witnessed the intricacies of the Yakuza culture, its complex system of loyalty, honor, and tradition. I had seen Kenji navigate the expectations placed upon him, the weight of family legacy, and the inherent dangers of his profession. My understanding of his world broadened my perspective, allowing me to appreciate the diverse tapestry of human experience, to recognize the complexities of cultural dynamics, and to accept the inherent imperfections within every system, every society, and every individual.

The cultural exchange between Kenji and myself became a constant source of enrichment. We explored each other's heritage, delving deep into the nuances of our respective cultures. He introduced me to the subtle art of Japanese tea ceremony, sharing the philosophy behind every graceful movement, the mindfulness inherent in every sip. I, in turn, introduced him to the vibrant rhythms and soulful harmonies of gospel music, sharing stories of struggle, resilience, and faith. This exchange strengthened our bond, fostering a profound respect for each other's backgrounds, differences, and experiences.

We learned to embrace the beautiful imperfections in our cultural differences, accepting the nuances of each other's upbringing and experiences. It was a testament to the power of open-mindedness, understanding, and unwavering love. The fusion of our cultures became a beautiful symphony of our unique identities and heritage, reflecting our relationship.

The threats remained, the shadows still danced at the periphery of our lives. The recording, the drug deal, the potential for betrayal—these were realities we couldn't ignore. But they no longer held the same power over us. We faced them together, our bond a fortress against the uncertainties of the future. The past, once a source of pain and trauma, became a source of strength, a testament to our resilience, our shared journey, and the unwavering strength of our love.

Our love story wasn't a fairy tale; it was a complex, imperfect, and deeply human experience. It was a journey of self-discovery, a testament to the power of vulnerability, and an affirmation of love's ability to heal, transform, and ultimately, set us free. And in the acceptance of our imperfections, both individually and as a couple, we found a depth of intimacy and a bond that transcended the superficial, revealing the true beauty of a love that embraced life's inherent complexities. This was not just survival; it was flourishing in the face of adversity, a testament to the strength of the human spirit, and the transformative power of accepting and embracing imperfections. The future remained unwritten, a blank canvas awaiting the strokes of our shared journey, a masterpiece in the making, imperfect, yet profoundly beautiful.

CHAPTER 10:
KENJI'S SACRIFICE

The humid Atlanta air still clung to my skin, a persistent reminder of the stifling heat that had become synonymous with the summer of our lives. But the heat felt different now, less oppressive, more like a warm embrace. The weight of uncertainty, the ever-present shadow of Kenji's world, still lingered, but it felt less heavy, somehow lighter, almost manageable. This shift wasn't due to any sudden resolution of the threats we faced, but rather to a profound transformation within Kenji himself, a sacrifice that had reshaped the landscape of our relationship.

It began subtly. Small gestures, quiet acts of consideration that spoke volumes about the depth of his love. He started taking more time away from his family business, more time spent with me, not in clandestine meetings or rushed stolen moments, but in genuine, unhurried companionship. He'd bring me breakfast in bed, a simple act, yet imbued with an affection so profound it brought tears to my eyes. He'd spend hours just listening, his quiet strength a comforting presence amidst the lingering anxieties that sometimes threatened to overwhelm me.

One evening, as we sat on our porch, the city lights twinkling like distant stars, he confessed something that shook me to my core. It wasn't a confession of wrongdoing, or a revelation of hidden dangers within his world, but something far more significant – a sacrifice that spoke volumes of his unwavering devotion. He spoke of a looming business deal, one that promised to secure his family's financial future for generations to come, a deal that demanded his full attention, his unwavering dedication. It was a deal that involved his uncle, a powerful and influential figure within the Yakuza, a man whose favor was both a blessing and a curse.

But the deal came with a condition, a steep price for his ambition. He had to relinquish his position within the family's beauty empire, a company that was not just a business, but a legacy, a testament to his family's history and heritage. He had to step aside, effectively giving up the birthright he'd been groomed for since childhood. It wasn't merely a financial sacrifice; it was a severing of ties to his past, a relinquishment of his identity, a shedding of his very lineage. The weight of this decision, the magnitude of his sacrifice, was palpable.

He spoke in quiet tones, his voice tinged with a hint of sadness, but his eyes, usually filled with the quiet intensity of a man accustomed to power, held a vulnerability I had never seen before.

He wasn't seeking my approval, or my understanding; he was simply sharing the burden of his decision, entrusting me with a piece of his soul, laying bare the profound depth of his love.

"I did it for us, Aisha," he whispered, his hand gently caressing my cheek. "For our future. This deal...it's too dangerous, too entangled with... with things I can't bring you into. It's a risk I'm not willing to take, not anymore."

His words hung in the air, heavy with meaning. I understood the immensity of his sacrifice, the magnitude of the choice he'd made. He was giving up everything he'd ever known, everything he'd worked for, to ensure our safety, our future together. It wasn't just a business deal he was abandoning; it was his life as he knew it. It was his legacy, his family, his very identity.

The next few days were filled with a whirlwind of activity. He arranged for the transfer of assets, dealt with the inevitable fallout from his decision within his family, and navigated the treacherous waters of the Yakuza underworld. He did it all with a quiet determination, a steely resolve that masked the inner turmoil I knew he must have been feeling. He faced his family's disapproval, the whispers of betrayal, and the potential for reprisal with a stoicism that was both admirable and heartbreaking.

The sacrifices extended beyond his family's business. He sold his prized possessions, items of significant value and sentimental importance. He released his hold on certain lucrative ventures, accepting a significant financial downturn as a necessary step towards building a life apart from the Yakuza. This wasn't simply about avoiding danger; it was an act of absolute devotion, a surrender of his own aspirations to create a safe and stable future for us.

He didn't complain, didn't seek pity. He simply bore the weight of his decision with a quiet dignity, a resilience that filled me with awe and gratitude. His love wasn't a grand gesture, a dramatic display of affection, but rather a series of small, meaningful actions, each one a testament to his commitment to building a life free from the shadows of his past.

There were moments of doubt, of course. Moments when I questioned his decision, when I felt the weight of his sacrifice pressing down on me. Moments when the fear of the unknown threatened to consume me. But his unwavering faith in our future, his quiet strength, always pulled me back from the brink.

His transformation wasn't just external; it was a profound shift in his inner landscape. He was no longer the enigmatic, reserved member of the Yakuza I'd initially fallen for. He was becoming someone new, someone unburdened by the expectations and constraints of his past, someone free to embrace a future built on love, trust, and a shared commitment to building a life together. The man who had once moved through the world with the quiet grace of a seasoned warrior now walked with a newfound lightness, a gentle warmth that emanated from his very being.

The transition wasn't easy. We faced financial challenges, and navigated the complexities of starting over. But we did it together, our bond strengthened by the very act of facing our new reality as a team. He learned to adapt, to embrace new challenges with an openness and enthusiasm I hadn't expected. He discovered a new sense of purpose, a passion for life outside of the Yakuza, a passion that was as captivating as the man himself.

He found joy in simple things, in the quiet moments shared between us, in the laughter and companionship that had once been overshadowed by the shadows of his life. He discovered a new depth of empathy, a sensitivity that had been carefully masked by his Yakuza exterior, and it was a stunning discovery. He embraced the domesticity of our life, finding satisfaction in shared chores and mundane routines, and it was within these moments that I truly saw him thrive. This new life was not a retreat from danger; it was a strategic advancement in building a safer and fuller life for us both.

Kenji's sacrifice wasn't a grand gesture meant for public display; it was a quiet act of devotion, a testament to the depth of his love. It wasn't just a change in his external circumstances but a fundamental shift in his being, a metamorphosis from a man bound by tradition and duty to a man liberated by love. And in that transformation, I saw a love that was both profoundly selfless and utterly captivating. It was a love that was, in its own quiet way, the most powerful force I had ever encountered. It was a love that would redefine not just our lives, but the very essence of our being.

The initial shock of Kenji's decision had begun to fade, replaced by a gnawing unease. His sacrifice, while breathtaking in its scope, had unleashed a maelstrom of unforeseen consequences. The quiet dignity he'd maintained throughout the initial upheaval began to crack under the pressure of his family's wrath. His uncle, a man whose shadow had loomed large over Kenji's life, was not one to forgive easily. Whispers turned to accusations, accusations to threats. The once-impenetrable wall of protection Kenji had enjoyed within the Yakuza was crumbling, leaving him vulnerable in ways I had never imagined.

The financial repercussions were immediate and stark. The sale of his assets, while strategically necessary, had left us with a significantly reduced income. The comfortable life we had envisioned was suddenly a distant dream, replaced by the harsh realities of budgeting and economizing. We moved from our spacious apartment, a symbol of our burgeoning love and shared success, to a smaller, more modest dwelling in a less affluent part of the city. The change was jarring, a stark reminder of the sacrifices we were making, not just financially, but emotionally.

The shift in our lifestyle wasn't simply a matter of adjusting to a smaller living space. It was a fundamental alteration of our routine, a shedding of the luxury we had both become accustomed to. Gone were the spontaneous dinners at expensive restaurants, the luxurious getaways, the seemingly endless supply of beautiful things. In their place were carefully planned meals, thrift store finds, and a renewed appreciation for the simple pleasures of life. It was a humbling experience, forcing us to confront the fragility of our newfound stability, a stark contrast to the opulent world Kenji had once inhabited.

But even more challenging than the financial adjustments was the emotional toll Kenji's decision had taken on him. The quiet stoicism that had masked his inner turmoil began to fray, revealing the deep wounds inflicted by his family's rejection. The man I loved, the fiercely independent and self-assured Kenji I had grown to adore, was struggling. He withdrew into himself, his usual warmth replaced by a chilling reserve. The lightness in his step was gone, replaced by a weariness that clung to him like a second skin.

His nights were filled with restless sleep, punctuated by fits of silent anguish. I'd wake up to find him sitting on the edge of the bed, staring out the window, his eyes reflecting the city lights that once held such promise, now seeming to mock our new reality. He didn't speak of his pain, rarely even acknowledging it, but the subtle tremors in his hands, the tightness in his shoulders, spoke volumes of the emotional burden he was carrying.

My heart ached for him, but I was helpless to alleviate his suffering. I could offer comfort, reassurance, and unwavering support, but I couldn't erase the pain he felt, the betrayal he had endured. I could only be there, a constant presence in his life, a silent testament to my love and unwavering commitment. It was a painful, slow process, a journey through dark valleys of despair and doubt.

My own fears, initially overshadowed by Kenji's sacrifice, now surfaced with a vengeance. The drug deal recording remained a ticking time bomb, a constant reminder of the dangers that still lurked in the shadows. While Kenji's departure from the Yakuza ostensibly reduced the immediate threat, it also exposed us to new vulnerabilities. Without the protective shield of his family's influence, we were more exposed, more vulnerable to the unpredictable forces that controlled the underworld.

The line between his past life and our present reality blurred. Occasional threats arrived anonymously— cryptic messages left on our doorstep, unsettling phone calls in the dead of night, a chilling reminder that the world Kenji had left behind wasn't so easily shed. Each incident was a sharp, painful stab, an unwelcome intrusion into our fragile peace. These threats were not just directed at Kenji; they were aimed at me, a constant reminder that I was caught in the crossfire of his past life, a pawn in a game I didn't understand.

My attempts to reassure him often fell flat, his silence a heavy blanket smothering my attempts at intimacy. Sex, once a vibrant expression of our love, became strained and infrequent. The passion that had burned so brightly between us seemed to flicker and dim, a casualty of the stress and uncertainty that permeated our lives. The physical intimacy we shared, once a sanctuary, now felt fraught with unspoken anxieties.

One evening, under the pale glow of a single bedside lamp, I finally broke through his defenses. He was sitting hunched over, his shoulders slumped in defeat, a stark contrast to the powerfully built man I knew. I gently took his hand, my touch hesitant, afraid to intrude on his private pain. "Kenji," I whispered, my voice trembling slightly, "it's okay to not be okay."

He looked up at me, his eyes filled with a profound sadness, a weariness that mirrored my own fears. The silence stretched between us, heavy with unspoken emotions. Finally, he spoke, his voice raspy and low.

"I failed, Aisha," he confessed, his voice barely above a whisper. "I failed my family, and now... I'm failing you."

His words hit me hard. I held his gaze, trying to convey the truth in my eyes. "You haven't failed anyone, Kenji. You made a sacrifice, a profound one. It takes immense courage to do what you did, to prioritize our future over everything else."

He didn't respond immediately. His eyes closed briefly before opening again. He took a deep breath and let it out slowly. "It wasn't just a business deal, Aisha. It was... my identity."

His words resonated with a deep sadness, a raw vulnerability that broke my heart. I pulled him close, holding him tight, letting him know that he wasn't alone, that I was there, unwavering in my love and support. The pain was still there, a constant undercurrent in our lives, but now it was shared, a burden we were bearing together. It wasn't a resolution, but the beginning of a healing process, a long, slow road towards rebuilding our lives, together. The future remained uncertain, but in the shared vulnerability and mutual love, we found a strength that would sustain us through the challenges that lay ahead. The weight of his sacrifice was immense, but so was the strength of our love, a love that was now forged in the crucible of adversity, a love that was ultimately more resilient and powerful than anything the past could throw at us.

The following weeks were a blur of quiet desperation and tentative hope. Kenji, stripped of his former life, found himself adrift, grappling with the profound loss of his identity. His family, once a source of pride and belonging, now represented a crushing betrayal. The weight of their disapproval pressed down on him, a suffocating burden that threatened to consume him. He had traded his birthright for our love, a choice that, while deeply personal, left him feeling profoundly alone.

My love for him deepened with each passing day, fueled by a fierce determination to see him through this storm. I watched as he fought to reclaim his sense of self, to forge a new identity independent of his family's legacy. It wasn't easy. The process was slow, painful, marked by fits of anger and despair, quiet moments of introspection, and the occasional flicker of a smile that hinted at the man I loved so dearly.

His work with me at the community garden became a refuge, a small patch of fertile ground where he could nurture something new, something entirely his own. The rhythmic work, the feel of the soil beneath his calloused hands, seemed to soothe his troubled spirit. He found a strange solace in tending to the plants, watching them grow, bloom, and bear fruit. It was a testament to the cycle of life, death, and rebirth, a mirrored reflection of his own journey. The vibrant colors of the flowers, the lush green of the vegetables, offered a vibrant counterpoint to the muted grays of his grief.

He began to paint again, a skill he had abandoned years ago in favor of the demands of the Yakuza. His canvases, once filled with the dark hues of his past, now blossomed with vibrant colors, expressing the raw emotions he had long suppressed. His paintings were less about the violence and power he once associated with his family and more about the tender emotions he was learning to embrace: the quiet love shared between two people, the enduring strength of the human spirit, the beauty of resilience.

We started small, hosting intimate gatherings at our new apartment, inviting friends from our community. The warm glow of candlelight, the shared laughter, the comforting aroma of homecooked meals helped to fill the void left by the opulent but empty extravagance of his past. He started to engage in the simple joys of everyday life, finding comfort in the rhythm of our shared existence.

I discovered a hidden talent in him. He was an exceptional baker. His hands, once adept at handling weapons, now delicately kneaded dough, creating exquisite pastries and cakes that were as beautiful as they were delicious. He found joy in the precision of his movements, the satisfying transformation of simple ingredients into something exquisite. The aroma of freshly baked goods became a constant reminder of the sweetness and warmth we were creating in our new life.

One day, while working in the garden, he found a small, fragile seedling pushing its way through the soil. He gently cradled it in his hand, his eyes filled with a newfound tenderness. "It's fighting to survive," he murmured, his voice soft and gentle. "Just like us."

The words resonated deeply. His struggle to find redemption wasn't just about escaping the shadow of his past. It was about embracing the present, and building a future that was both honest and fulfilling. He was learning to live authentically, to let go of the expectations and pressures that had defined him for so long.

His uncle's threats, though still present, seemed to lose their power. Kenji had stopped reacting to them with fear and instead responded with a quiet defiance, a quiet confidence in the life he was building. The anonymous phone calls and messages continued, a lingering reminder of his past. But they no longer held the same chilling effect. Kenji had found something far stronger, a love that was a force of its own, a love that was anchoring him.

The fear didn't completely vanish, but it was now manageable. We learned to recognize the signs—the tightening in Kenji's jaw, the way his eyes would momentarily darken— and we'd find solace in each other's embrace. Our intimacy returned, but this time it was different. It was slower, more deliberate, and filled with a deeper understanding and appreciation of the fragility and beauty of our love.

The drug deal recording continued to be a looming threat, a constant reminder of the precariousness of our position. But Kenji's actions, his willingness to sacrifice everything for our future, had shifted the dynamic. He had demonstrated a commitment to a life beyond the Yakuza's reach, and this new path, though uncertain, was brimming with a hope I had never thought possible.

His redemption wasn't a single event; it was a gradual process, a journey of self-discovery and personal growth. He was learning to forgive himself, to accept his past mistakes, and to embrace a future defined by love, honesty, and the unwavering commitment he had shown to me. His transformation was remarkable, a powerful testament to the human capacity for change, resilience, and love's unwavering ability to heal the deepest wounds. The future was still uncertain, but now, hand in hand, we faced it together, ready to navigate whatever challenges lay ahead.

His journey was far from over. The scars of his past were still visible, but they were no longer defining him. He was creating a new narrative, a story of redemption, of resilience, and of unwavering love. It was a testament to his courage, his strength, and the profound power of second chances. His sacrifice had not only secured our future, it had also set him free. He was finally finding peace, not in the illusion of power and wealth, but in the quiet dignity of a life lived authentically and with unwavering love. He had not only earned his redemption but had shown me the true meaning of strength and the boundless capacity of the human spirit to heal and transform. And in that, I found my own redemption, a testament to the healing power of love, loyalty, and the unwavering belief in second chances.

The quiet of our apartment was deceptive. The peace we had painstakingly built felt fragile, a thin veneer over a simmering tension. While Kenji's outward transformation was remarkable – the gentle smile replacing the hardened mask, the warmth in his eyes that once held only shadows – the threat of his family still hung heavy in the air. Their silence was a weapon, more potent than any shouted threat. It was a silence that spoke volumes about the unwavering power they wielded, the reach of their influence, and the price Kenji had paid for his defiance.

One evening, a single, crimson rose arrived, nestled in a simple, unmarked box. No note, no sender. Just the single, perfect bloom, a stark contrast to the understated elegance of our apartment. Kenji's hand trembled slightly as he picked it up, his face unreadable. The rose, a symbol of love and passion in many cultures, felt menacing in its simplicity, a chilling reminder of the precariousness of our situation.

"They're testing me," he finally said, his voice low and husky. His eyes, usually so full of warmth, were clouded with a mixture of fear and determination. The rose, a silent message, signified a challenge, a test of his loyalty. Were his actions, his sacrifice, truly enough to earn their forgiveness, or had he only earned their wrath?

The ensuing weeks became a subtle game of cat and mouse. Anonymous phone calls, laced with veiled threats, punctuated the otherwise quiet evenings. Subtle acts of intimidation – a slashed tire here, a mysterious package left on our doorstep there – served as chilling reminders of the reach of his family's power. These weren't blatant acts of violence, but calculated maneuvers designed to chip away at our newfound peace, to erode our confidence and sow seeds of doubt.

Kenji remained outwardly calm, his demeanor betraying none of the turmoil he must have been feeling. He refused to be drawn into a conflict he knew he couldn't win, at least not yet. He channeled his frustration into his baking, his hands moving with a practiced grace, transforming flour and sugar into exquisite works of art. He was building a wall, not of stone or steel, but of quiet resilience and unwavering love for me. He was demonstrating his commitment not only to me but to this new life he had painstakingly crafted. This was his silent rebellion, a quiet defiance against the suffocating power of his family.

However, his composure couldn't completely mask the deep-seated anxieties that gnawed at him. He would wake up in the middle of the night, his body tense, his eyes wide with unspoken fears. He confided in me, sharing his fears in hushed whispers, his vulnerability as captivating as his strength.

He spoke of the code, the unspoken rules that governed the Yakuza, the unwavering loyalty demanded of its members.

He spoke of the shame he had brought upon his family, the disappointment that weighed heavily on his heart. He carried the weight of centuries-old traditions, the burden of expectations that were as ancient as they were unforgiving. His sacrifice was not just about me, but about his own sense of honor, however twisted that sense might be.

The pressure mounted, forcing him to make impossible choices. He received a cryptic message, demanding his presence at a family meeting. The message held no promises, only threats masked as invitations. He wrestled with his decision, the conflict tearing at his soul. He was torn between his loyalty to his family and his loyalty to me, his past and his future.

His internal conflict was palpable, a tempest raging within him. He knew that attending the meeting would be tantamount to surrendering, to accepting the conditions his family would undoubtedly impose. But he also knew that ignoring their summons could have devastating consequences for us. It was a classic dilemma, a test of his allegiance on a monumental scale.

His internal struggle manifested in his art. His paintings became a mirror to his soul, reflecting the torment he endured. The once vibrant colors dulled, replaced by muted grays and somber hues. The images themselves became distorted, reflecting the internal struggle he was battling, the impossible choices he was forced to make.

His hesitation, his fear, was understandable, even rational. His family had a reputation for ruthlessness, for dispensing brutal punishment to those who dared to defy them. Their power was not to be trifled with. Yet, his love for me, his commitment to a life free from their shadow, fueled his resolve. He knew, despite his fear, that he could not go back. He had chosen a path, and despite the risks, he would not deviate.

Ultimately, he decided to face them, to test the boundaries of his family's unforgiving loyalty. This was not a surrender, but a deliberate act of defiance. He went not to submit but to negotiate his terms, to demonstrate the unwavering strength of his character. He would show them that while he might have stepped outside the accepted parameters of the Yakuza, his loyalty, redefined and re-focused, was not something to be broken.

The meeting itself was a tense affair, a clash of wills between tradition and a burgeoning, modern love. Kenji faced his family, not with fear, but with a quiet dignity, a strength born from his love for me and his determination to create a life on his own terms. His choice to defy them, to choose love over family loyalty, created a dramatic shift.

His sacrifice was not a simple act; it was a complex tapestry woven with threads of tradition, love, and self-discovery. He tested the limits of his family's authority, exposing the cracks in their seemingly impenetrable power structure. It was a profound act of self-assertion, a testament to his unwavering belief in his chosen path. His loyalty had been redefined, reevaluated, and re-purposed. And, importantly, his loyalty to himself, to his own integrity, became the defining trait of his character. The outcome of this confrontation would shape not only his future but the future of our relationship, a future that remained as uncertain as it was electrifying.

The air in the ancestral home hung thick with the scent of incense and unspoken resentments. Kenji sat rigidly, his posture betraying none of the turmoil churning within. He'd chosen this path, this confrontation, not out of bravado, but out of a desperate need for understanding, a yearning for a reconciliation that might feel impossible. His family, steeped in the rigid traditions of the Yakuza, were known for their unforgiving nature, their adherence to a code older than most nations. Yet, Kenji, in his heart, held onto a sliver of hope, a fragile belief that even the most hardened hearts could be softened by genuine remorse.

His father, a man whose eyes held the icy glint of decades spent navigating the treacherous waters of organized crime, sat at the head of the long, polished table. His gaze was unwavering, piercing, a silent interrogation that spoke volumes about the weight of Kenji's actions. The other family members, uncles and cousins, sat in stoic silence, their faces impassive masks, revealing nothing of their thoughts. The atmosphere was suffocating, the silence a tangible entity pressing down on Kenji, weighing him down.

He began to speak, his voice low and measured, a carefully constructed plea for forgiveness that echoed the years of careful planning and internal struggle. He didn't begin with apologies, but with a meticulously detailed account of his actions. He spoke of the challenges, not as excuses, but as explanations, painting a picture of the suffocating pressure of expectation and the allure of freedom. He detailed the allure of Aisha, not as a justification but as a testament to the power of love, a force strong enough to challenge the iron grip of tradition. He spoke of her intelligence, her strength, her compassion, her unwavering support in the face of his own insecurities.

He described the recordings, not as a careless act, but as a desperate attempt to protect himself and Aisha from the dangers of a world he now understood far too well. He articulated his apprehension, his fear, and the constant weight of the threat hanging over them. He described the calculated risks he'd taken, the calculated moves to protect her and simultaneously mitigate the damage to his family's reputation. He hadn't sought to betray them, but to protect himself from a betrayal that would have undoubtedly destroyed them all.

He spoke of the Yakuza code, not to seek refuge behind its rules, but to highlight the hypocrisy he had witnessed within its ranks. He spoke of corruption, of brutal acts sanctioned in the name of tradition, acts of violence perpetrated against innocents. His voice gained strength, not from defiance, but from a conviction born of a deep understanding of both the code's supposed virtues and its inherent flaws. He wasn't challenging the Yakuza; he was seeking to reform the system from within.

His speech was not a confession, but a meticulously crafted explanation, a measured articulation of his choices, presented with both humility and a quiet defiance. He was not begging for forgiveness, but earning it. He was not simply seeking pardon, but asking for understanding. This was not about erasing the past but about integrating it into a new narrative, one where he could reconcile his past with his present and his future.

His father remained impassive, his expression unreadable.

The others, too, remained silent, their faces offering no clues to their thoughts. The silence stretched, tense and heavy, punctuated only by the rhythmic ticking of an antique clock, each tick a hammer blow against the fragile hope building within Kenji's heart. The silence wasn't necessarily hostile; it was the silence of deliberation, of men wrestling with the weight of generations of tradition and the implications of Kenji's choices.

The tension reached a fever pitch, a tangible force in the room that felt almost physical. Kenji waited, his heart pounding in his chest, his breathing shallow. He'd bared his soul, his vulnerabilities laid bare for all to see, and he now awaited the judgment of those whose acceptance he desperately craved. This wasn't simply about his future, but about his identity. This was about claiming his place, not just within his family, but within the world.

Finally, after what felt like an eternity, his father spoke. His voice was still and measured, devoid of the harshness Kenji had expected. There was no thunderous condemnation, no fiery outburst.

Instead, his words were surprisingly soft, laced with a weariness that spoke of years spent carrying the burden of responsibility.

He spoke of the traditions, the unyielding expectations, and the difficult path Kenji had chosen. He didn't condone Kenji's actions, but acknowledged the circumstances that led him to defy the family code. He spoke of the risks Kenji had taken, the dangers he'd faced, and the courage he'd shown in the face of overwhelming odds. He acknowledged Kenji's love for Aisha, not with approval or disapproval, but with a grudging recognition of its power to transform even the most entrenched beliefs.

The ensuing discussion was not a simple exchange of apologies and forgiveness. It was a delicate negotiation, a careful balancing act between tradition and modernity, between the rigid demands of the Yakuza and the fluid nature of love and understanding. It was about finding common ground, about acknowledging the conflicts and complexities of a life straddling two vastly different worlds.

It was a conversation laced with unspoken nuances, a dance around centuries of cultural weight and personal experiences. They delved into the intricacies of their relationships, acknowledging the sacrifices made on both sides. It was a testament to their strength and resilience, to their capacity to adapt and to find new paths through the labyrinth of their shared history. It was a recognition of the enduring strength of family, even in the face of profound differences.

The conversation stretched into the night, fueled by shared memories, unspoken resentments, and a growing understanding. Kenji, having laid his heart bare, now witnessed the slow unfolding of his family's own vulnerabilities. He learned of their regrets, their unspoken fears, and the sacrifices they themselves had made in the name of tradition and duty.

By dawn's first light, a fragile peace had been established. It was not a complete absolution, not a return to the way things were. It was a beginning, a new chapter in their relationship, built on a foundation of understanding, mutual respect, and a shared recognition of the complexities of their lives. The lingering tensions remained, the wounds were deep and the scars would remain, but there was a sense of hope, a possibility of healing and reconciliation. Kenji had sought forgiveness, and he had received, not a full pardon, but a measured acceptance, an understanding that extended beyond the rigid boundaries of the Yakuza code. It was a step toward healing, a journey toward a future where love and tradition might find a way to coexist. His sacrifice had been profound, and it had borne fruit, not in a complete erasure of the past, but in a recalibration of loyalty, love, and understanding. The future remained uncertain, but for the first time in a long time, Kenji felt a glimmer of hope, a sense of peace that had been hard-won, but ultimately, deeply satisfying.

CHAPTER 11: SHADOWS OF DOUBT

The fragile peace forged in the ancestral home felt brittle, like a newly mended vase poised on the edge of shattering. The lingering silence between Aisha and Kenji, even amidst the intimacy of their shared bed, spoke volumes. It wasn't the comfortable silence of lovers deeply entwined, but a tense quietude, punctuated by unspoken anxieties. Aisha, nestled against Kenji's warm body, felt the phantom weight of his family's scrutiny pressing down on them, a heavy cloak woven from centuries of tradition and unspoken rules.

Kenji's confession, his meticulously crafted plea for understanding, had seemed to appease his family, but Aisha couldn't shake the feeling that something remained concealed, a shadow lurking just beyond the reach of the flickering candlelight. His carefully constructed narrative, while convincing, hadn't fully erased her doubts. The details, though flawlessly delivered, held a carefully calibrated ambiguity, a subtle lack of complete transparency. The narrative felt controlled, almost rehearsed, and the memory of the fear in his eyes, before the family meeting, still haunted her.

His love for her felt genuine, undeniable in its intensity, yet its very strength amplified her unease. Could this overwhelming passion be a calculated move, a performance designed to protect his position within the Yakuza hierarchy? The question gnawed at her, a persistent irritant in the midst of their passionate embraces. She couldn't dismiss the possibility that she was merely a pawn in a larger, more dangerous game, a beautiful prize strategically deployed to secure his family's position.

Their intimacy, once a refuge, now felt laced with a subtle undercurrent of suspicion. The sensual exploration of their bodies, the blending of Western and Eastern traditions, had always been exhilarating, a testament to their mutual attraction. But now, each touch, each whispered word, felt subtly measured, guarded. The intense passion that had initially drawn them together had morphed into something more complicated, a delicate dance between desire and distrust.

She recalled the night she'd accidentally recorded the drug deal, the chilling moment when her life had teetered on the precipice of destruction. The subsequent events, Kenji's carefully orchestrated intervention, his protection, had initially seemed like acts of selfless love. Now, however, that narrative seemed less certain, clouded by a pervasive doubt. Had he been acting out of love, or was his intervention a strategic move to safeguard his family's interests, and her unwitting role within it?

The weight of his family's legacy bore down on her, a tangible presence in every stolen moment, every whispered conversation. The Yakuza, with its intricate code of conduct and ruthless pragmatism, felt like a vast, shadowy entity that constantly threatened to engulf them. She understood the profound weight of tradition, having grown up surrounded by the complex dynamics of her own African American community, its strong family ties, and the pressures of societal expectations. But the Yakuza was different. It was a world ruled by a distinct set of values, a world where loyalty and betrayal were often intertwined, where familial bonds were forged in violence and maintained by fear.

The cultural clash between their worlds only heightened her uncertainty. Kenji's world, steeped in centuries of tradition and power, felt like a foreign land, despite the intense intimacy they shared. His explanations, while eloquent, often fell short of resolving her nagging questions. The subtle shifts in his demeanor, the fleeting expressions that crossed his face, were like cryptic clues scattered in a puzzle she couldn't solve. The language barrier, while overcome by their physical connection, sometimes felt like a wall between their minds, impeding the easy flow of communication that true intimacy requires.

She sought solace in the familiar comfort of her own community, finding solace in the genuine acceptance she received from her friends and family. Their unwavering support provided a counterpoint to the uncertainty she felt in Kenji's world. Yet, even amongst her loved ones, she found herself unable to articulate the full extent of her anxieties. How could she explain the intoxicating pull of a man who belonged to a world so inherently dangerous, a world that thrived on deception and violence? How could she express the exhilarating fear of falling in love with someone who was both her protector and a potential threat?

The fear wasn't purely for her physical safety. It was a fear of being manipulated, of being used, of discovering that her love had been a carefully orchestrated illusion. The possibility that her emotions were being played upon, that her heart was being exploited for Kenji's own ends, was a chilling thought that haunted her waking moments and disrupted her sleep. She longed for clarity, for a certainty that would dispel the shadows of doubt that clung to their relationship like a persistent fog. Yet, the more she searched for answers, the more elusive the truth seemed to become.

Kenji's attempts to reassure her felt inadequate, his gestures of affection tinged with a forced calmness that couldn't completely mask the underlying tension. His love for her, she knew, was real, but its manifestation was distorted by the complex web of family obligations and the ruthless pragmatism that defined his world. The fear that he might be forced to choose between her and his family gnawed at her, a constant undercurrent in their relationship. The weight of his dual allegiances felt heavy, a silent pressure that threatened to pull them apart.

The very intensity of their passion seemed to amplify her suspicion. Was this powerful connection an escape from the responsibilities of his world, a temporary distraction from the dangerous game he played? Or was it a genuine, deeply felt love that could transcend the rigid confines of his family's expectations? This question, unanswered, hung between them like a sword of Damocles, threatening to shatter the fragile peace they had so painstakingly constructed.

Aisha found herself caught in a web of conflicting emotions, torn between her deep love for Kenji and the gnawing suspicion that she was playing a part in a game far beyond her comprehension. The lines between love and betrayal blurred, the boundaries between intimacy and manipulation were almost indistinguishable. Her feelings for Kenji were as intense as the fear of the future, a future where love and danger were inextricably intertwined. The uncertain path ahead was fraught with peril, and yet, the thought of abandoning Kenji, of walking away from the intoxicating fire that burned between them, was equally unbearable. She was adrift in a sea of uncertainty, her compass spinning wildly, pointing in multiple directions at once. The journey ahead promised both breathtaking highs and heart-wrenching lows, and Aisha, with a mixture of apprehension and fierce determination, was ready to face whatever lay ahead. The lingering suspicion, however, remained a dark shadow, threatening to engulf her at any moment.

The following days were a slow unraveling, a gradual erosion of the fragile trust they had painstakingly built. It began subtly, with missed cues and unspoken anxieties. Kenji, usually so attentive, seemed preoccupied, his gaze drifting away during their conversations, his responses often clipped and brief. The vibrant energy that had once filled their interactions had dimmed, replaced by a cautious reserve that chilled Aisha to the bone. The vibrant laughter that had echoed through their shared space was replaced by a heavy silence, punctuated by the occasional nervous cough or the restless shifting of limbs.

Aisha tried to bridge the growing chasm, initiating conversations, offering gentle touches, but her attempts were met with a hesitant response, a guardedness that felt like a physical barrier between them. She longed for the easy flow of communication that had once defined their intimacy, the effortless exchange of thoughts and feelings that had been their refuge. Now, even the simplest exchanges felt fraught with unspoken tension, a silent battle waged in the space between them.

One evening, while preparing dinner, Aisha attempted to

break the silence. "Kenji," she began, her voice soft, "is something troubling you? You seem distant."

He turned from the window, where he'd been staring out at the bustling city below, a flicker of something unreadable in his eyes. "Nothing, Aisha," he replied, his voice flat, lacking the warmth that usually infused his words. "Just tired."

But Aisha knew better. She knew the difference between physical exhaustion and the weariness of the soul. This was something deeper, something that he wasn't willing, or perhaps able, to share. The lie hung heavy in the air, a silent accusation that shattered the fragile peace she had been trying to maintain.

"Don't lie to me, Kenji," she said, her voice rising slightly, a hint of frustration creeping into her tone. "We built this on trust, on honesty. If something is wrong, tell me."

His silence was a deafening response, a confirmation of her unspoken fears. The carefully constructed walls he had built around his emotions seemed impenetrable, leaving Aisha feeling increasingly isolated and alone. The cultural differences that had initially intrigued her now felt like insurmountable barriers, hindering their ability to communicate effectively.

The unspoken language of touch, once a bridge between their cultures, now felt strained. Their intimate moments, once filled with a passionate blending of Western and Eastern traditions, felt mechanical, devoid of the emotional connection that had previously defined them. The physical intimacy that had once been a refuge from the pressures of their respective worlds now felt like a performance, a hollow imitation of the genuine connection they once shared.

She sought answers in his family, reaching out to his older sister, hoping to find some explanation for Kenji's sudden withdrawal. But even his sister's carefully chosen words offered little solace. She spoke of the pressures of the Yakuza, the weight of tradition, the unspoken rules that governed their lives. The conversation, though polite and cordial, left Aisha feeling more lost and confused than before. The veiled allusions and cautious phrasing only heightened her sense of unease, confirming her suspicions that something was being deliberately concealed from her.

Frustration mounted, fueled by a growing sense of alienation. The cultural gap, once a source of fascination, now seemed to widen with every passing day, creating a chasm between them that threatened to swallow their relationship whole. The idioms and unspoken nuances of his culture, the subtle body language and indirect communication styles, felt like cryptic messages she couldn't decipher. The language barrier, which they had seemingly overcome, suddenly presented itself as a formidable obstacle, obscuring the true nature of their connection.

Aisha's frustration boiled over during a particularly tense evening. The air hung heavy with unspoken accusations, the silence punctuated by the clinking of glasses and the rhythmic ticking of the grandfather clock in the corner of the room. "I don't understand you, Kenji," she cried, her voice raw with emotion. "We're supposed to be partners, lovers, but you're shutting me out, building walls around yourself."

Kenji flinched, his face etched with pain. "It's not that simple, Aisha," he whispered, his voice barely audible. "There are things I can't tell you, things I can't even explain."

"But you have to try," she pleaded, tears welling up in her eyes. "This isn't working. Our communication, our intimacy... it's all falling apart."

He reached out to touch her, but she recoiled, the gesture feeling more like an intrusion than an act of comfort. The walls between them, once invisible, had solidified into an insurmountable barrier. The emotional distance between them was now a tangible presence, a palpable void that consumed the space between their hearts.

The ensuing days were filled with intense arguments, tearful reconciliations, and a growing sense of despair. Aisha found herself questioning the very foundation of their relationship, wondering if the intense passion they had shared had been merely a fleeting illusion, a temporary distraction from the harsh realities of their vastly different worlds. The weight of unspoken words, the burden of unshared anxieties, threatened to suffocate them both.

The silence lingered, a heavy cloak that smothered their once vibrant connection. The chasm that had opened between them seemed unbridgeable, the emotional distance echoing the cultural divide that separated them. Aisha struggled to reconcile her deep love for Kenji with the insurmountable obstacles that threatened to tear them apart. The pain was acute, a constant reminder of the fragility of their bond and the devastating consequences of miscommunication.

The stark realization that they were failing to communicate effectively shook her to her core. She had always understood the importance of open dialogue and honest expression, especially after her past experiences. But with Kenji, the cultural differences and his inherent reticence were creating a seemingly insurmountable barrier. The very foundation of their relationship, a foundation built on mutual respect and understanding, now felt threatened by a deep-seated inability to share their innermost thoughts and feelings.

The weight of this communication breakdown bore down heavily on Aisha, filling her with a profound sense of loneliness. She missed the easy intimacy they once shared, the effortless understanding that had blossomed between them. Now, every shared moment felt burdened by a heavy silence, a constant reminder of their fractured bond. She realized that love, even the most passionate love, couldn't survive without open communication, without the unwavering honesty that formed the bedrock of any healthy relationship. The future of their relationship, once a vibrant tapestry of dreams and desires, now seemed uncertain, the threads of their connection frayed and loose, threatened by a chasm of unspoken words and unresolved anxieties. Their journey together had taken a dangerous turn, and only through honest communication could they hope to navigate the turbulent waters ahead. The question remained: could they mend the broken bridge, or were they destined to drift apart, forever separated by the shadow of their unspoken fears and misunderstandings?

The following days were a painstaking dance of apologies and hesitant reassurances. Kenji, finally breaking his silence, confessed to the weight of his family's expectations. The Yakuza, he explained, wasn't just a business; it was a way of life, a complex tapestry woven with ancient traditions and unwavering loyalty. His silence, he admitted, stemmed not from a lack of caring, but from a deep-seated fear of jeopardizing his family's standing. Revealing his relationship with Aisha, a Black woman from a vastly different background, was a risk he hadn't been prepared to take. The weight of this secret, the fear of judgment from his family, had been a heavy burden, suffocating his ability to connect with Aisha on a truly open level.

He spoke of the subtle nuances of communication within the Yakuza, the unspoken codes and carefully chosen words that governed their interactions. Direct confrontation was often avoided, replaced by indirect suggestions, and veiled meanings. He apologized for his perceived coldness, explaining that his communication style wasn't a reflection of his feelings for her, but rather a product of his upbringing and the cultural context in which he'd lived. He'd been taught that showing vulnerability was a sign of weakness, a lesson that had deeply affected his ability to express his emotions openly.

Aisha, while initially hurt and frustrated, listened intently, trying to understand the cultural complexities behind Kenji's actions. She acknowledged the deep-seated fear that fueled his silence, realizing that his reticence wasn't a personal rejection, but rather a complex interplay of cultural expectations and ingrained habits. Her own past experiences with betrayal and mistrust, though different in context, provided a surprising point of connection. She understood the fear of vulnerability, the pain of keeping secrets, and the devastating consequences of unspoken anxieties.

Their conversation, though painful, became the turning point. It was a slow, arduous process, filled with tears, reassurances, and a mutual commitment to overcome their differences. Aisha made an effort to understand the nuances of Kenji's culture, spending hours studying Japanese customs and learning to interpret his subtle cues. She delved deeper into his world, learning about the complex relationships within his family, the unspoken rules that governed their behavior, and the weight of tradition that rested heavily on Kenji's shoulders.

Kenji, in turn, made a conscious effort to break free from the constraints of his upbringing. He started to communicate more openly, expressing his feelings with a newfound vulnerability. He learned to appreciate the directness and honesty of Aisha's communication style, realizing that it was a reflection of her strength and authenticity. He began to understand that vulnerability wasn't weakness, but a testament to the strength of their bond.

Their intimacy, once strained and mechanical, rekindled with a newfound passion and depth. They explored new ways to communicate, blending their cultural backgrounds to create a unique and fulfilling intimacy. They found common ground in their shared experiences of pain and resilience, forging a stronger connection that transcended cultural differences.

Their process of reconciliation wasn't without its challenges. There were moments of doubt, fleeting anxieties, and the occasional resurgence of old patterns. But they learned to navigate these challenges together, using their newfound understanding as a guide. They learned to express their emotions with greater clarity, to listen more attentively, and to appreciate the nuances of each other's communication styles. They learned to forgive each other's shortcomings, accepting that perfection was an illusion, and that genuine connection thrived in the midst of imperfections.

Aisha's understanding of Kenji's cultural context also helped her address the lingering issues stemming from the drug deal recording. She understood that his reluctance to involve the authorities wasn't solely rooted in loyalty to his family but also in the Yakuza's intricate web of power and its intricate system of justice. This understanding allowed her to approach the situation with greater empathy and a more nuanced perspective. She recognized that a direct confrontation might jeopardize both their safety and their relationship. Instead, she opted for a more cautious approach, using her intelligence and her knowledge of the underworld to find a solution that minimized the risks. This collaboration, this shared strategizing, became another bonding experience, further solidifying their trust and partnership.

Their journey towards reconciliation involved more than just overcoming communication barriers. It was about embracing differences, celebrating individuality, and creating a space where both their cultures could coexist and thrive. Aisha brought her strength and directness, her openness and capacity for emotional expression. Kenji countered with his quiet strength, his unwavering loyalty, and his deep understanding of the intricate world he inhabited. Together, they created a unique and powerful dynamic, a testament to the resilience of love in the face of overwhelming obstacles.

They began to blend their cultures in unexpected and

delightful ways. Kenji introduced Aisha to the beauty of Japanese tea ceremonies, the elegance of traditional calligraphy, and the meditative power of Zen gardens. Aisha, in turn, introduced Kenji to the vibrant energy of gospel music, the soulful rhythms of blues, and the rich culinary traditions of her Southern heritage. These cultural exchanges not only enriched their lives but also deepened their understanding and appreciation for one another.

The previously insurmountable walls between them crumbled, revealing a foundation of mutual respect, deep affection, and an unwavering commitment to their relationship. They understood that love wasn't simply about passion and attraction; it was about empathy, understanding, and a willingness to bridge cultural divides and overcome personal limitations. The challenges they had faced had made their bond stronger, forging a connection that was deeper and more meaningful than anything they could have ever imagined. The shadows of doubt had receded, replaced by the radiant glow of a love that had been tested and refined, emerging stronger and more vibrant than before. Their journey was far from over, but they were now equipped with the tools – communication, understanding, and forgiveness – to navigate the future together. They had faced the darkness and emerged into the light, their love a beacon of hope, shining brightly against the backdrop of their contrasting worlds. Their love story became a testament to the resilience of the human spirit and the unifying power of love. The cultural differences, once a source of conflict, were now celebrated as part of their unique and beautiful narrative. They had found a way to honor their individual identities while forging a shared future, a testament to their enduring love. Their story became a powerful narrative of bridging cultures, overcoming obstacles, and finding strength in vulnerability. The shadows of doubt had indeed been overcome, paving the way for a brighter, more fulfilling future together.

The air between them crackled with a newfound energy, a stark contrast to the tense silences that had previously defined their interactions. It wasn't a sudden, dramatic shift, but a gradual thawing, a slow unveiling of their true selves. Aisha, ever the pragmatist, initiated a conversation about the lingering unease surrounding the drug deal recording. She'd spent days researching, poring over articles about the Yakuza's internal justice system, the intricate web of alliances and betrayals that governed their world. She understood now that Kenji's reticence wasn't simply about family loyalty; it was a deep-seated understanding of the potential consequences, the ripple effects that could devastate his family and possibly endanger her as well.

"I've been thinking," Aisha began, her voice soft but firm. "I understand why you hesitated to go to the police. It's not just about protecting your family; it's about navigating a world where the rules are different, where the consequences are far more severe than in the outside world."

Kenji looked at her, his eyes filled with a mixture of relief and admiration. He'd expected accusations, anger, perhaps even a demand for him to abandon his family for her sake. Instead, he found understanding, a willingness to see his world through his eyes, not judge it by the standards of hers.

"You... you understand," he whispered, the words catching in his throat. The weight of his secret, the burden he'd carried alone for so long, seemed to lighten with each word Aisha spoke. He'd always valued loyalty more than anything else, a trait ingrained in him since childhood. The thought of betraying his family, of exposing them to the potential consequences of his actions, had paralyzed him. But Aisha's understanding was a lifeline, allowing him to breathe freely for the first time in weeks.

"I understand the complexities," Aisha continued, her gaze unwavering. "And I understand the risks. But I also know that we can't just ignore what happened. We need a plan, a way to protect ourselves without jeopardizing your family or exposing ourselves to unnecessary danger."

This wasn't just a discussion about a crime; it was a declaration of partnership, a testament to their evolving bond. It was a step beyond romance, into the realm of shared responsibility, mutual trust, and unwavering commitment. They spent the next few hours strategizing, pooling their knowledge and resources. Aisha, with her sharp mind and street smarts, offered solutions Kenji hadn't considered. He, in turn, provided insights into the Yakuza's inner workings, the unspoken rules and channels of communication that could be leveraged to their advantage. Their collaboration was seamless, their minds melding together in a harmonious effort to navigate a dangerous situation.

Their conversations extended far beyond the immediate crisis, delving into the depths of their individual pasts. Aisha spoke openly about her own experiences with betrayal, the scars left by her previous relationship. She described the emotional turmoil, the feeling of being used and discarded, the lingering distrust that made intimacy challenging. She hadn't shared this level of vulnerability with anyone before, not even her closest friends. It was a profound act of trust, a willingness to expose her most vulnerable self to Kenji.

Kenji, in turn, revealed aspects of his upbringing that had shaped his reserved nature. He spoke of the strict code of conduct within the Yakuza, the emphasis on self-control and emotional restraint, the pressure to maintain a facade of unwavering strength. He confessed that his seemingly cold demeanor wasn't a reflection of his feelings, but a defense mechanism, a way of protecting himself from the harsh realities of his world. He admitted that he'd never truly allowed himself to be vulnerable, that the fear of showing weakness had always held him back.

Their shared vulnerabilities became a bridge, a connection that transcended cultural differences and past traumas. They found solace in each other's stories, a shared understanding of pain and resilience. Aisha's directness and emotional honesty helped Kenji to unlearn some of the ingrained habits of his upbringing. He learned that vulnerability wasn't weakness, that showing his true emotions wasn't a sign of failure but a testament to the strength of their bond. He began to express his love for Aisha not through grand gestures, but through quiet acts of devotion, thoughtful words, and unwavering support.

Their intimacy deepened, moving beyond the physical to encompass a profound emotional connection. They explored new ways of communicating, learning to understand each other's unspoken cues, their subtle gestures, the nuances of their respective cultures. Their lovemaking became a sacred ritual, a blending of Western and Eastern traditions, a testament to their mutual respect and acceptance. They discovered that their differences, once perceived as barriers, were now sources of enrichment and fascination. They celebrated their individuality, embracing the unique aspects of their respective cultures and forging a shared identity that was both distinct and unified.

Aisha introduced Kenji to the rich tapestry of African American culture, taking him to gospel services, introducing him to soul food, and sharing stories of her family history. Kenji, in turn, introduced Aisha to the beauty of Japanese art, the elegance of traditional ceremonies, and the serene tranquility of Zen gardens. These cultural exchanges weren't just superficial; they were deep dives into their respective heritages, forging a deeper appreciation for the richness and diversity of human experience. Kenji learned to appreciate Aisha's directness, her passionate expression of emotions, understanding that it wasn't a sign of disrespect, but a testament to her authenticity. Aisha, in turn, learned to appreciate Kenji's quiet strength, his unwavering loyalty, his ability to find peace amidst chaos.

Their journey wasn't without its bumps. There were moments of doubt, of insecurity, of lingering anxieties. Old patterns resurfaced, moments when the weight of their pasts threatened to overwhelm them. But they learned to navigate these challenges together, using their newfound understanding as a compass. They communicated openly, honestly, and with empathy. They listened to each other, offering support and reassurance. They learned to forgive each other's imperfections, recognizing that true love was not about finding perfection, but about embracing the imperfections and growing together.

Their love story became a testament to the power of vulnerability, the strength found in honesty, and the resilience of the human spirit. The shadows of doubt had indeed receded, replaced by a radiant glow of love that had been tested and refined, emerging stronger and more vibrant than before. They had faced the darkness together, emerging into the light, their love story a beacon of hope, a celebration of cultural diversity, and a powerful reminder of the unifying force of love. Their journey was far from over, but they faced the future hand-in-hand, armed with the tools of communication, understanding, and a love that transcended cultural differences and past traumas. They were a testament to the enduring power of love, a love story that was both deeply personal and universally resonant. Their love story became a testament to the fact that love could indeed conquer all, bridging cultural divides and overcoming personal limitations. The world around them might be complex and dangerous, but in each other's arms, they found a sanctuary, a place where love thrived amidst chaos. They understood that true intimacy wasn't just about physical closeness, but about emotional vulnerability, honesty, and a willingness to share their most vulnerable selves. Their unique blend of cultures became the cornerstone of their relationship, a celebration of their individual identities and a testament to the unifying power of love.

The quiet hum of the city outside their apartment window was a stark contrast to the tempest of emotions swirling within Aisha. She'd never been this vulnerable, this open with anyone before. Sharing her deepest fears, her past traumas, had felt like peeling back layers of hardened skin, revealing the raw, tender flesh beneath. Yet, in Kenji's embrace, it hadn't felt like exposure, but like a homecoming. His quiet strength, his unwavering gaze, had provided a safe harbor, a place where she could finally let go of the armor she'd built around her heart.

Kenji, in turn, was experiencing a transformation. The

rigid walls he'd erected around his emotions were slowly crumbling, revealing a depth of feeling he hadn't allowed himself to explore. He'd spent his life adhering to the strict code of the Yakuza, suppressing his emotions, believing vulnerability to be a weakness. But Aisha's unwavering honesty, her willingness to embrace her emotions, was chipping away at his ingrained beliefs. He was learning that true strength wasn't about suppressing feelings, but about acknowledging them, understanding them, and navigating them with grace.

Their conversations became a ritual, a sacred space where they explored the intricacies of their pasts, their present realities, and their hopes for the future. They delved into the nuances of their cultural backgrounds, appreciating the subtle differences in their communication styles. Aisha, accustomed to the directness and emotional expressiveness of African American culture, initially found Kenji's reserved nature puzzling. But she came to understand that his quiet contemplation wasn't a lack of engagement, but a unique way of processing information, a reflection of his Japanese heritage, where subtle gestures and unspoken cues carried weight.

Kenji, in turn, was fascinated by Aisha's emotional openness. He found himself drawn to her passionate nature, her unwavering honesty, her ability to express her feelings without reservation. He began to understand that her directness wasn't a sign of disrespect, but a testament to her authenticity, a reflection of her upbringing in a culture that valued open communication. He learned to appreciate the vibrancy of her spirit, her unwavering commitment to her beliefs, and her capacity for both fierce love and fierce independence.

Their physical intimacy deepened, mirroring the growth of their emotional connection. Their lovemaking became a fusion of cultures, a blend of Western and Eastern traditions, a testament to their shared respect and understanding. They explored new sensations, new ways of expressing their desires, pushing boundaries, and transcending limitations. They learned to read each other's bodies, anticipating needs and desires, creating a symphony of touch and passion. The physical intimacy wasn't just about pleasure; it was a language of love, a testament to their unwavering commitment to each other.

Aisha introduced Kenji to the world of African American soul music, the rhythmic heartbeat of gospel hymns filling their apartment. She shared stories of her family history, tracing the lineage of her ancestors through the struggles and triumphs of the African American experience. She showed him the beauty of Black art, the power of Black literature, and the resilience of the Black spirit. Kenji, in turn, took Aisha to traditional tea ceremonies, where the ritualistic movements and quiet contemplation brought a sense of serenity. He introduced her to the elegance of Japanese calligraphy, the graceful precision of ikebana, the art of flower arrangement. He shared stories of his family's history, the complexities of his upbringing within the Yakuza, and the unwavering loyalty he felt towards his family. They explored the beauty of different artistic forms, learning to appreciate the nuances of each culture, recognizing that art transcends language and geography, bridging cultural divides.

One evening, while sharing a quiet dinner, Aisha confessed a lingering fear. The drug deal recording still weighed heavily on her mind. Despite their meticulous planning, the constant threat of discovery hung over them like a dark cloud. Kenji, holding her hand, reassured her with unwavering confidence. He explained that the Yakuza had a complex system of internal justice. Although the consequences of violating the code were severe, the focus was usually on internal resolution. His family had considerable influence and could potentially navigate this delicate situation without resorting to extreme measures.

He outlined his strategy, detailing the channels of communication he would utilize, the key players he needed to engage. His explanation was not only reassuring, but also revealed a level of strategic thinking that Aisha hadn't previously realized. She had always appreciated his strength and loyalty but hadn't fully grasped the extent of his intellect, his ability to maneuver the complex landscape of the Yakuza world. This new understanding, this glimpse into his mind, further deepened her respect and admiration.

Their conversations extended beyond their immediate concerns, exploring the broader themes of trust, loyalty, and vulnerability. They discussed the importance of open communication, of acknowledging insecurities and fears without judgment. They learned to navigate their differing communication styles, finding ways to bridge the gap between Aisha's direct approach and Kenji's more subtle style. They realized that trust wasn't simply about belief, but about consistent actions, consistent vulnerability, and mutual support.

They celebrated each other's differences, recognizing that their unique cultural backgrounds enriched their relationship, fostering growth and understanding. They learned to negotiate their contrasting personalities, respecting their individual needs and desires. Their intimacy wasn't just about physical closeness; it was about emotional connection, about mutual respect and unwavering support. They supported each other's dreams and aspirations, cheering each other on during setbacks and celebrating triumphs.

One evening, under the soft glow of candlelight, Aisha confessed a deep-seated insecurity about her body. The scars of her past relationship, both physical and emotional, still lingered. Kenji, gently cupping her face in his hands, reassured her with unwavering affection. He traced the delicate lines on her skin, whispering words of love and admiration. He spoke of her strength, her beauty, both inside and out. His words were not empty platitudes, but heartfelt expressions of genuine affection. His love wasn't about physical perfection, but about the beauty of her spirit, her resilience, and her unwavering love for him.

Their intimacy continued to evolve, deepening with every shared experience, every whispered secret, every act of kindness. They were forging a relationship that transcended cultural differences, personal traumas, and the dangers lurking in the shadows of Kenji's world. Their love story was a testament to the power of communication, the importance of vulnerability, and the resilience of the human spirit. Their love was not just a passionate affair but a testament to the enduring power of connection, a beacon of hope shining brightly against the backdrop of the uncertainties they faced. They knew their journey wouldn't be easy, but they were ready to face whatever came their way, hand in hand, their hearts intertwined in a bond that grew stronger with each passing day. Their love was a testament to the beautiful complexities of human connection, a love that celebrated differences, nurtured vulnerabilities and thrived in the face of adversity. It was a love that whispered promises of forever, a love etched into their souls, a love for the ages.

CHAPTER 12: THE WEIGHT OF SECRETS

The weight of unspoken words pressed down on Aisha, a heavy cloak she couldn't quite shed. Kenji's assurances about navigating the Yakuza's internal justice system had offered temporary solace, but the underlying threat remained, a constant hum of anxiety in the background of their otherwise idyllic life. The fear wasn't just for herself; it extended to Kenji, to the fragile equilibrium they'd painstakingly built. She knew the Yakuza world was a labyrinth of loyalty, betrayal, and unforgiving consequences. One wrong move, one misplaced word, could unravel everything.

One rainy afternoon, while curled up on their plush sofa, lost in the comforting rhythm of jazz, Kenji received a cryptic call. His expression hardened, the calm facade he usually presented dissolving into a mask of controlled intensity. He excused himself, retreating to his study, leaving Aisha with a knot of apprehension tightening in her stomach. The air crackled with unspoken tension, the silence punctuated only by the relentless drumming of rain against the windowpanes. The call, she sensed, had to do with the recording. The secret that bound them together, and could just as easily tear them apart.

Hours later, he emerged, his features etched with a weariness that went beyond physical fatigue. He sat beside her, his hand finding hers, his touch conveying a gravity that silenced any attempt at casual conversation. He spoke then, his voice low and measured, revealing a truth that chilled her to the bone. His family, the formidable Yakuza clan, wasn't simply involved in legitimate businesses. They were deeply entangled in the very drug trade that had nearly claimed Aisha's life.

The revelation was a seismic shock, shattering the carefully constructed world Aisha had begun to build around her newfound love. The man she'd fallen for, the man who had offered her sanctuary, was inextricably linked to the very darkness she was desperately trying to escape. The beautiful, serene moments they had shared, the quiet evenings filled with laughter and whispered secrets, were now overlaid with a layer of suspicion, a chilling uncertainty about the true nature of their relationship.

The silence that followed was heavier than the storm raging outside. Aisha felt a familiar wave of nausea rise in her throat, a bitter taste of betrayal mixing with the lingering fear for her life. The recording, a desperate attempt to protect herself, had unwittingly entangled her in a web of deceit far more complex and dangerous than she could have ever imagined. She had sought refuge in Kenji's arms, only to find herself caught in the crosshairs of his family's clandestine operations.

Kenji, sensing the storm brewing within her, pulled her close, his embrace both comforting and suffocating. He explained, his voice thick with a mixture of regret and desperation, that he had tried to distance himself from the family's illegal activities, but the bonds of loyalty, forged in blood and tradition, were not easily broken. His position, he confessed, was precarious. He walked a tightrope, attempting to maintain a semblance of normalcy while battling the shadows of his heritage.

He confessed his struggle to reconcile his love for Aisha with the inescapable realities of his upbringing. The conflict tore at him, a constant internal battle between the man he wanted to be and the man he was expected to be. He revealed the pressures he faced, the expectations placed upon him, the threats that loomed constantly over his head. His words were a painful admission of his own vulnerabilities, a stark contrast to the stoic image he had presented to the world.

Aisha listened, her heart aching with a mixture of anger, fear, and a deep, unsettling empathy. She saw the pain in his eyes, the burden he carried, and for the first time, understood the complexity of his world, the weight of his legacy. The realization didn't excuse his family's actions, but it did offer a glimpse into the intricate tapestry of loyalty and obligation that governed his life.

The revelation spurred a period of intense introspection for Aisha. She wrestled with her emotions, grappling with the implications of her discovery. Her feelings for Kenji were real, profound, but they were now tinged with a daunting uncertainty. Could she reconcile her love for him with the morally questionable actions of his family? Could she trust him completely, knowing the insidious nature of his world? The questions haunted her, twisting her insides with a mixture of fear and confusion.

She spent days lost in thought, wandering through the streets of the city, the rain a constant, melancholic backdrop to her internal turmoil. She revisited her past, the trauma she had suffered, the lessons she had learned. She realized that her initial attraction to Kenji had been a mixture of allure and a desperate need for escape. But now, she had to confront the harsh reality that her escape had led her into a new kind of danger.

In the midst of her internal struggle, Aisha sought solace in her closest friends, sharing her burden with those she could trust. Their perspectives were diverse, reflecting the varied experiences and worldviews within the African American community. Some urged caution, urging her to distance herself from Kenji and the dangerous world he inhabited. Others, understanding the complexities of love and loyalty, counseled patience, urging her to confront the issues head-on.

Their advice, while conflicting, helped Aisha gain a clearer perspective. She realized that the decision wasn't about choosing between love and safety; it was about navigating the complexities of her relationship, understanding the forces at play, and making informed choices based on her own values and aspirations. The issue wasn't about Kenji himself but the insidious world he was a part of. It was about determining if a future with him was possible, if their love could overcome the daunting obstacles they faced.

The weight of secrets continued to loom, but Aisha began to feel a shift within herself. Fear remained, a constant shadow, but it was tempered by a newfound determination. She recognized that Kenji was not solely defined by his family's actions. He was a complex individual, capable of both great love and profound internal conflict. Their journey together would not be easy, it wouldn't be straightforward, but she was ready to face it, hand-in-hand with the man she loved, even if that love was navigating a perilous path. The future remained uncertain, but Aisha understood one thing with unshakeable clarity: she would face it with strength, and with love. Her love for Kenji was a powerful force, one that she was determined to harness in the face of the uncertainties that lay ahead. The road ahead was fraught with peril, but it was a journey she was willing to embark on, fueled by love, hope, and an unwavering determination to forge her own path, even amidst the darkness. The secrets unveiled had only strengthened her resolve, her love for Kenji a beacon guiding her through the storm.

The following days were a blur of uneasy silences and stolen glances. Kenji, usually so effortlessly charming, was withdrawn, his usual playful banter replaced by a quiet intensity that mirrored the storm raging within Aisha. He tried, God knows he tried, to bridge the chasm that had opened between them. He brought her extravagant gifts – a diamond necklace that shimmered like captured starlight, a silk kimono so soft it felt like a lover's caress – gestures that felt both lavish and hollow in the face of his family's dark secret.

His attempts at intimacy felt forced, a clumsy dance around the unspoken truth. The passionate nights that had once been a fiery testament to their connection now held an undercurrent of unease, a haunting reminder of the precariousness of their situation. The physical act, once a refuge, was now fraught with tension, the pleasure tinged with fear. Each touch carried the weight of his family's actions, a subtle reminder that their love was built on shifting sands.

Aisha, in turn, found herself oscillating between anger, hurt, and a baffling, persistent loyalty. Her upbringing, steeped in the strong, resilient spirit of the African

American community, taught her the value of forgiveness, of understanding the complexities of human nature. But forgiving Kenji's family for their involvement in the drug trade, for their callous disregard for human life, felt like a betrayal of everything she stood for. Yet, the thought of abandoning Kenji, of severing the connection that had blossomed between them, felt equally painful.

One evening, she found herself at her grandmother's house, seeking solace in the comforting familiarity of her childhood home. Her grandmother, a woman whose wisdom had guided her through countless storms, listened patiently as Aisha poured out her heart, the words tumbling out in a torrent of frustration and confusion. Her grandmother, a matriarch steeped in both Southern tradition and a deep understanding of human resilience, didn't offer easy answers. She simply listened, her presence a quiet anchor in the tumultuous sea of Aisha's emotions.

"The heart, child," her grandmother finally said, her voice low and resonant, "is a fickle thing. It loves where it loves, regardless of the darkness that may surround it. But the mind, that's where the strength lies. The mind must guide the heart, keep it from straying too far into the shadows."

Her grandmother's words resonated deeply within Aisha. It wasn't about blindly forgiving or abruptly rejecting Kenji; it was about making a conscious choice, a decision rooted in clear-headedness and a strong understanding of her own needs and boundaries. She had to navigate this treacherous terrain with both her heart and her mind working in harmony.

The next day, Aisha sought out Kenji, not with accusations or recriminations, but with a newfound clarity. She confronted him, not with the anger she felt, but with a quiet, unwavering resolve. She didn't mince words; she spoke of her fear, of her hurt, of the betrayal she felt. She didn't demand answers, but expressed her need for understanding. She wanted to know, not just the extent of his family's involvement, but the depth of his own commitment to separating himself from their illegal activities.

Kenji listened, his usual stoicism crumbling under the weight of her words. He confessed the details of his family's operations, revealing the intricate web of power and influence, the intricate dance between legitimate businesses and illicit dealings. He spoke of the inherent risks, the threats, and the sacrifices, painting a picture far more complex than Aisha had previously imagined. He revealed his own internal struggles, his attempts to maintain a semblance of morality within a system that rewarded ruthlessness and treachery. He spoke of the pressure from his elders, the weight of tradition, the deep-seated cultural obligations that bound him to his family. He spoke of the shame he carried, the guilt that gnawed at his conscience.

He spoke of his love for Aisha, how it had become a lifeline, a beacon of hope in a world of shadows. His voice was raw with emotion, his vulnerability a stark contrast to the hardened image he usually projected. He admitted that he had been hesitant to reveal the full extent of his family's involvement, fearing that it would push Aisha away. He confessed that he loved her so deeply that the thought of losing her was unbearable, but he also understood the gravity of her concerns and respected her need for clarity.

Aisha listened intently, her heart aching with a mix of empathy and apprehension. She understood, perhaps more than she ever thought possible, the suffocating weight of cultural expectations, the almost impossible task of breaking free from a deeply ingrained system of loyalty and tradition. She recognized the internal conflict that tore him apart, the constant battle between the man he wanted to be and the man he felt obligated to be. It wasn't a simple case of black and white; it was a complex tapestry woven with threads of love, loyalty, fear, and duty.

Their conversation lasted for hours, a raw and honest exchange of emotions that cleared the air between them, though not without leaving a lingering residue of uncertainty. The weight of secrets remained, but it was no longer a suffocating burden; it was a shared challenge, a joint responsibility to navigate. Their relationship had shifted, evolving from a passionate romance to a complex partnership, forged in the crucible of trust, understanding, and a deep-seated love that transcended cultural differences and the dark undercurrents of the Yakuza underworld.

The revelation of Kenji's family's involvement wasn't just a plot twist; it was a catalyst. It forced Aisha to confront not only her own past trauma but also the complexities of her relationship with Kenji, testing the strength of their connection and ultimately deepening their understanding of each other. The journey wasn't over, far from it. New challenges lay ahead, new secrets yet to be unearthed, but they faced them together, their bond strengthened by the crucible of shared experience and a mutual commitment to navigating the treacherous path that lay before them. The erotic connection that had initially drawn them together was now interwoven with a profound emotional intimacy, a shared vulnerability that forged a bond stronger than any external force could break. The weight of secrets had changed their relationship profoundly, but it hadn't destroyed it; it had, in its own paradoxical way, strengthened it. Their love story was no longer simply a passionate affair; it was a journey of self-discovery, of overcoming cultural barriers, and of confronting the shadows of their past to forge a future built on mutual respect, understanding, and unwavering love.

The silence in the aftermath of Kenji's confession hung heavy, a palpable tension that vibrated between them like a taut string. The luxurious suite, usually a haven of sensual delights, felt stark and cold. Aisha traced the delicate pattern of the silk kimono Kenji had gifted her, the soft fabric a stark contrast to the harsh reality of their situation. The diamond necklace, a symbol of lavish affection, felt like a weight around her neck, a constant reminder of the opulence built on a foundation of illicit dealings.

Kenji watched her, his usually sharp features softened by a mixture of vulnerability and apprehension. He knew that the truth, however painful, was a necessary step towards preserving what they had. He understood that his actions, his family's actions, had jeopardized everything. The weight of his family's legacy, a heritage steeped in both tradition and criminality, pressed heavily on his shoulders.

"I'm sorry," he whispered, the words barely audible above the pounding of his heart. "I should have told you sooner. I was afraid... afraid of losing you."

His confession wasn't a simple recitation of facts; it was a raw, emotional unveiling, a deep dive into the complexities of his world. He painted a vivid picture of the Yakuza's intricate web of power and influence, its tentacles reaching into every facet of their lives. He spoke of the constant pressure to conform, the ingrained sense of duty and loyalty that bound him to his family, despite his own moral reservations. He spoke of the cultural nuances, the expectations placed upon him as the heir apparent, the near-impossible task of navigating the treacherous waters of his family's business while trying to retain his own sense of integrity.

He described the internal battles he waged daily, the internal conflict tearing him between his desires for a life free of violence and corruption and the obligations imposed by his birthright. He admitted that he had often felt suffocated by the expectations of his family, the constant threat of violence looming over him. He explained that his attraction to Aisha, a woman from a completely different world, had been a beacon of hope, a breath of fresh air in his suffocating reality.

Aisha listened, her heart aching with a complex mixture of empathy, anger, and a persistent, baffling affection. She understood, in a way she never anticipated, the cultural constraints that weighed so heavily on Kenji, the deep-rooted traditions that shaped his world. She saw beyond the carefully constructed façade of the powerful Yakuza member, recognizing the man struggling within, battling his conscience and his heritage.

She had grown up in a community steeped in resilience and

fortitude. She knew the strength of family, the unwavering bond of loyalty that often blinded individuals to the realities of wrongdoing. She recognized the complexities of Kenji's situation, the almost impossible choice between loyalty to his family and loyalty to himself, to their love.

However, understanding was not the same as forgiveness. There was a deep anger simmering beneath the surface, a righteous indignation at the callous disregard for human life that was inherent in his family's operations. The knowledge that they were involved in the very drug trade that had nearly cost her life sent a fresh wave of fear coursing through her veins. Her past trauma resurfaced, the memories of violence and betrayal flooding back.

The fear, however, was not only for herself. She was now intimately involved with this world; she had to face the possibility of losing Kenji, or even worse, becoming a pawn in the family's dangerous games. The implications of her involvement, the possible consequences, were becoming alarmingly clear. The initial thrill of their forbidden romance was now replaced by a chilling awareness of the potential danger she was in.

She confronted him with her fears, her anxieties expressed with a measured calm that belied the turmoil within her. She didn't lash out or accuse; her questions were pointed, direct, and focused on the future, not the past. She needed to know the extent of his involvement, the steps he was taking to distance himself from his family's criminal enterprise, and most importantly, what his intentions were regarding their relationship.

Kenji answered honestly, revealing more than he'd initially intended, laying bare the intricacies of the Yakuza's power structure. He admitted that it was a challenge to completely extricate himself from their dealings, but he was actively working towards it. He emphasized his commitment to their relationship, his love for her so profound that it had become his main driving force for change. He spoke of a desire for a life beyond the shadows, a life where their love could flourish free from the constant threat of violence and betrayal.

The night stretched on, a continuous ebb and flow of confession and understanding. They talked for hours, baring their souls to each other, navigating the treacherous landscape of their pasts, and forging a path towards an uncertain future. Their discussion was not about assigning blame or finding fault; it was about facing reality and accepting the weight of consequences.

As dawn painted the sky in hues of orange and pink, they reached a fragile, yet deeply meaningful understanding. Their love was not a simple fairytale romance, but a complex tapestry woven from love, danger, and a shared commitment to forging a future together, free from the shadows of the past. The weight of secrets still loomed, but it was no longer a burden they carried alone. It was a shared responsibility, a joint endeavor to navigate the treacherous path ahead. Their journey was far from over; it was just beginning. The road ahead was fraught with uncertainties, but they faced it together, their bond reinforced by their shared vulnerability and the powerful, unwavering force of their love. Their connection transcended the cultural differences, the dangers, and the secrets; it was a testament to the enduring power of human connection, a love story as complex and captivating as the lives they lived. The passionate erotic connection that had drawn them together had evolved into something deeper, more profound, a testament to their shared vulnerability and commitment. Their love story was far from over; it was a story of resilience, transformation, and the enduring power of love amidst the darkness.

The fragile peace established at dawn shattered like delicate porcelain under the weight of a new dilemma. Aisha awoke to the insistent ringing of her phone, a jarring contrast to the lingering warmth of Kenji's embrace. It was her best friend, Chioma, her voice tight with urgency. "Aisha, it's about the recording," she whispered, her words laced with fear. "Someone found out. They know you have it."

The blood drained from Aisha's face. The recording – her accidental capture of a crucial Yakuza drug deal – was the ticking time bomb she'd been desperately trying to ignore. The knowledge of its existence hung over her like a dark cloud, threatening to engulf her entire world. Now, it was no longer just a secret; it was a weapon, a dangerous piece of evidence that could destroy not only her but Kenji, and potentially expose his family's illegal activities on a massive scale.

The weight of her moral dilemma pressed down on her. The recording could bring down Kenji's family, but it could also condemn her to a fate worse than death, at the hands of ruthless criminals. The decision was stark: betray Kenji, potentially saving herself but destroying him and his world, or keep the secret and risk her own life and possibly others.' The ethical considerations were mind-boggling, laced with fear, loyalty, and a deep sense of self-preservation.

This new threat forced Aisha to re-evaluate everything. Kenji's confession had opened her eyes to the complexities of his world, but it had also illuminated the terrifying realities of the Yakuza. She had initially focused on the personal aspect of their relationship, on their love, but now the larger implications of her involvement became overwhelmingly clear. She was not merely caught in the crossfire; she was the target.

Kenji, sensing the shift in her demeanor, pulled her close. He'd seen the fear in her eyes, heard the tremor in her voice. He knew, instinctively, the weight of this new development. He understood the ethical tightrope she was walking, the precarious balance between love and survival. He, too, faced a profound moral crisis. He had confided in Aisha, hoping for a path to redemption, a way to escape his family's shadow. Now, his confession risked exposing him even further, potentially drawing his family's wrath down on Aisha, the woman he loved.

His own moral struggle deepened. He'd been trying to disentangle himself from his family's criminal network, but the possibility of Aisha being harmed because of him sparked a desperate resolve. The deep-seated loyalty he felt towards his family warred with his love for Aisha, creating an excruciating internal conflict. The cultural pressures that had shaped his life, the expectations placed upon him, now felt crushing. He was torn between his tradition and his desires, between loyalty and love. Choosing Aisha meant risking everything, a potential act of rebellion that could shatter his entire world.

Days turned into weeks as Aisha and Kenji grappled with the situation. They spent countless hours discussing their options, weighing the potential consequences of every decision. They sought counsel from trusted advisors, people who understood both their worlds, bridging the gap between Western ideals and the complex realities of the Yakuza culture. Their discussions were far from simple; they involved an exploration of Eastern and Western philosophies, of duty versus personal freedom, of loyalty versus love.

One advisor, an elder from Kenji's family, surprisingly offered a path of negotiation. He revealed a feasible way to protect Aisha while avoiding open conflict with the Yakuza's powerful leadership. This path, however, came with its own ethical complexities. It involved making a deal, a Faustian bargain that would require Aisha to compromise her ideals, making her a part of the system she despised. The choice was agonizing. Would she exchange one moral compromise for another?

Aisha's African American heritage, marked by generations of struggle and resilience, played a significant role in her decision-making. She understood the necessity of survival, the need to fight for what one believed in, even when the odds were stacked against them. But her background also instilled in her a deep sense of justice, a commitment to doing what was right, even when it was difficult. She saw the deep-seated corruption within Kenji's family as an affront to humanity, but also recognized the complex cultural pressures that contributed to their choices.

She didn't want to simply destroy, but to seek a way to heal, to bring about lasting change within the Yakuza, and maybe even prevent future tragedies. The potential for both personal and social transformation was enormous, but the risk was terrifying. She might fail in both goals and risk losing her life in the process.

Kenji, witnessing Aisha's internal battle, was reminded of his own struggles. The weight of his family's expectations had shaped his life, but he was beginning to question those very foundations. Aisha's influence was significant, transforming his view on loyalty and tradition, challenging his deep-seated beliefs. He found himself drawn to her vision of a different future, one that allowed for personal growth and moral integrity even within the constraints of his heritage.

Their love story, once a passionate exploration of sensual pleasure, had transformed into a deep philosophical quest. They were no longer merely lovers, but partners in a dangerous fight for their lives, their loves, and their souls. The erotic bond that had ignited their relationship now served as a grounding force, a source of strength amidst the ethical maelstrom. Their shared vulnerability, their willingness to confront their inner demons, strengthened their resolve. Their physical intimacy became a refuge, a way to connect on a deeper level as they navigated this intricate web of moral dilemmas. Each touch, each kiss, was a silent affirmation of their shared commitment, a testament to their love's enduring power against the looming threat. The future remained uncertain, but they faced it together, hand in hand, navigating the complex landscape of love, loyalty, and the overwhelming weight of secrets. Their journey was not only a testament to the strength of their bond, but a powerful exploration of the intersection of culture, love, and moral responsibility. Their story was far from over; it was a testament to human resilience in the face of profound ethical challenges, a love story that was as potent and gripping as the dangerous world they inhabited.

The elder's proposal hung in the air, a heavy, suffocating silence filling the opulent, traditionally decorated room. The scent of incense and aged wood did little to mask the tension radiating from Kenji, his usually impassive features etched with worry. Aisha, her heart a frantic drum against her ribs, felt the weight of centuries pressing down on her – the legacy of slavery, the fight for civil rights, the constant struggle for survival within a system designed to oppress. This wasn't just a matter of life and death for her and Kenji; it was a battle against the very systems that had shaped their lives, systems steeped in secrecy and corruption.

The elder's plan was a carefully crafted web of deceit, a dance with the devil that demanded Aisha's complicity. She would become an informant, feeding information to the Yakuza leadership in exchange for her protection and Kenji's freedom. It was a compromise that felt like a betrayal, a violation of her deeply held moral compass. The idea of working within a system she despised, of aligning herself with the very people who sought to exploit her, revolted her. Yet, the alternative – facing the wrath of the Yakuza without any protection – was terrifying, a prospect that could lead to her brutal demise and possibly endanger Chioma and others caught in the crossfire.

Days bled into sleepless nights. Aisha found herself wandering through the city, the neon lights a stark contrast to the shadowed corners of Kenji's world. She sought solace in the vibrant tapestry of her African American community, finding comfort in the shared experiences of struggle and resilience. In the soulful rhythms of gospel music, in the comforting embrace of her family, she found the strength to confront her inner demons, the courage to make a decision that would forever shape her destiny.

Kenji, meanwhile, was torn between his loyalty to his family and his love for Aisha. The Yakuza's code was deeply ingrained in him, a complex tapestry of honor, duty, and obedience that had shaped his life since birth. But Aisha had shown him another way, a path that prioritized love, justice, and personal integrity. He had begun to question the very foundations of his world, realizing the devastating consequences of blind loyalty to a corrupt system. He was caught between two worlds, struggling to reconcile his heritage with the woman he loved.

Their conversations became intense, passionate debates filled with love, fear, and the weight of their shared predicament. They explored the cultural differences between their backgrounds, examining the deep-seated patriarchal structures that both oppressed and empowered them. They delved into the complexities of their own internal struggles, acknowledging the conflicts between their desires and the expectations placed upon them. Their love, born amidst danger and secrecy, deepened, transforming into a powerful bond that anchored them amidst the chaos.

The physical intimacy between them evolved as well, reflecting the depth and complexity of their emotional journey. The once fiery, spontaneous encounters now carried a profound weight, each touch a testament to their shared vulnerability and mutual strength. Their bodies, intertwined in passionate embraces, became a sanctuary, a place where they could find solace and reassurance amidst the uncertainties of their lives. The erotic bond between them became a source of strength, a reminder of their shared humanity, and a powerful expression of their love in the face of impossible odds.

Aisha, drawing upon her heritage, sought a different approach. She recognized the elder's offer as a stepping stone, a path towards a broader goal – not just survival, but the possibility of reform within the Yakuza. She proposed a counter-offer – a chance for the Yakuza leadership to make amends, to choose a different path, to break free from the cycle of violence and corruption. Her plan was audacious, a gamble that involved utilizing her knowledge of both the Yakuza's inner workings and the intricacies of Western law enforcement. It was a daring strategy, one that required a deep understanding of both cultures, a delicate balance of negotiation and threat.

The negotiations were agonizing, a tense dance on the razor's edge of betrayal and redemption. Aisha, relying on her sharp wit and negotiating skills, skillfully played both sides, using her knowledge of the recording as leverage. She pointed out the immense risk to the Yakuza's reputation if their illegal activities were exposed, highlighting the catastrophic consequences of continuing down a path of violence and deceit. She offered a way out, a chance for redemption, a path towards a more just and ethical future.

Kenji's support was crucial throughout this delicate process. He used his influence within the Yakuza to subtly steer his family towards a compromise, using his newfound perspective to challenge the traditional power structures. His willingness to break with family tradition, to risk everything for Aisha and his own conscience, was a testament to the transformative power of their love. His presence, a silent affirmation of Aisha's approach, helped sway his family's decision.

The outcome was a delicate compromise. The Yakuza agreed to drop their pursuit of Aisha, acknowledging the potential damage her recording could inflict. In return, Aisha agreed to cooperate with a select group within the organization, helping to dismantle some of their illegal activities from within, while shielding the family's reputation from major exposure. It wasn't a perfect solution, but it was a beginning – a path towards healing and reform within the corrupted heart of the Yakuza. The journey ahead was still fraught with peril, but they had managed to avert a devastating conflict, choosing a path that balanced survival with the pursuit of justice.

Their love story, forged in the crucible of danger and deception, had evolved into something profound. They had confronted their personal demons, navigated the complexities of their cultures, and ultimately, chosen to fight for a better future, together. Their erotic connection, once the fiery heart of their relationship, had become a source of strength, a testament to their resilience, their mutual respect, and their unwavering love amidst the chaos. The weight of secrets, once a crushing burden, had been transformed into a shared responsibility, a challenge they faced together, hand in hand, their journey a powerful testament to the enduring strength of love, resilience, and the transformative power of shared purpose. Their future, though uncertain, held the promise of a new beginning, a love story etched not just in passion, but in courage, forgiveness, and the unwavering pursuit of a more just world.

CHAPTER 13:
FORGIVENESS AND
ACCEPTANCE

The air in the small, dimly lit temple hung heavy with the scent of incense and unspoken words. Kenji knelt before a small, intricately carved Buddha statue, his posture rigid, his normally expressive eyes cast down. The weight of his actions, the betrayal of his family's trust, pressed heavily on him. He'd lived his life by a code, a rigid set of rules dictated by the Yakuza, and yet, Aisha had irrevocably shattered that code, introducing chaos and a love that felt both forbidden and utterly essential.

Aisha sat beside him, the worn wooden floor cool against her skin. She watched him, her heart aching with a mixture of love and concern. His quiet desperation mirrored her own. She hadn't just endangered herself; she had risked Kenji's life, his family's standing, and the precarious balance they had painstakingly crafted. The recording, a desperate act of self-preservation, now hung between them, a constant reminder of their shared vulnerability and the precariousness of their situation. The guilt gnawed at her, a relentless beast feeding on her already fragile sense of self-worth.

The silence stretched, broken only by the rhythmic chanting from a nearby monastery, a gentle counterpoint to the storm raging within them. Finally, Kenji spoke, his voice barely a whisper, the words tinged with the unfamiliar vulnerability that Aisha had come to cherish and yet simultaneously fear. "I failed you, Aisha," he confessed, his voice thick with emotion. "I should have protected you, kept you safe from the dangers of my world. I let my loyalty to the family blind me, and in doing so, I almost lost you."

Aisha reached out, her hand covering his, her touch gentle yet firm. "You weren't alone in that," she replied, her voice soft but resolute. "I put you in danger, too. I acted recklessly, without considering the consequences. I was so focused on my own survival, I forgot about yours, about us." She squeezed his hand, offering him the comfort she so desperately needed herself. "We both made mistakes, Kenji. But we can fix them. Together."

Their shared confession opened a floodgate of emotions. Tears welled in Kenji's eyes, tears born of remorse and the overwhelming weight of his responsibilities. He spoke of the suffocating pressure of Yakuza life, the ingrained sense of duty that often overshadowed compassion and empathy. He spoke of the strict hierarchy, the unwavering loyalty demanded, and the unspoken consequences of disobedience. He confessed his fear, not just of failure, but of losing the woman who had shown him a separate way, a path illuminated by love, respect, and a sense of individual worth that he hadn't known existed.

Aisha listened intently, her heart filled with a mixture of empathy and understanding. She spoke of her own struggles, the trauma of her past, the deep-seated fear that had shaped her life. She recounted her experiences of racism and poverty, of navigating a world where survival often felt like a daily battle. She described the fear of being betrayed, the constant vigilance required to navigate a society that sought to minimize her. She shared the scars of a previous relationship that had left her damaged, wounded, and cynical, revealing the deep-seated insecurities that often made her fear intimacy.

Their conversation flowed seamlessly from personal struggles to shared aspirations. They discussed their hopes for a future free from violence and oppression, a future where their love could flourish without the constant threat of danger. They spoke of the importance of forgiveness, not just for each other, but for themselves and the mistakes they'd made along the way. Forgiveness, they realized, was not about forgetting the past, but about acknowledging it, learning from it, and moving forward.

The next few days were a blur of intense conversations and quiet introspection. They sought out elders in both their communities, seeking guidance and understanding. Aisha spoke with her grandmother, a matriarch of her family, a woman who had weathered countless storms. Her grandmother listened patiently, offering words of wisdom rooted in generations of resilience and the strength of the African American community. She reminded Aisha of her inner strength, her capacity for forgiveness, and her inherent ability to overcome challenges.

Kenji, following tradition, sought guidance from his own elders within the Yakuza. This was a treacherous path, a delicate dance between tradition and change. The elders, steeped in the ancient codes and customs of the Yakuza, were initially resistant to Kenji's pleas for understanding, for leniency, for a different approach. The weight of their traditions and the deeply ingrained power structures were formidable. Yet, Kenji's unwavering conviction, his heartfelt apologies, and his love for Aisha, slowly began to chip away at their resolve.

The process of seeking forgiveness from Kenji's family was slow and painstaking. It involved deep apologies, acknowledging the harm caused and offering amends where possible. It involved accepting responsibility and acknowledging the weight of his actions. He had to demonstrate his sincerity and his commitment to changing the path of the Yakuza, moving away from violence and deception. He proposed initiatives designed to assist the community, emphasizing the importance of social responsibility and a commitment to making amends for the Yakuza's past transgressions.

Aisha, drawing on her background in social work and activism, played a crucial role. She helped Kenji articulate his vision for a more ethical and responsible Yakuza. Her expertise in community engagement and conflict resolution proved invaluable. She facilitated discussions between Kenji and his family members, mediating tense encounters and fostering a dialogue based on empathy and understanding. Her presence, a silent testament to Kenji's transformation, helped to soften the hearts of the elders, convincing them that his remorse was genuine.

The road to forgiveness was not easy. It required self-reflection, honest apologies, and a commitment to changing behavior. But eventually, through their combined efforts, they began to mend the fractured relationships, slowly rebuilding bridges that had been shattered. They found a new purpose in their shared quest for justice, finding a renewed strength and shared determination to transform their individual worlds. Their love story, forged in the crucible of danger and deception, became a beacon of hope, a powerful testament to their capacity for forgiveness, their resilience, and their unwavering love for one another. The erotic bond that had initially brought them together now served as a foundation for a deeper, more profound connection, a love that was not just physical, but deeply spiritual, a testament to their shared journey of healing and transformation. The future remained uncertain, but it now held the potential for growth, healing, and a new beginning, built on a foundation of mutual respect, understanding, and a shared desire for a better future. Their journey would continue to be challenging, but they faced it together, hand-in-hand, their love a powerful testament to the enduring strength of the human spirit.

The weight of unspoken words finally lifted, replaced by a quiet understanding that settled between them like a gentle snowfall. The temple, once a symbol of Kenji's internal struggle, now felt like a sanctuary, a place where their shared vulnerability had been laid bare and ultimately accepted. The scent of incense, once heavy with the unspoken guilt, now carried the faint, sweet fragrance of hope.

Aisha, remembering the harsh words exchanged during their earlier conflict, felt the sting of her own culpability. Her sharp tongue, born from a lifetime of defending herself against a world that often felt hostile, had wounded him deeply. She hadn't considered the impact of her words, the way they sliced through his carefully constructed armor, exposing his vulnerabilities. She'd forgotten, in her fear and desperation, the importance of empathy, of understanding the weight of his responsibilities within the Yakuza. The understanding was not just about forgiving Kenji, but forgiving herself for her own harsh judgments, her own lack of compassion in that moment.

She reached out and gently took his hand, her touch conveying a depth of understanding and remorse. He squeezed back, his fingers intertwining with hers, a silent acknowledgement of their shared pain, and the road to healing that lay ahead. They spent the rest of the afternoon in quiet contemplation, the rhythmic chanting of the monks a soothing balm to their troubled souls.

Later, as the sun dipped below the horizon, casting long shadows across the temple grounds, they walked hand-in-hand through the serene gardens, the tranquility of the landscape mirroring the peace they were slowly finding within themselves. They spoke of the past, not with recriminations or blame, but with a shared understanding of the circumstances that had led them to where they were.

Kenji spoke openly about his life within the Yakuza, the rigid code of conduct, the unwavering loyalty demanded, and the constant threat of violence. He detailed the intricate power dynamics, the unspoken rules, and the treacherous path he'd walked to protect those he loved, even as those same actions had endangered Aisha. He confessed that his initial hesitation to involve the police had been motivated by fear, not just for his own safety, but for the potential ramifications for his entire family. He revealed that many Yakuza families had developed a system of community support to reduce their dependency on the legitimate government. They often provided help to members of their communities, especially the vulnerable ones. This system, despite its problematic origins, had helped them foster community support.

Aisha listened intently, her heart aching with empathy. She understood his loyalty, his commitment to family, and the immense pressure he was under. She saw, beyond the fearsome exterior, the man she loved, a man struggling with the conflict between his ingrained loyalty and the burgeoning love that had blossomed between them. She understood the weight of his heritage, the legacy he carried, and the challenges he faced in reconciling tradition with his own evolving sense of morality. Her own understanding of the societal pressure Kenji was under deepened when she realized the parallels with her own community. The pressures to conform to certain stereotypes within her own community were as fierce, even if the mechanisms were different from the Yakuza.

In turn, Aisha shared her own story, the scars of her past, the trauma of her relationship with the drug dealer, and the deep-seated fear that had shaped her life. She described the constant vigilance, the ever-present sense of danger, and the crippling sense of vulnerability that had haunted her for so long. She recounted how racism had shaped every aspect of her life, from the systemic inequalities she faced to the micro-aggressions that constantly eroded her self-esteem. It was a painful confession, a raw unveiling of her deepest wounds, but it was also a necessary step in the process of healing. She spoke of her hopes and dreams, her desire for a life free from fear, a life where she could feel safe, loved, and accepted.

Their confessions intertwined, creating a tapestry of shared experiences, vulnerabilities, and mutual understanding. They discovered a depth of empathy that transcended their cultural differences, forging a bond that was stronger than any perceived divide. The act of sharing their stories wasn't just about confession; it was an act of mutual support, a recognition of their shared humanity. It was about acknowledging the pain, embracing the vulnerability, and recognizing that healing was a shared journey.

The following days were dedicated to a deliberate process of reconciliation and forgiveness. Aisha sought out her own elders, wise women in her community who offered guidance and support. They listened patiently, offering comfort and reassurance, reminding Aisha of her strength and resilience, echoing Kenji's own emotional journey. They spoke of the importance of forgiveness, not just for Kenji, but for herself, for the self-doubt and fear that had shaped her choices. They helped her reclaim her own narrative, celebrating her resilience and strength.

Kenji, too, sought counsel from respected figures within his community. It was a fraught process, fraught with the complexities of tradition and change, loyalty, and love. The elders, initially skeptical of his newfound commitment to change, were eventually swayed by his sincere remorse and his demonstrable commitment to reform. His actions spoke louder than words. He initiated various community initiatives, focusing on education and providing support for underprivileged children. His actions demonstrated not only his desire for personal redemption, but his determination to create positive change within the Yakuza, to transform its image and purpose.

This was a long, slow process, a journey of gradual understanding and mutual respect. The wounds of the past could not be erased overnight, but they slowly began to heal, as they worked together towards a shared future. The physical intimacy between them, once a source of both passion and vulnerability, became a grounding force, an embodiment of their evolving relationship. It was a testament to their strength, a source of comfort, a symbol of their commitment to healing together. The love that had drawn them together, once tested by fear and uncertainty, grew deeper, broader, more profound. It was a love built on mutual respect, understanding, forgiveness, and a shared commitment to building a life beyond the shadows, a love that promised a new beginning, a future of hope and healing.

The air hung heavy with the unspoken, a silence pregnant with the echoes of their past conflicts. Yet, it was a different silence now, devoid of the sharp edges of accusation and resentment. It was a silence that hummed with the quiet strength of their shared journey towards healing. Aisha, gazing at Kenji's profile as he sat cross-legged on the tatami mat, saw not the fearsome Yakuza member she had initially encountered, but a man grappling with his own demons, a man who was bravely facing his past.

She watched as he meticulously arranged a small bonsai tree, his movements slow, deliberate, almost meditative. Each tiny adjustment spoke of patience, of a willingness to nurture and cultivate growth, a metaphor for their relationship, their shared struggle towards a more peaceful future. His usually steely gaze was softened, reflecting a newfound tranquility. The shadows that had once haunted his eyes seemed to have receded, replaced by a quiet confidence, a sense of inner peace that resonated with her own growing serenity.

The acceptance didn't come easily. It was a gradual process, a peeling away of layers, a slow unfolding of understanding. They spent hours in quiet contemplation, sharing their thoughts and feelings without judgment, without the need for grand pronouncements or dramatic gestures. Their communication was subtle, a language of shared glances, gentle touches, unspoken affirmations. It was a testament to their growing intimacy, a deepening connection that transcended words.

Aisha began to understand the nuances of Kenji's world, the intricate web of loyalties and obligations that bound him to the Yakuza. She learned about the familial structure, the emphasis on honor and tradition, the complex system of unwritten rules that governed their lives. It wasn't just about power and violence; it was about a deep-seated sense of community, a network of support that, despite its darker aspects, provided a sense of belonging and security. She recognized that his actions, though often harsh, were rooted in a loyalty that mirrored her own fierce protectiveness of her own family and community.

She saw the parallels between the pressures Kenji faced and the challenges she'd navigated within her own community. The expectations, the stereotypes, the unspoken rules—they were different in form, but similar in their intensity. The weight of conforming, the fear of judgment, the constant struggle to be accepted—these were experiences they shared, a bridge of understanding spanning vastly diverse cultural landscapes.

Kenji, in turn, deepened his understanding of Aisha's past. He learned about the systemic inequalities she faced, the racism that had shaped her life, and the trauma she'd endured. He listened patiently, his heart aching with empathy for the struggles she'd overcome. He saw the resilience in her spirit, the strength that had allowed her to survive and thrive in the face of adversity. He learned about the importance of sisterhood and communal support within her culture, a strength that often went unrecognized by those outside of their circles. He began to appreciate the deep spiritual practices that grounded her and empowered her resistance.

He began to understand the depth of her fear, the justifiable caution that shaped her interactions with the world. He saw that her sharp tongue, which had initially grated on him, was a shield forged in the fires of past hurts, a protective armor against a world that had often treated her with cruelty. He recognized her vulnerability, not as a weakness, but as a testament to her courage, her ability to bear the weight of her experiences and still remain open to love.

Their journey towards acceptance wasn't merely about forgiving past mistakes; it was about understanding the roots of those mistakes, the complex interplay of cultural influences, personal trauma, and societal pressures. They acknowledged the hurt they had inflicted on each other, but they did so without blame, without the need for recriminations. It was an act of mutual self compassion, a recognition of their shared humanity.

They sought out guidance from their respective communities, finding solace and support in the wisdom of their elders. Aisha's community offered her spiritual guidance, reminding her of the power of resilience, forgiveness, and the enduring strength of her heritage. Kenji's community, though initially hesitant, eventually embraced his sincere remorse and his commitment to positive change. The elders, recognizing the depth of his transformation, offered him support, guiding him on a path of both personal and communal redemption.

The physical intimacy between them, once a source of intense passion and vulnerability, evolved into a symbol of their shared healing. It wasn't just about physical pleasure; it was about comfort, connection, and a shared affirmation of their love. It became a sanctuary, a space where they could nurture each other, offering solace and support in their mutual journey towards growth.

Acceptance, for Aisha and Kenji, wasn't about erasing the past. It was about integrating it, understanding its influence, and using it as a foundation for building a stronger, more resilient future. It was about recognizing that their love was not a rejection of their heritage, but an embrace of their unique experiences, a testament to the power of human connection across cultural divides. It was a love built not on the illusion of perfection, but on a foundation of mutual understanding, empathy, and the shared journey of letting go. Their past experiences, once sources of pain and division, now served as a testament to their shared resilience, forging a bond that was stronger, more profound, and more meaningful than either could have ever imagined. The future, though still uncertain, now held the promise of a love built on forgiveness, understanding, and a commitment to building a life together, free from the shadows of their past.

The scent of jasmine tea hung in the air, a delicate fragrance that seemed to mirror the subtle shift in their relationship. They sat on the veranda of Kenji's family home, overlooking the meticulously manicured garden. The rhythmic chirping of crickets provided a soothing soundtrack to their quiet contemplation. Gone were the fiery arguments, the explosive clashes of wills. In their place was a comfortable silence, punctuated by shared glances and gentle touches.

Aisha found herself increasingly drawn to the quiet strength of Kenji's family. Initially, she had been wary, seeing them as symbols of a world she didn't understand, a world that felt both alluring and threatening. But as she spent more time with them, she began to see the complexities of their relationships, the intricate web of loyalty and responsibility that bound them together. She witnessed the quiet acts of kindness, the unspoken gestures of affection, the unwavering support they offered each other.

She learned about the traditions that shaped their lives, the ancient customs that had been passed down through generations. She participated in tea ceremonies, learning the delicate art of preparing and serving the sacred beverage, a ritual that emphasized mindfulness and respect. She listened to stories of their ancestors, tales of resilience and perseverance, tales that spoke of a rich cultural heritage. She began to appreciate the beauty of their traditions, the depth of their history, and the profound connection they held to their roots.

Kenji, in turn, discovered a new appreciation for Aisha's strength and resilience. He had been captivated by her beauty and her spirit, but he had also underestimated the depth of her pain, the scars that ran deep beneath her confident exterior. He had initially viewed her as an exotic prize, a woman he desired to possess. But as he learned more about her, he came to see her as a woman of profound strength, a woman who had overcome incredible hardship.

He learned about her unwavering commitment to her

family and her community. He saw how she navigated the complexities of being a Black woman in a world that often sought to define and limit her. He witnessed the subtle ways she used her intelligence and wit to overcome obstacles, to navigate a world that wasn't always welcoming. He learned about the rich tapestry of her cultural heritage, the vibrant traditions that shaped her identity, and the deep-rooted sense of community that sustained her.

Their conversations, once filled with heated debates and misunderstandings, now flowed effortlessly. They talked about their childhoods, their dreams, their fears. They shared stories of their families, their triumphs, and their failures. They discussed their cultural differences, celebrating the unique aspects of their heritage, while also acknowledging the challenges of navigating those differences. They learned to appreciate the richness that came from their diverse backgrounds, a richness that strengthened their connection.

Kenji began to understand the weight of Aisha's past trauma, the deep-seated fear that had shaped her perceptions and actions. He saw how her experiences with racism and violence had left lasting scars, scars that were not always visible but deeply affected her sense of security and trust. He learned about the importance of validating her experiences, of acknowledging the injustices she had faced, and of offering her unwavering support. He realized that his initial attempts to protect her had often inadvertently minimized her pain, and he committed to a more sensitive and empathetic approach.

Aisha, in turn, began to see the complexities of Kenji's world. She had initially viewed the Yakuza as a violent and ruthless organization. But as she learned more about their internal structures, their codes of conduct, and their sense of community, she began to see a different side to their lives. She saw how their loyalty and dedication to their family and their community often overshadowed the violence and crime associated with the organization. She understood that Kenji's actions, though often morally ambiguous, were often driven by a deep sense of responsibility and a desire to protect those he loved. She learned to recognize the nuances of his life, the complexities of his choices, and the challenges he faced in navigating his family's legacy.

Their physical intimacy, once a source of intense passion and excitement, evolved into something more profound. It became a space of comfort, security, and shared vulnerability. Their lovemaking was no longer merely a physical act; it was an expression of their growing emotional intimacy, a testament to their shared journey towards healing and understanding. They communicated through touch, through whispered words, through shared moments of quiet intimacy. Their physical connection deepened their emotional bond, reinforcing their commitment to each other.

They sought guidance from trusted mentors within their respective communities. Aisha found solace in the wisdom of her elders, women who had navigated similar challenges and offered her invaluable support. They reminded her of the resilience of her ancestors, the strength of her heritage, and the enduring power of love. Kenji sought counsel from respected elders within his community, men who understood the complex dynamics of the Yakuza and offered him guidance on navigating his family's legacy while pursuing a more ethical path.

Their journey towards forgiveness and acceptance wasn't linear; it was a winding path filled with difficulties, moments of doubt and moments of clarity. There were times when old wounds resurfaced, times when past traumas threatened to derail their progress. But through it all, they held onto each other, offering unwavering support and understanding. They learned to communicate their needs and desires openly and honestly, creating a space where vulnerability was embraced, not feared.

The process of forgiveness wasn't about condoning past actions but about acknowledging the complexities of human experience, understanding the influence of past traumas, and finding a way to move forward together. They acknowledged the pain they had inflicted on each other and the pain they had experienced individually, without resorting to blame or recrimination. Their shared journey was a testament to the transformative power of love, a love that transcended cultural differences and healed deeply ingrained wounds. It was a love built on mutual respect, understanding, and a shared commitment to creating a better future, together. The shadows of their past experiences remained, but they no longer defined them. Instead, they served as reminders of their strength, their resilience, and the enduring power of their love.

They were ready to face the future, together, their love a beacon of hope illuminating their path.

The cool evening air carried the scent of blooming wisteria, a stark contrast to the heat of their earlier arguments. They sat on the veranda, the meticulously crafted Japanese garden bathed in the soft glow of lanterns. The silence wasn't tense this time, but a quiet understanding, a shared space where unspoken words hung heavy with the weight of their journey. The past few weeks had been a crucible, forging a bond stronger than either had anticipated. It hadn't been easy. The chasm between their worlds, the stark differences in their upbringings, and the weight of Kenji's family's expectations had threatened to tear them apart. But in the quiet moments of shared reflection, a profound realization dawned on them both: shared responsibility.

Kenji, with his carefully cultivated composure, finally admitted to the manipulative undertones in his initial approach. "I saw you, Aisha, and I wanted you. I wanted to possess that strength, that fire...I didn't see the scars, the pain beneath the surface. I objectified you, and for that, I am terribly sorry." His voice was low, a confession etched in genuine remorse. He spoke of the pressure within his family, the expectation to maintain their status, the inherent dangers of his world. But his words weren't excuses, they were admissions of culpability. He wasn't seeking absolution, but acknowledgment of his flaws and a commitment to change.

Aisha listened, her heart a complex tapestry of emotions. Anger, hurt, and a flicker of understanding intertwined. She saw the genuine regret in his eyes, a reflection of her own self-blame. She'd been running from her past, from the trauma of her previous relationship, seeking solace in the thrill of the forbidden, the allure of a world vastly different from her own. She had consciously chosen to ignore the red flags, the unspoken warnings of Kenji's world, blinded by passion and a desperate need for connection. "I wasn't a victim, Kenji," she said, her voice steady, "I made choices. I knew the risks, and I took them anyway. I allowed myself to be swept away, to lose myself in the excitement, ignoring the danger signs."

This acknowledgment was not a deflection of responsibility, but a crucial step towards genuine healing. She spoke of her own insecurities, her fear of vulnerability, and how her past experiences had shaped her desperate search for love and acceptance. She'd been so focused on escaping her past that she hadn't paused to consider the potential consequences of her actions. The recording, the near-fatal encounter with the drug dealers— these were not mere accidents; they were the direct result of choices she had made. She owned them, fully and completely.

Their shared confession wasn't a theatrical display of remorse, but a deeply personal accounting. They spoke not only of their actions but also of the cultural forces that had shaped them, the societal expectations they had both internalized. For Aisha, it was the pressure to be strong, independent, and self-sufficient, a pressure stemming from societal expectations placed upon Black women. The need to appear invulnerable had masked her vulnerability, making her susceptible to Kenji's initial charm.

For Kenji, it was the suffocating weight of tradition, the unshakeable code of the Yakuza, and the unwavering loyalty he felt towards his family. The expectations placed upon him to uphold his family's honor had blinded him to the humanity of Aisha, reducing her, initially, to a symbol of status, a prize to be won. Acknowledging these pressures didn't excuse their actions; it provided a context, a deeper understanding of the motivations behind their choices.

This shared acknowledgment of responsibility became a

foundation for their rebuilding. It was a testament to their maturity, a willingness to confront their flaws and work towards a healthier, more equitable relationship. They delved into the intricate details of their pasts, not to assign blame, but to foster empathy and understanding. Aisha recounted the brutality of her former relationship, the insidious cycle of abuse that had left her scarred and wary of trust. Kenji, in turn, spoke of the sacrifices he had made for his family, the internal conflicts he'd faced between tradition and his evolving feelings for Aisha.

The conversations weren't easy. Tears were shed, silences stretched, and emotions ran high. But within the vulnerability, a profound connection strengthened. They were not simply apologizing for past actions; they were actively working to understand the root causes of their behavior, taking ownership of their part in the unfolding drama, and making a conscious effort to avoid repeating past mistakes. This involved not just verbal apologies, but tangible changes. Kenji started distancing himself from the more dangerous aspects of his family's business, seeking less compromising avenues to satisfy his responsibility. Aisha started attending therapy, confronting her past trauma with the help of a therapist specializing in trauma recovery and interracial relationships.

The process wasn't quick or painless. It required consistent effort, a willingness to listen without judgment, and a commitment to open and honest communication. They explored the impact of their cultural backgrounds on their perceptions, challenging their preconceived notions and biases. Aisha educated Kenji on the historical context of racism against Black people in America, its pervasive impact on societal structures and individual lives. Kenji, in turn, guided Aisha through the complexities of Japanese culture and traditions, helping her understand the nuanced social hierarchy and the pressure of maintaining family honor.

They sought guidance from respected elders in their respective communities. Aisha's grandmother, a woman of remarkable strength and wisdom, offered unwavering support, reminding her of the resilience of their ancestors and the importance of self-forgiveness. She emphasized the necessity of self-care and healing, urging Aisha to confront her trauma and find peace within herself. Similarly, Kenji sought counsel from a respected elder in his community, a man who understood the Yakuza code but also recognized the importance of ethical conduct. This elder provided Kenji with a framework for navigating his family responsibilities while upholding his commitment to Aisha.

Their shared journey wasn't just about individual accountability; it was about mutual growth and transformation. They both understood that forgiveness was not a single event, but an ongoing process, a continuous commitment to understanding and supporting each other. It wasn't about erasing the past, but integrating its lessons into a more mature and responsible future. The past still cast a shadow, but it no longer dictated their present or future. It was a constant reminder of their vulnerability and the importance of navigating their relationship with empathy, respect, and a shared commitment to growth. Their relationship was no longer just about love and desire; it was a testament to resilience, healing, and the profound power of shared responsibility. They were forging a future built on accountability, understanding, and a love that had survived the crucible of their past, stronger and more profound than ever before. The jasmine scent, once a symbol of their initial tentative steps toward understanding, now carried the fragrance of hope, renewal and a shared future built on a foundation of genuine accountability and mutual respect.

CHAPTER 14: A NEW DAWN

The rising sun painted the sky in hues of apricot and rose, a vibrant contrast to the somber palette of their recent past. Aisha woke nestled against Kenji's warmth, the familiar scent of his skin a comforting anchor. The lingering fear, the constant shadow of their precarious situation, felt less oppressive this morning. A fragile peace had settled between them, a quiet understanding that transcended the tumultuous weeks that had passed. It wasn't a naive optimism, but a cautious hope, built on the foundations of shared accountability and a mutual commitment to building a future worthy of their love.

The following days were filled with a gentle rhythm of rediscovery. They explored Tokyo together, venturing beyond the opulent confines of Kenji's world. They wandered through bustling markets, the vibrant colors, and exotic aromas a stark contrast to the sterile elegance of Kenji's usual surroundings. Aisha, initially hesitant, found herself captivated by the intricate details of Japanese culture, the meticulous artistry in the simplest objects, the profound respect for tradition interwoven into the fabric of daily life. Kenji, in turn, reveled in the unfiltered authenticity of Aisha's spirit, her infectious laughter echoing through the crowded streets, a testament to her resilience and her growing capacity for joy.

They discovered shared passions, unexpected common ground that cemented their bond beyond the initial allure of forbidden desire. They spent hours in quiet tea houses, savoring the delicate bitterness of matcha, their conversations flowing effortlessly, unburdened by the weight of their past. They visited ancient temples, the serene atmosphere fostering a sense of peace and reflection. In these sacred spaces, surrounded by the echoes of history, they found solace and a renewed sense of perspective. Their conversations weren't always easy; the scars of their past still lingered, surfacing in moments of unexpected vulnerability. But the difference was in their approach. They no longer avoided the difficult topics, instead facing them with a newfound maturity, a willingness to listen and understand.

Kenji, particularly, was undergoing a profound transformation. He was slowly distancing himself from the more dangerous aspects of his family's business, navigating the complexities of his loyalties with careful consideration. He found solace in his family's legitimate enterprises, his passion for the beauty industry rekindled, the creativity and artistry providing a welcome contrast to the shadows of his past. He spent more time working in his family's beauty stores, immersing himself in the details of operations, learning the intricacies of business management. This new focus brought him a sense of fulfillment, a feeling of purpose beyond the constraints of his family's expectations. The pressure to uphold the Yakuza code remained, but it no longer held the same suffocating grip. He was beginning to carve his own path, forging his own identity independent of the dangerous legacy that had defined him for so long.

Aisha, too, embraced a new chapter in her life. She continued her therapy, the sessions providing a safe space to confront her past trauma and build a healthier foundation for her future. She discovered a newfound confidence, a strength born not from invulnerability, but from embracing her vulnerability. She started volunteering at a local community center, working with young women from disadvantaged backgrounds. She found a purpose in helping others, using her own experiences to empower and inspire. Her past relationship, once a source of deep shame and pain, was slowly transforming into a catalyst for growth, a testament to her resilience and her unwavering spirit. She learned to channel her anger into productive action, advocating for social justice and empowerment within her community.

Their relationship evolved, moving beyond the initial tempestuous passion into something deeper, more enduring. The erotic element remained, of course, but it was now infused with a profound sense of intimacy and understanding. Their lovemaking became a sacred ritual, a celebration of their connection, a testament to their shared journey. It was no longer a frantic escape, but a deliberate expression of affection, a shared exploration of pleasure and vulnerability. Their intimacy was a reflection of their journey, each touch carrying the weight of their shared past and the promise of their shared future.

They faced challenges, naturally. The shadow of Kenji's family loomed large, their disapproval a constant reminder of the risks they were taking. Whispers and warnings circulated within the family, but Kenji stood his ground, his commitment to Aisha unwavering. He learned to navigate the conflicting demands of his family and his personal life, prioritizing open communication and setting boundaries, a feat of balance that both surprised and impressed even him. He utilized his influence within the Yakuza to protect Aisha, ensuring her safety without directly compromising his integrity. This delicate dance required immense skill and strategic thinking, a testament to his growing maturity and self-awareness.

Aisha, in turn, learned to navigate the complexities of Kenji's world, understanding the nuances of Japanese culture and the deeply ingrained traditions that shaped his life. She learned to appreciate the strength of his family's bonds, the intricate network of loyalty and responsibility that bound them together. This understanding didn't erase the initial discomfort she felt, but it provided a new perspective, allowing her to engage with Kenji's family with greater empathy and respect. She still felt a sense of caution, a wariness of the power dynamics at play, but she also felt a growing connection with Kenji's mother, who, despite her initial reservations, began to see the depth of Aisha's character and her genuine love for her son.

As their relationship strengthened, their respective communities began to play a more significant role in their lives. Aisha's grandmother, a pillar of wisdom and support, embraced Kenji with open arms, sensing the genuine depth of his love for Aisha. She offered him insight into the African American experience, bridging the cultural gap between them and fostering a sense of mutual understanding and respect. Similarly, Kenji's mother, initially wary of Aisha's background, gradually warmed to her, recognizing her resilience and compassion. She saw in
Aisha not just a potential daughter-in-law, but a woman of extraordinary strength and character.

The process of building a future together wasn't a simple, linear journey; it was filled with twists and turns, unexpected challenges, and moments of profound vulnerability. But the foundation they had built – a foundation of mutual understanding, respect, and shared responsibility – proved resilient. They navigated the complexities of their cultural backgrounds, the lingering shadows of their pasts, and the ever-present threat of Kenji's dangerous world. They emerged stronger, their love deepened by the crucible of their shared experiences. They found solace in each other, a sanctuary from the storms of their lives. They found a shared purpose in creating a life together, a life built on love, respect, and a shared commitment to building a future worthy of their love story, a future as vibrant and hopeful as the sunrise painting the Tokyo sky. Their love story was a testament to the power of resilience, the transformative potential of shared responsibility, and the enduring strength of a love that had survived the storms and emerged stronger than ever before. This was not simply a new dawn; it was the beginning of a breathtaking new chapter in their extraordinary love story, a testament to the enduring power of love in the face of adversity.

The crisp autumn air carried the scent of fallen gingko leaves as Aisha and Kenji strolled hand in-hand through a secluded park in Tokyo. The vibrant reds and golds of the foliage mirrored the warmth that now permeated their relationship. Gone was the chilling uncertainty that had once clung to them like a shroud; in its place bloomed a quiet confidence, a shared belief in their ability to navigate the complexities of their lives together. They spoke little, their silence comfortable and companionable, a silent acknowledgment of the journey they had shared and the future they were building. The occasional brush of their hands, a fleeting touch of their shoulders, spoke volumes more than words ever could.

Kenji, visibly relaxed and at peace, watched as Aisha laughed, her joy infectious. He had never seen her so genuinely happy, so free from the shadows of her past. The weight of his family's expectations still pressed upon him, but it no longer held the same paralyzing grip. He had found a new purpose, a sense of self beyond the confines of the Yakuza, a purpose fueled by his love for Aisha and his growing passion for his family's legitimate business. He was not abandoning his family, but forging a new path, carving out a space for himself and Aisha within the complex tapestry of his heritage.

He had begun to delegate more responsibility within the Yakuza, focusing his energy on overseeing the expansion of his family's beauty empire. The creative process, the meticulous attention to detail required in the beauty industry, offered a welcome counterpoint to the harsh realities of his past. He found satisfaction in the artistry, the transformation, the opportunity to create beauty where before there had only been darkness. He even began to appreciate the cultural fusion his business offered, incorporating elements of both Japanese and Western aesthetics, much like his own relationship with Aisha.

Aisha, too, was thriving. Her therapy sessions had become less about processing trauma and more about building a durable foundation for her future. She was no longer defined by her past relationship; instead, she had transformed it into a source of strength and resilience. Her volunteer work at the community center flourished; she had established a successful mentorship program for young women, using her experiences to guide and empower them. Her voice, once silenced by fear and insecurity, was now a powerful advocate for social justice and personal growth within her community. She was making a difference, not only in the lives of the young women she mentored, but also within the broader fabric of her community.

Their cultural differences, once a source of apprehension, had become a source of mutual enrichment. Aisha had embraced Japanese culture with an open heart, learning the language, exploring the culinary traditions, and appreciating the intricate details of Japanese art and design. Kenji, in turn, delved deeper into understanding the nuances of African American culture, fascinated by its rich history, vibrant music, and powerful resilience. They learned from each other, celebrating their differences while cherishing their shared humanity. Their home, a beautiful apartment overlooking the Tokyo skyline, reflected this cultural fusion – elements of Japanese minimalism blended seamlessly with touches of Aisha's vibrant style.

They began to discuss the future, not with trepidation, but with a shared sense of excitement. They talked about starting a family, envisioning a life filled with love, laughter, and shared adventures. They imagined raising children who were grounded in both their cultures, children who would embody the best of both worlds. These conversations weren't always easy; they acknowledged the challenges that lay ahead, the potential difficulties of raising a family within the complex dynamics of Kenji's family, the inevitable cultural adjustments they would need to make. But their optimism remained unshaken, their commitment unwavering. They understood that building a future together would require patience, compromise, and an ongoing effort to communicate and understand each other's perspectives.

Aisha's grandmother, a cornerstone of strength and wisdom in her life, had become a cherished confidante for Kenji. She shared stories of her own life, her struggles, and her triumphs, helping him to understand the depth of Aisha's resilience and the unique challenges faced by African American women. Kenji's mother, initially hesitant about Aisha, had also come around, impressed by Aisha's strength of character and her genuine love for her son. The initial reservations had melted away, replaced by a cautious respect and a growing fondness for the young woman who had captured her son's heart. Family dinners, once fraught with tension, became occasions for laughter, shared stories, and the slow, careful weaving of two worlds together.

Their intimacy deepened, moving beyond the passionate encounters of their early relationship to a profound and tender connection. Their lovemaking became a sacred ritual, a celebration of their shared journey, a testament to their enduring love. It was a space where they could express their vulnerability, their joy, their profound connection. It was a fusion of their cultural backgrounds, a blend of Eastern and Western traditions, a testament to the beauty of their unique relationship. Their physical intimacy mirrored the emotional intimacy that had blossomed between them – a profound and enriching aspect of their life together.

Their happiness, however, wasn't without its challenges. The whispers and warnings from within Kenji's family persisted. There were still those who disapproved of their relationship, who saw Aisha as an outsider, a threat to the established order. But Kenji was resolute, his commitment to Aisha unwavering. He continued to navigate the complexities of his family's expectations, carefully protecting Aisha while also building his own independent life. He learned to set boundaries, to prioritize his own happiness without sacrificing his responsibilities to his family. This delicate balance required immense skill and unwavering determination.

Aisha, in turn, continued to navigate the subtle power dynamics within Kenji's family, understanding their traditions and showing respect for their beliefs. She didn't shy away from the challenges, but embraced them, viewing them as opportunities to build bridges and foster understanding. She understood that acceptance wouldn't come easily, but she was committed to earning their respect and demonstrating the depth of her love for Kenji. She learned to appreciate the strength of the familial bonds, the intricate web of loyalty and responsibility that bound them together.

Their relationship, though challenging at times, became a beacon of hope, a testament to the power of love to transcend cultural differences and heal past wounds. They found joy in the small moments – a shared cup of tea, a quiet evening at home, a spontaneous trip to the countryside. Their love was a testament to their resilience, their commitment, their willingness to embrace the future together, hand in hand, navigating the challenges and celebrating the victories, their love story woven into the vibrant tapestry of their lives. The new dawn had broken, and their future shone with the promise of a love that was both profound and enduring.

The Tokyo sky, a canvas of deepening twilight, painted hues of lavender and rose across the cityscape as Aisha and Kenji sat nestled on their balcony, a steaming mug of matcha tea warming their hands. The city lights twinkled below, a dazzling backdrop to their intimate conversation. Tonight, they weren't discussing the complexities of the Yakuza or the challenges of bridging two vastly different cultures; tonight, they were dreaming.

Kenji, his eyes reflecting the city's glow, spoke first, his voice low and tender. "I've been thinking...about our future. About what we want to create together." He paused, taking a slow sip of his tea, the warmth spreading through him, mirroring the warmth blooming in his heart. "I want a family, Aisha. A family filled with love, laughter, and the vibrant tapestry of our cultures."

Aisha leaned against him, her head resting on his shoulder, the scent of his cologne a comforting presence. "Me too, Kenji. I've always dreamt of a big family, filled with noise and chaos and unconditional love. I want children who grow up knowing both their Japanese and African American roots, children who understand the beauty of diversity." Her voice was soft, yet laced with conviction, a testament to the strength she had cultivated from her past struggles.

They talked for hours, their voices a low hum against the backdrop of the city's symphony. Kenji spoke of his vision for their home, a place where modern design would blend seamlessly with traditional Japanese aesthetics, a space where the vibrant energy of African American culture would intertwine with the quiet serenity of Japanese tradition. He envisioned a garden, bursting with color and life, a tranquil sanctuary where they could escape the hustle and bustle of city life. He imagined family dinners where the aroma of his mother's traditional Japanese dishes would mingle with the rich flavors of Aisha's grandmother's soul food, a culinary fusion reflecting the beauty of their combined heritage.

Aisha described her hopes for their children, their education, their exposure to both cultures. She envisioned them spending summers in America, exploring her vibrant family history, attending festivals, and immersing themselves in the richness of African American culture. She dreamed of them learning Japanese, spending winters in Japan, mastering the art of calligraphy, and exploring the ancient temples and serene gardens. She envisioned a childhood where they felt equally at home in both worlds, understanding and appreciating the unique beauty of each. She saw them speaking multiple languages, embracing diverse perspectives, and becoming citizens of the world, embracing the interconnectedness of humanity.

Their conversation flowed seamlessly, their dreams intertwining, becoming a shared vision of their future. They discussed the challenges they knew lay ahead, the potential for conflict, the cultural adjustments required, and the ongoing negotiation of their respective family expectations. They acknowledged that building a strong foundation would require patience, compromise, and constant communication. But their shared dream, so clearly defined and deeply felt, fueled their determination to navigate these challenges together.

They talked about work, too. Kenji expressed his desire to gradually transition away from the more dangerous aspects of his family's business, focusing more on the legitimate beauty empire. He envisioned a future where he could dedicate his time and energy to fostering creativity and innovation within the company, and where he could use his influence to uplift others. He wanted to use his platform to promote diversity and inclusion within the beauty industry, showcasing the beauty of different cultures and ethnicities. He wanted to create a space where people felt seen, heard, and celebrated, reflecting the principles of inclusivity he championed in his personal life.

Aisha, energized by her own success with her mentorship program, planned to expand her community initiatives. She dreamt of creating a foundation dedicated to supporting young women from underprivileged backgrounds, empowering them to pursue their education, achieve their dreams, and find their voices. She planned to incorporate aspects of both American and Japanese cultural values in her approach, recognizing the importance of self-reliance and resilience, paired with a commitment to community and collective well-being.

Their combined ambitions, their dedication to personal and professional growth, and their unwavering commitment to supporting each other fueled their optimism. They realized that building a life together required more than just love; it demanded a shared vision, a commitment to growth, and a willingness to face any challenges hand-in-hand.

As the night deepened, they moved from their balcony to the cozy comfort of their living room, the conversation shifting from ambitious dreams to more intimate hopes. They talked about the simple joys they anticipated: morning coffees overlooking the city, quiet evenings spent reading together, spontaneous weekend getaways to explore the beauty of Japan. They visualized cozy nights in, surrounded by the warmth of family, laughter echoing through their home.

Kenji, his voice filled with affection, gently traced Aisha's hand.

"I love you, Aisha. More than words can ever express."

Aisha squeezed his hand, her eyes brimming with emotion. "And I love you, Kenji. With all my heart." Their eyes met, a silent acknowledgment of the profound depth of their love, a love that had blossomed from unexpected circumstances, a love that had transcended cultural boundaries, a love that held the power to shape their future and build a world of their own making. They shared a kiss, long and tender, a seal upon their shared dreams, a testament to the love that would guide their journey, a promise of a future filled with love, laughter, and the intertwined beauty of their cultures.

Their conversation wasn't just about the future; it was about the present, too. They discussed the need for open communication, for honesty and vulnerability, for navigating the complexities of Kenji's family and the ever-present threat of his past life. They knew that challenges would arise, that unforeseen obstacles would test their strength and their resolve. But they approached these considerations not with fear, but with a shared understanding and a determination to face them together.

The night continued, the conversation shifting from dreams to practicalities, from grand aspirations to the minutiae of daily life. They planned their next trip to America, deciding on visiting Aisha's family and exploring her hometown, a bustling urban center quite different from their life in Tokyo. They planned their next trip to Kenji's family's ancestral home in the countryside, imagining the serenity and tradition they would encounter. They planned small things, and big things. They planned a future, step by step, moment by moment, weaving their individual threads together to form a strong, vibrant tapestry.

Their plans were not simply about constructing a future; they were about building a foundation of trust, respect, and unwavering support. They discussed the importance of maintaining their individual identities, their cultural heritage, while simultaneously creating a unique identity as a couple. They were not blending cultures into a homogenous whole, rather they were crafting a space for coexistence and appreciation, where each culture retains its distinct flavor and beauty. Their relationship was a mosaic, a beautiful and diverse collection of unique perspectives, forming something entirely new and magnificent.

The night eventually wound down, exhaustion settling upon them as the first rays of dawn began to break. They drifted to sleep in each other's arms, their bodies intertwined, a physical manifestation of their intertwined destinies. Their shared dreams, once a whisper of possibility, were now firmly planted, roots stretching deep into the rich soil of their love, bearing the promise of a future as breathtaking and beautiful as the Tokyo skyline that spread before them. Their love story was not simply a tale of two people finding love; it was a testament to the power of cultural understanding, personal growth, and the enduring strength of a shared vision, a potent combination destined to bear plentiful fruit. The new dawn, indeed, was theirs.

The days that followed were a whirlwind of activity, a testament to their burgeoning ambition and the sheer force of their shared vision. Kenji, true to his word, began strategically divesting himself from the more volatile aspects of the family business. He channeled his considerable energy and influence into expanding the legitimate beauty empire, focusing on ethical sourcing, sustainable practices, and promoting diversity within the company's marketing and product development. He implemented new initiatives, showcasing models from a wide range of ethnic backgrounds, and incorporated traditional ingredients and techniques from various cultures into the company's product line. This wasn't just a business decision; it was a personal commitment, a reflection of his growing understanding of the importance of inclusivity and representation.

Aisha, meanwhile, threw herself into her mentorship program with renewed vigor. She secured additional funding, expanding the program to reach more young women, offering a wider range of support services, including tutoring, career counseling, and financial literacy workshops. She incorporated elements of Japanese philosophy into her teaching, emphasizing concepts like perseverance, self-discipline, and the importance of community. She organized cultural exchange programs, pairing her mentees with Japanese students, fostering cross-cultural understanding and collaboration. Her work transcended mere mentorship; it became a powerful movement, inspiring young women to dream bigger, reach higher, and embrace their unique identities.

Their personal lives were as vibrant as their professional endeavors. They explored Tokyo together, discovering hidden gems and experiencing the city through each other's eyes. They visited traditional tea houses, learning the art of the tea ceremony, and savored the subtle flavors and refined elegance of Japanese culture. Kenji introduced Aisha to his extended family, navigating the complex dynamics with grace and patience, and Aisha, in turn, shared aspects of her own family history and cultural traditions with him. There were moments of awkwardness, of cultural misunderstandings, but they met these challenges with open communication and a willingness to learn. Their differences, far from being a source of conflict, became a source of mutual enrichment, deepening their bond and fostering a richer understanding of each other.

Aisha's past continued to cast a long shadow. The lingering fear of retribution from the drug dealers she had inadvertently implicated never completely vanished. Kenji, ever vigilant, ensured her safety, but he also encouraged her to confront her past, to acknowledge the trauma she had endured, and to move forward with strength and resilience. He listened patiently as she recounted her experiences, offering solace and support without judgment. He helped her to understand that her past didn't define her; it had shaped her, made her stronger, and fueled her compassion. Together, they explored methods of healing, seeking solace in meditation, in long walks through Tokyo's serene parks, and in the intimacy of their shared love.

Their sexual relationship also deepened, evolving beyond the initial intensity and passion into a more profound connection of trust and mutual respect. They experimented with new forms of intimacy, blending their cultural backgrounds and exploring different sexual practices with openness and curiosity. Their lovemaking wasn't just a physical act; it was an expression of their mutual admiration, their growing understanding of each other, and a testament to the powerful bond they had forged. It was a celebration of their combined heritage, a fusion of Eastern and Western sensibilities, a unique and beautiful expression of their love.

Kenji's relationship with his family also evolved. He found ways to reconcile his loyalty to his family with his desire for a more ethical and equitable business. He engaged in open dialogue with his father and elder brothers, explaining his vision for the future, and successfully negotiated a more balanced approach to the family's business operations. He earned their respect, not through brute force or intimidation, but through demonstrating his competence, his integrity, and his unwavering commitment to the family's long-term success. His success was not just a personal triumph; it was a testament to his ability to navigate the complexities of a patriarchal system while upholding his own values.

Aisha's journey was equally transformative. She discovered a newfound confidence and self-assuredness, a strength born from overcoming adversity and embracing her true identity. She found her voice, not just as a survivor but as a leader, an advocate, and a beacon of hope for other young women. Her experiences had taught her the importance of resilience, perseverance, and the power of self-belief. She learned to trust her instincts, to stand up for what she believed in, and to navigate complex situations with grace and determination.

Their combined journeys of self-discovery fueled their shared ambitions. They worked tirelessly, supporting each other's endeavors, celebrating each other's triumphs, and offering solace during moments of doubt. They had become more than just lovers; they had become partners, collaborators, and lifelong companions. Their love story wasn't just a romantic fairytale; it was a testament to the power of personal growth, cultural understanding, and the enduring strength of a love that transcended boundaries and challenged expectations.

Their future was no longer a hazy dream; it was a concrete vision, a tangible reality shaped by their shared efforts and mutual aspirations. They planned their wedding, a celebration that would honor both their cultures, blending traditional Japanese customs with elements of African American heritage. They envisioned a future filled with family, laughter, and the comforting familiarity of their shared home.

They began planning their family. Aisha, having finally found peace with her past, embraced the prospect of motherhood, envisioning a future where she could share her love and wisdom with her children, teaching them the importance of cultural diversity and the beauty of embracing one's heritage. Kenji, too, looked forward to fatherhood, eager to impart his own wisdom and values, to instill in his children a sense of responsibility and a commitment to making a positive difference in the world. They visualized their children, a vibrant blend of their heritages, growing up in a loving and nurturing environment, surrounded by the beauty of both Japanese and African American cultures.

Theirs was a love story that defied expectations, a testament to the transformative power of personal growth and the enduring strength of a relationship built on mutual respect, understanding, and a shared vision of the future. The new dawn wasn't just a metaphor; it was a reality, bright and promising, filled with the warmth of their love, the richness of their cultures, and the endless possibilities that lay before them. It was a dawn that illuminated not just their own lives but the lives of those they touched, a dawn that promised a future as bright and beautiful as the love they shared. Their journey had just begun, and the world held its breath, waiting to see the extraordinary tapestry they would weave together.

The scent of cherry blossoms drifted through the open

windows of their modern Tokyo apartment, a gentle perfume that mirrored the peace that had settled over Aisha and Kenji's lives. It wasn't the absence of challenges, but a hard-won serenity, a quiet understanding that bloomed from the fertile ground of their shared journey. The echoes of Aisha's past, once a haunting symphony of fear and uncertainty, had faded into a distant hum, replaced by the steady rhythm of their present happiness. Kenji, with his quiet strength and unwavering devotion, had been the conductor of this harmonious transformation. He had not erased her past, but rather, he had provided the space, the empathy, the unwavering support she needed to process it, to integrate it into the rich tapestry of her life, rather than letting it define her.

Their days unfolded with a gentle grace, a rhythm orchestrated by their mutual love and respect. Mornings were spent in quiet intimacy, the slow awakening shared with soft touches and whispered words, a subtle symphony of affection that warmed their souls before the day's demands. Evenings were dedicated to shared passions – exploring the hidden culinary delights of Tokyo, losing themselves in the vibrant energy of the city's nightlife, or simply curling up together with a book, the quiet comfort of shared silence a testament to their deep connection. Their intimacy was no longer a desperate clinging to one another for solace but a celebration of their union, a testament to their shared growth and mutual understanding.

Kenji's family, initially wary of Aisha, had come to accept her, not entirely welcoming, perhaps, but certainly acknowledging her presence and her impact on Kenji. There were still moments of subtle tension, cultural misunderstandings that sometimes bubbled to the surface, but these were now navigated with a patience born of mutual respect and a willingness to learn. The formal bow and the warm hug, the traditional tea ceremony, and the spontaneous laughter over a shared joke – these were the bridges they built, a testament to their ability to bridge the gap between two vastly different worlds. Aisha had found a home within this complex family structure, a space where she was not merely tolerated but increasingly understood and appreciated.

Aisha's mentorship program blossomed under her unwavering dedication. The young women under her wing thrived, inspired by her unwavering belief in their potential and her commitment to empowering them to overcome societal obstacles. Her work had expanded beyond the local community, gaining national recognition and attracting funding from various organizations impressed by her innovative approaches and dedication. The program had become her legacy, a testament to her resilience and her desire to give back to a community that had once given her so little. She had transformed her past trauma into a wellspring of empathy and action.

Kenji's business endeavors continued to flourish. The beauty empire, once mired in the shadowy world of the Yakuza, had been successfully transitioned into a reputable, ethical enterprise, lauded for its sustainable practices and inclusive marketing. Kenji's commitment to ethical sourcing, diversity in representation and environmental responsibility had not only bolstered the company's image and profitability but also demonstrated his evolution from a powerful figure within a problematic family structure to a conscious and responsible leader. He was no longer solely defined by his family's legacy; he was forging his own, a legacy built on integrity and positive change.

Their shared success was a testament to their teamwork, a dance of mutual support and unwavering encouragement. They celebrated each other's triumphs, offering solace during moments of doubt, recognizing that their shared journey was not a race to the top but a collaborative process of growth and discovery. Their love was not merely romantic; it was a powerful partnership, a bond forged in the fires of adversity and nurtured by the nourishing waters of mutual respect and unwavering support.

Evenings often found them on their balcony overlooking the sprawling cityscape of Tokyo, the shimmering lights a mesmerizing backdrop to their intimate conversations. They would share their day's events, their dreams, their fears – each vulnerability met with an equal measure of empathy and understanding. These moments were not merely a recounting of their daily experiences; they were a reaffirmation of their commitment to each other, a silent acknowledgment of the shared journey that had brought them to this point.

Aisha had healed, not from forgetting her past but from embracing it, integrating it into the rich fabric of her present. The scars remained, a reminder of the battles fought and won, but they were now badges of honor, a testament to her resilience and her indomitable spirit. The fear remained a subtle undercurrent, a shadow lurking in the periphery, but it no longer dictated her life; it had become a constant companion, a reminder of how far she had come and a motivator to continue to build a life free from its oppressive grip.

Kenji had transformed, his journey leading him from the rigid confines of his family's expectations to a place of self-acceptance and authentic self-expression. He was still keenly aware of his familial responsibilities, but he had found a way to reconcile his loyalty to his family with his own evolving values. He embraced the challenges of navigating complex cultural dynamics, finding strength not in dominance or control, but in understanding and communication. He wasn't merely a powerful man; he was a compassionate partner and a leader guided by his principles, as much as by his family's traditions.

Their weekends were an exploration of both their cultures, a joyful dance of tradition and modernity. They learned from each other, sharing stories of their families, their heritage, their childhood experiences. The differences, once a potential source of conflict, now became a source of mutual fascination and shared learning. They celebrated festivals together, attending traditional Japanese ceremonies and lively African American gatherings. These events were not merely cultural experiences; they were a testament to their commitment to each other and their mutual respect for each other's heritage. They built bridges between two worlds, creating a unique cultural tapestry rich in tradition and vibrant with diversity.

One evening, as the sun dipped below the Tokyo skyline, painting the clouds in hues of fiery orange and soft lavender, Aisha turned to Kenji, her eyes sparkling with unshed tears. "I never thought I'd find this," she whispered, her voice choked with emotion. "This peace, this happiness. It's...earned."

Kenji reached for her hand, his touch gentle but firm, a comforting reassurance. "We earned it together, Aisha," he replied, his voice soft and filled with tenderness. "Together, we faced our demons, we navigated our differences, and we built something extraordinary. This peace…this love…it's the culmination of our shared journey."

Their love story was not a fairy tale; it was a testament to the power of resilience, the beauty of cultural understanding, and the strength of a love that had transcended boundaries, expectations, and the lingering shadows of their pasts. It was a love born from adversity, nurtured by compassion, and strengthened by the unwavering commitment they shared. It was a love that had given them both the strength to find their own peace, their own dawn. And in that shared peace, they found a happiness that resonated not only in their hearts, but also in the lives of those they touched. Their future stretched before them, a limitless canvas waiting for their next brushstroke, their next shared adventure, a testament to the enduring power of their love.

CHAPTER 15: EPILOGUE

The Tokyo skyline shimmered, a million tiny diamonds scattered across the velvet night. From their balcony, Aisha watched the city breathe, its pulse a steady rhythm mirroring the beat of her own heart. It was a heart that had once raced with fear, a heart that had been shattered and mended, a heart that now beat with a quiet, profound contentment. Looking back, the path hadn't been easy. The scars remained, etched onto her soul like delicate, silver filigree, reminders of a past she couldn't erase but had learned to embrace.

She thought of the young Aisha, the girl who'd fled a broken home, searching for belonging in the wrong places, a desperate hunger masked by a brittle exterior. The Aisha who'd found herself entangled with Marcus, that shadow of a man who'd left a trail of wreckage in his wake. The memory of his touch, once a source of fleeting pleasure, now felt like a brand, a painful reminder of her vulnerability and naivete. But that girl, that lost and frightened young woman, was not the woman she was today. That Aisha was merely a stepping stone on her journey, a necessary chapter in the larger narrative of her life.

The encounter with Kenji, initially a collision of worlds, had been her unexpected salvation. His world, steeped in the traditions and complexities of the Yakuza, had initially seemed so alien, so daunting. Yet, within that seemingly harsh landscape, she had discovered a depth of emotion, a capacity for loyalty and love she'd never anticipated. The cultural clashes, initially jarring and disorienting, had become opportunities for growth, for understanding, for the building of bridges between vastly different worlds. She'd learned to navigate the nuances of Japanese culture, to appreciate the intricate beauty of their traditions, the quiet strength of their spirit.

Kenji himself had been a revelation. He had challenged her perceptions, forced her to confront her own biases and preconceived notions. He'd shown her that strength wasn't about dominance or control, but about vulnerability and understanding. His unwavering support, his quiet empathy, had been the balm that healed her wounds, the gentle hand that guided her through the darkest hours. His love hadn't been a rescue, but a partnership, a shared journey of self-discovery and growth.

She remembered the initial hesitancy of Kenji's family, their veiled disapproval, the subtle challenges they'd presented. But through patience, through a willingness to learn and adapt, she had earned their respect, their grudging acceptance. She had come to appreciate the strength of their family bonds, the unwavering loyalty that bound them together. The tea ceremonies, the formal bows, the shared meals – these had become not just cultural rituals, but acts of connection, of mutual understanding.

Her mentorship program, born from a desire to give back, had flourished, becoming a testament to her resilience and her unwavering commitment to empowering young women.

Seeing these young women thrive, seeing them overcome their own challenges, had filled her with a sense of purpose, a sense of satisfaction that transcended her own personal triumphs. It was a legacy she hoped to leave behind, a tangible representation of the strength she had found within herself.

The near-fatal incident, the accidental recording of the drug deal, had been a constant reminder of her past, a shadow that lingered in the periphery. It had been a catalyst, pushing her to confront her fears, to embrace her vulnerabilities, and to fight for her own survival. The trauma had not broken her; it had tempered her, forging her into a woman of unwavering resolve. She had emerged from the ashes, stronger, wiser, and more resilient than she had ever imagined.

Kenji's transformation had been as profound as her own. The young man she'd first met, shrouded in the shadows of his family's legacy, had evolved into a leader of integrity, a man guided by his own moral compass, not just by familial expectations. He had successfully steered his family's business away from the dark underbelly of the Yakuza, transforming it into a model of ethical and sustainable practices. His leadership was a testament to his ability to reconcile tradition with modernity, family loyalty with personal integrity.

Their love story wasn't a fairy tale; it was a testament to the power of resilience, the importance of cultural understanding, and the enduring strength of a love that defied all odds. It was a love born from adversity, nurtured by shared experiences, and strengthened by the unwavering support they offered each other. It was a love that had healed their wounds, both visible and invisible, that had given them the courage to confront their demons and embrace their future. It was a love story still unfolding, a testament to the ongoing journey of self-discovery and shared growth.

The past still held its power, but it no longer defined her. It was a tapestry woven into the rich fabric of her present, a reminder of the strength she had discovered within herself. She had learned that healing wasn't about forgetting, but about integrating, about finding peace within the chaos, about embracing the complexities of life and love. The scars were a testament to her journey, badges of honor that marked her resilience.

Their love story was a beacon, a shining example of a relationship that blossomed amidst cultural differences, past traumas, and societal expectations. It was a testament to the healing power of love and acceptance, a testament to the beauty of embracing both oneself and another. It proved that love could overcome the darkest shadows, that true connection could transcend boundaries and create a future stronger and more vibrant than ever imagined. The city lights, sparkling below, mirrored the brilliance of their shared future, a future built on a foundation of mutual respect, unwavering love, and the resilience of two souls who had found peace in each other's arms. And in that peace, Aisha knew, lay the true promise of forever.

The morning sun, a gentle caress on her skin, woke Aisha. It wasn't the jarring alarm clock of her past, the frantic rush to escape a life she no longer recognized. This was a different kind of awakening, a peaceful surrender to the quiet beauty of a new day, a day filled with the promise of shared laughter and whispered secrets. She stretched, the movement languid and deliberate, feeling the warmth of Kenji's body nestled close beside her. His breath, soft and even, tickled her ear as he slept, a comforting rhythm against the stillness of the room.

She traced the lines of his face, the subtle creases etched by time and laughter, the strength that lay hidden beneath the calm exterior. He was a man of contradictions, a warrior with a gentle heart, a leader born into a world of shadows who had chosen the path of light. And in his embrace, she found a solace she'd never known before. His love wasn't a possessive claim, but a shared journey of growth, a mutual respect that transcended cultural differences and the scars of their pasts.

Aisha's gaze drifted to the balcony, the Tokyo skyline still shimmering in the distance, a panoramic masterpiece painted in shades of gold and rose. The city that had once felt so alien, so daunting, now felt like an extension of herself, a vibrant tapestry woven from the threads of her experiences. She thought of the mentorship program, of the young women she guided, their faces filled with a newfound strength and confidence. It was a testament to the ripple effect of kindness, the power of believing in someone's potential, the profound impact a single act of compassion could have.

She remembered the hesitancy, the fear, the uncertainty that had once plagued her. The fear of judgment, the fear of failure, the fear of not being worthy of love. Those fears, once all-consuming, now felt distant, mere whispers in the wind. She had faced them, confronted them, and emerged victorious. The scars remained, but they were no longer symbols of defeat; they were reminders of her resilience, testaments to her strength.

The appreciation for life wasn't just a feeling, it was a

conscious choice, a daily practice of gratitude. It was in the quiet moments, the shared laughter, the tender touches, the unspoken understanding. It was in the way the morning sun warmed her skin, the way Kenji's hand rested protectively on her waist, the way the city hummed with a life force that resonated deep within her soul. It was in the simple act of breathing, of being present, of cherishing the gift of another day.

She thought of her mother, her image a faded photograph in the recesses of her memory. The pain of her absence, once a gaping wound, had begun to heal, replaced by a quiet acceptance. She carried her mother's memory within her, a silent tribute to a life lived under different circumstances. She sought to honor her legacy, to create a life worthy of the sacrifices her mother had made. This wasn't about forgetting, but about healing, about finding peace within the complexity of memory and emotion.

The cultural exchange, once a daunting prospect, had blossomed into a rich tapestry of shared experiences and mutual respect. Kenji's family, initially hesitant and reserved, had grown to embrace her, their acceptance a testament to her unwavering commitment to understanding their traditions, their history, their way of life. The tea ceremonies, the formal bows, the shared meals – these weren't just cultural rituals, they were acts of connection, building bridges between vastly different worlds. She learned to appreciate the subtle nuances of Japanese etiquette, the importance of respect and hierarchy within the family structure. And in turn, she had introduced them to the vibrancy and warmth of her own culture, sharing her stories, her music, her food, bridging the chasm between two seemingly disparate worlds.

The accidental recording of the drug deal, a near-fatal event, had been a turning point. It had forced her to confront her past, to acknowledge the lingering shadows that haunted her, to face the demons she had so carefully tried to bury. But it had also been a catalyst for growth, a moment of reckoning that had strengthened her resolve, emboldened her spirit. It had shown her the importance of trusting her instincts, of speaking truth to power, of refusing to be silenced. The ordeal, though terrifying, had empowered her, making her a stronger, more resilient person.

She had learned that true strength wasn't about physical power or dominance, but about vulnerability and resilience. It was about acknowledging your fears, confronting your weaknesses, and emerging stronger from the experience. Her scars, both physical and emotional, served as reminders of her journey, badges of honor that marked her resilience. She had learned to embrace the beauty of imperfection, the grace of vulnerability, the power of acceptance.

Kenji's evolution had been equally remarkable. The man she had first encountered, shrouded in the shadows of his family's legacy, had emerged as a leader of integrity and compassion. He had navigated the treacherous waters of his family's history, challenging the old ways, implementing ethical and sustainable practices within his family's business. He had shown her that change is possible, that tradition and modernity can coexist, that family loyalty doesn't require the sacrifice of personal integrity. His transformation reflected her own: a journey from fear to empowerment, from uncertainty to acceptance, from survival to thriving.

Their love story wasn't just a romance; it was a testament to the human spirit's capacity for resilience, its ability to overcome adversity, its endless capacity for love and growth. Their connection wasn't a mere physical attraction, but a deep and abiding respect, a mutual understanding that transcended cultural and personal differences. It was a love that had healed old wounds, a love that had nurtured their individual growth, a love that had become a powerful force for good in the world.

Aisha smiled, the memory of their shared moments flooding her senses. The laughter, the tears, the quiet moments of shared intimacy – these were the treasures she held close to her heart. They were the building blocks of their relationship, the evidence of their enduring connection. They were the moments that defined their love, that gave it meaning, that made it a love story worthy of being told.

She looked at Kenji again, his face still soft in sleep, his body radiating a warmth that embraced her. She leaned in, pressing a kiss to his forehead. It was a silent declaration of love, a grateful acknowledgment of the journey they had shared, a promise of the future they would build together. The future stretched before them, a vast and uncharted territory filled with untold possibilities. And as she gazed at Kenji, she knew they were ready. Ready to face any challenges, ready to embrace any opportunities, ready to continue writing their own unique love story, one chapter at a time. And in this moment of profound appreciation, of unshakeable contentment, Aisha knew that she was finally, truly, home. The city lights twinkled below, a radiant reflection of the peace and love that filled her heart. This wasn't just an ending, but a beginning; a new chapter in a life filled with endless possibilities, a life lived to the fullest, a life deeply and profoundly appreciated.

The sun dipped below the Tokyo skyline, painting the clouds in hues of fiery orange and soft pink. Aisha sat on the balcony, a warm cup of chamomile tea warming her hands. The city hummed with a quiet energy, a comforting rhythm that mirrored the peace within her heart. Kenji joined her, his arm settling gently around her waist. The silence between them wasn't awkward; it was a comfortable companionship, a shared understanding that transcended words.

They watched the city lights twinkle into existence, each tiny spark a testament to the millions of lives unfolding beneath them. Aisha thought of the journey they had shared, the obstacles they had overcome, the love that had blossomed amidst the chaos. It hadn't been easy. There were moments of doubt, moments of fear, moments where the weight of their pasts threatened to overwhelm them. But they had persevered, their love a beacon guiding them through the darkness.

Kenji's hand caressed her cheek, his touch light yet reassuring. "Remember that first meeting?" he asked, his voice a low murmur against the backdrop of the city's hum.

Aisha smiled, the memory vivid. The accidental encounter, the immediate spark, the undeniable pull. It had been a whirlwind, a collision of two vastly different worlds. Yet, amidst the cultural differences, the language barriers, the inherent risks of their respective lives, something extraordinary had taken root. A love that defied logic, a connection that transcended boundaries. "I do," she replied, her voice soft. "I remember thinking you were the most intimidating, yet intriguing man

I'd ever met."

He chuckled, a deep, resonant sound. "And I remember thinking you were the most fiercely independent, yet vulnerable woman I'd ever seen." He leaned in, pressing a kiss to her forehead. "We were both a little scared, weren't we?"

"Terrified," Aisha admitted, a laugh escaping her lips. "But also...excited. There was an adventure in it, a risk worth taking."

Their adventure had been fraught with peril. The threat of the Yakuza's rivals, the lingering danger from Aisha's past, the constant pressure to conform to expectations – these had tested their relationship, pushed them to their limits. But each challenge had only strengthened their bond, forging a love that was unbreakable, resilient.

The mentorship program flourished. Aisha watched as young women, once trapped in cycles of abuse and despair, found their voices, their confidence, their strength. She saw herself in their eyes, the echoes of her own journey mirrored in their struggles and triumphs. It was a powerful reminder of the ripple effect of kindness, the transformative power of believing in someone's potential.

Kenji, too, had undergone a significant transformation. He had embraced change within his family's business, implementing ethical and sustainable practices, challenging the outdated traditions that had perpetuated cycles of violence and exploitation. He was no longer just a member of the Yakuza;

he was a leader, a reformer, a man who used his power and influence for good.

Their cultural exchange continued, a vibrant tapestry woven from shared experiences and mutual respect. Aisha had introduced Kenji's family to the rich tapestry of African American culture, sharing her music, her food, her stories. Kenji, in turn, had deepened Aisha's understanding of Japanese traditions, customs, and history. They had built bridges between two vastly different worlds, proving that love could indeed transcend cultural boundaries.

The scars of their pasts remained, but they were no longer defining features. They were badges of honor, reminders of their resilience, testaments to their strength. They had confronted their demons, faced their fears, and emerged victorious. They had found peace in vulnerability, strength in acceptance, and a love that was as profound as it was transformative.

The future stretched before them, a canvas waiting to be painted with the vibrant colors of their dreams. They had plans to travel, to explore new cultures, to continue their work with the mentorship program. They were building a life together, a life rooted in love, respect, and shared purpose.

The city lights twinkled, mirroring the joy in Aisha's heart. She snuggled closer to Kenji, feeling the warmth of his body, the steady rhythm of his heartbeat. It was a comforting presence, a grounding force. This wasn't just the end of a chapter; it was the beginning of a new era, a testament to their resilience, their love, their enduring hope.

Their love story wasn't just a romance; it was an exploration of self-discovery, a testament to the healing power of love, and a beacon of hope for a future filled with endless possibilities. It was a story about overcoming adversity, about bridging cultural divides, about finding strength in vulnerability, and about the transformative power of a love that transcended all boundaries.

Aisha's past, once a source of pain and insecurity, had become a catalyst for growth and empowerment. She had confronted the shadows of her past, transforming her experiences into a source of strength and resilience. The fear and uncertainty that had once defined her had been replaced by a quiet confidence, a self-assuredness that radiated from within.

Kenji's journey was equally profound. He had shed the image of the ruthless Yakuza member, embracing a more compassionate and ethical path. He had used his position of power to effect positive change within his family and community, proving that tradition and modernity could coexist. His transformation was a testament to his personal growth, a testament to the power of love and redemption.

Their relationship wasn't without its challenges. The cultural differences, the language barrier, and the complexities of their respective lives tested their commitment, forcing them to confront their own insecurities and biases. Yet, their love had persevered, thriving in the face of adversity. They learned to communicate, to understand, and to appreciate the unique perspectives that shaped their identities.

The city lights continued to shimmer, a backdrop to their quiet conversation. They talked about their dreams, their hopes, their plans for the future. They shared stories, laughed, and held each other close, their bodies a testament to the intimacy that bound them. It was a love built on trust, respect, and a shared vision for a brighter tomorrow. It was a love that had healed old wounds, that had nurtured their personal growth, and that had given them both a sense of belonging they had never known before.

As the night deepened and the city lights began to fade, Aisha and Kenji stood hand in hand, gazing out at the horizon. Their future was uncharted territory, full of uncertainty and endless possibilities. But as they looked into each other's eyes, they knew they were ready to face whatever lay ahead, together. The past was behind them, their present was filled with love and contentment, and their future was a boundless expanse of hope and promise. Their love story, unique and powerful, was a testament to the enduring strength of the human spirit and the transformative power of love. It was a story that deserved to be told, a story that inspired hope, a story that ultimately, celebrated the promise of a future lived to the fullest, a future where love conquered all.

The morning light filtered through the sheer curtains, painting the room in soft, ethereal hues. Aisha woke to the gentle touch of Kenji's hand on her hip, his breath warm against her skin. She smiled, the memory of the previous night's intimacy still lingering, a warmth that spread through her like sunlight. Their love had been a tempestuous journey, a whirlwind of passion and peril, but it had forged a bond that felt unbreakable.

She traced the lines of his sleeping face, the subtle shadows beneath his eyes hinting at the weight he carried, the burdens of family and tradition that still clung to him. But even those shadows couldn't diminish the light that shone in his eyes, the love that radiated from his very being. He had chosen her, chosen a life beyond the confines of his world, a life where love and loyalty were the guiding principles.

The transformation in Kenji had been nothing short of remarkable. He had moved beyond the shadows of the Yakuza's more ruthless practices, channeling his influence toward ethical reform within his family's business. He'd faced the opposition, endured the skepticism, and ultimately, emerged victorious, a leader who championed fairness and sustainability. His journey was a testament to the power of redemption, a beacon of hope for those who believed change was impossible.

His family, initially resistant, had slowly come to accept Aisha, recognizing the depth of their love and the positive influence she had on Kenji. The cultural exchange continued to flourish, a beautiful tapestry woven from two distinct worlds. They celebrated each other's traditions, shared stories, laughed together, and slowly, painstakingly, built a bridge between their cultures, demonstrating that love could indeed transcend differences.

Aisha's mentorship program had blossomed into a beacon of hope for young women, providing guidance, support, and a safe space for healing and growth. It had become a testament to her resilience, her unwavering belief in the power of redemption. She poured her heart and soul into the program, helping young women navigate the complexities of their own lives, empowering them to break free from cycles of abuse and find their own path to self-discovery.

The scars of their pasts remained, a tangible reminder of the challenges they had overcome. Aisha's past relationship had left its mark, a constant reminder of the pain and betrayal she had endured. But those scars were no longer wounds; they had transformed into badges of honor, symbols of their resilience, reminders of how far they had come. They were a testament to the strength of the human spirit, a powerful symbol of the healing power of love.

Kenji's past was equally complex, shrouded in the shadows of the Yakuza's world, a world filled with violence, exploitation, and betrayal. But his transformation, his decision to embrace ethical practices, had shown the world that change was possible, that redemption was within reach. He had faced his demons, confronted his past, and emerged a stronger, more compassionate individual. His journey was a story of hope, a testament to the transformative power of love and self-reflection.

Their love story was far from a fairytale. It was a gritty, realistic portrayal of a love that had blossomed amidst adversity, a love that had weathered storms, and a love that had emerged stronger, more resilient than ever before. It was a story of cultural exchange, a story of self-discovery, a story of redemption, and ultimately, a story of hope.

Their days were filled with a quiet contentment; a simple joy found in the shared moments of their lives. They took walks in the serene gardens of Tokyo, hand in hand, their bodies intertwined, their souls connected. They cooked together, sharing recipes and stories from their respective cultures, blending their culinary traditions into a delightful fusion. They spent countless hours engrossed in each other's company, sharing their dreams, their fears, and their hopes for the future.

Evenings were often spent sharing laughter with close friends and family, bridges built between their worlds. Aisha introduced Kenji's family to soul food, gospel music, and the vibrant tapestry of African American culture. In return, she was immersed in the rich traditions of Japanese culture, learning the nuances of tea ceremonies, traditional arts, and the quiet beauty of Japanese gardens.

Their communication wasn't always easy. There were moments of frustration, misinterpretations, and the inevitable challenges of bridging two vastly different cultures. But they persevered, working tirelessly to understand each other, to appreciate the differences that made them unique individuals. Their patience and respect for each other were the foundation of their enduring love.

Their journey was a testament to the power of resilience, a powerful reminder that love could conquer all. They faced their fears, confronted their pasts, and emerged victorious. They had healed old wounds, transformed their lives, and ultimately, found love in the most unexpected of places. Their story was a beacon of hope for those who believed in second chances, for those who sought redemption, for those who yearned for a love that transcended all boundaries.

The future stretched before them, an uncharted territory brimming with possibilities. They had plans to travel the world, to continue their work with the mentorship program, to share their stories with others, and to continue to build their lives together. Their love had transformed them, shaped their destinies, and given them both a sense of belonging and purpose.

Their love story wasn't just their own; it was a testament to the universal power of love, a beacon of hope for those who sought connection, understanding, and acceptance. It was love that defied expectations, challenged boundaries, and ultimately, triumphed over adversity. Their story, unique and powerful, was a reminder that even in the darkest of times, love can illuminate the path toward redemption and a brighter tomorrow. Their love story was a celebration of resilience, a testament to the healing power of love, and a beacon of hope for the future. It was a story of two souls finding solace in each other, embracing their differences, and creating a life filled with love, laughter, and unwavering support.

As they stood hand-in-hand, watching the sun rise over the Tokyo skyline, painting the sky in hues of gold and crimson, they knew that their journey was far from over. Their love story was an ongoing narrative, a testament to their enduring commitment, their unwavering hope, and their unwavering love for one another. It was a story of resilience, a story of redemption, and a story of love that had conquered all. It was a love story worth telling, a love story that deserved to be celebrated, a love story that would inspire hope and faith in the power of love to transform lives and heal the soul. A love story for the ages.

Five years later, the Tokyo skyline shimmered beneath a twilight sky, the city lights reflecting like fallen stars in the tranquil waters of the bay. Aisha, draped in a silk kimono Kenji had gifted her – a vibrant crimson that mirrored the passion still burning between them – stood on their balcony, a gentle breeze ruffling her hair. Beside her, Kenji, his dark hair streaked with silver at the temples, held her close, his hand resting warmly on her lower back. The years hadn't dulled the intensity of their gaze, the unspoken language that passed between them, a silent testament to the enduring power of their love.

Their life together was a tapestry woven with threads of joy, understanding, and unwavering support. The initial challenges – the cultural differences, the lingering shadows of Kenji's past, the scars of Aisha's own trauma – had become stepping stones, each hurdle surmounted forging an even stronger bond. The fear and uncertainty that once clouded their relationship had given way to profound and unshakeable trust. Their love wasn't simply a feeling; it was a conscious choice, a daily affirmation, a steadfast commitment to weathering any storm that life might throw their way.

Aisha's mentorship program thrived, expanding beyond its initial scope to include workshops on financial literacy, self-defense, and emotional well-being. She had become a beacon of hope for countless young women, her own experiences serving as a potent catalyst for change. The program wasn't just about providing shelter and support; it was about empowering women to reclaim their agency, to break free from the shackles of societal expectations and patriarchal norms, to discover their inner strength and build lives on their own terms. Kenji, ever supportive, had helped secure funding and partnerships, leveraging his influence in the business world to amplify Aisha's impact. He understood the importance of her work, not just for the women it served, but for the broader societal shift it represented.

Kenji's transformation continued to unfold, his leadership within his family's business solidifying his position as a force for positive change. He successfully steered the company towards sustainable practices, prioritizing ethical sourcing and fair labor standards. He had faced significant opposition, even threats, but his unwavering commitment to integrity, fueled by his love for Aisha and his desire to create a better world, had proven unyielding. The family business, once synonymous with the shadows of the Yakuza, now stood as a symbol of corporate responsibility and social consciousness, a testament to the power of one man's transformation.

Their cultural exchange had blossomed into a vibrant celebration of two distinct worlds. They regularly hosted gatherings, inviting friends and family from both sides of the globe to share their unique blend of traditions. Soul food feasts were followed by elegant Japanese tea ceremonies; gospel music echoed through the same rooms that once housed hushed conversations about Yakuza business. Their home, a sanctuary of love and acceptance, became a microcosm of a world where cultural differences were celebrated, not feared. They instructed their children, a beautiful blend of their heritage, to embrace both cultures, instilling in them a profound appreciation for diversity and a deep understanding of their shared history.

Their love life continued to evolve, adapting to the changing seasons of their relationship. The initial tempestuous passion had matured into a deep and abiding intimacy, a quiet understanding that transcended the physical. Their intimacy was as multifaceted as their lives, a dance of tenderness and exploration, a journey of continuous discovery. It was a love that nourished their souls, strengthened their bond, and served as a constant source of comfort and reassurance.

The scars on Aisha's back, a testament to her past trauma, served as a reminder of the strength she'd discovered within herself, of the resilience that had allowed her to survive and ultimately thrive. The memories weren't erased, but they were no longer defining elements of her identity; they were simply a part of her story, a narrative that had led her to the profound love and happiness she now embraced.

Kenji's past, the whispers of the Yakuza world, still existed, but the darkness had receded, replaced by the radiant light of his new life, a life built on integrity and love. He had faced his demons, accepted his responsibility, and emerged victorious, a testament to the power of redemption and the transformative potential of love. The weight of his past still occasionally surfaced, but Aisha's unwavering support was his anchor, guiding him through the choppy waters of memory and remorse. Together, they had navigated the treacherous currents of their pasts, emerging stronger and more resilient than ever.

Their children, now teenagers, mirrored their parents' remarkable blend of cultures, fluent in both English and Japanese, deeply rooted in their heritage, yet embracing a global perspective. They moved effortlessly between two worlds, their lives enriched by the richness of their parents' combined experiences. They were a living testament to the enduring power of love, a symbol of hope for a future where cultural understanding and acceptance were the norm, not the exception.

Their love story was not merely a tale of romance; it was a testament to the power of resilience, the transformative potential of love, and the enduring strength of the human spirit. It was a narrative that transcended boundaries, challenged assumptions, and celebrated the beauty of diversity. It was a love story for the ages, a story that would continue to unfold, each chapter written with unwavering commitment, enduring passion, and a profound appreciation for the journey that had brought them together. The sunset painted the sky in hues of orange and purple, mirroring the rich tapestry of their lives, a vibrant testament to a love that had conquered all, a love that would last a lifetime and beyond. Their love was a legacy, a beacon of hope shining brightly against the ever-changing skyline of life, a love that defied boundaries, embraced differences, and ultimately triumphed over adversity. It was a love story worthy of celebration, a story that would resonate through generations, reminding us of the incredible power of love to heal, transform, and inspire.

BACK MATTER

Primarily, I extend my deepest gratitude to my family and friends, whose unwavering love and support have been my constant source of strength throughout this writing journey. Your patience, understanding, and belief in me fueled my creativity and helped me navigate the challenges of bringing this story to life. A special thank you to my cousin, whose insightful critiques and unwavering encouragement pushed me to explore the depths of this narrative.

My sincere appreciation also goes to my editors at Staten House, whose expertise and guidance shaped this manuscript into its final form. Their keen eye for detail and unwavering commitment to excellence significantly enhanced the quality of my work. I am especially grateful to my mom for her invaluable contribution and unwavering belief in this project.

Finally, I want to acknowledge the numerous individuals within the African American and East
Asian communities who generously shared their experiences, perspectives, and cultural insights. Your contributions enriched the authenticity and depth of this story, and I am deeply honored to have learned from your wisdom and knowledge. This book is dedicated to you.